The Captain-General brought the king a letter. It was bound with a strip of leather to the shaft of an arrow; the watch had found it embedded in the trunk of a plum tree. In the night an archer had fired it across the moat.

The letter was written in an Eildon hand and addressed to "The High and Mighty Prince, Sharn Am Zor, King of the Chameln, who shares the double throne."

You will bring no bride out of Eildon. Know this and, while you can, hold yourself and your champions far from the Tourney of All Trees and the vigil that will follow. Do this for those who love you and respect your ancient line. There is still time for you to forswear this tournament because of the injury to the Lord Denwick or for some other ground. For if you once take part in these ceremonies, you will be bound, by Eildon custom, to follow the ritual or suffer a disgrace that is worse than death for a true knight. Heed this entreaty, noble Sharn, and know that the one who risks great pain and penalty to send this warning is your true friend.

D0631224

The <u>RULERS OF HYLOR</u> Series

A Princess of the Chameln
Yorath the Wolf

CHERRY WILDER

THE SUMMER'S KING

BAEN BOOKS

THE SUMMER'S KING

This is a work of fiction. All the characters and events portrayed in this book are fictional, and any resemblance to real people or incidents is purely coincidental.

A Baen Book

Baen Publishing Enterprises
260 Fifth Avenue
New York, N.Y. 10001

First Baen printing, February 1987

ISBN: 0-671-65617-1

Cover art by Stephen Hickman

Printed in the United States of America

Distributed by
SIMON & SCHUSTER
1230 Avenue of the Americas
New York, N.Y. 10020

∽ PART I ∽

THE KING'S PLEASURE

CHAPTER I

ACHAMAR

IN ACHAMAR, IN THE WOODEN PALACE OF the Zor, the young King Sharn lies asleep. His chamber, widened at his own command, is a lake of quiet with the huge curtained bed, rich with the shining cloths of Lien, floating like a barge upon the lake. Prickett and Yuri, the two valets, make excursions to peer at their master, stepping on the scattered fur rugs. The pillow beside his own is dented; Yuri, a boy from the northern tribes, reaches in and lifts a long shining hair from this pillow. Prickett, an older man, from Lien, catches the boy's wrist. He takes the long, dark hair, winds it round his finger and casts it on the floor.

The king lies on his back, uncovered to the waist. Relaxed in sleep he is still as beautiful as a god, his features strong and regular, his lips perfectly shaped, his teeth white and even. His golden hair clings to his forehead in damp peaks; on a thin golden chain about his neck he wears some small token. His hands are large and well-shaped; he wears no rings. Under blue-veined lids his eyes move: the king is dreaming.

He is a boy, running through a maze of roses. He comes up against a smaller boy, his brother Carel, and pushes him into the thorny wall of the maze. He runs

3

and runs, and no one can catch him; women in billowing gowns snatch at him, screaming half in anger, half in admiration. He runs on over sand, over grass, over thick carpet embroidered with flowers, and behind him he hears the sound of hoofbeats. The giant horse, riderless, pounds after him. It is a light bay, strong and fierce, with a wild bloodshot eye and bared teeth. He is trapped now, the dream has become a nightmare. He runs through a ruined building, shadowy and terrifying, and sees a man dressed in motley beckoning from an arched doorway. "Here, lad . . ." But as Sharn darts into cover, he trips over a rope hidden in the grass and brings down a wooden stand piled with arms and armor. The swords, spears, shields, helmets, suits of mail, come cascading down upon him with a loud, brazen clangor that dwindles into the gentle tinkling of a silver bell . . .

A shaft of sunlight touches the king's face as he opens his eyes. Yuri has hauled back the long hanging at a southern window and Prickett has drawn the bed curtains. He gives the silver bell a final shake. Sharn, awake on the instant, raises a hand to shield his face from the sunlight. A new day as king. He remembers what day it is. He remembers his dream. Straightaway he gets up, steps down from the high bed, thrusts his arms into the silken bedgown the valets are holding for him. Halfway to his bathroom he smiles and speaks, his eye lighting upon Yuri, as if seeing him for the first time.

"The trumpeters . . ." he says.

"Yes, Dan Sharn," says the boy, bobbing his head. "Yes, all ready."

Beyond the carved and painted door of the bedchamber, there is a murmuring and a rustling. Sharn moves deliberately from the bathroom back to his bed again. The pillows have been turned and piled high, the curtains drawn back. He settles himself comfortably; Prickett smoothes the featherbed and the embroidered coverlet. Yuri pulls on the wrist-thick bellcord that hangs beside the fireplace. The doors of the bedchamber are flung wide; twenty people in livery or court dress come tumbling into the room. It is the king's awakening.

There is no need for the king to speak to any of those who have come to dress him and offer him drinks, perfume. Sometimes, after a festival, when everyone, the king included, has had far too little sleep, he may go through the whole awakening, the bath, the robing, without a word. But if the ritual falters—Prickett has said this to Yuri more than once—if even a close friend or the privileged lady who has not long left the King's side forgets the order of the vessels on the tray, lets fall a towel, trips on the steps of the bed, then watch out for fireworks. Yuri watches hopefully, day after day, but the king is gracious, pleasant.

On this day of all days, one of the new torch-bearers, Denzil of Denwick, drops the tray with a clatter. Beakers of fresh milk, wine, fruit juice go crashing down to the polished floor.

"Zilly, you clumsy idiot!" shouts Sharn Am Zor. "Are you trying to kill me!"

He bounds out of the other side of his bed and strides off to his bath, with those gentlemen whose duty it is to wash the king stumbling after him. The remaining courtiers step back; the liveried servants clean up the mess. Yuri wants to leap forward and help, but Prickett holds him back.

"*Their* duty," he whispers. And when the silver tray is carried away and the floor cleaned, "*Now . . .*" he says.

The two valets march forward, strip the bed, hand part of its linen to a waiting laundrymaid. Prickett flashes a glance to remind the new Master of the Bedchamber, the young Count Caddah, a gangling southerner, of his duty. The signal is given for the royal wardrobe and four servants wheel from one of the adjoining rooms the wooden rack bearing the king's attire for the day, together with a tall draped mirror upon a stand.

As the courtiers and servants hang about waiting for

the king to return, a very old and privileged lady, the
dowager Countess Palazan Am Panget, Holder of the
Royal Jewels, is heard to make a loud remark in the Old
Speech. None of the newcomers from Lien understand
her and those Chameln nobles who do look shocked.

"What was that?" hisses Prickett.

Yuri cannot keep a grin off his face. "She said, 'How
much more simply this is done in the Palace of the
Firn, without all this Lienish ceremony.'"

"Old hag!" murmurs Prickett. "She thrives on ceremony."

The king returns at last. He is in an angry mood, and
the reason is plain to see. He wears Chameln under-
wear: a short linen chemise, linen underdrawers to the
knee and white silk and wool stockings. The fine clothes
waiting on the rack are Chameln clothes fit for a king,
and the king hates them. He is almost pouting as the
ladies and gentlemen persuade him into the long white
doeskin breeches, the long, heavily embroidered tunic
of blue velvet and softest yellow leather, and, at last,
the brown and gold boots.

The clothes fit perfectly and are very becoming. Sharn
Am Zor allows his hair to be brushed and combed. He
selects from the tray offered by the Countess Am Panget
a gold ring with a ruby, a silver ring in the shape of a
fox's mask, with eyes of amethyst, a heavy gold chain
with a pendant of amber. He waves away the tray,
refuses a hand mirror, a glass of wine, an elixir to give
sweet breath, but accepts a lace-edged handkerchief
offered by the dark-haired beauty, Lady Seyl. At last
the king, gorgeously arrayed, stands poised before the
long mirror. Caddah again gives the signal, and Yuri
reefs away the silken cloth.

Sharn Am Zor reels back with a cry; a woman screams,
other nobles and servants gasp or cry out. Even Veddera
the palace barber, the man with the steadiest hand at
the court of the Zor, drops his tray of instruments.
Yuri, in terror lest he has done something wrong, is
ready to fling himself down on the polished floor. He
peers at the mirror and cries out.

"Cover the glass!" shouts the king.

Prickett snatches the cloth from Yuri and blots out the sight.

"Out! Clear the chamber!" cries Sharn Am Zor. "Zilly, Seyl . . . stay with me. . . ."

There is a blind rush for the door. Some of the courtiers are insulted; others, who were not following, are baffled. The Countess Am Panget spills the jewels; Prickett rescues a pearl ring and pockets it. The old lady is borne on out of the room crying, "What was it? What did he see?"

The three young men, Sharn and his two closest companions, stand before the mirror, and Yuri is told to lift the cloth again. They behold, as calmly as they can, a sparkling mist, and in it a dark point of light. It grows quickly into the figure of a man in a robe of midnight-blue. He is pale-faced, with flowing hair of a distinctive dark red. Yuri has never seen the man, the sorcerer, before, but Prickett trembles. He recognizes Rosmer, the Vizier of the Markgraf of Lien.

"What do you want with me?" demands Sharn Am Zor.

In spite of the wild extravagance of his sudden appearance, Rosmer is matter-of-fact.

"Majesty," he says, "I must speak of your sister and brother, Princess Merilla and Prince Carel."

"What about them?"

"They are gone," says Rosmer. "They went riding yesterday afternoon and did not return to the royal manor."

"Alldene?" asks the king.

"Hodd," says Rosmer. "They have ridden off, I believe, in the direction of the Nesbath road."

"You believe!" cries the king. "Should I believe you, old toad!"

"Majesty," says Rosmer humbly, "I tell you for their safety. The princess has run off to join you and taken her brother . . ."

"Are they alone?" ventures Denzil of Denwick. "No servants?"

"One servant, lord," says the magician, "and they are all well mounted."

"I will see to them," says the king. "I will receive them. I hope this is not another of your damnable tricks. The princess was summoned to Achamar, but my Uncle Kelen would keep her in Lien!"

"The Markgraf Kelen and the Markgräfin Zaramund are gravely concerned," says Rosmer, smooth as ever. "They send their greetings to the Daindru . . ."

Sharn inclines his head, barely acknowledging the greeting. With an effort, twisting the rings upon his fingers, he asks in a low choking voice, "How fares Queen Aravel, my mother?"

"The queen is quiet," says Rosmer. "She has not been told."

There is a moment of silence. Outside in the palace garden an officer shouts a command.

"Majesty," says Rosmer, "that is my message, brought in haste, for the safety of the princess and the prince."

"I have the message then!"

"Majesty . . . Dan Sharn, may I say—"

"Get out of my sight!"

The magician raises a hand, veiling his face with a wide blue sleeve. As he turns himself about, the mirror clouds and presently gives back the image of the young king, magnificently dressed, frowning and pale.

Sharn turns to his companions. The three young men talk softly, their heads together, and Prickett sighs and smiles. This is how they took counsel as boys, in Lien, in the schoolroom at Alldene. Seyl is the most sensible and cool-headed; Denwick is rueful, anxious. The leader, then as now, is the king. He walks through the royal apartments, flanked by the two torch-bearers, with that proud, swift, striding walk that carries him ahead of every gathering, past every outstretched hand and eager glance.

"Send Engist to the garrison at once," he says. "Company of kedran to ride south. Curse Rilla and Carel for putting me to this trouble."

Yuri and Prickett fling open succeeding doors, and

the king marches down a deserted corridor, newly paneled to hide the Chameln walls of intricate reedwork over the ancient wood. Guards shout, bells ring, the king is proceeding to breakfast.

In the sunlit lower eastern hall the commotion of the king's approach can be heard far off, and the hearts of all the petitioners beat faster. They do not know that their case is hopeless. Tradition permits a few chosen petitioners of every estate to stand in this hall before the green saloon where the king breakfasts, but there is no power in heaven and earth to make the king speak to a petitioner before breakfast. They are permitted to stand in the hall every morning for eight days, hoping for the royal lightning to strike before they take their petitions through other, more tedious channels.

When the king comes down a few steps into the lower eastern hall, he passes within a few feet of a short, dark young man in the riding dress of the northern tribes. He is booted to the thigh and wears a short flaring tunic of dark red and a blue cloak embroidered with stags. His draped scarlet hat with a jeweled band marks him out as a chief's son. Today is his last day. He has been standing in the hall every morning for seven days, poised, alert, hopeful, holding in his right hand a scroll of parchment: his petition.

Sharn Am Zor strides on without catching the eye of any suppliant. Then the miracle occurs. He checks, midway to the door of the green saloon, just as the guards are preparing to strike the ultimate gong. The king turns back, murmuring to Seyl, and approaches the suppliant.

The young man from the north looks up at the young king. Their interchange, the words they must speak, are firmly laid down by custom, and the king sweeps the custom aside.

"Your name, I pray?" he says.

Sweeping off his red bonnet the young man falls to his knees. "Tazlo Am Ahrosh, my king! Your liegeman from the loyal feoff of Vedan!"

"Come up!" says the king. "A petition?"

"My land right in the matter of . . ."

The king takes the scroll and hands it to Seyl of Hodd.

"It will be studied," he says. "Count Ahrosh, tell me plainly—are you a good horseman?"

Tazlo smiles, a flash of white in his handsome, dark Firnish face, and says, "The best, Dan Sharn!"

"Then you can do me a service," says the king. "Come in to breakfast, and I will explain the matter."

As the king strides on with three men in his wake, a middle–aged woman, the widow of a carpenter, runs mad with despair. Before the servants can hold her, she flings herself, shrieking, at the king's feet. Guards and servants pluck at the sobbing woman, but the king smiles.

"Good mother," he says, following the ritual, "what is your will?"

The woman can only shudder and sob. The guards raise her up gently; she whispers her reply: "I crave your help, my king, in the name of the Goddess!"

"Come," says Sharn, "I will take your scroll. Be of good cheer!"

He raises his voice.

"Let all those who wait here give their scrolls into the keeping of the Third Steward. Do me the favor of leaving this room free for others who will come to me. Wait for answers in the outer ward."

An old man waves his hat and cries, "Hold high the Daindru!"

The king goes into breakfast to the sound of the two-fold cheer for the rulers of the Chameln land.

Tazlo Am Ahrosh, following the king into the delicious reek of Lienish bread, apple curd and hot tea, has had his life changed as if by magic. He sits at the king's right hand, hears his commission, and is sent off with a guard captain, still clutching a bread roll. Long before the kedran troop, the battlemaids on their small grey horses, set out for the south, Tazlo has ridden forth. He takes his own fine Chameln grey for the first lap and wears the cockade of a royal courier on his hat. He rides breakneck out of the southern gates of the city and takes the highroad. In eight or nine days of hard riding, with changes at every relay post, he will come to the borders of the Chameln land. Somewhere along the way he must meet the runaways: Princess Merilla, the Heir of the Zor, and the young Prince Carel.

Now the king and his court hurry on to the great business of the day. It is the second quarter of the Hazelmoon in the year 1172 since the laying of the stones in the south wall, as time is reckoned in Achamar, and the Dainmut has been summoned. It is the third year since the invading armies of Mel'Nir were humbled and driven from the land. In Mel'Nir the year is given as 328 since the Farfaring; and the civil war between Ghanor, the Great King, and Valko Firehammer, Lord of the Westmark, has just worn out a second season. In Lien, it is the year 2221 of the Annals of Eildon, for Lien shares its dating with its ancient liegeland; and Kelan, the Markgraf and his lady, the fair Zaramund, have given up hope of an heir. The Vizier, Rosmer, is dreaming of his grand design: the expansion of Lien into a kingdom. In the peaceful land of Athron, it is the year 37 since the Carach tree returned, and the feast of Carach Troth is not far off.

Sharn Am Zor goes straight from the bathroom beyond the green saloon, where he has been combed and put to rights like a child, to his private stableyard. His four torch-bearers, his companions of honor, are waiting beside their mounts for the king. There is Old Zabrandor, the only torch-bearer inherited from Esher Am Zor, the king's late father; there is the southern lord, Effrim Am Barr; and the two new men, Denzil of Denwick and Jevon Seyl of Hodd, who is the king's cousin. The king has many cousins, including his co-ruler, the Queen Aidris Am Firn, and a little tribe of Chameln poor relations, the children of Esher's two sisters, whose husbands came down in the world. Some, the Inchevin, remain on their rundown estates in the northeast, but the king's aunt, Parn Am Chiel, has sent her eldest son to court, and the king has advanced him modestly. The head groom who holds the king's horse is Esher Am Chiel, seventh in succession to the throne of the Zor.

The king's horse is a ten-year-old roan gelding captured in the central highlands during the fighting with Mel'Nir. It is a trooper's horse, heavily built, handsome, intelligent, and above all, docile and good-mannered. It is the first horse with which the king has had a friendly relationship. His memories of horses go back to his third year and are a long record of discomfort, misery and terror. Between his father, who forced him to ride, and his mother, who shrieked when she saw him walking a pony, Sharn's long martyrdom began and was not ended until he found this kind horse that he calls Redwing, bred in the Eastern Rift on the High Plateau of Mel'Nir and brought into the Chameln lands by an unknown trooper.

So the king, well-built and strong, often in his young life doubted if he could ever be a king because he rode so ill. He will not hunt, joust on horseback or ride at the ring, but has trained tirelessly at all the knightly pursuits that can be practiced on foot. He is an excellent archer with the longbow, the short bow and the crossbow. He loves hawking, a sport not much practiced in the Chameln lands, but now becoming more popular. He fences and handles a broadsword quite respectably. He excels in the novel pursuit of swimming, an activity that the common folk of the Chameln undertake mainly when they fall into a lake. Now there are bathing parties of lords and ladies to be seen on every strand from Lake Musna to the Danmar.

Now the king, after a quick glance at his favorite hawks in the royal mews, mounts up on Redwing. The heralds of the Zor are fretful, but the procession is only a few minutes behind time. The king, preceded by his own horseguards, moves off at last through the outer wards of the palace at a gentle pace.

It is a perfect autumn day in Achamar; the maples are beginning to turn red. From the northern wall the city sweeps down in a series of shallow terraces, each with its ringroad; and from the southern walls a watcher can see almost as far as the Danmar, the inland sea. The two royal palaces, which dominate the city, are vast irregular buildings made of oak logs, dressed and undressed. Sharn cannot look at his palace rearing up like a barn or a tribal lodge without a twinge of irritation. Let no one tell him of the beauty, the quaintness, the cool-in-summer, warm-in-winter qualities of his home: for the king, true palaces are built of stone.

He rides in a slow circle on the uppermost ringroad, thronged with citizens of the better sort who live near the palace. Ahead ride the hundred guardsmen and the heralds; behind the king and his four companions come fifty nobles, those men and women who sat down to breakfast with the king. The guardsmen wear green and gold, the courtiers are a blaze of color: the rich dyes of the Chameln land—dark red, purple, blue, emerald— lit with the springtime colors of Lien, yellow, turquoise, apricot, lilac, rose-pink. The ladies of Lien ride sidesaddle in their elaborate gowns; the ladies of the Chameln land, in breeches and jeweled tunics, sit astride on small horses, the Chameln grey. The lords and gentlemen of Lien are fine in puffed and slashed costumes and short cloaks; their Chameln counterparts are more soberly clad, their cloaks are longer, they wear short swords.

The two races of the Chameln land, the tall blond folk of the Zor and the short dark folk of the Firn, can be singled out, but there are many in Achamar who are middle-sized and brown-haired. Here and there among the courtiers and the spectators are the changelings, giant tawny men of Mel'Nir who have forsworn their country and their king for love of the Chameln lands.

The ceremonial ride ends in a round park with an enclosure for horses and a crowd of grooms and pages waiting. At this point the procession from the palace of the Firn can be seen dismounting in a similar park three streets away. The king gets down, feeds Redwing a tidbit, and leads off on foot, chatting easily with his torch-bearers. The mounted guard has quickened its pace and come to the huge courtyard outside the meeting hall, another towering structure of ancient wood, with banners of the Daindru spread out upon its flat grey facade like tribal markings upon a birch lodge.

At last a group of five other persons on foot, divided by a good distance from the mingling crowd of courtiers, can be seen converging on the courtyard. A small dark woman in Chameln dress of emerald green and grey walks ahead with a light springing step in her high-heeled boots. Behind Queen Aidris Am Firn come her torch-bearers: Bejan Am Nuresh, her consort; Jana Am Wetzerik, the kedan general; and two newcomers, Nenad Am Charn and Count Zerrah, an Athron knight. Behind the king's back, Seyl of Hodd whispers to Zilly of Denwick, who hides a grin. Seyl has murmured, "Ah . . . the bright sparks . . ." The two young men of Lien find the torch-bearers of the Firn, with the possible exception of Count Zerrah, a dull lot.

The king has eyes only for his cousin Aidris; she is one of the few persons in the world whom he trusts, one of the few for whom he can feel love. The queen comes forward eagerly, and after their ritual embrace, she takes Sharn's hands.

"Rilla and Carel!" says Aidris Am Firn. "I have heard . . ."

It is to be expected. She has heard by magic or from one of the hundreds of royal servants and soldiers crisscrossing the city.

"No cause for alarm," says Sharn, smiling down at her. "A kedran troop has set out, and I've sent a rider, a wild young courser from Vedan, to fly ahead and meet them. Rilla has managed the escape, the hoyden. I am sure she will come to no harm."

He likes to reassure the queen. Aidris smiles. She has a striking face, youthful and fresh, and remarkable green eyes. The queen is twenty-eight years old and has borne two children; Prince Sasko, Heir of the Firn, aged three years; and his sister, Princess Micha, one year old; both safely tucked away in the huge, beloved palace of the Firn, far from the tumult of the Dainmut. The cheers from round about are deafening. Aidris and

Sharn walk hand in hand, flanked by their torch-bearers, through the long column of cheering citizens and the guards for both their escorts. They pass through the doors of the meeting hall.

The hall of the Dainmut is a vast, vaulted structure, dark as a cavern after the sunlit streets, with a fresh tang of pine garlands masking the musty reek of age. The Daindru are officially alone except for a shaman from the northern tribes who holds up an oak bough and gives them the blessing of the Goddess. They bow to him and to each other; then part and turn aside to go to their robing rooms. Aidris goes to the left, Sharn to the right, each striding down a narrow, creaking, dark corridor. Then he is in the sunlit robing room that gives on to the dias with the double throne.

Yuri and Prickett are in the robing room to meet the king, together with Iliane Seyl, Mistress of the Royal Robes and two of her ladies, blonde Xandel and dark Veldis. All three women are so wrapped and swirled in shining Lienish cloth that they almost fill the small chamber. When they sink down before the king, they billow and rustle. Sharn raises up Lady Seyl with a cool, impatient smile and stands like a rock in the ocean as everyone goes to work on him.

The king has been surrounded by beautiful women like these for as long as he can remember. His curiosity is dulled; the edge has long since been taken off his appetite. Yet he acknowledges his relationship to Iliane Seyl. As she bustles about in her seagreen gown, showing off perfect white arms, he thinks of those secret bathing parties at Alldene. Three children, three half-grown young people, two boys and a girl, Sharn, Jevon and Iliane, among the reeds, deep in the soft grass. He has even wished that he had married Iliane himself instead of leaving her to Jevon Seyl. She raises dark eyes to him, dimpling, as she sets straight his tabard; he feels her breath upon his cheek. No, it would not do. Iliane, beautiful, high-born Iliane, is a silly goose, vain and empty-headed. As the king's mistress and the wife of his torch-bearer, she has reached her zenith. Of course her marriage to Seyl of Hodd was arranged in childhood; Iliane could count herself lucky that her husband was a good friend. They are all three good friends, old friends. The king, who is twenty-three years old, suddenly longs for times past, for the deep grass in the shade of the trees and a plunge into cool water.

Over his clothes the women have placed a long tabard of felt encrusted with jewels. A trailing robe of dark green cloth edged with golden fur is fixed to his shoulders, and a tippet of brown velvet is arranged over it. Prickett girds him with a golden belt, and Yuri, lips drawn back in concentration, sets the first of the heavy gold chains about the king's neck and fastens it into place with golden pins and twists of thread. Sharn moves a little to make sure that the garments sit well, that his hands are free for the sword and the silver dipper that he must carry.

Beyond the robing room the hall is filling up. Greater and lesser nobles are crowding the massive oaken benches tiered behind the double throne. Below them in the body of the hall jostle the merchants and their wives, dressed in their best, and further back the common folk of the city and the followers of the landowners. In the galleries under the roof are waiting women, pages, scribes, musicians. A team of nimble fellows, the climbers, perch and swing on the beams of the hall, operating the shutters that admit light and air, driving away the rooks and pigeons.

Prickett, the valet, gets the sign of readiness from the king and passes it through a shutter in the robing room to the trumpeters on the steps of the dais. There is no waiting, for Queen Aidris is ready, too. The wooden trumpets of the Chameln land blend with the silver notes of King Sharn's new trumpeters from Lien. The king and the queen enter slowly from either side of the platform and move across the old, dark boards to stand before the double throne. The twofold cheer rises for the Daindru. To a long, wild trumpet call, two honored nobles, Lingrit Am Thuven and the Countess Caddah, emerge from the shadows behind the throne and hold aloft the two ancient crowns. Shutters overhead send down beams of light upon the dark gold, the round emeralds, the yellow diamonds that encrust these treasures.

For a few moments only Sharn feels the cap of leather slip onto his head and the immense weight of the crown. It is a weight too great for Queen Aidris to bear even for a short time, and Lingrit, her chancellor, supports the crown upon her head. Then the crowns are upheld a second time and carried away. Two other favored personages, Iliane Seyl and Sabeth of Zerrah, both beautiful women, come forward and set simple diadems of gold and pearls upon the heads of the Daindru. At last the king and the queen sit down upon the double throne, holding their swords of office. Aidris Am Firn carries a silver bough for her office as Lady of the Groves, just as the king bears a silver dipper as Lord of the Wells.

The cheers and shouting rise to a thunderous climax that seems to shake the hall; the king and the queen smile and nod to their subjects. Sharn can see very clearly in memory two men seated stiffly upon the throne as he sits now: his father, Esher Am Zor, and Racha Am Firn, father of Aidris. The Daindru has prevailed: they reign in Achamar as they have done for a thousand years. There are tears of joy still among the citizens as there were at the coronation two years past. A kedran with a strong sweet voice, below the dais, begins to sing the last verse of a battle song, an anthem for the restoration of the Daindru, and the whole multitude take up the strain:

> Far off, far off in Achamar
> The fires are lit,
> The king and queen have come home,
> O let me live till that moon!

The ceremony lasts six hours. The closest advisors of the queen and the king have worked hard to cut it to this length. The Daindru are no longer force to remain before their subjects for ten, twelve, twenty hours at a time, eating and sleeping on the double throne with only a gold screen hiding them now and then so that they might answer calls of nature. Queen Charis Am Firn, grandmother of the present queen, almost gave birth before the Dainmut on one occasion, and at another meeting her co-ruler, King Vavar Am Zor, was seized by a fit of apoplexy.

Even now, with hourly pauses, brief forays to the robing room, Sharn Am Zor is tormented by the ceremony. Aidris talks to him, they smile, they listen to the loyal addresses, accept oaths of fealty, name officeholders. More than two hours after noon, a trio of lesser lords from the town of Winnstrand on the Danmar are permitted to read a loyal address. They are liegemen of Sharn Am Zor, for the town lies within one of his personal feoffs. After the usual expression of love and fealty, the third lord appeals to the king. On behalf of his fellow lords he urges the king to marry and secure the succession of the Zor.

Sharn is furious. After enduring the discomfort of the long meeting, now he is harassed by these presumptuous fools. Aidris, seeing his handsome face dark as a thundercloud, clasps his hand firmly on the throne bench.

"Hold firm!" she whispers.

"Curse them!" he says aloud.

He leaps to his feet before the loyal address is done and speaks in a voice taut with anger. "Good lords of Winnstrand, I see you are all old men. You cannot earn the respect due to your grey beards if you do not respect your king and liege. I will marry when it pleases me. My sister, Princess Merilla Am Zor, is my heir, and my brother, Prince Carel, is in good health, too. Do not think that because I am your king I can be commanded in any matter!"

Aidris quickly rises, and she too is inwardly cursing the clumsy lords of Winnstrand.

"Sharn Am Zor is my co-ruler and my dear cousin," she says firmly. "If it please the lords of Winnstrand

and any other lords or citizens who presume to consider the matter of the king's marriage: I will advise the king. I will find out and set forth for him the names and estates of any maidens fit to be honored as his wife!"

There is a murmur of satisfaction. The Winnstrand lords are rebuked. Sharn, still furiously angry, asks Aidris for the ending of the ceremony, and she nods. He gestures to the trumpeters, and they blow up "The Daindru Goes Out." The Dainmut is at an end. The king stalks perfunctorily through the closing ceremonies; he disrobes so hastily that the floor of the robing room is covered with scattered seed pearls and scrapings of felt. He leaves the meeting hall down his private corridor at the double; his horse guards are thrown into confusion when he appears.

Still the king strides on without a page or an esquire, let alone a courtier. Seyl and Denwick, seeing how things have gone, are trying to extricate themselves from the hall. Sharn, already at the stabling park, setting the grooms into confusion this time, mounts Redwing. Behind him he leaves cheering citizens, cursing guardsmen and grooms, disturbed horses. His two closest followers continue to fight their way after him, and indeed they catch up on their own horses, trotting back to the Zor palace followed by a demoralized guard escort.

Inside the meeting hall Aidris Am Firn bids the trumpeters sound the call for order and has the heralds cry out for a peaceful departure. She and her consort Bajan stay an hour or so longer, talking to those greater or lesser landowners who have come from a distance.

The city of Achamar now prepares for a great feast. The tables are being decked in each of the royal palaces for a hundred nobles and their servants. In the meeting hall itself, as soon as the merchants and citizens have made place, the trestles are flung up and food brought in from the High Reeve's Hall nearby to feast three hundred lesser lords. Merchants of any worth provide a banquet table in their houses, and in every city square oxen or sheep are roasting and barrels of apple wine are tapped.

"Well, Zilly," says the king, close to home, as they catch a whiff of roast meat. "Are you for the feast? Are you, Seyl?"

Someone must preside at the banquet table in the palace, but the king cannot be reminded of his duty. Seyl says with a smile, "I will dine, my king, and so will Iliane."

"Take the head of the table then," says the king. "Zilly, bring me some good company to the bend in the path by the old elm. I'll get out of this rig."

He goes by swift and devious ways to his chambers again. Yuri and Prickett await him, panting a little. They have run and jostled through the crowded streets while the king rode home on the ringroad. Sharn Am Zor begins to strip off his clothes; again beads jingle on the polished floor. He splashes his face in a bowl of perfumed water held by Yuri.

"I will have a tray," he says, "and the stirrup cup . . ."

"They are ordered, Sire," says Prickett.

Sharn begins to relax, to smile as he dons his Lienish hunting breeches and is helped into his most comfortable boots. When the tray of hot meat, bread and greens together with a few sorbets and sweetmeats arrives, he eats sparingly. Prickett covers the dishes. He and Yuri will clear the tray when the king is gone.

There is a moment's disturbance when a party of nobles including the Countess Caddah present themselves at the outer door of the royal apartments. All the screens are up however, and Prickett could hold the doors against an army. No, there will be no audience, and no, the king will not dine, and no . . . no one may ask to accompany the king if he rides out.

Sharn sprawls in the chair, eats a lamb chop and picks his teeth dreamily. Then with a new burst of energy he springs up, dons cloak and hat, takes his gauntlets. With only two guards, he returns to the maze of corridors and comes to his own stable yard by the lower eastern hall. He must play hide-and-seek

once or twice with parties of nobles struggling to reach
the banquet table in the great hall. The stable yard has
been kept very quiet; Redwing is waiting and the two
hawkmasters, the brothers Réo, and their servants. A
page hands the king his stirrup cup of apple wine once
he is in the saddle.

"Go ahead, Hawkmasters!" cries the king. "Carry
their cradles down to the gate. We'll try the Chernak
road, what d-ye say? That valley I've been saving . . ."

"My king . . ."

The swarthy elder Réo grins and bows. Four men
bear out the long wooden cages, hitch them to their
shoulders; two others handle the dogs, cheerful black
pointers, waving their tails. They all set off through the
palace grounds to a private gate out of the city.

The king smiles down at the head groom. "Master
Chiel," he says, "we must have some decent mounts,
some tall horses, I think. My sister Merilla is coming
and Prince Carel."

"My pleasure, Dan Sharn," says Esher Am Chiel.
"Does the princess ride in the manner of Lien?"

"Not if she can help it," says the king. "She hates the
sidesaddle."

He laughs in fond irritation thinking of Merilla, riding so coolly out of Lien.

"She rides a great deal better than I do," he says,
"and young Carel has been known to ride at the ring.
Goddess, they may even join the hunt . . ."

He rides out of the stableyard and follows the
hawkmasters down a broad path. The palace stands in a
gentle landscape: grassy slopes, ponds, flowering groves.
Apart from an orangery and a display of roses in stone
urns, there are no formal gardens. The attempt to plant
a garden in the manner of Lien was made at the palace
of the Firn, and it was not a success. The king does not
know it, but the lovely Chameln park that lies about
him is a memorial to his mother, Aravel of Lien. The
queen complained long over her exile in the barbarous
Chameln lands, but before her mind clouded, she showed
an instinctive appreciation of their beauty. The rare

conifers, dwarf maples, ash trees and every sort of birch were brought at her command from the far corners of the realm to enhance this park of the Zor and its ancient oak trees.

Now the king sees below him, by the old elm, a little knot of ladies and gentlemen . . . the "good company" hunted up by Denzil of Denwick. Indeed, Zilly, who knows his master's habits well, might be accused of advance strategy. How else did Count Zerrah and the Countess Sabeth happen to be prepared to ride out in Athron hunting dress, following an invitation to dine at the Zor palace? There is of course a great deal of invitation and counterinvitation between the two palaces. On this day General Zabrandor sits at the left hand of Aidris in her banquet hall. Sharn notes the Zerrahs with approval and sees that dark Veldis of Wirth, Iliane's waiting woman, is there, and the handsome widow, Lady Hargren, and Engist, the king's master at arms. Zilly has done well. As Sharn rides down to join the company, which is well prepared with two packhorses, bearing food and drink, all that is necessary for a picnic, he sees that they are staring into the park.

"Sire!" exclaims Engist. "Your tree of doom . . . look there . . ."

In an open space there stands a stockade and a shallow ditch; in the midst of the enclosed plot, on a hillock, there grows a solitary dark tree. It is gnarled and spiny, but not unshapely, and about fifteen feet in height. Its trunk is black and grey; the smooth black patches of bark seem to absorb the light. The leaves are of a papery texture, resembling just a little the leaves of a plum tree, and in color they vary from deep purple to midgreen. Queen Aravel's call for rare trees had an unexpected success; the seedling that the gardeners thought was a wild flowering plum was instead the rarest of trees. Harts Bane is one name for it or Wanderers Bane or Blackthorn, Killing Thorn; in some tales it is the Morrichar, the tree under which unwanted children were exposed. Its best-known name is Skelow.

Leaves, bark, flowers and the very exhalations of the
tree are held to be deadly poison; and if this were not
enough, the tree is credited with magic powers. Danu
Araval would have uprooted the thing as soon as it was
identified, but this was held to be a dangerous provoca-
tion of the tree and the Dark Huntress to whom it was
sacred. It was, after all, an honor to have such a tree.
The stockade and the ditch were set in place to keep
children away from the Skelow, the black tree.

Sharn sees that now, after years of slow growth, a
change has come to the tree. The leaves are turning to
their autumn color, a coppery purple-brown, and as
they fall it is clear that for the first time the Skelow has
brought forth fruit. Two gardeners with long-handled
rakes and a basket on the end of a long pole are scrap-
ing away fallen leaves and taking up a few of the long
black fruit.

Sharn Am Zor has a special relationship to this tree;
it haunts his dreams and is woven into the painful
memories of his childhood. He bids the gardeners take
care of the Skelow and burn its fruit and leaves upon
the stone altar by the long pond.

He is still in high good humor and leads his party of
good companions out of the park into the countryside.
They follow the hawkmasters, the cagers and the dogs
sedately along a road through the cornfields. They can
look to the northeast and glimpse the Hain, the royal
hunting grove, and the blue waters of Lake Musna, but
their way lies to the south. They leave the road and
climb a low hill; before them lie broad slopes of grassland and a long valley, a deep grassy ravine, dotted
with trees. A brook pushes through reeds and sedges in
the valley floor. It is a place that must teem with birds
and other small game.

The king rides to a chosen spot, a natural platform on
the side of the valley. The party dismounts and the
ladies and gentlemen turn to and set out their own
comforts; blankets to cover the grass and baskets of
good things. The king is already engrossed in his hawking: the blue-black wanderers have been set free to fly

high, the dogs are off with their handlers into the thick grass. The two great hillfalcons have been uncaged. The dogs point at once and their handlers begin to flush out the hurtling grouse and woodcocks. Sharn, whispering to the bird perched on his gauntlet, removes its hood, meets its dark eyes, raises his hand. The hillfalcon soars away.

All eyes are on the young king. Engist, the burly master at arms and Gerr of Zerrah join the hunt, running to retrieve game. As a wanderer hurtles down upon a grouse and the male hillfalcon takes a woodcock, very high, the ladies cry out in admiration. Sharn Am Zor is in his element, striding about on the hillside. And in the minds of those ladies watching—Sabeth of Zerrah or Veldis of Wirth or the Widow Hargren— perhaps this autumn day, the wide sky, the rich, sheltered valley, the king, with his bright head uplifted, smiling at last, remains as an image of a golden time.

Yuri, who has been sound asleep on a fur rug beside the fireplace in the king's bedchamber, wakes up with a start as the lamplighters raise up the candlerack. Late, late, and the king will be back from his hawking and the bath not yet hauled . . . There is a laugh from a settle by the window. The king sits there in his dressing gown, and Prickett is going about gathering up bath towels and muddy boots. They have allowed the boy to sleep. Through the open doors onto the balcony comes the sound of the guard changing in the palace gardens; lanterns glow in the dusk.

Sharn Am Zor, fresh and tireless, quaffs off a drink of apple brandy and changes his clothes for the third time. Now he is garbed in the manner of Lien, with satin doublet and hose, all in pale gold, splashed with white, and a short cloak of dark gold and apricot. Prickett brings out the tray of jewels from their locked press, thinks of the pearl ring he rescued and fishes it from his pocket. The king chooses this ring and another with a topaz set in gold and a round pin for his cloak with faceted diamonds in the manner of Lien.

There is a light tapping at the inner door, and Jevon Seyl looks in, resplendent in blue and white.

"Ready for your evening stroll, my king?"

"Ready!" says Sharn. "And hungry. I can't eat while I'm hunting. At least Aidris has good food at her country dance . . ."

The two young men, preceded by the same commotion of guards and trumpets as at breakfast, turn up another way that brings them into the entry hall of the Zor palace. A procession of ladies and gentlemen in evening dress awaits the king, and he receives their greeting. He marches off, with Seyl and his lady to his right and the Countess Caddah and her son to his left. The evening stroll takes the glittering company clear across the city to the palace of the Firn for an evening of dancing. The pace is gentle, but many ladies of Lien have their maids carry a change of shoes. The people of Achamar, not yet worn out with feasting, cluster along the way to cheer the king. Music reaches out to Sharn and his courtiers: fiddles, bagpipes, flutes, the music of Achamar with a touch of Athron.

In the palace of the Firn, all is ordered in the manner of the Chameln lands, and even the king has to admit that it is well done. In a beamed hall the size of the meeting house, decked for autumn with maple leaves, the fires burn brightly. The dancing floor is polished and well swept, and there are pleasant bowers of greenery where the guests may disport themselves between sets. Aidris Am Firn and Bajan Am Nuresh, her husband, come forward smiling to greet the king and his court.

They are a fine-looking couple, and the king suddenly envies them, envies Aidris for having married, and wonders, almost for the first time, who will walk at *his* side in this way.

Then he has fresh grounds for envy: the young Prince Sasko, allowed to watch the dancing, breaks away from Nila, his nurse, and comes sliding and running across the dancing floor crying out; "Sharn! Sharn! Sharn!"

There is a burst of laughter, quickly hushed, for this

is no way to address the king even if he is a cousin. Sharn Am Zor greets the little prince with delight: how fine it is to be singled out and recognized by a child. They smile at each other, king and prince, and Sharn sees that Sasko is tall for his age with loose brown curls, his mother's green eyes, his father's sturdy good looks; though both his parents are of the Firn, he will grow taller than Bajan. The king reaches down and picks up Sasko, at the same time nodding to Denzil of Denwick, who gives a series of high signs. Two liveried servants from the Zor palace run up with a tall shrouded object: the prince's present.

"What can it be . . . eh?" whispers Sharn to the child.

Aidris, the queen, has a look, for a moment, that asks, "What indeed?" Presents for a little prince too often run to bejeweled weapons, savage pets, or fragile, elaborate toys meant only for ornament. Bajan, smiling, comes forward and removes the cloth. There are cries, and among them a few shrieks. The prince's expression of wonder as he is set down to look at the gift is Sharn's reward. In a high and airy wicker cage of many compartments, with nests, swings, mirrors, wheels—in a palace of a cage—there are several generations of white and parti-colored mice. They swing and run and twirl, oblivious of the godlike beings about them.

"Oh Sharn!" says Aidris.

"I always wanted one," says the king.

"A house of mice, my king?" asks Bajan, grinning.

"A mouse," says Sharn Am Zor. "Even one."

Sasko sits open-mouthed before the marvelous cage and presently is led away by his nurse, with the mouse-palace carried by the servants, in close attendance.

Now the music strikes up, after a round of ceremonial greeting, and Sharn leads out with the queen; the Daindru dance together. There follow the courtly dances of Lien, the tripping and leaping measures of Athron, and the dances of the Chameln land with many simple figures. The king spends some time stilling his hunger in his elaborate bower beside the bower of the queen.

The wine makes his eyes bright. He dances with Iliane Seyl, with Sabeth of Zerrah, with the Countess Barr and the Countess Caddah, and all these partners are carefully noted by the court gossips. The king is not neglecting his duty.

When he come to Queen Aidris again, she begs to be excused and introduces him to one of her attendant ladies. He leads out a young girl in Chameln dress, a tall, pale girl with grey eyes and short dark hair in a kedran's cut: Lorn Gilyan, the Heir of Chernak, grand-daughter of the late Lord Gilyan, a torch-bearer of Racha Am Firn. Here is something for the gossips at last: a girl who must be on the list of chosen maidens, who may even be the queen's choice.

The dance is a Chameln round called "The Maids of the North." The king speaks to his partner, who answers, smiling, a pretty flush rising in her pale cheeks. But the dance has many figures and after the first three, there is a longer pause. By accident or design, the king is distracted. The dancing floor is crowded now and certain courtiers who have been enjoying the wine indulge in horseplay round the edges of the floor. The king catches a flung fir cone, hurls it back to Zilly of Denwick, and turns aside, leaving Lorn Gilyan alone upon the dance floor when the music strikes up again. So she stands among the dancers, uncertain whether to go or stay, for who knows if the king will return? Iliane Seyl, passing in her set of dancers, brushes against Lorn Gilyan, her silken gown whipping over the girl's leather boots, and says loudly enough for all the world to hear:

"Why do you wait in the middle of the dance floor, my dear? Has your partner grown tired of you?"

Then Lorn Gilyan, with no sign of tears of confusion, walks from the floor and returns to the queen's bower. The dancing goes on. The king begins to dance again, this time with Lady Hargren. The queen, frowning, presses the hand of the young girl.

"It is nothing, my Queen," whispers Lorn. "It was an accident, nothing more."

She is soon dancing again. The queen's ladies, bonny Chameln girls and the beautiful Countess Zerrah, do not lack for partners.

There is the king, drawing all eyes as he leads the set of dancers. There is the king, and Aidris sees him as beautiful, proud, high-bred and high-spirited as her white stallion Tamir . . . and with as much sense of responsibility. The whole world must wait for him to grow up and try vainly to keep his attention. Her sigh of reproof draws a chuckle from the shadows of the royal bower. Bajan is off drinking a round with the chieftains of the northern tribes and now Nenad Am Charn sits beside the queen. He is a round, Firnish man, middle-aged, and one of her most trusted advisors. Sometimes, indeed, he can read her thoughts.

"The king," he whispers, "is in his own way very disciplined. We have heard of the ceremony of the court of the Zor, which in some way outruns our own."

"Tomorrow we have called a rest day," says Aidris. "The Dainmut will drag on for many days because we cannot hold long meetings. The king must swim and go hawking . . ."

"Long meetings are for the olden days," says Nenad Am Charn. "The work of government is done in small gatherings of the land's leaders, in local courts and moots. You must not fret, my Queen. We are at peace, and the harvest is good."

Aidris smiles again and sips her apple wine.

"I have glanced at the scrolls and books," pursues Nenad, "and given some thought to the *list* that must be prepared. I find some most interesting names upon it . . ."

"Tell me . . ." says the queen.

"Let me keep my thoughts to myself for a while, my queen, until you have prepared your own list."

"I must find a husband for the Princess Merilla Am Zor, as well as a wife for the king," says Aidris.

"Is she . . . headstrong?" asks Nenad.

"She has had the spirit to quit the land of Lien," says Aidris, "but perhaps this shows good judgment!"

Nenad Am Charn chuckles at this revealing comment by the queen. The dance goes on. The king leaves the set and takes a tour of the hall with Lady Seyl and her waiting women, then settles in his bower and allows them to feed him dainties.

The long day is not done. Sharn Am Zor leaves the ball two hours after midnight and returns to his palace in a closed carriage, a long, lurching, unsprung vehicle, in spite of its gilding and royal crests. At the king's couching, a number of the gentlemen are the worse for wear and take the opportunity to soak their heads in the bathroom. Prickett has had hot tea brought in. Sharn settles into his great bed again, dressed in his silken bedgown, and speaks a blessing to his attendants in this last ritual of the day.

When the courtiers have gone, he swings out of bed impatiently, takes more tea, and seats himself at a leather-topped writing desk. He gives a sign to Yuri, and the boy runs to the press where the jewels are kept. He brings out a chased silver coffer, which he carries reverently to the king. The servants lower the candlerack and snuff the candles; the only lamp still burning is a silver oil lamp on the king's writing table.

Now only Prickett remains, a thin, elderly man bowing to his master in the gloom. He approaches the circle of light.

"My king . . ."

"I won't forget to lock the press," says Sharn.

The valet holds up a piece of ribbon on which hangs yet another key. The king shakes his head impatiently. Prickett bids the king good night and slips away.

Sharn Am Zor is alone. He bends forward and unlocks the silver coffer with the small gold key that he wears about his neck. He dips into the papers and documents it contains and drinks his tea. The papers in the silver box are all so well-known to him that he hardly needs to read them; he fingers them like jewels or amulets.

He sets two small eight-fold pages side by side: both

bear the crest of a swan and are written in black ink in a flowing Lienish variant of the merchants' script called ladies' round. The page on the left bears the words:

"Give this cap and the belt of green leather to Prince Sharn, for I know he would have them. And thereto my love and care."

The signature is bold and simple: Aravel.

The paper on the right is torn and stained; the writing slants and shakes, and the pen has often pierced the paper. Some words are blotted out, some illegible because they are so ill-written. It is apparently a part of some longer letter.

" . . . to send help but they were waylaid and killed by fiendish *(or the word could be firnish)* traitors I would do very well if I could sleep sound but the dreams, pains, beasts, guardians *(words illegible)* that He sends will not let me rest. Let him spare the child, the first-born, the prince. He may kill the other in the womb and have the maid and myself to his will, to be his creatures. Only spare the prince. Bring this to him before new moon when he is not so angry *(or the word could be hungry)*

The signature, sprawled and trembling, is written twice. Aravel.

Sharn Am Zor stares at this dreadful document calmly. There is nothing to show for whom the letter was intended, and certainly it was never sent. Grisel Wyse, the queen consort's chief attendant, gathered up and burnt such outpourings, all save this page, stolen by Sharn: the first-born, the prince. Sharn does not reflect on the contents of the letter nor on the question of Aravel's madness. Was it in fact a sending from Rosmer, the magician, or, as many would have claimed, a natural womanish affliction?

He folds the letters together and takes from the coffer a scrap of parchment inscribed in clumsy straight-letter:

> "To my son Sharn Am Zor, this ivory bow and quiverful of arrows. Grow straight, ride well, hold to yr. right."
>
> Esher Am Zor.

He lays the letter aside, thinking of the bow, engraved with scenes of the hunting of the narwhal, which he still possesses in some chest or cupboard. The next letter, in fine bold straight letters, addressing him with all his titles, makes him smile. It came from Aidris Am Firn, in her exile in Athron, and bade him hold to his right if any tried to break the Daindru. The young queen gave no hint of her whereabouts but some proof of her identity:

That you will know that I live and that this letter comes indeed from my hand alone, I will recall to you the Great Oak where we sheltered, and how we spoke there of the Tulgai and I said they would do us honor if we came amongst them. And I will recall how we overturned a stone urn with a rose-bush in the garden of the palace of the Zor at Achamar and ran off and were never charged with the deed.

The king recalls that he never doubted that the letter came from Aidris; her unquenchable spirit spoke from every downstroke.

He sighs and stirs before reading the rest of his treasure trove. An imitation of a players' handbill printed on fine paper for a New Year's mask at the palace in Balufir. The manuscript copy of a song in a neat pointed merchants' script. The king is not musical, he can scarcely carry a tune, but he tries to hum the melody of the song. Almost smiling again, he reads another paper in the same hand:

A Death Spell
As told to Robillan Hazard by an old woman of the Chameln, said to be a witch, at Athory town on the Ringist.
When a witch or a sorcerer or one who shares the fairy blood is certain to die, then her enemies must beware, for there is a mighty working that can be turned against them. It is called the

Hunting of the Dark or, in the Old Speech,
Harkmor, the ox-felling. It works best when the
death is one of blood or fire, as sometimes comes
to a witch, and this is how it is done. The one
certain to die must be purified by fasting and
the casting off of all links to this dark and mor-
tal world. Then at the last, as it comes to the
final agony the victims, the death partners, are
named by their true names and tokens of the vic-
tims may be clenched in the hand or secreted else-
where upon the witch's person. Or if there are no
tokens the names of the victims may be written
upon a leaf of Carach, Ash or Thorn or the rare
Murcha tree. Then to make the spell complete, the
one dying shall utter these words.

(The old woman, wrote Hazard, would not utter the
words but wrote their runes upon a white stone that
she carried in her pocket and erased them as soon as
they were copied.)
There is a final notation from the poet at the foot
of the page: *Not used in a tale but the Lady G. had it*
copied.
Sharn Am Zor has written upon this page himself,
placing the letters of the common speech beneath the
runes of the Death Spell so that they can be sounded.
He mouths them now to himself, then frowns and re-
places the paper in his silver box. His distrust and
hatred of magic run so deep that he cannot recognize in
himself that condition of stillness where magic might be
worked. Yet he reaches out and takes a folded parchment from the box and reads these words:

> *To the most excellent Prince, Sharn Am Zor,*
> *Greeting!*
> *My dear Liege and your royal uncle, the Markgraf*
> *Kelen, bids you heartily welcome to the land of*
> *Lien and is pleased to grant you every freedom of*
> *this land. He awaits you in Balufir and his love for*
> *you will be made plain, for he will have you by his*

*side until that happy day when you return to your
throne as ruler of the Chameln lands. So let me
repeat his welcome and his summons and humbly
join with him in all good wishes for your health
and well-being.*

The signature, like the rest of the letter, is exquisitely penned, with interlocking serifs:

> *Ross Ap Tramarn Demerge, called Rosmer,
> Vizier of Lien*

The paper is folded away with the rest. The king
yawns at last and stretches. He thinks of his new day, of
swimming in Lake Musna. The night is very still, he is
alone and will remain so. It is his natural condition.
Indeed he has often had the strange notion that until he
sets eyes upon his friends and his servants they do not
exist, that they are new made every day. At this moment, unknown to him, Iliane Seyl, in a glorious
bedgown, dark hair unbound, comes through one of the
many secret passages in the palace of the Zor to a little
painted door that opens into the king's dressing room.
She finds the door locked; Prickett has put away the
key.

Sharn Am Zor reads the last letter from the box. It is
addressed to Jevon Seyl of Hodd.

> *To the Lord Seyl, Greeting!*
> *The money arrived at last and has been put to
> good use for the purchase of a settle and other
> necessaries. Our poor friend does as well as can be
> expected. More gold may work at the proper time.
> Discretion will be maintained, but one word from
> yr. liege would turn the trick.*
> *Hoping for a happy outcome I remain your obedient servant*

> *Dylan Buckrill, Printer
> Pen Lane. Balufir*

The king tucks away the letter, locks the coffer, returns it absently to its place and locks the press. Then suddenly he is overwhelmed with remorse and pain. It is as if Hazard stood before him, in his old bronze-colored cloak, tearing his hair, as he often did and crying out in his player's voice, "Lad, lad . . . this has gone far enough!"

"It could not be helped," whispers Sharn Am Zor. "It was the time . . . I held to my right . . ."

The lamp gutters upon his writing table, and the moment has passed. He turns out the lamp and stands in a thin ray of moonlight that comes through a gap in the hangings. He lets his bedgown fall to the floor and blunders into his bed through the silken curtains. He lies curled up thinking of the road to the border and the young courier pounding through the dark and his sister and brother sleeping in some flea-ridden inn with the common folk. He thinks of the land by Radroch, of the long valley where he went hawking, of the grasses of the plain, of the blue waters of the inland sea. The king sleeps.

CHAPTER II

BALUFIR

NIGHT IN THE CITY, THE WATCH CALLS THE hours in the dark streets. Candles blaze in the public rooms of the palace where Kelen and Zaramund are gambling, as they do every night with the ladies and gentlemen of the court. Late roses in the palace gardens are asleep, are dying and scattering their petals upon the walks. The park-keeper has closed the gates of the Wilderness, and a few pairs of lovers have hidden away so that they will be shut up in the park. They flit about like ghosts, over the humped bridge, through the long arbors, past the ruined tower. At the furthest border of the park in the west, by a sunken wall, there lurks a true ghost, the shade of a murdered lord, vanishing as he passes a certain tree.

Behind the towering half-timbered houses, brown and white, in the long street called Three Fountains, a lane runs into an old yard. The sign creaking overhead shows an open book and a quill pen. It is an old sign; books are printed here now, but Master Buckrill and his stable still make use of the pen. The printing house is two stories high, with a spreading, flattened look as if it had been stepped on by a giant. Under the rattling slates Buckrill sits alone in a torrent of paper and parchment, reading by the guttering light of a single thick candle in a wall sconce.

He is a big, paunchy man with deep lines etched upon his brow. He reads and rereads a crude book or "sheaf" of handwritten documents, then puts them under a paperweight. He snatches up a scroll from the pile before him, glances through it, smiles, growls, hurls it aside. There is a rustling, and the largest of his three cats, Ink, stalks insulted to a more comfortable corner.

Buckrill hears the watch in Three Fountains Street, calling the first hour of morning and a shower of rain. He takes up the sheaf of paper, girds himself with a bulging money-belt, swathes about him a dark cloak, pulls on his fine leather gloves . . . for Buckrill is a rich man . . . and hides a round token in his gloved left palm.

He goes down the creaking stair, stepping over Paper and Goldie, the two smaller cats, and, further down, over Jem Toogood, a poet of some reputation, sprawled asleep. A few candles still burn in the printing shop; a black-fingered apprentice is tidying up. The master printer, a lean, dark, dyspeptic man called Hogrim, is sleeping on a settle in a back room.

Buckrill takes up a thick staff from its place by the outer door, crosses his damp yard and steps out into the lane. There is a patter of footsteps, and he grasps the stick firmly, ready to step back on to his own premises; but the runner cries softly.

"Master Buckrill?"

"What d'ye want at this hour?"

For answer the man comes closer and holds up a dark-lantern. In its feeble light he is revealed as a player, still wearing the evening's motley and a painted face.

"Sir," he says, "I am Troy Loverose from the Tumblers' Yard. I have to tell you that Old Milleray is dead."

Buckrill gives a gasp of excitement and presses a coin into the player's hand.

"Poor old man," he says. "And is the scene unfolding as rehearsed?"

"It is," says Loverose. "The cart will wait at the corner of Ship Lane, by the chandler's shop."

"Come then . . ."

They hurry to the east along Three Fountains and turn down one street after another, each meaner and more threatening than the last. They are approaching the part of the city known as Riverside. From the top of a flight of ancient steps, pitchblack and slippery with rain, they can look down upon a part of the docks, a lively place with yellow light spilling onto the cobbles from a sailors' tavern. The player leads Buckrill down, deep down, into still meaner streets, and they come into the shadow of a huge building overhanging the river Bal. The waters of the river wash far up its stone walls. It is the Blackwater Keep, also known as the Wells.

There are four prisons in the city of Balufir, all far away from the palace and the gardens and the fine houses in the west. Buckrill recalls a jingle:

> Go to the Watch-house
> You'll not swing,
> Go to Motherhill
> The lash will sting,
> Go to the Wells
> Where the drowned men lie,
> Go to the Caltrap
> You're bound to die . . .

He is anxious to proceed with the plan, to come to the end of the journey, and at the same time fearful of what he might find. In a little square, beside the chandler's shop, another dark lantern blinks its eye. Two more cloaked figures stand beside a handcart on which there lies a shrouded bundle.

"Good cheer, Master Buckrill!" says a rich, sweet voice.

"You here, Lady?" says the printer. "Will you risk the streets and with a dead man for company?"

"Master Milleray's ghost will protect us!"

He sees her in the lantern light, a slight figure in tunic and hose under her cloak. She stands very light and straight to hide her injured side. Her face is pale and beautiful, her full lips painted red, her dark hair falling in a heavy fringe across a high forehead. Buckrill lifts her gloved hand to his lips, and she receives his salute like a queen.

"Taranelda . . ."

"You know Master Quaif . . ."

The third player is strong and darkly bearded, a heavy. He carries a very practical pike. Buckrill turns his attention to the fourth player; he bids Loverose hold up the lantern and lifts aside a fold of canvas. The old man, Milleray, newly dead, has a noble face and a white beard. Buckrill sighs, murmurs a blessing, covers the face again.

"We must serve the living," he says.

The strange procession moves on up to the very walls of the prison keeping a sharp look-out. A drab and a drunken sailor reel into an alley; a party of three men, muffled to the eyes, give the deathcart a wide berth. At the outer wards Buckrill calls a halt, goes forward alone to a certain low door hidden beside a buttress. He knocks in a special rhythm and speaks urgently into a drawn shutter. He turns and beckons the others.

Nothing loath the two men, Quaif and Loverose, lift the dead man from the cart and with the help of the actress arrange him between them, his hood drawn up, his arms about their shoulders, his poor old feet trailing in their long, fancy slippers. Carrying him thus, as a drunken or a senseless man is carried, they follow Buckrill, squeezing through the low and narrow door, Taranelda walks proudly after them, but there is a whispered argument. She must go back; no woman may enter the Wells. She turns aside and perches on the upturned handcart in the deep shadow of the wall. In a short time, while the low door is held open, the two players return and sit beside her, waiting patiently, as players have learned to wait.

Inside the yard, Buckrill is surprised again by its neatness and order. The body of old Milleray, lying untidily beside a refuse bin, is the only thing out of place. Two black-clad men with close hoods and close, brutish faces have the run of this small, neat yard, little more than a corridor leading to another low door. On the other side of a towering brick wall, Buckrill can hear movement in a larger space, orders, the sound of bolts being drawn and a strange high-pitched cry like the cry of a bird. He enters the door at the end of the yard and is confronted by another door, ironbound, that bars the way down to the dungeons. He turns aside and climbs up one flight to the quarters of Flood, the head warder. The jokers say that no one drowns so many men.

Buckrill knows that men of dreadful calling seldom look like monsters, that a murderer, a poisoner, may look quite unremarkable. Flood gives the lie to this; he is a creature of nightmare. He is a big misshapen old man with a thick neck, a quivering pale jelly of a face and bulging brown eyes. There is a wetness about him; his thin arms, with large, limp hands, the fingers bulbous at the tips, resemble the forelimbs of a frog. He sits in a room with old hangings of green leather, heated by two braziers, so that it is filled with steamy warmth. The tallow candles give off a sweetish stink. There is no day, no night in Flood's chambers, but a perpetual twilight. The head warder has a huge book chained to a stand beside his chair.

"Ah, Master Buckrill," he says pleasantly, "I was balancing my book. What can I do for you?"

"I have a piece of work for my poor friend," says Buckrill, "as I have had once or twice before."

"Yes," says Flood, slowly turning the crackling pages. "Yes, yes, yes. He was brought up, dried out, I remember. How long has he served in all?"

"Three years," says Buckrill. "I hope he—"

"Master Buckrill, you and other friends have made several payments," says Flood. "All has been done. Here I have listed floorboards, blankets, a settle, food of the first serving—namely bread, meat stew, apples. Trust me. What is it this time?"

"A final payment," says Buckrill. "This new work for the house of Denwick must be done elsewhere."

He begins to count out gold coins onto a clammy tabletop, and at Flood's shrill outcry he says, "Good Master Flood, your books will balance!" He points over his shoulder and adds, "In the yard." Flood knits his brows and whispers; "No violence?"

"A natural death."

"Very sudden," says Flood. "Sprung upon me. How can I . . ."

Buckrill, his gorge rising, peels back his glove and shows the jailer a round copper token with the sign of a hawk. It is the badge of the Harriers, a secret troop of the city watch.

"In that case," says Flood cheerfully, "with three years served *and* my books balanced, my precious numbers . . ."

He reaches for a pen and makes a very brief, neat notation in the middle of a page and rules off with a little rod of green marble. He pulls a bell-rope; the two black-clad men come running up the stairs. Buckrill turns his back politely while Flood gives them instructions; he catches only a few words of prison jargon. "*. . . the wakener . . . the sluice . . . not linked . . . a hull but no stones . . .*"

"Master Buckrill," Flood raises his voice. "Do you have a cart? Good. No corpse boards then."

After the men have gone, Buckrill waits uneasily, perched on the edge of a mildewed green stool. A long time passes, the silence broken only by crackling of the braziers, then a bell on the wall of the chamber rings softly.

"It is done," says Flood.

He struggles to his feet, collects the gold pieces, counts them into a leather bag beside his chair and holds out his hand. Buckrill, sweating, clasps the jailer's hand and finds it cool and dry. He blunders from the room in terror, races down the stairs. The heavy door

gapes now and from it comes the hideous reek of the
river cells, the dungeons of the Wells where men lie
half-drowned for years in weedy darkness.

The corpse of old Milleray, the player, has disap-
peared, and in its place lies a narrow sheath of sacking,
a death hull, open at the top and feebly twitching.
Buckrill flings himself down beside the river-smelling
bundle. He sees the blanched, thin, naked figure of a
man, the face half-hidden in lank hair, plastered to his
scalp and his wasted cheeks. Buckrill feels, with a stab
of pain, that whatever happens, whether the man lives
or dies, *it is too late*. Three years in the Wells are
enough to scar any man irrevocably.

He cries out, grasping the thin ice-cold arms; "Hazard . . . Hazard, it is all over . . . Hazard for the love of
the Goddess . . ."

The poet, Robillan Hazard, suddenly opens his eyes.
"Buckrill," he says loudly, "we can just make that
deadline . . ."

Buckrill heaves the poet into his arms and pushes
blindly past the men holding open the narrow door. It
clangs behind him; the three players come down like a
flock of birds. They lift up their comrade and bear him
tenderly to the waiting cart.

He hears Hazard's voice: *"Taranelda, I have found
you!"* and the murmur of her voice replying. Buckrill
turns back and scatters a few coins through the grating.
The journey is not yet done. He walks behind the cart
as it is wheeled swiftly out of the shadow of the Blackwater Keep, out of Riverside into the maze of streets by
the docks.

Hazard wakes again to the lap of water; he keeps his
eyes shut to make the dream last longer. Buckrill rescued him, yes, by the Goddess, a most tormenting
cruel dream. Two blackfrogs gave him the waking dose
of spirit, then stripped him and sluiced him down,
wrapped him up again, some sleight of hand in a cold
yard . . . and Taranelda, his lost love.

The poet utters a loud sob, and the light beyond his

eyelids grows painfully bright. He could swear he lies
in soft sheets; the dream clings so closely, but still he
hears the cursed water lapping, the waters of doom.
Come to the Wells where the drowned men lie. He
opens his eyes cautiously and sees a color, dark red,
and catchs a whiff of bacon.

"Oh Goddess," whispers Hazard, "it was no dream . . ."

There she sits by his bedside in a dark red robe,
older now and sad, with a proud tilt to her head.

"Rob, my dearest . . ."

He begins to laugh and to cry. Their hot tears mingle
as she leans across the bed and lays her cheek against
his, kissing his face.

"Draw the curtain," says Hazard, "draw the curtain,
my darling, the light hurts my eyes. Have you got me
on some sort of a boat?"

"A caravel. A tall ship."

As Taranelda moves to the cabin window, Hazard
gives a cry of pain.

"Nell . . . Nelda, little love, you're hurt, still hurt
from the fall, that damned balcony in The Masque of
Fair Ishbéla!"

"Hush," she says, "that was years ago, four years. I
do very well, though my ribs have mended somewhat
askew. Oh, Hazard, you know nothing and so much has
passed!"

"Tell me all!" he says eagerly. "Where is that bacon
cooking? Whose ship is this? Did Buckrill get me out of
the Wells?"

He struggles to sit up and falls back upon his pillows.
Taranelda fetches a tray with wine, bread, a few scraps
of the bacon and a strange black drink from the lands
below the world, which is said to have restorative powers.

"Buckrill brought you out. He will come soon," she
says. "He has an important commission from the
Denwicks."

"I might have known it!"

"He has remained true!"

"Who has not?"

Taranelda is silent.

Hazard says, "Where is he then? Where is our golden lad? Where is King Sharn?"

"On his throne, where else?" she answers bitterly. "And with Queen Aidris Am Firn at his side. The Daindru rules as it has done for a thousand years."

Her face has a stiff, dreaming look; she speaks in an altered voice: "It is the time of the Dainmut in Achamar. The queen is roused early with a milk posset. Her chambers have windows to the south, with golden hangings; they can be reached by the grand staircase from the north hall, by circling the galleries from the east, or by two sets of stairs from the kitchens and the servants hall. First, the chamber maid comes in, then the mistress of the robes with her attendants, and the queen may receive the chancellor or other officers while still in her bedgown, before she has bathed. A member of the house of Gilyan holds the jewels for her to choose. With green she may wear emerald, yellow beryl, jade or rubies, but the rubies are usually worn alone, without other jewels . . ."

"Where have you learned all this?" asks the poet. "Sweetheart, what became of you? You were healing, so they said, when I visited you in the Broad Street Infirmary. But when I returned from a four-day progress with the prince, with Sharn, you were gone. Released in the care of a man and a woman."

"So I was," sighs Taranelda. "I went with them willingly. They were part of the plan. I came into the power of a magician."

"Not the old scorpion himself!"

"There is more than one magician," she replies. "This one is a healer, too. He saw me on a chance visit to the infirmary, saw me too late to mend my ribs better. I was the answer to his prayer. Either my injury suggested the scheme to him, or he had it in his mind and chanced upon a girl of the right shape and coloring. She is older than I am . . . her hair grows curled from her head . . ."

"What magician? Whose hair?"

"I was in the power of a man called Jalmar Raiz," says

Taranelda. "The woman and the man who took me away were a gardener and his wife. The woman had been a nursemaid once to a Princess of the Chameln, Aidris Am Firn. This royal heiress had not been seen in her native country for several years, since she fled from the warriors of Mel'Nir."

"There were wild tales about," says Hazard. "I collected them for Sharn."

"Jalmar Raiz put a sleeping spell upon me; I was half in a dream. He taught me to be the Queen of the Chameln, Aidris Am Firn."

"You were ever a quick study," says Hazard.

"Hazard, I *became* the queen. I became another person. I remembered an endless torrent of sights and words, always at one remove from my true self. I even dreamed the queen's dreams. I forgot all my past life! I forgot Lien and Balufir and the players. Only a few true memories were spared to me. I dreamed of the balcony falling. I knew *you*, my love; I heard you cry out. I remembered your work when I saw the books. Yet I was the queen . . ."

"Where?" asks Hazard. "Where was all this done?"

"At Nesbath, I think. Do you know this Master Raiz?"

"Indeed I do!" says Hazard. "He had to do with the Chameln royals and with the palace set here in Balufir. Something of the showman about him. Yes, surely, he had a son, a tall yellow-haired player with some promise. He was never more than a walking gentleman here in town but might have done better."

"He played the king," says Taranelda.

"The king? Our king? Sharn Am Zor?"

"He played the king and I the queen," she says softly. "I was brought into an old keep, full of Moon Sisters in Dechar in the Chameln land. The good women knew me for their queen. They treated me according to my estate, and when the time was right, I was brought forth. I called upon the folk to throw off the power of Mel'Nir. I put in some part of your Queen Negartha . . ."

"Very suitable!"

"Oh Hazard, I played well! I was not playing at all. I

was the queen. Yet there were those who knew that I was not, that I was a puppet. I remember one old soldier who lectured me very sternly for my imposture. I thought he must be mad or a traitor."

"This *is* madness," says Hazard. "How did it serve Raiz? Who were his masters? What profit did he have?"

"The Daindru were restored," she says. "The king, the player king, Raff Raiz, came to the loyal city. I knew him at once for my cousin and co-ruler Sharn Am Zor . . ."

"Pah, he was nothing like . . ."

"He played well," says Taranelda. "He has a talent. He was acting the king, not under a spell as I was. What a precious pair we were. There was fighting. I had no fear; it was like a pageant. We were proclaimed as the Daindru, and the south rose up against Mel'Nir. Dechar held firm; we saved the city and drove the Melniros out."

"I see it more or less," grumbles Hazard. "I was half-mad searching for you. I fell out with Sharn-me-lad over this search. I heard something of this tale when I was returning from a wild goose chase to some hospital in Hodd. Pretenders. Yes, pretenders. A blow at the king's right, the dearest thing he had in the world."

"As you say," whispers Taranelda. "Dearer to him than any loyal servant. Why Rob, this was the whole reason: to rouse the Chameln and to summon the true king. So we ruled in Dechar till he came, landing at Winnstrand with his toadies: Seyl, Seyl's wife, young Denwick . . ."

"Nay, come," says Hazard, "they were not bad fellows . . ."

"The king came into his own," says Taranelda. "Jalmar Raiz should have brought us out, his two pretenders, but the plan went wrong. Sharn, the true king, sent kedran into the city and had us brought out. The play was done."

She begins to weep now, wringing her hands.

"I could not be anything but the queen. I knew nothing else. Oh what a figure I made them, what a foolish, lost creature. Oh unkind to leave me so, this Master Raiz, to be tormented, insulted, questioned, injured, with folk coming to stare at me in my cell and make me play the queen. I had only one friend, and it was the False Sharn, Raff Raiz. He did his best for me. He knew I was innocent."

"Sweet love," says the poet, "I pray you, do not weep . . ."

"I must; I cannot help but weep for that foolish False Queen . . ."

"Heaven help me, I was already in the Wells," says Hazard. "I was jumped by the watch for old debts, else I might have gone with the king and found you. I thought Rosmer was behind it, that *he* sank me in the Wells. I still think so. It was pure malice. I had led a racketty life: never enough gold, trouble with the scripts, insulting the court. Rosmer struck at me just at this time to embarrass the king, because I was his friend. I sent to Sharn at the last . . ."

"Sent to him?"

"A ring he had given me. A last appeal from the Wells. He knew what it meant to come into the Blackwater, that I was a drowned man. Perhaps the ring never came to him. He sailed off upriver to the Dannermere to reclaim his kingdom from the men of Mel'Nir and from the pretenders."

"It is a tangled web." She sighs. "Sharn had some notion of who I was. We spoke together of you, of the masques and songs. You are a most renowned poet, my dear. Even Aidris Am Firn, the true queen, had a book of yours. Can you guess which one? *Hazard's Harvest!*"

"There was magic in it," smiles Hazard, "for those who were interested. Did you see the Queen of the Chameln?"

"We were held in an old keep, Radroch, upon the plains," says Taranelda. "We were kept in the menagerie, the False Aidris and the False Sharn. We feared for our lives. There was an old, fat jailer there, Hazard, and I went to his bed to get extra food and to try to find a way out of the keep. He was not a bad man. I went up a little privy stair and came to his room and to the king's room when he visited."

"The king?"

"Have no fear. He had no wish to make love to me. He could not bear my crookedness. He teased me, saying I was an imposter. He showed me your books; we spoke of you. The king swore he was your friend. Perhaps he hoped that I would confide in him at last, tell him who had raised up the pretenders. But I could not shake off my enchantment. I believe he had your ring and knew that you were in prison."

"Hush, I never expected the lad to remain true. His kingdom was more important to him. This is how it must be with princes. For a handsome fellow, a rich and lively sovereign, Sharn is in some ways a shadow man. He suffered too much as a young boy. His mother is mad. His Uncle Kelen is a fool. Rosmer is his enemy. If there is one person the old Scorpion, the Night Flyer, should fear, it is Sharn Am Zor, King of the Chameln. But what of the true queen?"

"There was a mighty victory," says Taranelda. "The Great Ambush. The Red hundreds of Mel'Nir were overwhelmed by the Chameln at the Adderneck Pass. The queen led this ambush, and my stern old soldier Zabrandor. So Queen Aidris came to Radroch, the old tower upon the plain . . ."

"I have missed a good deal of excitement . . ."

"I came to the queen's chamber late one night, by the secret stair," says Taranelda. "I can see her now, sitting by the fire, mourning for some horse that was killed, or so the kedran said. I was very haughty. I queened it over her. But the sight of her sent a ray of light through my darkness. So many people—Zabrandor, the kedran, the jailer Sansom, the king, the False King—had told me my life was treason, my memories a pack of lies. I could hardly believe them until I saw this straight, pale woman seated by the fire. I knew she must be the true queen. I had a strange thought concerning Raff Raiz, my friend, the False Sharn. I believe those two, Aidris the Queen and Raff Raiz, were known to each other,

friends or even lovers during the queen's exile. I do not
know how this could be, and I have never questioned
him about it. At any rate the queen saved us both.
Sharn Am Zor might still have had us killed."

"No!" cries Hazard. "No, surely not! Could he be so
cruel?"

"We were pretenders, and you have said that his
right was very dear to him. The queen had us brought
out secretly by her kedran, her Athron kedran from the
time of her exile. It was deep winter upon the plain,
and I rode behind Raff Raiz upon a great horse of
Mel'Nir, so broad I could hardly straddle it. We came
to the Dannermere, and there was Jalmar Raiz in a boat
with his elder son Pinga, a greddle-dwarf. We came to
Nesbath again, to the Raiz mansion there, and at last I
was healed of my royal disease. Jalmar Raiz removed
his spell. He made me sleep, and when I woke, my
mind was healed. I was plain Nella Down of Denwicktown, stage name Taranelda, from your songs. Oh,
Hazard, Jalmar Raiz gave me gold, he knelt before me
and humbly begged my forgiveness for what he had
done and for the way things had gone wrong. I forgave
him; I could not do otherwise. But I still recalled all
that I had done as the False Queen. I felt, I still feel
. . . dishonored."

"We have been ill-used!" says the poet fiercely.

He struggles from his bed this time, covers his bones
with a woollen bedgown and stands embracing the slight,
crooked figure. Presently he manages to cross the cabin
to the small washroom and to blink from the two portholes at the docks and the sunlit surface of the river
Bal. The ship is not tied up to the wharf but moored
out in the stream. The sight of so much water makes
Hazard lower his eyes.

"There were comforts sent to me in prison," he says.
"Floorboards, most necessary at the second level, and a
settle. If the water comes up past the third mark you
can crouch on the settle. Blankets were sent; in good
weather they dry out completely. You need oil for the
skin, goose grease is best but it is dear. Someone sent

me a whole pot of goose grease. I wore it on my hands and feet and ate a few dabs of it every day for a year. I was dried out three times and brought up to a room with a brazier where I did some writing for Buckrill."

"I sent some of those things," says Taranelda. "I gave all the money I could spare to Buckrill and trusted him to spend it for your good. I had come back to the Tumblers' Yard, of course, and rejoined the company. I play the leading ladies. Goffroy is still the manager. We meant to give you a benefit, but it was not permitted. We petitioned the High Justiciar for your release and managed to wring from the courts a limit of sentence . . . five years."

"Now I am out in three years," ponders Hazard. "I begin to wonder why. Am I safe here, dearest? Will I bring you into danger?"

"You are safe on this ship," says Taranelda. "We will stay aboard while you do this work for Buckrill, then my season will be done as well. I thought we might go into Athron. This ship will travel there. Remember old Polken, who played clowns and went to be an inn-keeper in Varda? We might live quite well and cheap with him. You need rest."

"Athron . . . the magic kingdom," says Hazard dreamily. "Yes, we would be welcome with old Polly, I am sure. I would not take you from the stage, my dear. . . ."

"You must be cared for!"

Taranelda sighs and begins to weep again, clasping the poet about the waist.

"You are so thin . . . Oh Rob, what will become of us?"

As he comforts her, smoothing her hair with a bony hand, there is a discreet knock upon the cabin door.

"Who's there?" asks Hazard with a trace of fear.

"Mazura!" comes the firm reply.

"The captain," says Taranelda, smiling, in answer to the poet's questioning look.

"Come in, Captain Mazura!" she calls.

Mazura is a young man, still under thirty, well built and colorfully dressed as befits a merchant adventurer.

He wears a long seaman's doublet of crimson broad-cloth and a draped cloak of royal blue with a gold border. He has flowing locks of blond hair and blond moustaches. His pleasant face is tanned by the sun; his eyes are slate blue.

"Greetings, Master Hazard," he says. "You honor my ship!"

"Greetings, captain . . ." begins Hazard.

He breaks off and gives a laugh.

"It must be!" he cries. "Or else my wits are washed away . . ."

"No, Master Hazard," says the captain, "you know me as Raff Raiz. I have taken my mother's name. This ship is also named for her, the *Caria Rose*."

"A loss to the stage," says Hazard. "I saw you as a player of royal promise. But tell me, where is your father, Jalmar Raiz?"

"In Achamar, in the service of the Queen, Aidris Am Firn," says Mazura. "He is her healer."

"He serves the Daindru?"

"No, as I said, he serves only the queen. She values his art enough to overlook all his intrigues. I do not believe that the king, Sharn Am Zor, will have any dealings with him."

"The king is unforgiving," say Hazard. "But you, Captain, you have done well. Your merchant enterprise has prospered!"

He indicates the spacious cabin with its gleaming dark wood and polished brass. The effort of his grand gesture is too much; Taranelda and the captain assist him back to the bunk.

"I sailed to the lands below the world," says Raff Mazura, pouring wine, "and in a distant harbor I learned the culture of the Kaffee plant. You drank kaffee, a potion made from its roasted beans, for your breakfast, Master Hazard, and so does half of Lien for the past two years. We are in the midst of a kaffee boom. I have done well. I own a share of a plantation, and I own two ships."

There is bumping against the side of the *Caria Rose*.

"That reminds me," says the Captain. "I came to say that Master Buckrill, the printer, is coming aboard."

The poet has not heard. He has fallen sound asleep on his pillows.

"Buckrill will have to wait," says Taranelda softly.

"Do you know what day it is?" asks Mazura, his voice just as low.

"The day of the Dainmut."

"The Chameln lands and their rulers are at peace," says Mazura sadly. "In Mel'Nir, on the other hand, the civil war is growing hotter. Val'Nur of the Westmark strives to hold the free zone and the High Plateau."

"I have had battles enough!" says the actress, still with a touch of royal authority. "Come and let us speak to Buckrill."

Hazard remains asleep in the darkened cabin, and presently Buckrill comes in bearing a heavy satchel. He sets it down beside the bunk and slumps into a chair screwed to the floor, watching the sleeping poet. At last he can wait no longer; he shakes Hazard, and the poet wakes with a cry.

"Hush, Rob . . ."

Hazard swings upright, blinking, and shakes his shaggy head like a dog coming out of water.

"Thanks," he says. "I am in your debt, old friend."

Buckrill waves away the poet's thanks.

"How do you fare?" he asks. "Have you eaten?"

"I am stronger," says Hazard, "and I will not be put off. I will thank you most heartily for bringing me out and for providing me with all those necessaries while I was sunken in the Wells. You remained true."

"I did what I could," acknowledges Buckrill, "but do not think I was the only one."

"Taranelda has told me. The players . . ."

"The players are loyal comrades," says the printer in his deep, wheezing tone, "and Taranelda would have given her last groat; but help for prisoners comes very dear. The greater part of your comforts *and* the bribes needed to have them brought in were paid for with gold sent from Achamar, from the king, Sharn Am Zor."

"From the king?"

The poet smiles and shakes his head.

"I have misjudged our young friend," he says after a pause.

"He would not have it known," says Buckrill. "It was all under cover, the letters from Seyl of Hodd."

"Yet he did not fail me," says Hazard. "He will make a proper man yet. Goddess knows how he is faring as king."

"See what I have . . ." says Buckrill mildly.

He lays a few small leather-bound books, and also a larger parchment in Hazard's lap. The poet fingers these offerings, catching his breath; a tear rolls into his beard.

"Great goddess . . . my books . . ."

He turns the pages reverently.

"How often have I dreamed of that place, my old mousebrown room, high and dry over Ratcatcher's Row, and my shelves of books. Who had my room while I was away?"

"One of the players," says Buckrill. "The old heavy, Milleray. Ondo Milleray."

The name does not bring forth any particular reaction from Hazard, who has not heard of Milleray's last service. He is looking through the books. Buckrill has brought along: *The Rose Garden*, a book of verses by Lienish poets, *The Annals of The Falconers*, a famous book of knightly tales from Eildon, *Tales of the Isles*, a book of Chyrian legends done into the common speech and also a Chyrian wordbook. A last book and the parchment "sheaf" are by Hazard himself: *Verses for the Seasons* and *The Masque of Fools*.

"Chyrian?" asks Hazard. "This work for the Denwicks . . . is it something from the Chyrian?"

Buckrill nods gravely.

"Holy Tree," says Hazard, "I'm rusty. It is a twisted tongue!"

"Wheesht," says Buckrill, "hear me out. There's money in it."

He lays another sheaf of parchment before the poet.

"This is part of what they call in Eildon a troth gift. Do you know what that is?"

"Of course," says Hazard. "A bunch of poems or pretty addresses sent by a would-be suitor to a lady at the beginning of a courtship. There was a nicely illuminated troth gift in the library at Alldene, for the Markgrafin Guenna, our poor ill-used sovereign, from her prince of Eildon, Edgar Pendark."

"Just so," continues Buckrill. "These works you see are both old and new, some are done into the common speech, some in the original Chyrian. There are maybe ten or twelve pieces of mixed quality so far as I can see. And it is to be a troth gift for a lady of Eildon of the same family that joined with the house of Vauguens years ago: the Princess Moinagh Pendark. Now this fair maid is a match of which princes dream, and Denwick, the new duke . . ."

"What, is the old man gone at last?"

"For more than a year. This is our own Hal of Denwick, the thirteenth duke, and he will have this lady to wife. For his troth gift, his first embassy to Princess Moinagh, he will send his own garland of poems. He will have some of these Chyrian works done into the common speech . . ."

"Better done than this, I hope," says Hazard, peering at the sheaf. "This is no more than a rough translation."

"Of course, of course," says Buckrill. "And he will have some new works praising the girl or yearning after her or describing the land of Lien. He will pay for the best. He will have it all done by Robillan Hazard."

Hazard gives the printer a small abstracted smile.

"So you will do it? I may bring word? Will you sing a bond?" asks Buckrill, masking his impatience.

"Yes, yes, I'll do it," says the poet. "But give me as much time as you can. The duke must know my situation."

"I can get you fifteen days, no more no less," says Buckrill.

"And the money?" asks Hazard.

"One hundred royals in gold," says Buckrill, grinning. Hazard whistles softly.

"He'll have his troth gift," he says.

Buckrill pours them both a stoup of Mazura's excellent wine, and the poet eats some buttered oat cakes along with it.

"And you think this is a bonny Eildon lass?" Buckrill asks cheerfully.

"Hush," says Hazard with a wink. "You are speaking of the morning star and the daughter of the sea otters. . ."

"Discretion," says Buckrill. "Secrecy. Eildon loves secrecy. Slip in a few lines on the princess. Rich, of course, with vast estates. Beautiful, so they say. Eighteen years old, gently reared and so on."

"A bride," says Hazard softly, "fit for king."

"What do you mean?" asks Buckrill.

There is a queer light in his eye, but perhaps it is only the sun of early afternoon stealing into the cabin past the drawn curtains.

"As I have said, Denwick will have this troth gift . . ."

"Ah, but who will win the lady? I may just take a copy of these poems and Chyrian conceits, together with your lines concerning the princess, and bring fair Moinagh's name to a more worthy bridegroom."

"No more of your wild talk!" cries Buckrill, covering his ears. "I hear nothing, I know nothing. I cannot hinder you if you take a copy. I will collect your scripts, have them approved by Denwick, fairly printed, and bound in a jeweled book. This is all my undertaking."

"I must have an advance!" says Hazard.

"I can see that you are becoming your old self again," says Buckrill. "I'll be plain with you. The entire sum was a hundred and fifty royals in gold. I paid out fifty to get you from the Wells . . . including a payment to the players who assisted. I will not receive a penny from Denwick until the work is done. Then I will keep ninety. Here I have ten of your remaining sixty. You are lodging free aboard this ship. Guard your advance well."

"Pens and paper from you . . ."

"Yes, yes," grumbles Buckrill.

"I am content," says Hazard.

The bond is signed, and Buckrill tucks it away and pays over the money. So the making of the troth gift is arranged and goes forward almost from that hour. When Taranelda returns to the cabin, Hazard already has the distant look she remembers. His head is full of strange numbers and wild figures of speech from the Chyrian. When she is rowed back to the city with Buckrill for her evening performance at the Tumblers' Yard, Hazard is already sharpening his first bunch of pens and balancing an inkhorn on the edge of his bunk.

Buckrill is pleased to see, in the days that follow, how quickly Hazard regains his health. Freedom, work, Taranelda's love and care restore the poet to something of his former swaggering self. His translations from the Chyrian, in prose and verse, forming "Songs for the Morning Star," are very fine and of the six or seven original lyrics he appends to them, one at least, "Returning to Balufir in Autumn," is his best work.

At some point in his brief "return season" Hazard has a package sent off in the care of Starling Brothers, a firm of cloth merchants and tailors who regularly send fine stuffs, patterns and made-up garments into Achamar, for the use of Sharn Am Zor and his court.

As he grows stronger, life on shipboard chafes Hazard a little. He steals into the city by day and by night roams the streets. For the first time he notices the presence of the brown brothers, going about collecting alms and preaching in the open spaces of Balufir. He disputes a little with a scrawny fellow who stands before the Tumblers' Yard urging the passersby to forgo worldly pleasures and turn to the light of the spirit.

One day Hazard and Taranelda picnic in the Wilderness, and there, among the bright maples, beside the artificial ruins, they are passed by another pair of lovers. It is one of the memories of this "false summer" that the poet will always cherish. They come softly through the golden haze of late afternoon like an elf-king and his queen, a tall man dressed all in amber, darkly bearded, with a lovely woman leaning upon his arm, her brown head drooping upon his shoulder, her silken gown, the color of a yellow rose, trailing over the grass. Kelen and Zaramund pass by, nodding at Hazard and his fair Taranelda. Only a page and a single waiting woman bear them company.

Captain Mazura makes ready for the journey downriver to the western sea and the passage to Westport in Athron. Hazard is persuaded to attend the new play at the Tumblers' Yard, his own work *The Masque of the Three Queens,* old Eildon stuff that he reworked. Taranelda would gladly have taken the role of Negartha, the Warrior Queen of the Southland but she has let it go to another. She sits with the poet in the curtained stage box where nobles and sometimes royal personages sit. The company plays up well and send many speeches and warm glances towards the box. Hazard, breathing in the warmth, the reek of paint, oranges, candles, is moved to tears in the half darkness. Afterwards there is a long revel at the Tumblers' Arms, adjoining the yard, and Hazard is king of the revel. Buckrill appears, other poets, scribblers, pretty women, friends and fellow mountebanks whom Hazard has not seen for years. He is presented with a fools' baton, a metal sphere filled with bells upon a painted stick.

So in the light of early morning they trail down to the wharves, a little knot of strayed revelers, not so much the worse for wear as they might have been thanks to a property, soon discovered, of the new drink, kaffee. It sobers one up. Buckrill clutches the poet's arm; he has seen that which is sobering indeed.

A litter curtained in midnight-blue is drawn up, waiting. There are four bearers in the livery of the Markgraf, with the emblem of the silver swan. Taranelda cannot hold back a faint cry of fear. The players who have accompanied Hazard to the dock shrink and fade away like dewdrops. The curtains of the litter are parted, and out into the light of the risen sun there steps a gentleman in a black scholar's robe. He is of middle height, balding, with a longish fall of greying auburn hair about his high forehead and his pate. His dark gaze is striking because it is slightly off-center, he squints; one is never sure where Rosmer is looking.

"I have been waiting for you, Master Hazard," he says mildly.

Hazard is a brave man. With the lap of river water in his ears, plagued by memories of a thousand days in the Wells, he steps forward boldly, shielding Taranelda and Buckrill.

"I cannot say that I am at your service, Master Rosmer," he says, smiling, "but I bid you good morning."

"You have served me nevertheless," says Rosmer, smiling in his turn. "I have come to tell you how you may serve me in the future."

"Sir, I must disappoint you," says Hazard. "I am about to go on my travels. The caravel waits."

"What, will you leave Balufir? When this next year, fast approaching, is our jubilee, our Year of Changes. Stay, Master Hazard! There will be rich commissions."

"You must pardon, me," says Hazard, "my health is not good."

"Stay!"

"No!" cries Hazard. "I can never serve you!"

"Go then," says Rosmer flatly. "I have asked not for myself but for the Markgrafin Zaramund. I will tell her of your ill-health, that you have looked your last upon our fair city."

It is a sentence of banishment, and Hazard accepts it, smiling. He bows ironically to the vizier, casts a wistful glance at the proud houses, the towers and gables touched by the sun, the noble trees in the west, about the domes of the palace. He hands Taranelda down into their waiting boat. They exchange a whispered farewell with Buckrill, who looks sick and frightened. The sailors from the *Caria Rose* lean to their oars, and the boat moves swiftly towards the caravel.

Buckrill stands reluctantly side by side with the Old Scorpion himself, watching the boat haul away.

"A discontented fellow!" says Rosmer, mild as ever. "Thank you, Master Buckrill, for concluding our business so successfully."

Buckrill nods, shamefaced, making some gruff sound. Hazard is out of prison at least and that must be good. What does it matter if the King of the Chameln is persuaded to court a certain Princess of Eildon? Can it be certain that Sharn Am Zor will rise to the bait offered in good faith by Hazard? He takes his leave now as hastily as the players, swathes his cloak about him and hurries off into the chill morning.

Rosmer remains in the sunlight, gazing after the boat that bears Hazard to the caravel. He leans upon a silver-bond staff and gives a sigh, a sigh of contentment or longing or of weariness. He is an aging man with an office that becomes more and more burdensome. He turns his head, and for an instant surveys the beautiful city of Balufir, his chosen city, rising up among its hills. He performs one of the cruelest acts of a life riddled with cruelty. He lifts a hand and extends it towards the river, moving his fingers in a certain manner and uttering a few words under his breath. In a breath, in the blink of an eye, there comes a low cry ringing across the water. Rosmer smiles and turns aside, back to his litter. The boat, which has checked briefly, goes on its way, and presently the caravel spreads its sails for the journey downriver.

CHAPTER III

EARLY SNOW

A COLD MORNING IN THE SECOND QUARTER OF the Maplemoon. The "false summer" has faded, and it is not the time of year to be hanging about in the vast, unheated entrance hall of the palace of the Zor at Achamar. Yet the court is all here, following an early breakfast, and now the king himself appears, unaffected by the cold in a satin doublet. There is a flurry of hoofbeats in the forecourt: the escort. A single trumpet call sounds, and boots ring out on the tiled floor of the hall. Tazlo Am Ahrosh strides ahead and flings himself at the king's feet.

"My king," he cries, "I have done as you asked. Here is your noble sister, the Heir of the Zor, Princess Merilla, and your noble brother, Prince Carel Am Zor!"

"My thanks, Count Ahrosh," says the king. He is in a good humor, and the dashing young courier, his face alight with devotion, cuts a pleasing figure. All eyes turn to the newcomers. How will they be received? Will they have to be taken into account, in the future, in the continual striving for the favor and recognition of the king? The courtiers from Lien, the inner circle of the court, might suppose that Sharn will have as little time for his brother and sister as he has had in the past. But times change. The exiled prince, fretting in a school-

room at Alldene, has become a man and become a king.
The princess, though this was hardly believed in Lien,
is his heir; her estate, the honors paid to her, reflect
the honors paid to the king and the house of the Zor.

Merilla Am Zor, whose mother, aunts and grandmother in Lien were renowned beauties, has the reputation of being plain. In a way this works to her good.
When it is seen that, far from being ugly, she is well
grown and pleasant-looking, those who meet her are
relieved and pleased. At eighteen she is above average
height, slender and shapely, with a straight fall of golden-
brown hair, rounded features, in which some of the
court see a likeness to the late King Esher Am Zor, a
clear brow and grey-blue eyes. She wears Chameln dress,
and it becomes her very well. The fourteen-year-old
Prince Carel bears a striking family likeness to his
brother. If Sharn, perfectly handsome, did not shine
forth so brightly, the boy would be called a comely
prince. He is a plump, full-faced lad with a mop of
curly brown hair; he wears Lienish hunting dress.

The princess, smiling, advances with her brother,
and the two young people kneel before the king, who
quickly raises them up.

"Accept our duty, Dan Sharn, dearest brother!" says
Merilla.

The king smiles. He gives Merilla a kiss on the cheek
and claps the prince on the shoulder.

"Look at Carel!" he says. "How he has grown. Did
you have a good journey?"

"We had the finest journey," bursts out the prince.
"It felt a little like campaigning. Tazlo, Count Ahrosh,
was a splendid guide. We rode out to hunt—had
campfires—"

"My king," says Merilla, "I will ask leave to present
two loyal servants. Master Aram Nerriot, who came
with us out of Lien, and Captain Draker, who led the
kedran escort."

At some distance a dark man of about thirty with a
lute case slung across his shoulders bows to the king,
and the captain, a tall kedran, gives a salute.

"Well then," says the king impatiently, "we must get on. Your household will be arranged in the west wing. Here is your chief attendant, the Countess Caddah . . ."

The Countess, a small, straight-backed woman in Chameln dress comes forward; and a sigh, soft as autumn mist, can be heard. The die is cast. The princess is unfashionable, is not an intimate of her brother. Merilla raises up her new lady in waiting, who bids her welcome to Achamar.

"The city is so beautiful," says Merilla, "and the palace is just as I remember it!"

"Remember it?" Sharn laughs. "You can't remember it. You left the place when you were six years old."

"I have a long memory," says Merilla simply.

Then she speaks to the king again, more earnestly.

"My king, we have been so happy during our journey through these Chameln lands. Pray you, let Count Ahrosh continue to ride with the prince. . . ."

Sharn Am Zor laughs aloud.

"I have chosen a fine courier," he says. "Everyone clamors for your services, Ahrosh!"

Tazlo Am Ahrosh bows again and smiles, his eyes never leaving the king. Merilla Am Zor moves in and speaks privately with her elder brother for the first time. The king laughs again.

"Behave yourself, Rilla," he says. "Carel will do very well with the people Seyl has chosen. Count Ahrosh must ride with me!"

Perhaps no one but the princess sees the light go out of Prince Carel's face, leaving it sad and petulant, more than ever like his brother in certain moods.

"So!" says the king. "The west wing. Get along, there's a good girl. I must hunt. The days are drawing in . . ."

The princess, perfectly good-humored, speaks up to all the company.

"My dear friends and fellow countrymen, I am pleased to have come home. Let me bid you all good morning!"

There is a murmur of greeting, and Merilla, drawing Carel after her, moves towards the grand staircase. She receives the carefully judged curtsey of Iliane Seyl and the Lienish waiting women and the duty of Seyl himself. She embraces the Countess Barr, who served her mother, Queen Aravel. She speaks briefly with Denzil of Denwick, offering her sympathy for the loss of his father, a year past, and making some polite reference to his brother, the present duke. She turns aside to a tall and burly old man and embraces him.

"My dear Lord Zabrandor."

The good old lord returns the greeting heartily, and Merilla laughing and crying, takes the trembling arm of a bedizened old woman.

"Surely . . . surely it is the Countess Am Panget!"

The terrible old creature, an embarrassment to everyone, begins to weep and presses a welcome gift into Merilla's hand. She makes one of her pronouncements in the Old Speech as Merilla moves on greeting other older retainers. At the foot of the stairs there lurks a tall young man in riding dress. The princess gives him a nod, rises up two steps and turns back.

"*Esher?*" she asks. "Cousin Esher Am Chiel?"

"At your service, Princess!" he says, smiling. "I am surprised that you remember me."

"Of course I remember," says Merilla Am Zor. "How could I forget the day we pushed my brother Sharn into the garden lake!"

And with this artless piece of lèse-majesté the princess goes up the stairs followed by a small group of most unfashionable people. The king has gone, accompanied by his favorites. Among the departing courtiers there are those amused and disaffected enough to laugh at this last remark and to ask what it was that old Lady Panget had said. "*A true princess of the Chameln, although she has come out of Lien!*"

Above stairs, pacing the wide, rush-paneled corridors and airy chambers of the west wing, Merilla Am Zor comes upon a round window set in an alcove. She bids Carel and the rest go on, all but the Countess Caddah.

"You are weary, Dan Merilla," says the countess. "Let me have a cordial fetched . . ."

"No, thank you," says Merilla. "Sit here with me, Lady Caddah. I am sure I sat here as a child. There is the garden: the trees have all grown taller, even the black tree, the Skelow, has grown a little. Countess, we must trust each other . . ."

"I can be trusted, Princess," says the countess. "You may put all your trust in me."

Merilla studies the firm chin and steady black eyes of this Firnish noblewoman.

"I see that it will be nearly impossible for me to speak privately with the king," she says, "although I am his sister and his heir. He has hedged himself about with his old friends from Lien. I knew them in the schoolroom; they were never *my* friends."

"Princess," says the countess with restraint, "the king does what he will."

"I worry over my brother Carel," says Merilla. "I had charge of him as a little child. I have seen him passed over and mishandled by bad governors as a boy. I know that I can have some kind of life here in the Chameln lands, and I pray to the Goddess that he can do the same."

"Oh my dear, my dear princess," says the countess earnestly, "you will both be happy; I swear it! The arrangements Seyl has made will do very well. My own son will ride with the prince. He is a good fellow: no use to the king and his circle because he is a plain man, no courtier, but there is not a better rider nor a kinder heart anywhere. So it is with the others Seyl has chosen: young Barr, the Mechan brothers and so on. They are all good Chameln folk, believe me."

"And the queen?" asks Merilla in a low voice.

The countess smiles and pats the hand of her liege lady.

"You will see!" she says. "Queen Aidris Am Firn sees all and understands. She has the ear of our king, and she has his measure. You must send your duty to her at once and ask for a family meeting."

"I hardly remember her at all," says Merilla. "She left the city when I was only four. I have heard wild things; in Lien she is called the witch-queen."

"She studies magic," says the countess, "but only for knowledge and protection. The kind magic of the Goddess. Who has told you otherwise?"

"I think you know that, Countess," says Merilla. "My mother was no friend to the house of the Firn."

She casts a glance about the room they are in as if she expected to see ghosts of a bygone day roaming through the shadows.

"I remember my dear father in this room," she says, "and my mother . . . more than once she wandered about in the night, distracted. All would be well for a while, then the dreams, the voices, the terrible visions would come again. She was recovered for the longest time when we first went into Lien after my father died. Now it is hopeless. I had thought of bringing her home to Achamar, but Achamar was never her home. Now she is cared for in Swangard, a royal prison, not far from Alldene where she was happy once with her sisters. I have prayed to the Goddess all my life for a miracle, that my mother should be healed of her madness, but now I feel it is too late."

"Alas, poor lady," sighs the countess. "And is it true what they say, what the king himself believes, that it was all an evil spell, the work of that terrible old man?"

"I have puzzled about it and read many scrolls and spoken with healers when I could," replies the princess. "It began with magic, with demands and nightmares sent by Rosmer. Then she could not wake. A weakness, a woman's sickness, made the evil dreams return, clouded her mind forever."

"Dear child," says the Countess Caddah, "you must continue your prayers and live your life, your own life, in the present."

"As the king does?" Merilla smiles.

She stands up, casts a glance through the round window and gives her hand to the countess.

"The west wing is a fine place!" she says. "I am well pleased with my household."

The Maplemoon and the Aldermoon that follows have a dark reputation: the moon of blood and the moon of death. Now the house of Achamar are shuttered against the approaching cold, the keeps and fortresses, the villages of the highland and the plain are stocked with provisions. The lodges of the northern tribes are insulated with turf and boughs, and the best furs are brought out of their cloth bags. It is the time of year that Sharn Am Zor likes the least because he must forgo the pleasures of hawking and swimming.

The royal calendar is full of disagreeable tasks that cannot always be put off or delegated to others. The Merchants' Reckoning, for instance, involves the Daindru in hours of wearisome debate in the Wool Hall. The Honoring of the Stones means another lost morning by the south wall. The distribution of winter gifts for the poor in Achamar is, thank the Goddess, an excellent thing for Merilla, Heir of the Zor, and Aidris the Queen has always undertaken the autumn progress through the highlands as far as Zerrah.

This year of the "false summer" Aidris has made this autumn progress early and is settled in Achamar again to receive the Princess Merilla and Prince Carel. The family meeting takes place, and the queen is well pleased with her cousins. Sharn strides about, half-quarrels with everyone by the queen's fireside. He radiates unease, a physical irritation as if all his fine clothes chafed and constricted him. Only music seems to soothe him a little, and this year the music is particularly sweet.

When Aram Nerriot, the lute-player who accompanied the runaways out of Lien, begins to play, the very trees upon the tapestries bend down to listen. Servants lay by their tasks, the guards peer round the door, the sounds of dishes, voices, even the clatter of Prince Sasko's little wheeled horse, all are hushed. It is like a scene from an old tale where the musician casts a spell over all who hear him. Good old Nerry, as Carel calls him, that easygoing companion who was more or less browbeaten by Merilla into making the escape into the Chameln lands, is clearly a great master of the lute.

He plays on: a duet with Merilla, who is herself no mean performer, then the accompaniment for many songs. Merilla and Carel sing together in close harmony: sweet airs of Eildon and Lien and the folksongs of the Chameln lands. Aidris the Queen sings a song from Athron, and when she has done Nerriot improvises upon "The Fair Maid of Steyn," enriching the simple melody.

When at last the sound of the lute dies away, when all have applauded, Count Bajan speaks for the whole company: "By the Goddess, I have never heard such artistry! We are honored, Master Nerriot, to have such a performer in Achamar."

Sharn, relaxed at last, long legs stretched out towards the fireplace, smiles at Merilla, his sister.

"You must send Nerriot to my suppers in the winter!"

Merilla bows her head in assent, but Carel bursts out in anger, "No, this is too bad! Sharn will steal away our good Nerriot! He will have our servant to his wretched suppers, but I swear *we* will not grace his table. He will have everything, every friend and servant for himself!"

To everyone's surprise, Sharn is surprised and hurt by his brother's outburst. He protests that he meant only to borrow the services of Nerriot. Aidris, watching, sees Merilla soothe the embarrassment of the poor musician with a gesture and a glance. She sees that the young king is quite incapable of straightaway inviting his brother and sister to sup with him. These wintery rituals belong to him, to his exclusive circle, they are *his suppers*. She wonders if he caught the reference to a friend stolen away: Tazlo Am Ahrosh. For the young man from the north has become the king's constant companion. Not a friend of the same order as Seyl and Denwick, more of a henchman. No prank is too wild, no horse too difficult, no night too long for Tazlo.

In the last days of the Maplemoon the weather prophets talk of a hard winter. Suddenly the tribal lands in the north are smothered in early snow. The saying is that Garm, the giant who guards the lands against the onrush of winter, is asleep. Still, the skies over Achamar are clear and the frosts are mild so that the king takes

out his hawks even longer than usual. At last he allows
them to remain in the mews and simply takes the air,
riding or driving in his carriage.

On the tenth day of the Aldermoon, near the anniver-
sary of that great victory at the Adderneck Pass, the
king rides and rambles on foot the whole length of his
favorite valley by the Chernak road. In the forenoon he
sets out with Tazlo Am Ahrosh, Engist, the Master-at-
Arms, and two officers of the palace guard and, in an
open carriage, the dark beauty Veldis of Wirth with
Denzil of Denwick, now a betrothed pair. The sky is
clear, giving the lie to rumors of another early snowfall;
and as the king's party turns out of the east gate, they
meet two other riders also setting out: Prince Carel and
his attendant Count Caddah. Greetings ring out, and
Sharn, with unpredictable generosity, calls for the prince
to join him. Caddah, unwanted, goes in, gives the word
for the prince to Esher, the head groom. It is an hour
or so before noon, and the sky is slowly beginning to
cloud over.

The king and his party take the road to Chernak, to
that long valley where Sharn has flown his hawks all
summer. It is not the day for a picnic, but some food
has been brought along in the carriage. Tazlo and Prince
Carel race about, hallooing in the frosty silence and
help the officers bring wood for a fire. When all have
feasted off a hearty "firepot" of quail and a firkin of
dark, mulled wine, the Lady Veldis gathers an autumn
bouquet of dried leaves, seed-pods and grasses. She
confides to Zilly of Denwick, who is bemused with
love, that she is cold. The pair of lovers ask the king's
leave and are driven back to Achamar.

The day has indeed become much colder, but there
is no wind. The whole party leaves the campfire and
moves due east along the steep side of the valley. The
king and his brother are walking with the mounted
officers leading their horses. Ahead ride Engist on his
black charger and Tazlo on his Chameln grey. Sharn is
happy, striding along in the cold, climbing down further to examine rocks, animal tracks, the bones of an

old kill from his hawking expeditions. He talks freely with his brother, and the boy gives back the same youthful spirit that he enjoys in Tazlo. Everything is new to Carel; he loves woodcraft and hunting. The Chameln lands, spreading out before the royal brothers as far as eye can see, promise a freedom that the Mark of Lien could never offer. So they wander on for more than five miles, the whole length of the valley.

They reach an open space at the valley's end with a stone monument. It is not a dolmen but a huge boulder, purple-black, having roughly the shape of a head. It is hollow and has been lined with fireclay, like a kiln, and stacked inside with firewood. This is the Beacon Head. The king mounts Redwing again and Carel swings up on to his horse, Tempest, the elegant gray gelding that brought him out of Lien. It is about the second hour after noon; the sky is hard and white. Small, hard flecks of snow are beginning to fall.

The six horsemen look out at the plain, still green in places, stretching away before them. Maple trees cluster about a mile away about a stone wall. The low downs shimmer a little in the greyish light, deceiving the eye; distances are hard to judge.

"Well, my friends," says Sharn Am Zor, "this is the end of the season."

He takes his leather flask of apple brandy from the officer who carries it, drinks and passes it around.

"Come, my kings," cries Tazlo, "let us ride to the maple trees!"

"No more, Count Ahrosh," says Engist. "It is time to turn back. We must have the prince back home!"

Carel accepts this with a shrug; for him the day has already gone marvelously well. But Tazlo gallops downhill a little and turns back towards his king.

"One last ride, my king!" he calls.

Sharn Am Zor laughs and wheels Redwing about to follow him.

"Sire!" says Engist. "Dan Sharn . . . we must turn back. I don't like this snow."

"Snow?" echoes Tazlo Am Ahrosh, the man from the north. "Are you afraid of a breath of sleet, Engist?"

He gallops away down the slope, and the king rides after him, letting Redwing have his head a little.

"My brother is riding better than ever," says Carel. "Redwing is a fine fellow."

The two officers, ensigns of the royal escort, hide their smile. Engist watches in irritation as Tazlo spurs away to the maple trees, and the king, riding better than ever, thunders after him. He sees the two riders— Tazlo's red bonnet, the king's brown cloak—through a film of light, crystalline snow. It has whitened the clearing and is stacking up against the northern side of the beacon. Once the riders are out of sight Engist is faced with other decisions. Should he send an officer after them and risk the king's displeasure? Should he send Prince Carel back at once with one of the officers? He waits, they all wait, expecting the king and Tazlo to come riding back, having rounded the maple trees. How far away are the trees? A mile?

"Come boy," says Engist to Carel, "Let us wait in shelter."

The snow, still dry and fine, is beginning to whiten the plain itself and settle upon the clothes and harness of the men and their horses. Engist leads the way to the only shelter at the end of the long valley, a stand of fir trees.

"If this keeps up," he says, "you'll have to ride back with Ensign Bladell."

"Sharn bade me come!" says the prince. "I must stay!"

Engist meets the eyes of Bladell, a tall man of the Zor, a southerner, and Féjan, dark and Firnish. He sees that they are anxious. They wait behind the trees; time spins out; the king does not return.

Presently Carel, who loves to play with fire, asks if he may light the Beacon Head. They have been waiting almost half an hour in the cold with the light beginning to fade. Engist sends the boy off to light the beacon— the prince has his own tinderbox—then turns to the two ensigns.

"Enough!" he says. "What lies beyond those maple trees, Fréjan?"

"Downland, Captain Engist," says the ensign, "smooth, low hills. Further off are sheepfolds, cottages. To the southeast there are trails and a road leading to Chernak Hall."

Prince Carel has lit the beacon. Now he gives a cry and points to the northeast.

"Engist, look there!"

The three officers ride out of the shelter of the fir trees. In the northeast they see thick cloud, white and wet, mantling earth and sky. A wind has sprung up; the snow is falling heavily.

"Bladell, Fréjan," orders Engist, "ride after the king. Find him and bring him into shelter if you cannot come back to this beacon."

The two men plunge off at once and are lost to view before they have reached the maple trees.

"Carel," says Engist, riding to the glowing beacon, "mount up!"

When the prince has scrambled on to Tempest again, the master-at-arms reaches out and seizes the boy by the arm.

"You're a brave fellow," he says, "and you have a good horse. You must ride back alone along the ridge and bring word to the palace."

He stares so wildly that the young prince realizes the danger for the first time.

"I would not send you," says Engist panting, "but it is for the king. He is the king, you understand, and your brother. If he is lost . . ."

"I can do it!" cries Carel.

"Go then! Go along this ridge. Stop any rider, any cart and ask their help to get you to the palace. Tell those at the palace to send help at once. The king is lost upon the plain, beyond the Beacon Head."

Carel urges Tempest gently onto the path that runs along the edge of the valley. The snow is steady, but the going is quite easy. He is warmly clad with boots, a lined mantle, thick gloves, but the northern cold of

Achamar is starting to seep into his bones. His face is numb, his ears sting, his teeth ache if he breathes through his mouth. Halfway along the valley he feels as if the way will never end.

He is stricken by a shameful thought. If he goes slowly, falters, falls, old Sharn will be truly . . . lost. Merilla will be Queen of the Zor. Tempest shudders and stumbles as if he shared the boy's imaginings. Carel urges him on, looking about at the pressing whiteness, and comes at last to the remains of their campfire. With a sob he remembers the day he has spent, so fine, with Sharn and Tazlo. Surely, surely it will not end so badly. He gallops along the Chernak road crying out at the dark shapes of stones or trees. The city, when he can see it, seems to be crested with a heap of white cloud, and the plain, the way he has come, is lost in whiteness. He pounds on, as fast as Tempest will go, seized by a deadly fear.

Achamar, mired in two feet of the sudden early snow, is in a slow, numbed state of chaos. Distress builds slowly in the clogged streets, among spoiled market stalls and collapsed balconies, slowest of all in the royal palaces. Merilla Am Zor, dreaming by her fire with a book of new songs and Carel's lurcher pup, seems to wake suddenly. She sees that the Countess Caddah has dozed off in her winged chair.

Without waking the good woman, Merilla wanders the cold corridors, passing the common room where servants are clustered by their fire and the room where Nerriot is practicing his lute all alone. She comes to that anteroom with the round window. She looks down at the snow and is delighted with it. Snow in Lien is uncertain. She still recalls the snow houses built for the royal children in the palace grounds and lit with red candles for the Winter Feast.

Merilla Am Zor sees the Skelow tree, bare and black as if the snow could not settle on it. Beyond the snow-filled ditch is a patch of whiteness, for all the world as if a figure is lying crumpled beneath the tree. She screws up her eyes, knowing it is a trick of the light, but the image will not fade. Her breath catches in her chest; she is filled with a paralyzing fear, half-formed. She springs up from the window seat and sees the king, her brother. He stands across the room before a wall of pale rushes woven in a diamond pattern. There is a snowy brightness about him; she can see the snow on the shoulders of his brown cloak and on his golden hair. He has an expression that is soft, pleading, rueful—an expression that she has never seen upon his face.

Merilla does not speak but mouths the name of her brother: "*Sharn!*" The king passes to the right, out of sight in the corridor. Merilla cries out, knowing what she has seen and what she fears.

She rushes to the empty corridor crying out, "Where is the king? Where is Prince Carel?"

The servants come tumbling out of their room. Merilla goes running headlong down the gallery from the west wing to the head of the grand staircase. The guards in the hall are clustered about one of the doors to the courtyard dragging a stone urn with a rose bush into shelter. A lord and his lady, in their furs, are standing with their servants exclaiming at the snow. Seyl of Hodd and his wife Iliane look up at the princess.

"The king!" cries Merilla. "Seyl, where is the king? Where is Prince Carel?"

"Are they not returned?" echoes Jevon Seyl cheerfully. "I have seen Denwick, and he was with the king."

Merilla comes down the stairs, still crying out.

"The king is in danger! Seyl, Iliane, we must send out!"

Iliane Seyl is shocked and frightened by the princess, her wild air, her undignified shouting.

"Be still, Highness," she says smoothly and contemptuously. "Who has brought you word?"

At that moment far off in the reaches of the palace a trumpet call rings out. The guards in the hall recognize their call to arms. It is repeated over and over again, discordant and shrill together with shouts and cries, the tramping of feet. The wave of sound comes nearer and

from the darkness of a corridor bursts a party of men:
Britt, Captain-General of the Guard, his two lieuten-
ants, a red-faced trumpeter, then Esher Am Chiel and
young Caddah supporting a pale, damp, gasping boy!
Prince Carel.

Merilla runs to her brother, and he gasps out his
news again.

"Sharn is lost in the snow. The king is lost upon the
plain, beyond the Beacon Head . . ."

Britt salutes Seyl.

"Mustering," he says. "First party has ridden out.
The sleighs will take some time to prepare!"

Iliane Seyl slips to the ground in a dead faint. Merilla
Am Zor has pressed her hands to her brother's face to
warm him. She speaks to Caddah, then confronts Britt
and Lord Seyl.

"How will you come to this place, the Beacon Head,
Captain? What will serve best in the snow?"

"There are pack sleds at the garrison in the South
Hall, Dan Merilla!"

Britt is a man of Lien, almost out of his depth,
suddenly, in the snowy wastes.

"Send for them!" orders Merilla.

Britt exchanges a glance with Seyl before he sends off
a lieutenant.

"We must not alarm the city," murmurs Seyl. "Merilla,
care for your brother."

"Seyl, care for your wife!" snaps Merilla. "Captain,
we must send out across the city at once to Queen
Aidris Am Firn!"

Again there is a shade of hesitation, the vain hope
that this can be kept within bounds, a household matter
of the Zor.

"By the Goddess!" cries Merilla, "will you obey,
Captain?"

A new voice sounds from the stairs.

"Do you not hear the Heir of the Zor?" calls the
Countess Caddah.

Merilla's title strikes fear into everyone. The captain
shouts into the darkness of the corridor, and troopers

come forward leading their horses. The growing crowd presses away from the steaming beasts. The palace has thrown off its Lienish decorations: it is the old oaken hall of another king where horses are commonly led through the lower floors in winter or in time of war.

"Build up the fires," say Merilla. "Let food and drink be brought here to this hall! A watch will be kept until we have word that the king is safe."

The bustling, the muffled cheers, cannot ease her painful anxiety. Carel is being borne off by the Countess and her son. Merilla sees a face in the crowd that she can trust.

"Esher . . ."

"Come, Princess," says Esher Am Chiel. "Here is a place by the fire."

"Esher," she whispers when he has settled her before the broad hearth in a tall golden chair that is too big for comfort, too much like a throne. "Where *is* the king? How can he be lost?"

Lost indeed and cold, yet with a burning in his fingertips, a pulsing ache in his head. He cannot believe what he feels, his wits are clouded. He is conscious of an enormous discomfort. The world has turned upside down, all is very white and cold. A horse is plodding through a winter landscape carrying a heavy burden. He hears groaning, and a voice that might be reassuring if he could understand the words. The horse stumbles, he feels the jolt through all his bones, and the mists clear for an instant. He is slung across a horse's back, moving through thick snow.

" . . . *not far, my king!*"

The voice brings no name with it, but an image of the downs, another easy slope with a flash of red: a red bonnet, a maple tree. What has happened? Did he cry for help? If he can reach the bridge, only stay on long enough to reach the bridge. The air is full of swans, swansdown, white feathers, and he comes into the shelter of an archway over the road. But that was long ago. He sinks into his cold dream again and is brought out of it by the noise of bells and voices. He sees a dark face suspended sideways, a young man in a red hat.

"My king! My king!"

"Tazlo?"

Many hands fasten on him. As he is lifted down from his horse, Sharn Am Zor cries out in pain and loses his senses.

He comes to himself again in a room that is strange to him, a warm, spacious chamber with russet hangings. It is night; a fire glows on the hearth; there are old-fashioned candleracks. He lies in a warm bed with constricting bands around his chest. His head aches intolerably, his back and limbs burn with pain. He hates the bed, he will not have it, they must do better than this.

He is gathering strength for a furious complaint when a voice whispers, "My king?"

She stands at his bedside bearing a silver cup between her hands. She is all softness, a slight, dark-haired girl, prettily flushed, clad in a grey bedgown furred at neck and wrists.

"Lady," he says, "I should know you. What place is this?"

"Sire, you have come to my house, to Chernak Hall. I am Lorn Gilyan, the Heir of Chernak."

She bends down and gives him drink from the silver cup. The potion it contains is thick and sour; he thinks of striking the cup aside but does not do so.

"You will sleep, my king."

"Pray you, lady, tell me how I came here. My head aches . . ."

She has a cloth wrung out in icy water that she lays across his brow.

"You went riding near the long valley, Dan Sharn. You were caught by this sudden snowstorm that has fallen upon the countryside about Achamar."

"Snow!"

"It is thought that you were thrown by your horse," she says warily.

"No," he says. "No, Redwing is a good fellow. More likely I fell off. I remember nothing."

He closes his eyes trying to remember, but nothing comes.

"Am I badly hurt?"

"No, Sire, praise to the Goddess! You have two broken ribs; you will be bruised and you have a slight brain-shaking. We will heal you."

"Healers?"

He fears and distrusts them.

"This is my healer," says Lorn Gilyan.

A middle-aged woman in a green coif sits on the side of the bed, gazing steadily at him.

"This is Granja Am Gilyan, my cousin, and a member of my household."

"My king." The woman bows her head briefly. "Have you much pain?"

She presses her fingertips to his wrist and gazes at him with a considering look.

"Not much pain. The drink—"

"Sleep, Dan Sharn."

"My people," he says, fighting sleep, "are they safe? Engist and the escort? Who brought me in?"

"Count Tazlo Am Ahrosh brought you in on one of the garrison sleds," says Lorn. "The search has been called off."

"Carel, was Carel lost too? Merilla will worry."

"The prince is safe."

"The search has been called off." It was as prompt, far-reaching and courageous a search as could be expected. Parties of the palace guard of the Zor came on their heavy chargers to the Beacon Head and found Engist, half-mad with anxiety, at his post. The king was lost indeed, and the two ensigns had not returned, only Tazlo had ridden back, found that the king was missing and ridden out again. The sleds from the garrison and two sleighs from the palace of the Firn came from the city to join the search. The freakish snowfall continued far into the night, lying wet and slippery on the downs, drifting deeply in the hollows. The search went too wide: there were none of the original escort to tell where the king had ridden. A riderless horse was found, but it was not the king's horse.

At last, in among the sheepfolds and small trails to the southeast, the kedran in the second garrison sled heard a thin hail and came upon Tazlo Am Ahrosh leading Redwing with the king slung over his back. It seemed that Sharn had fallen from his horse and rolled down a bank, there to be covered with snow. Redwing, trained to stand, had come into the shelter of an old windbreak beside his master. So the sled brought the injured king swiftly to Chernak Hall and sent out riders from the hall to spread the good news and call off the search.

Many of the searchers, in a desperate state themselves, found their way to Chernak and were revived and warmed by the Gilyan household. There were injuries among the searchers: Engist, the king's master-at-arms, was brought back to Achamar nearly dead from cold and exhaustion. The Ensign Bladell, the tall southerner, never returned. It was his horse that had been found riderless upon the plain. The palace guard sent out parties in the days that followed, when a thaw set in as bad as the snow itself. The body of Bladell was found in a ditch and brought back for a soldier's funeral.

The searchers brought back strange tales of lights in the snow, visions of the king and riders upon dark horses moving through the upper air. The power of the Goddess was abroad. A woman in a green cloak, glowing with unearthly light, had pointed the way to Chernak and had told the weary searchers that the king was safe. Some took this to be the queen, Aidris Am Firn, working her magic, but others swore it was not so.

In the aftermath of all this magic and misadventure, it was difficult to get a clear report of what had happened. Britt, the Captain-General of the Palace Guard of the Zor, did his best and gave it out that Engist had handled well from first to last. Seyl of Hodd and Denzil of Denwick, working as closely as they dared with Princess Merilla and her adviser the Countess Caddah, rewarded the searchers and declared, more or less, that all was well that ended well.

It was plain that the early snow was most to blame in the matter, the early snow and the king himself, urged on by his reckless young friend Tazlo Am Ahrosh. Tazlo had redeemed himself; he had found the king and brought him to safety. He was now, Seyl murmured to Denwick privately, more firmly entrenched than ever. Probably sleeping like a faithful hound across the threshold of the king's door in Chernak. All that the king's Heir and the king's torch-bearers and the palace guard could do was to guard his person more carefully in the future, even at the risk of his displeasure.

Yet there was one who could do more. Queen Aidris Am Firn, torn between relief and anger when the tale was told, was the first to take a sleigh and come to Chernak. She was not displeased at the thought of Lorn Gilyan caring for Sharn Am Zor. She hoped some good would come from all this foolishness. She saw the king alone, bruised, docile, and so far as those clustered at the closed doors could tell, she upbraided him fiercely. The king was told his duty in no uncertain terms; he was scolded like a child. Then when the doors were open, the king, somewhat pale, and the Queen, with tears in her eyes, sat holding hands. The Daindru were one and would always remain so.

The queen found occasion, at Chernak, to speak with Tazlo Am Ahrosh. The charm and modesty of the young man from the north did not cut so much ice with Aidris Am Firn as they did with others. She questioned him about his life in Vedan, his family of proud and warlike chieftains, perpetually on the verge of quarrelling with their neighbors, the Oshen and the Durgashen. His view of the world was narrow; it reached no further than Achamar and contained no one more perfect than King Sharn Am Zor. He took in all her entreaties concerning the king's safety with lowered eyes; he swore to protect the king's life with his own and never to lead him into danger again.

Back in the city, Aidris could not let the matter rest until she had spoken with Engist, the king's master-at-arms. She had never cared for this hardy veteran from

Lien, but the sight of him, still grey-faced from his ordeal, aroused her pity. He had brought along the young Ensign Fréjan. She received the two soldiers in her workroom at the palace of the Firn, where years before she had recovered from the arrow of an assassin. So the tale of the king's ride was told again, and when it was done Engist nudged his companion.

"You must tell the queen!"

"There is no proof," said Fréjan miserably.

"Speak," said Aidris Am Firn. "Anything you say is safe, Ensign."

"My comrade, Ensign Bladell, rode off to the southeast," said Fréjan. "We had been searching far out over the downs, but then we had returned almost to that first group of maple trees. So Bladell rode out, and I remained to show the way for other searchers. Count Ahrosh came by at a distance and shouted to me and then set off to the southest himself. The searchers did appear, and Captain Engist. Dan Aidris, I believe that Ensign Bladell found the king."

"But Count Ahrosh . . ."

"I believe that Bladell found the king and set him across his horse, Redwing. Bladell was found dead in the snow by the wall of an old sheepfold and his head was broken as if from a blow. I believe Ahrosh struck him down from horseback, to have the honor of bringing in the king for himself alone. He could not have lifted the king onto Redwing's back by himself."

"Is that all you have? This suspicion?"

"I came to it first through the king's leather bottle," said Fréjan. "It was carried first of all by Bladell, but at the Beacon Head the king gave us all a drink. I swear that he did not give it back but kept it himself. Yet Bladell had it in his hand when he was found. He took it from the king's saddle to revive Dan Sharn as he lay in the snow."

"Engist?" murmured the queen.

Engist shook his head.

"I remember the flask going round but nothing more."

They were all silent, thinking of this strange deed of

blood. Was it possible? Was the young man from the north so mad, so tenacious of "honor"?

"There is no proof," said the queen. "We must keep silent."

The king lies safe and warm in Chernak Hall and is tended by Lorn Gilyan and her healer Granja. He sees no one else at first save for Queen Aidris and then Tazlo, who tells him all that has passed. Sharn is puzzled by the Lady Lorn: she has such a straightforward Chameln way with her, like a kedran. Yet she is attractive, even beautiful, and he believes that she has come down with a familiar sickness. He sees that she is in love with him. He has seen it happen in an instant to all kinds of people: men and women, old, young, noble or humble, they have looked at him, and in their own way been stricken with love. To have his will with the young women of the court in Lien, he had only to turn the light of his presence upon them: a smile, a word. Now, almost for the first time, he feels sympathy and tenderness for one so afflicted. For hours together they are happy as two children, reading old tales, playing Battle.

After ten days, near the end of the Aldermoon, the king has another ordeal. He has promised to submit to an examination by the Queen's Healer before he returns to Achamar. The Healer comes riding on a tall horse through the icy sludge on the Chernak road, a pale-haired fellow with dark almond eyes who goes by the name of Jaraz. The king knows him as Jalmar Raiz, a man of magic and intrigue from Lien, a man who struck at Sharn Am Zor's sacred right, who set up the False Sharn and the False Aidris, those two sorry pretenders, in the city of Dechar. The sight of him entering the sickroom fills Sharn with hatred.

"Dan Sharn," says Jalmar Raiz, bowing deeply.

"Get on with your task!" orders the king. "I will not have you in my presence any longer than I can help, Raiz!"

With the aid of Granja, the Healer of Chernak, Jalmar

Raiz makes the examination. He compliments Granja; they consult together.

"You are healed well, Dan Sharn," he says. "Do you have any memory of the fall that caused all this?"

"None!"

"Yet memory of such an accident may return."

So the healer goes on his way, and it is time for the king to return to his palace. A procession of sleighs and carriages decked out with bells, pine boughs and banners makes its way to Chernak. There they stand in the old hall, raising a cheer as he appears upon the stairs in the fine clothes that Prickett and Yuri have brought: Seyl of Hodd, Zilly of Denwick, the ladies of the court, magnificent in their furs and jewels. Merilla and Carel bring the king down the stairs proudly, and behind him, bearing his ermine cloak, comes Tazlo Am Ahrosh. The king, perhaps a shade paler than usual, moves towards the blazing hearth of Chernak Hall where Lorn Gilyan stands in a long golden robe, the mistress of the household. When he takes her hand and speaks his thanks aloud for all to hear, Iliane of Seyl twists her hands tightly inside her sable muff to think of such a whey-faced creature tending the king.

But any fears the king's intimates may have had are dispelled at once. Sharn claps Tazlo on the back, is received into the arms of his friends, strides out to the waiting procession. He complains of the weather, will not wear his gloves, demands candied apple for Redwing, whom Tazlo is leading home. He upsets the order of the procession, sets off at once in the sleigh with Seyl and Iliane without another word to his sister and brother, who must ride last of all in an old carriage. Lorn Gilyan comes to stand on the steps of her house, but Sharn Am Zor does not look back. The king is himself again.

The people of the Chernak estate line the way to cheer the king; and when the procession reaches the south gate of Achamar, there is a great noise of trumpets and voices. Sharn Am Zor is much loved; the thought of losing him through accident or sickness is

not to be borne. The king is driven slowly to the palace
of the Firn; he goes in with only Jevon Seyl and appears
upon the balcony with Queen Aidris Am Firn. The
cheers are raised for the Daindru.

Sharn comes at last to his own palace, and after he
has dined, he confesses himself too tired for any further
celebrations. He retires to his apartments—he has missed
them—and settles down by his own fireside. Only the two
valets are allowed to remain. The king sips mulled wine.

"Now behold, Sire," says Prickett gently, "the new
stuffs and patterns have arrived from Balufir."

"What, those slow birds, Starling Brothers?"

The king begins to lay the swatches of silk and velvet
along the arms of his chair.

"A packet was sent," says Yuri, offering it on bended
knee. "A packet of books and writings . . ."

The king sees the writing upon this packet, seizes it
with an oath of surprise and strips off the wrapping. He
reads the letter first, and then, between laughter and
tears, dips into the sheaf of other writings. He returns
to the letter over and over again, as if this short screed
and the wine and the fire's warmth had made him a
little drunk. He looks up, more than once, as if he
expected to see a friend, a companion with whom he
can share his good fortune—but that other warm room
and Lorn Gilyan are far away. He turns back to his
letter: one for the silver casket.

> *To the most excellent and mighty King Sharn
> Am Zor: Greeting!*
> *It is the privilege of poets and fools to address
> their betters familiarly so I will say at once—Dear
> lad, I have come out of prison. Think of me as a
> half-drowned sailor taken from some dark ocean. I
> am warmed by the sun of this "false summer" and
> by the reports that you have come into your king-
> dom. Most of all I am comforted by the thought
> that the Lord of the Wells in Achamar did not
> forget his old companion, that unhappy prisoner in
> "the Wells," the Blackwater Keep.*

Buckrill has fished me out, then, to cobble up a troth gift out of some new and old Eildon stuff, and it shall be for the new Duke, Hal of Denwick. Yet the fair maid that is praised in these pages, the lovely dark princess, far off as dreams, deserves a better suitor. If I am not mistaken, the Princess Moinagh Pendark is a bride fit for a king, especially if that king be her own blood cousin.

Balufir is a melancholy place these days, however tall the roses grow; I hear the brown brothers at the corners of the streets exhorting one and all to forgo every pleasure. I will go into Athron and see what they have to offer in the way of homespun magic, garrulous nut-trees and the like. An old friend is host at the Owl and Kettle Inn, near Varda, but if you would favor me with a reply, send it first through Buckrill.

So I wish you well for the New Year, the year of changes in old Eildon and in Lien. There will be no change, come wind and weather, in the unswerving love and duty of one who is bold still to call himself

Your friend,
Robillan Hazard

Sharn Am Zor dips into the sheaf of parchment. He skims through at first, then begins to read more carefully. At last he calls Prickett to his side and asks:

"Who do we know from Eildon?"

The valet tugs at his lower lip a moment and replies, "No one of name, sire. A few kedran in the queen's guard. But wait . . . the lute-player, Princess Merilla's lute-player, Aram Nerriot. . ."

"Excellent!" says Sharn. "Send for him! No, wait . . ." He is in a kind and reflective mood.

"Send first for Count Ahrosh. He must take my compliments to Rilla and Carel, and yes—I will send them each a gift. Do we have one of those leather baldrics with a dagger for young Carel? I will choose a ring for Merilla. Then the count can ask for the musician, to play to me in my sickness."

Prickett bows deeply and goes about his business. A log crashes down in the fireplace, sending a shower of sparks up the chimney. Far out in the gardens of the Zor palace, cold but not snowcovered, there is a soft thump and a frantic rustling. Some animal has been caught in one of the gardeners' pitfalls.

Snow fell again at the proper time, and Achamar celebrated the Winter Feast. When Aidris raised the question of the king's marriage and the promise she had made to the Dainmut regarding a list of suitable maidens, Sharn Am Zor was surprisingly keen. He proposed an immediate meeting with those members of the inner council who were wintering in the city.

They sat down together in the palace of the Zor, in that pleasant room above the royal apartments where the king gave his little suppers. It was the third festival day, given over to fasting and long wintery sleeps in preparation for the New Year celebration. In the warm anteroom the royal attendants whiled away the time with dice games and fortune-telling for the season; the musician Nerriot waited to play for the Daindru.

The king welcomed Lingrit Am Thuven, the Chancellor of the Firn, and Nenad Am Charn. Of his own torch-bearers only Seyl of Hodd was present; Denzil of Denwick and his betrothed were visiting in Lien, and Count Barr was not expected until the New Year. Sharn had invited his sister Merilla and the Countess Caddah, and now he spoke kindly to them. He was so agreeable that Aidris wondered if he might still be sick. He talked aside with Jevon Seyl, and they seemed to share a secret.

Aidris spoke some words of welcome herself and then said to the king, "My good torch-bearer Nenad Am Charn has an interest in family history, and I have asked him to prepare a list of maidens suitable to be your wife."

Nenad bowed to the king a little warily, and Sharn gave an encouraging smile.

Nenad Am Charn chuckled sadly.

"Sire," he said, "I have ransacked the archives of Achamar, and I must say that we live in a time of bad harvest. Ten years earlier or later, and you would have had a wider choice."

"Perhaps I should wait ten years," said Sharn, "and wed Imelda of Kerrick, Zerrah's lovely daughter."

"For shame!" said Aidris. "Let me hear your list, Nenad, and compare it with my own."

So Nenad, moving from north to south, presented such names as: Jamilar, High Chieftainess of the Durgashen, niece of Ferrad Harka; and Natocha, High Chieftainess of the Ingari; and Dan Sharn's cousin of the Inchevin, Derda, aged seventeen, not well-endowed with the world's goods but a beauty: The Starry Maid of Inchevin.

"Were the others *not* beautiful?" inquired Seyl of Hodd in an undertone.

"Each of these maidens has her own qualities, Lord Seyl," replied Nenad seriously.

"On the southern plains," he pursued, "there is indeed a dearth of daughters in the great families, but if we move nearer to Achamar, we find a lady who fulfills all hopes. I mean of course Lorn Gilyan, the Heir of Chernak."

There was an uneasy silence.

Sharn Am Zor cleared his throat and said, "The lady is my true friend, I hope."

Aidris, the queen, could not repress a sigh. Still the list went on, corresponding with her own. The greatest prize in the land of Athron was a certain Baroness Ault, a battlemaid, who had fought in the late conflict with Mel'Nir as the esquire of her kinsman, Sir Jared Wild of Wildrode, but she had been spoken for half a year past by Prince Terril of Varda.

Bajan laughed and looked at the queen.

"The prince had always a weakness for battlemaids," he said.

"Go along with you," said Aidris, blushing a little as she bent over her list.

Nenad Am Charn moved on into the Mark of Lien,

where women were famed for their beauty, but even here there were no more than three or four families who could hope to wed their daughters to a king of the Chameln. He spoke of the twin sisters of Duke Hallem of Denwick and his brother Denzil, Rose and Anne-Rose of Denwick, sixteen years old. Merilla and her brother laughed aloud.

"What, the twins?" asked the king. "We used to tease them in the schoolroom at Alldene. Have they lost their baby fat, Merilla?"

"Yes," said Merilla, "but they are still a pair of silly geese."

"In the family of Grays," said Nenad, "there is a daughter of the younger son, one Zelline of Grays. She is a beauty and attends her cousin, the Markagrafin Zaramund."

"No," said Sharn Am Zor, shortly. "Out of the question."

"Is it a matter of pre-contract?" inquired Nenad. "I have heard a rumor that she will be given to the Duke of Chantry."

"Zelline is a splendid girl," said the king, "but as a queen . . . I mean, she is not . . ."

"She has been too long at the court in Balufir," put in Lingrit Am Thuven helpfully.

Now the king seemed to blush a little, but it may have been only the firelight.

Nenad Am Charn, coming to the end of his list, made mention of a princess of Mel'Nir. There could be no question of an alliance with the Duarings, he said, but Ghanor, the so-called Great King, had one grandchild, eighteen years old, Princess Gleya, called "the un-marked child," the daughter of the Princess Merse and Kirris Hanran, the general defeated at the Adderneck Pass.

"Goddess forbid," said the Countess Caddah, who had suffered at the hands of the Mel'Nir landlords in the south. "They are surely the blood enemies of the Daindru."

"Yet it might have been otherwise," murmured Aidris.

"Suppose the Lady Elvédegran of Lien had lived or had borne a living child, a son, a giant warrior prince, to Gol of Mel'Nir. . . ."

She broke off, and Nenad took up his list again.

"We must move over the western sea, my king, for the last and, some say, the loveliest of all high-born maidens. We must speak of Eildon, and of the family of your royal grandsire, Prince Edgar Pendark."

"Speak on, Count Charn," said Sharn Am Zor softly. "Tell us of Eildon, of the Eildon blood that we inherit, and of the family called Pendark."

Aidris looked at the young king in surprise and at her own list again. As Nenad began to speak, everyone listened closely, as if the very name of Eildon had cast a spell upon them.

"The Pendark lands," he said, "lie in the southwest of Eildon, a rich and beautiful inheritance of which bards have sung from old time until this day. When Edgar Pendark crossed the seas to wed Guenna of Lien, he left behind two brothers and a sister, all older than himself and with families of their own. It might have been thought that fortune had smiled upon the Pendarks. Yet all was changed in the space of a few years. Prince Edgar, that comely and beloved young man, died of the sweating sickness before he was five and twenty. More than that, his brothers and sisters fell victim to accident and disease. A tournament took the life of the eldest, Prince Morr and his young son; the sister and her children died in the old water-fortress of the Pendarks from a poisonous fever. So only the second son, Prince Kilnan, survived, and raised one son, Prince Thorm, who married twice. With the second lady, Merigaun Ap Llir, he had a son and daughter and died himself only a few years past. The family now consists of Prince Kilnan, relict of that time of misfortune, the aged great-uncle of the Daindru; his widowed daughter-in-law, Merigaun; and those two bright hopes of the house of Pendark, Prince Beren and and Princess Moinagh, who will one day divide all the lands between them, according to Eildon custom. Many hopes and wishes center upon

these two: not only upon Prince Beren, a knight of the
Order of the Fishers, but upon his sister. She is eighteen years old, born in the Birchmoon, and a being
without fault if we are to believe the slight reports we
have. She is your cousin, my King, and she is, more-
over, the only princess of marriageable age in Eildon . . ."

"So you have placed her name upon the list," said
Sharn Am Zor.

"So have I, cousin," said the queen.

"It is the only name I will hear!"

Jevon Seyl rose up from the long table where they
were sitting, crossed to a press by the window and
brought out a thick sheaf of parchment which he carried
to the king.

"I have received this book from an old companion in
Lien," said Sharn eagerly. "It is a copy of a troth gift
made by Hal of Denwick. As I read the poems addressed to Princess Moinagh and the descriptions of
this dark, sweet girl, it came to me that I must ask for
her hand."

He stood up and spoke directly to the queen.

"Oh, Aidris, you will say that the way is too long,
that it will take half the revenue of the Chameln lands
to fetch her home, but I must attempt to win her! Do
you not believe that I may be preferred, as King of the
Chameln and as a cousin, to other suitors?"

The king stood in the candlelight holding his book.
Those watching had seldom seen him so moved. There
was in his question a kind of modesty. It took no
account of those things that could win the heart of a
young girl and that might weigh with her family. Sharn
Am Zor was tall, straight, the height of manly beauty,
and his charm overrode all the vagaries of his character.
He was the Summer's King, and to all those watching
he was at that moment an irresistible suitor.

"*Eildon!*" said Aidris Am Firn.

Other voices echoed her cry. She saw the king's look
of certainty and excitement. She knew that he would
persuade them all, the Council, his own liegemen and
women, the people of the Chameln lands. She had no

thought to hold him back, only an inner fear. Was it simply a woman's fear, like a mother's for her child? She caught the eye of the Princess Merilla and wondered if the Eildon blood that they all shared had given her a warning, too.

"My King," said Bajan, "you have been in danger lately. This journey far beyond the kingdom to find a bride must be undertaken step by step with particular care."

"I will bear all," said Sharn Am Zor. "I have set my heart on this marriage."

Then Jevon Seyl gave the signal for refreshments to be brought in, for a pause in the proceedings. Aram Nerriot came in and played sweetly while they all ate and drank, working his magic upon the company. He played airs of Eildon and answered a few questions about the customs of his native country. There was an air of lively congratulations at the table, as if the king had already won his dark princess. Yet when Nenad Am Charn mentioned slyly to the Princess Merilla that Prince Beren Pendark was also of marriageable age, she laughed aloud.

"No, Count Charn," she said without a blush, "do not add the poor prince to my list of suitors, for they were a sorry lot however high-born. You may depend upon it; if I marry, it will be a man of the Chameln lands."

When the pleasantries were done, Lingrit Am Thuven was the first to comment seriously on the king's plan. The trusted advisor of Queen Aidris was a thin, refined, rheumatic man who had spent many years in Lien as Envoy. He knew Sharn Am Zor well, from the time he had come into Lien as an exiled prince, aged eleven. Lingrit had some knowledge of Eildon and had travelled once to the magic kingdom of the west when he was a young man. His approval was guarded.

"My king," he said, "you must be prepared for a stiff and formal reception from those of high estate. And you must remember that the courts of Eildon know little of the Chameln lands. They will expect something of the order of Voyvid, The Wild Warrior King."

"Strange," said Sharn loftily, "that is rather how I see one rival of whom I have been told, the King of the Isles!"

"Lord Lingrit," asked the Countess Caddah, "can you tell us from your knowledge of Eildon who will decide the match? Will it be the princess's widowed mother? Her grandfather, Prince Kilnan? The councils of the realm?"

"I cannot tell," said Lingrit. "I would say all of these, plus the knightly orders and the religious colleges."

"And the princess herself?" asked Aidris. "Could she express a preference?"

"Of course," said Lingrit sadly, "but where in the world would a young girl of high estate be permitted to choose all by herself? Even here, where women have many rights, a princess of the blood would be . . . assisted."

The Princess Merilla seemed about to speak but thought better of it.

Lingrit went on, "Your own marriage, my Queen, was arranged in your cradle."

"The queen could have let the bond lapse when she was of age," put in Bajan Am Nuresh drily. "She could have thrown me over . . ."

"I never thought of that," said Aidris.

Bajan and the queen smiled at each other in perfect understanding. Seyl of Hodd was the next to speak.

"I have heard of tournaments, knightly games and strange vigils held in Eildon to decide many things, even the succession in noble families. Would the king take champions with him? Would there be limits set to the number of his followers?"

"By the size of his fleet of ships at least," said Lingrit.

"Goddess preserve us," said the Countess Caddah, shivering. "A journey over the western sea!"

"It has been done before," put in Nenad Am Charn, "and in such a manner as surely to weigh with the rulers of Eildon if they set store by tradition. I speak of course of the Sea-Oak twins, the Tamirdru, the Prince and Princess of Eildon who braved the seas in old time and came to Achamar to wed the Daindru."

"I have thought of them," said Sharn eagerly. "Are they creatures of legend? When did they come?"

Nenad Am Charn shook his head.

"I must search the scrolls more thoroughly," he said, "and bring you the answer when next we meet, my King. We know too little of these ancient times."

"We know too little of Eildon," said Aidris, "but we have one friend in that land, and it is Prince Ross Tramarn. I spoke with him in Athron, at Kerrick Hall, and he brought comfort to me in exile. Count Zerrah, son of Lord Kerrick, went on his wedding journey with the Countess Sabeth to the Tramarn estates in Eildon. They found the country beautiful and the hospitality of the prince very warm. Perhaps the tales we hear of stiff formality and strange rituals are not true. I will send for the messengers of Prince Ross and speak frankly with them of Dan Sharn's courtship."

Sharn Am Zor said as lightly as he could: "You must use magic to fetch them."

"They are magical creatures," said Bajan, "as strange as the snow demons. I remember the time they found me in the mountains and brought me this ring from my dear queen, in exile. See, it is a black pearl, the ring of Tamir, the Sea-Oak Prince, according to Prince Ross, but how it returned to Eildon we do not know."

The heavy silver ring, patterned with oak leaves and containing a splendid pearl, dark and lustrous, was passed from hand to hand.

"Perhaps it is a homing ring," said the Countess Caddah, "like the homing cup of gold in another legend."

Sharn Am Zor gazed into the black pearl before he returned the ring to Bajan.

"The Princess Moinagh is beautiful as this pearl," he said, "and I will bring her home to Achamar."

PART II

THE EILDON BRIDE

CHAPTER IV

MESSENGERS

IT WAS MORE THAN FOURTEEN DAYS LATER, on a bright winter's morning at the end of the Tannen-moon, that the Messengers put in their appearance. The Daindru were walking together in the grounds of the palace of the Firn; at a distance Tazlo Am Ahrosh was building a snow goddess with Prince Sasko. Nila, the child's nurse, a woman from the northern tribes with black braids and bright cheeks, suddenly gave a cry. There in a grove of birch trees stood three persons wrapped in snow-colored cloaks. Aidris took Sharn by the hand.

"They have come," she whispered. "Hold firm!"

The king saw that one of the messengers was an old man with hawklike features and white hair; next to him stood a woman, tawny-haired, with a silvery glint to her complexion; and farther off a dark man with his hands resting on a wooden flute that hung on a thong about his neck. Slowly they approached the Daindru and bowed to them.

Aidris said, "Greetings to you and your companions, Master Dravyd!"

The old man bowed again and murmured their names: Nieva, the woman, and Gil, the dark man.

"Greetings to King Sharn, in the year of changes," said Nieva, her voice strange and sweet, like bell-chimes.

"I have told you my reason for this summons," said Aidris. "King Sharn Am Zor has heard of the Princess Moinagh Pendark, his cousin, and will sue for her hand. Will your master, Prince Ross Tramarn, help us in this matter?"

"The Prince sends a New Year greeting to the Daindru," said Gil, the dark man. "This is our last errand in his service."

"How can this be?" asked Aidris. "Surely the Prince is not . . ."

"He is well." Dravyd smiled. "Yet his estate will soon be changed. The Priest-King Angisfor of the house of Paldo goes forth, and his place will be taken by Prince Ross Tramarn."

"He will be king!" said Sharn.

"And therefore he can no longer help you," said Nieva, spreading her silvery hands.

"I do not understand . . ."

"He will go into retreat, beyond the sacred wood," said Dravyd, "and have no more to do with worldly things. We are the messengers of the knightly Order of the Falconers and served the Prince when he was the patron of that order. Now the new patron will be the Eorl Leffert, and we will be his servants, his messengers."

"Can you commend us to the new Prince of the house of Tramarn?" asked Aidris.

"The new head of the house is the Princess Gaveril," said Nieva, "the niece of Prince Ross, for he had no true-born son. She is widowed and has one son, Prince Gwalchai; and he too is a suitor for the hand of this pearl of the house of Pendark."

"There are ladies of high degree in the Chameln lands," said Dravyd, "and King Sharn might have any one of them for a wife."

"Alas," said Sharn Am Zor impatiently, "is this all the help you have for me?"

Aidris laid a hand on his arm and said to the Messengers, "Come into the palace of the Firn. Accept our hospitality. We will speak further . . ."

The old man inclined his head, and the three walked

with the queen to a pathway where three kedran of the royal guard had appeared almost as suddenly as the messengers themselves. So they were escorted into the palace and settled down to enjoy Chameln delicacies, sampling the apple wine and the brandy. Gerr of Kerrick, Count Zerrah, came with the Countess Sabeth and paid his respects to the messengers, who were welcome guests in his Athron hall. Presents were given. The Daindru spoke several times with the Messengers but received little in the way of firm advice.

Once Gil, the dark man, said: "Dan Sharn, the land of Eildon makes no alliances these days with the lands of the continent of Hylor. Some would say there is no benefit for Eildon in such a marriage."

Sharn went from red to white and his torch-bearer, Seyl of Hodd, answered smoothly, "Marriage with the reigning king of a wide, rich and secure kingdom, even a distant one, would seem a benefit."

"Do you mean," asked Sharn, controlling himself, "that we have nothing that you want?"

"Perhaps," said Nieva, smiling.

She walked or floated to the window of the painted room in the king's apartments, where the Messengers had been received, and gazed out into the snowy gardens.

"Give us your Skelow tree, Dan Sharn!"

"What, only that?" asked the king. "Why will Eildon have my tree?"

"There is a vacant place for it in the garden of the White Tower, where all the sacred trees of Hylor are growing," said Nieva earnestly. "We lost the Carach; it was brought home to Athron, but a seed was soon found to be replanted. But the Skelow is still lacking. This may be the last Skelow in all the world."

"I doubt that," said Sharn. "My gardeners have the care of the young trees, perhaps there is a Skelow among them."

"You mean that the tree has borne fruit?" asked Dravyd.

Sharn and his friend, Jevon Seyl, both smiled, believing they had something to bargain with at last.

"A seedling, a healthy seedling," said the king, "might be added to my troth gift of pearls for the Princess Moinagh."

The Messengers bowed solemnly.

"We would take care that this part of the gift came safely to Eildon," said Nieva.

"It is not a thing to be carried by any mortal man," said Gil.

"The gardeners take care, with gloves and wooden tongs and so forth," said Sharn, "but some persons must be immune. I have no fear of the Skelow tree. It will not harm me."

He walked quickly through the open doorway into his bedchamber and went to the press where jewels were kept. He came back and extended his hand to the Messengers. On his open palm lay a single black leaf.

The Messengers stared at Sharn Am Zor as if seeing him for the first time. They murmured together in Chyrian, and Nieva said, "Dan Sharn, you have a rare gift as well as a rare tree. It is from the Eildon blood; a power of resistance to many influences."

"Well, I am proof against this tree. Some are not harmed by stinging nettles!" laughed the king.

"You are proof against much more than that," said Dravyd sadly.

"Against magic, are you saying?" asked the king. "Well and good. You know I will have no truck with it."

Dravyd quelled his fellow Messengers with a glance and said, "Choose an envoy from your court, King Sharn, to deliver your troth gift. We will see that your embassies come safely to Eildon!"

It was all the encouragment that the king needed. The envoy was already chosen: Count Effrim Barr, one of the king's torchbearers. There was much to recommend the choice. Count Barr was a man of forty, handsome and urbane, with something of a Lienish air about him. He was dignified, fluent and, it was hoped, discreet and sensible. His wife, Countess Madelon, who had attended Queen Aravel, was held responsible for some of her husband's good qualities or at least for his stylish dress.

Sharn Am Zor concentrated all his energy upon the preparation of the troth gift, and the letters that would accompany it. Nothing else was undertaken in the palace; all ceremony was set aside. Count Barr was instructed by the king daylong and nightlong. When at last he rode out with this escort, those watching remarked how he smiled.

"Count Barr seems glad to be on his way," said Bajan Am Nuresh. "Are you sure he has been thoroughly instructed, my king?"

"He is a worthy envoy," said Aidris with a warning glance at her husband.

Sharn Am Zor, nervous and withdrawn, put on a smile and raised his hand to those departing.

"Surely I know that tall young fellow on the bay," said Aidris.

"Yes," said the king, "it is Esher Am Chiel. I had him here as a head groom. Merilla suggested him as Barr's esquire. She has this fancy to do more for the cousins, to set things right."

The true reason for the virtual banishment of King Esher Am Zor's two sisters was known to Aidris, and it had little to do with the lost land of the Chiel or the money troubles of the Inchevin. Queen Aravel had conceived a jealous hatred against her two sisters-in-law and their children.

Behind the Envoy and his escort rode the Messengers of the Falconers upon their borrowed horses, leaving the Chameln lands in an everyday fashion, however magically they had first appeared. Gil, the dark man, carried a wooden coffer containing a seedling of the Skelow tree, carefully packed to keep out the cold. Those watching upon the bastion of the south wall, above the sacred stones, saw the procession out of sight. The way led to Count Barr's villa on the Danmar, then by pinnace or pleasure boat down the Bal to Balufir, where the party would take ship for Eildon.

"The Messengers have their own boat," said Sharn Am Zor.

"Yes, Sire," said Gerr of Zerrah, who stood nearby.

"My father saw that boat once, long ago, when he was plain Huw Kerrick, a poor sailor, near Port Cayl."

"Tell me . . ." said the king.

"It came by night," said Gerr, "a small boat with a painted sail. It moved upon the sea by magic . . ."

Sharn Am Zor made some incredulous noise, and Zerrah smiled.

"The messengers stepped out," he said, "and once they were safely on land, the empty boat sailed away again to the west, or so my father said. I have no reason to doubt him."

Now there was nothing to do but wait.

Afterwards it seemed to the court of the Zor and even to the court of the Firn that the whole year was spent in a dream of Eildon. Sharn Am Zor planned and replanned his entourage for the journey. He had sent letters through Buckrill, the printer, to his old companion Hazard, suggesting that a poet would be no bad thing to take along, and at last he had a reply directly out of Athron, carried by a merchant. It was a short letter in a clear round script, not the poet's hand; and though the king drew encouragement from it, he was a little disappointed.

I cannot write, lad, because my arm is swollen. An aftermath of my captivity is a plague of boils. This will pass, the leeches say, but meantime I must eat greens and use salves. I am delighted that you have come so far with the Eildon bride and will send more songs, as you have asked, and hope they find favor with you and with the princess. But for the journey I must humbly beg to be excused. An old tattered hack, a patched thing like myself, will be no ornament to your royal entourage. Think of me, if you will, as I was in the old days in our bright city, when I took to the boards and played Wanthor, the Poor Knight, in the Masque of Warriors. So I will say, in this character, and as myself:

*"The sun may darken, lord king, and the stars
fall into the abyss of night,
But my love and duty will never fail!"*

The poet had made an effort to sign the letter, but the small, neat signature wandered and sprawled as it had not done before even when Hazard had had too much to drink. With the letter, copied, the king did not doubt, by one of the poet's light-o-loves, were three lyrics: "Moonlight Remembered," "The Common Day," and "The Colors of the Springtime," all counted as the finest work of his middle period.

At last, towards the end of the Birchmoon, in bright spring weather, Count Barr returned. The Council, hastily summoned, sat down in the cold hall of the Dainmut.

"I will let Count Barr, my good torch-bearer speak," said the king. "Our embassy has been crowned with success!"

So, nothing loath, Effrim Am Barr told of his winter journey. The caravel, captained by a certain Master Dynstane, a friend of the Chameln, made good time: ten days from the port of Balamut, in Cayl, to the great and ancient city of Lindriss upon the Laun.

"The Messengers of the Falconers," said Count Barr, "parted company from us at Balufir to take their own boat, and they came to Eildon before us. So our way was prepared. Lindriss is a large city; the port is busy and foreign visitors might be lost without a guide and a full purse. As it was, there were horses waiting and a kedran captain of the Falconers. We had planned to go straight to the Pendark Court, but our guide led us another way. We had come to Lindriss just in time to lay our suit before the Banquet of the Long Board, a meeting of all the nobility of Eildon, and the Messengers were insistent that we should not let slip this chance.

"So we set out in midmorning, and when the mist cleared, we saw all about us the hills and towers of Lindress, a city larger than Achamar or Balufir. The citizens hailed us as we passed, and a few seemed to grasp what we said and called us Kemmerlonders or Chemlings. We came at last to the Hall of the Kings, a long grey pile with a wooden dome, set in green meadows.

"There is a custom at this Banquet of the Long Board for the Lord of the Revels to call for a wonder, some piece of magic or good news. Our Embassy from the Chameln Lands was this wonder for the year of changes. At a given moment, our trumpeter sounded the call of the Daindru and of the Zor; we entered the hall and stood before the noble company while our herald cried out the names and titles of King Sharn Am Zor and my own name as envoy.

"Dan Sharn, Dan Aidris. I need to be a poet, a minstrel of old time to do justice to that brave sight: the long, draped festive board, the noble hall, the princes and princesses, together with their nobles, all richly dressed in blazoned surcoats and flowing raiment—all the pride of Eildon was there.

"I marked out first Prince Beren Pendark, a handsome open-faced young man under the baldachin of the Fishers, then in the center of the board Prince Borss Paldo, broadly built and auburn-haired. It was this prince who bade me welcome with a great display of knightly courtesy. He said that it was a great wonder we had come so far and asked certain simple questions about the Daindru, the double sovereignty.

"There was an interjection from a nobleman, the Duke of Wencaer, who asked: 'Had the Kemlings not lately destroyed the armies of a neighboring kingdom with their wild hordes?' My good esquire, Esher Am Chiel, plucked me by the sleeve and bade me mark the crests beside Prince Borss. There, next to the prince sat a handsome dark lady and a young girl with long, blonde braided hair; theirs was the crest of the Duarings of Mel'Nir. It was the Princess Merse of Mel'Nir, daughter of Ghanor, the so-called great king, and her daughter Princess Gleya, the betrothed of Prince Borss.

"So I replied to Wencaer, 'The lands of the Chameln are at peace, and we bear no present enmity to any

here. The Daindru rules in Achamar as it has done for a
thousand years.'

"So Prince Borss asked me plainly what the King of
the Zor had to seek in the land of Eildon. I saw then
that the Messengers of the Falconers had appeared in
the hall, and I went on according to their instructions. I
begged the Courts of Eildon to accept the king's gift of
a young Skelow tree. The elder messenger, Dravyd,
came forward and laid the coffer with the tree before
Borss Paldo, and by magic, for it had never done so
before, the coffer glowed with a dark radiance, and all
the company gave a gasp of wonder.

"Prince Borss expressed thanks for this great gift and
said that it increased the honor of King Sharn, as the
giver, and the honor of the Falconers, whose Messengers had brought it into Eildon. He gave the tree into
the care of the High Priest of the Druda and the White
Prophetess, who both stood by, ready to speak a grace
at the banquet.

"Then I spoke again, and this time I addressed Prince
Beren Pendark, saying the words that were agreed
upon. I told how the beauty and virtue of the Princess
Moinagh Pendark were known to the king and humbly
begged, on his behalf, that he be allowed to sue for the
hand of this princess, to make her his queen. Here I
disgressed a little and set forth the qualities of the king,
my master, and also the benefit to both kingdoms of
this loving and peaceful bond. Then I opened the silver
casket of pearls, the troth gift, and set them before the
Prince of Pendark.

"Prince Beren was taken by surprise. He sprang up
as I spoke, and when I had done he cried out, 'Who has
done this to my kinsmen?' I could not understand this
cry. Prince Borss said, 'Your honor is increased, Prince
Beren!' and Princess Gaveril Tramarn laughed and said,
'Now there are two kings and a duke of Lien who all
seek the pearl of Pendark!' Then the young Prince
Beren seemed to recollect himself. He greeted me heartily and said that he longed to hear of his cousin, Sharn
Am Zor. He accepted the king's suit and praised the

troth gift. More than that he spoke of the laws of hospitality, saying that he would fail in them if he did not bid the envoy of King Sharn to lodge in the Pendark Court. So I accepted his offer with fair words. I was led with my esquire to the seats of Destiny, and our escort were taken to the place where the followers had their own feast. So I accepted his offer with fair words and the first part of our embassy was successfully concluded."

Aidris felt herself join in the general sigh of relief. Sharn was still on his feet, glowing with excitement.

"There, you see?" he cried. "The Messengers have served us well! And what a happy chance that allowed our envoy to be the wonder at this banquet!"

Count Barr cleared his throat discretely.

"It was not quite a happy chance, my king," he said. "The Messengers had smoothed the way for us. I paid over half of the gold that I brought into Eildon to the Lord of the Revels for the privilege of being the wonder. I understand that others coveted this place."

"Count Barr," said Aidris, "I know you must be weary from your long journey, but I would hear more of Prince Beren. Why did he hesitate? Why did he cry out when the king's suit was proclaimed?"

"My queen," said Barr, "I cannot tell. I never spoke to the prince again."

There was a certain discomfort at the Council board, but the king looked undisturbed. Count Barr went on with his story.

"We were taken to the Pendark Court when the banquet ended by a young esquire of the Fishers. He told us that Prince Beren was required to go into a knightly retreat, a vigil, after the banquet. He carried a letter, written in the Prince's tiring room, to be delivered to his mother, Princess Merigaun.

"The Pendark Court, when we came there, was a fair white mansion, very old, and the lady of the house came out to greet us: Princess Merigaun. She is well-made, small and fine, with hair of an ashen fair color. Many of the Eildon nobility used magic to smooth away their wrinkles, but Princess Merigaun always 'wore her years,' for she is of a beauty that resists age.

"She was plainly delighted to receive a visit from such a great distance and spoke of the king at once as a cousin of her house. So I followed her into a spacious bower, and there, with one or two ladies in waiting, I first beheld the Princess Moinagh, sitting by a little stone pond in the floor of the chamber watching the golden fishes in the water. Truly she is an enchanting creature; she outshone all those ladies present though some were very beautiful.

"She is of the middle stature and very slender. Her hair is brown-black; it was drawn back from her face with a jeweled clasp and then fell loose, almost to her waist. She is pale, her eyes large and widely spaced, of a soft grey or grey-green. Her teeth are small and even, her voice sweet, childlike, yet she speaks well.

"When Princess Merigaun read her son's letter, her look became more grave and formal. She sighed and said that she understood what had passed. I presented the troth gift again, and I am sure Princess Moinagh was pleased with the pearls. Then, saying that tradition must be observed, Merigaun sent her daughter away with her ladies.

"Then I sat alone, at the fireside, with Princess Merigaun, and told her of the Chameln lands and of the Daindru and of King Sharn Am Zor. She heard me out gravely and said, 'The Land Pledge will not be a burden to such a king.' I swore that it would be worth any parcel of land of the king to have such a bride. Then Merigaun said, 'It cannot be helped.' She asked if I had anything about me that belonged to the king or anything that he had touched. I had, of course, the king's ring with the crest of the Daindru, for sealing documents, so I let her hold the ring.

"She clasped it in her hand, shut her eyes for a moment, then said at last, 'Your king is all that you say and more, Count Barr. I believe it is his destiny to journey to Eildon.'

"I felt this was a most hopeful reply that augured well for the king's suit."

Count Barr who had spoken with great concentration and eagerness, paused for breath. The Council board stood in a circle of daylight shining down from open shutters overhead, in the midst of the dark hall. There was a murmur of voices in the darkness where the guards were standing, and a figure strode out of the shadows into the light. It was Jaraz, the queen's healer, with a long dark cloak, richly lined, over his customary robe of homespun wool. He carried a staff and held it up urgently.

"My queen! My king!" he said. "I beg leave to speak to you and to this Council!"

Aidris recalled with a twinge of old fear the very first time that she had set eyes upon this man, Jalmar Raiz, as he rose up in the path of the royal hunt. She wondered if Bajan and Sharn, who had ridden at her side, could recall this moment.

Sharn said angrily, "Aidris, have you bidden Raiz to this Council?"

"No, Cousin," she said, "but I would hear him speak."

The king glowered at Jalmar Raiz then gave a curt gesture of assent.

"I have come against my will," said the healer, "for I know that the king will not hear reason from a man he hates. Yet I must implore the Daindru and the Council to turn back from this act of folly. King Sharn Am Zor should not go into Eildon. He will never be permitted to wed the Princess of Pendark."

"You are mad, old man!" said Sharn Am Zor. "Aidris, your healer presumes too much!"

"Why do you say this?" the queen asked Jalmar Raiz. "Count Barr's embassy . . ."

"The Count is an honest man," said Jalmar Raiz, "but he is no diplomat. He was paraded before the Banquet of the Long Board straightaway with no chance to consult with the house of Pendark, and he did not even check the crests of those at table. He was brought in by the Messengers of the Falconers to embarrass both Paldo and Pendark; as the envoy of the King of the Chameln he could not be welcome to the Princess of Mel'Nir."

"And Pendark?" asked Lingrit Am Thuven, following closely. "What do you say to Prince Beren's reaction?"

"He was trapped," said Jalmar Raiz. "As soon as Count Barr put forth the king's suit before that company, Prince Beren was honor-bound to accept it, even if he knew that King Sharn had little chance of marrying his sister and must incur the loss of land and goods."

"But why? Why?" exclaimed the king. "Am I so unworthy a suitor?"

The Council chimed in with the king, challenging the boldness of Jalmar Raiz, assuring the king of his worthiness.

"Eildon is old and its ways are strange," said Jalmar Raiz. "The Princes of Eildon are not close even to Lien, their former tributary. Dealings with the Chameln lands lie far in the past. Eildon has its own cult of honor and a lasting prejudice against foreigners. No princess of the blood would be allowed to wed beyond the borders of Eildon!"

"Great Goddess!" said the king. "I share that blood! I am cousin to the princess!"

"This brings me to a further danger," said the healer. "You are known, my King, for a hatred of magic. Yet in Eildon magic is widely used in everyday life."

"The king will take magical protection!" said Aidris.

"Yes," said Sharn Am Zor. "Yes, if it must be. In any case I am proof against magic. The Messengers of the Falconers, whom I trust at least as much as I trust you, Raiz, have told me this is a rare thing."

"This was known to me," said Jalmar Raiz, sadly. "You are a bandhul, one dark and light at once. It is indeed a rare condition. My King, I beg you not to go into Eildon!"

"Be damned to you, traitorous fellow!" cried Sharn Am Zor. "You know nothing. You have not heard all of Barr's report. I am pledged to take part in a tournament and a knightly retreat. I may bring seven champions. Here is the invitation, a fair parchment, richly illuminated . . ."

"Fit for a king," said Jalmar Raiz. "I hope a copy was taken at once, in Eildon."

"No," said Effrim Am Barr, alarmed. "No, we did not take a copy. Why should we? Could the letters change upon the page? Could the ink fade? I protest, my King. This healer goes very sharply against my honor, as well as your own!"

Jalmar Raiz caught the eye of the queen and bowed his head. Sharn saw that the healer was deeply moved, and this increased the anger and revulsion he felt. The young king could not bear to be pitied by this man any more than he could accept the sharp warning he had given. Now the healer bowed deeply to the Daindru and returned to the shadows.

There was an uneasy silence, then Nenan Am Charn asked, "Has Count Barr anything to tell us about the land pledge?"

The Council turned to this matter with relief. Only Aidris, the queen, sat still and white in her gilded chair. Bajan pressed her hand, and Sharn whispered, "Do not heed this Raiz! I have sworn to take care of myself . . ."

"The land pledge," said Count Barr cautiously, "is a further and greater troth gift. My King . . ."

"It is some kind of bride price," said Sharn Am Zor. "I do not fear it."

"No, my king," put in Nenad, "as Barr has said, it is a gift, a gift of land offered by a suitor. It is paid before the courtship or the marriage arrangements begin. A piece of land equal in value to some named possession of the lady's family."

"Equal in this case to the Cantry of Tallien," said Barr. "It is a mining district not far from the old Pendark fortress in the southwest."

"My land pledge must exceed this, of course. I think of the Adz, or that part of it with the Silverbirch Mine."

"We must hope that the pledge is redeemed," said Aidris, "for this is indeed a rich part of our kingdom. I wonder if this custom was used in old time, in the time of the Sea-Oak Twins? What was the pledge given for Princess Eilda, the sister of Prince Tamir?"

"I know more about these two, my Queen," said

Nenad Am Charn. "They lived during the reign of Voyvid, the Wild Warrior King of the Zor, who ruled with Nagra, a King of the Firn. The Sea-Oak Twins wed the children of these two rulers. It was long before the coming of the men of Mel'Nir, and the Chameln lands extended far beyond the inland sea. The Daindru was allied with the rulers of Eildon; the alliance was sealed with the legendary double marriage. The land pledge for Princess Eilda, who wed Prince Ayvid Am Firn, was given long before marriage. I have it marked on this map."

"Was this her true name?" asked Aidris. "Eilda of Eildon?"

"No, my queen," said Nenad Am Charn, busily unrolling his map. "Her name was Eidalin I believe, or Ydillian."

"*Ydillian!*" exclaimed Lingrit Am Thuven.

He bent over the map as the others did.

"You see," said Nenad, "it is listed as well in other ancient documents. 'All the land between the rivers.' "

Lingrit Am Thuven began to laugh, and all the members of the Council joined in a little apprehensively. It was clear that 'Ydillian's Pledge' was nothing more nor less than the Mark of Lien, the richest land in Hylor.

"It has remained bound to Eildon," pursued Nenad, "almost to this day. The land pledge, my king, is not a bride price but a gift, an earnest to prove a suitor's worth. There is no tradition that a land pledge should be redeemed or returned, even if the noblewoman in question weds another."

In after years Aidris the Queen thought of this moment in the hall of the Dainmut. She wished that it could be set down that she herself or any of the others . . . Lingrit, Nenad, Seyl . . . had seen into the matter, grasped its meaning. Yet no one did, and least of all the king who smiled at Count Barr, his torch-bearer.

"I am well pleased with Count Barr's embassy," he said. "We will speak further . . ."

Aidris and Sharn walked side by side out into the sunshine, where Tazlo Am Ahrosh and others were

waiting for the day's hawking. The queen asked after
Esher Am Chiel, Barr's esquire.

"Merilla and Carel have carried him off to ride in the
Hain," said Sharn cheerfully. "Perhaps I will take him
into Eildon again. This is a year of changes, Cousin,
and you will see how generously I can behave."

In the Hain, the royal grove, on this spring day,
changes are working like the sap in the tall old trees. A
young girl on a roan horse and a young man on a bay
amble down the royal ride. Prince Carel and his riding
companion, Count Caddah, have galloped away on a
kind of mock hunt, following a cub fox. Esher Am Chiel
brushes back his fair hair in exasperation.

"Barr does not understand," he says. "I spent my
time with servants and soldiers. Often we were treated
as if we had the plague or had lost our wits. The Eildon
soldiery, even in the Pendark court, were all on tiptoe
ready to fight for what they called honor. To keep any
large body of followers in Linriss would need magic
indeed."

"You must tell this to the queen," says Merilla. "Sharn
will never hear it."

"Lady, how can I? Barr is the best of men. Among
the nobles themselves it may be different. Certainly the
princess and the knights and ladies that we saw were all
comely and fine."

"Tell me again of Moinagh Pendark," begs Merilla.

"I found her passing strange," says Esher, "a fairy
creature, not of this mortal world. I saw her but once,
and it was the second time Count Barr met with her.
We walked in the garden of the Pendark court, a very
fair, soft, green place even in winter, with trees and a
pond that they called the lake. Beyond the wall, in
Lindriss, it was snowy and grey. The princess came
down to walk by the pond every afternoon. She wore
this day a green silken gown and green jewels; everything about her had a greenish tinge from the light in
the garden. She trailed her small white hands and her
sleeves in the water. When Count Barr bade her good

day, she smiled and spoke to him of his journey over the western sea."

"But she is beautiful?" asks Merilla rather gruffly.

"Yes," says Esher Am Chiel, "very beautiful. Not to my taste, of course, but perhaps the king . . ."

Two birds burst noisily from a tree, just over Merilla's head, and her well-trained mare takes fright, shies, is brushed by a spray of briar, and bolts away. Merilla, a good horsewoman, is surprised and can only cling onto Rondella's neck and bend low to avoid the overhanging boughs. She hears Esher thundering after her, calling her name. Then there is a twist in the path the mare has taken, a tall thicket and one last branch. She cries out, and as the mare checks, she comes off, sliding sideways to the ground in a heap, and for a few moments the breath is knocked out of her. She has never fainted in her life, and the fall does not make her faint, but she comes close to it soon afterwards. Esher Am Chiel is beside her, taking her in his arms, calling her name still in a voice that trembles with anxiety.

"Merilla . . . my dear love . . ."

"Esher . . ."

"Are you hurt?"

"No, not hurt."

She clings to him.

"Oh I have missed you, Esher!"

They kiss and kiss again in the heart of the grove. Merilla says in a wondering voice, *Oh Goddess . . . what will we tell the king?*

A good question. They tell the king the truth; and at once, without any consultation, coming before him hand in hand like two children, still with leaves in their hair. They have plighted their troth; they will marry; they ask the king's blessing. Sharn Am Zor takes it badly. He says harsh and destructive things to his sister and heir, Merilla, worse things to his cousin Esher Am Chiel. No one overhears except Nerriot the lute player.

The cloud of the king's displeasure hangs over the palace of the Zor; the Countess Caddah is distracted with anxiety; even Queen Aidris is vaguely displeased,

although she quickly sees the suitability of such a match.
After days of separation and secret meetings, the two
are married, suddenly and with little ceremony in the
west wing of the palace, giving rise to unfounded rumors. The king himself performs the marriage and stays
only long enough after it is done to suggest that Count
Am Chiel take his bride home to his miserable estates
until such time as he is summoned to court again. In
short the young pair are banished from Achamar, and
they ride off happily with a very small number of
attendants.

Merilla has knelt before her brother Sharn, subdued
her will, which is as strong as his own, and humbly
begged one favor: that Prince Carel will not suffer any
evil consequences of this rash marriage. She goes off
into exile believing that the king has given her some
brusque assurance on this point. But Sharn Am Zor is
not yet satisfied, and the brunt of his unreason falls
upon poor Carel. The Caddahs, mother and son, are
sent home to their estates, too, and Carel is not permitted
to accompany them. When he tries to ride after Count
Caddah, his friend, he is brought back in disgrace by
Engist and the palace guard.

Yet when all this excitement has died down, there is
another wedding to look forward to, one of which the
king approves. At Midsummer, Denzil of Denwick is
married with great pomp to Veldis of Wirth at the Zor
palace. The bride's family is an old one, distantly con-
nected to the royal house of Lien; the bride's father, Sir
Berndt, her two young sisters, Mayrose and Fideth,
attend upon her. One thing is unusual: the pair are not
married by a shaman, a moon sister or even by the king
himself, but by a housepriest of the Wirth family, a
follower of Inokoi, the Lord of Light. The seat of the
Wirths happens to be at Larkdel, not far from the First
Hermitage of Matten. The long summer festival for this
wedding seems a fitting rehearsal for the wedding of
Sharn himself in another summer not far distant.

CHAPTER V

LINDRISS

SHARN WAKES IN THE DAWN AND HEARS THE
lap of water: the great adventure is beginning. He looks
out at the river Bal and sees that his flagship, the
Golden Oak, has come to a mooring, while the smaller
caravel, the *Nixie,* sails on downriver. They have moored
at Larkdel, that pretty, unpretentious town upon the
Bal, west of Balufir.

The king's ship has come to bear a bridegroom of less
than a year away from his bride. Sharn rings impatiently for his valets. Ceremony is reduced on board
ship: he is sparing of his linen and wears few jewels.
But today he must be fine to receive Zilly of Denwick,
his bride and her family. The king has once again
chosen Chameln dress; he is proud to have overcome
his distaste for it.

Presently Gerr of Zerrah and Tazlo Am Ahrosh attend the king in his cabin, brimming over with that
excitement that has carried them all the way from
Achamar. After a first breakfast of new-baked ship's
bread, Sharn goes on deck with his two companions.
The spring sunshine, the simple beauty of Larkdel, the
keen sweet air are fitting accompaniments for this marvell-
lous journey. Now the procession is approaching from
the manor house. There is the good, old knight, Sir

Berndt, all in the panoply of the Falconers, for he is the last member of this order in the land of Lien. There are the new-wed pair, Zilly and his dark beauty, the Lady Veldis. The king receives Sir Berndt upon the after deck of the *Golden Oak* and exchanges many civilities with him. He embraces Lady Veldis and begs her forgiveness for taking her husband across the western sea.

Times presses; the wind is freshening, and Captain Dynstane is eager to take advantage of it. The ship's trumpets are sounded to call back the crewmen who have gone to light candles at the sanctuary for a safe voyage. Zilly, his honest, freckled Denwick countenance dark with emotion, draws his lady aside, kissing her and drying her tears. At last her old nurse takes her ashore. The last sailor scrambles aboard after the gangway has been shipped. To a burst of song the *Golden Oak* sails off from Larkdel, westward to the sea.

Zilly can no longer contain himself. He bursts out with a piece of good news. His brother, Duke Hal of Denwick, is no longer a suitor for Princess Moinagh.

"What was the reason?" asks Sharn. "Was the land pledge too much for him?"

"Maybe," says Zilly. "I think he loves another. Tall red-haired girl from over the river. Nothing to look at, but she rides well."

"From Mel'Nir?"

"Dame Brond, a soldier's widow. Owns half of Balbank. I think he will have her."

"Good luck to him," says Sharn.

It is vaguely troubling, upon the Bal, to look into the rough green hills and pastures of Mel'Nir, stretching away from the distant south bank, and think of the civil war still raging. There are tales of dead men and dead horses fouling the fishers' nets, of deserters and fugitives swimming over to Lien.

The king is glad to have Zilly aboard. Zerrah and Tazlo are the best of men, but he has known Denwick much longer. His little court lacks balance: There are no women aboard, and Sharn misses the presence of women. He misses poor Iliane Seyl, now definitely an

ex-mistress, and he misses even more his good friend
Lorn Gilyan. She has proved a true and forthright
companion during the year just past, ready to give
advice or simply to listen to his plans and dreams
concerning Eildon. He cannot think, as he once did,
that his good friend is in love with him. She is much too
good-humored and clear-eyed to be that yearning maid
in a knightly tale who "loves on though hope is gone."

Lack of entertainment has not really been a problem
on the journey. When Sharn Am Zor arrived at Balufir,
where his caravels were waiting, he was welcomed by
his uncle, the Markgraf Kelen and by fair Zaramund,
who had always had a tender regard for her handsome
nephew. Rosmer presented himself, urbane and quiet,
for his ritual snub from the young king, then made
himself scarce. The king was royally entertained at the
palace for several days. It was just like old times: The
ball that became a revel, the gaming tables, the billowing featherbeds of Lien, the masques, dawn breaking
while the candles still burned.

There was an old flame, beautiful Zelline, betrothed
to the Duke of Chantry, more than twice her age and
confined to his estate with an attack of gout. Somehow
the king and Zelline managed to be locked into the
Wilderness, the rose park, for one whole night, consol-
ing each other against the approach of marriage. There,
shivering in their fur cloaks in the spring dawn, they
stood on the humped bridge, and Zelline begged her
old friend Sharn to forgo a small part of his journey. He
should not do it, she said; nothing would be served, no
one would think ill of him, if he did not visit Swangard.

The king would not be persuaded. He sailed off with
his fleet and dropped anchor again by a little river that
ran into the Bal. The swans were returning from their
winter in the Burnt Lands, settling upon the water and
the sedgy meadows. Swangard, the royal folly, sat very
square and white upon its plot of ground. Sharn Am
Zor was rowed to the landing place with a small escort;
he went into the white central tower alone.

He returned after some hours, frowning, pale, ut-

terly unapproachable. Even the valets, Prickett and
Yuri, had never seen their royal master stricken in this
way. It was feared, as he sat silent in the bow of the
ship, that the sight of Queen Aravel in her madness had
stolen away her son's wits. Yet Sharn recovered his
composure and his good humor. The journey to Eildon
was physic enough; the caravels sailed on, and now
after some days they had collected Denzil of Denwick
from the arms of his bride at Larkdel.

After dinner there is sword practice on deck. The
king does not like to be reminded that Effrim Barr did,
in fact, make an error in the reading of the invitation to
the Tourney of All Trees. When the king himself came
to read the illuminated scroll, there it was plain for all
to see: not seven champions but four. Gerr will fight in
the lists; Tazlo will ride at the ring and in any horse
races; the king himself will show off his prowess with
the bow; Zilly will be the king's esquire and take part in
the sword play.

The king retires early to his cabin, reads Hazard's
verses and daydreams of the Princess Moinagh. He
does not quite delude himself into thinking that he is in
love; he has recognized long ago that his capacity for
love has been injured. Yet he feels an odd stirring in his
cold heart; *she* may awaken his true feelings.

King Sharn does not dream as much as other people.
Fearful nightmares, sent by Rosmer, heralded his mother's madness; in his exile he experienced a few bad
dreams and blamed the old Scorpion for them. Now he
has controlled his dreams, he believes, by the exercise
of his strong will. Yet sometimes he suspects that he
does dream and simply fails to recall his dreaming.

Now, aboard the *Golden Oak* he has one sweet dream,
puzzling, warm, often repeated. He lies in bed in his
old room at Alldene, the royal manor where he spent
his exile, and a lady in a Lienish gown brings him a cup
of milk. He is a child, yet not a child. The lady is not
his mother yet she speaks to him in a motherly voice,
calls him by name. "*Sharn . . . Little Sharn . . . Sharn
Kelen, my Prince, how you have grown . . .*"

*   *   *

So the journey continues: The weather is good, the winds favorable, and with only a brief mooring at Balamut for the lashing of the cargo, the two caravels and the pinnace set out over the western sea in the dark of the Willowmoon in the year 1174 since the laying of the sacred stones in Achamar, also called the year 2223 of the Annals of Eildon.

The difference between a sea and a river journey is apparent at once. Even before the winds freshen and the sea becomes choppy, there are those who turn green about the gills. Some of the Chameln folk are so sick that Captain Ruako, the healer of the guard escort and his assistants fear for their lives. Yuri, the young boy, is unable to lift his head and prays for the Goddess to cast him into the waves. Even Gerr of Zerrah is not quite himself. Denwick lies with his face to the wall, groaning; and Nerriot's lute falls silent. Only the king, Sharn Am Zor, is unaffected and not quite able to understand what all the fuss is about. He strides about on deck in wind and weather and eats heartily with the sailors.

The journey lasts ten days, and one by one the king's champions gain their sea legs. Tazlo, who was never very ill, is first to stand beside the king, then Gerr, then Zilly. They laugh and drink schnapps like old sea dogs, and at last, far in the sunset troughs of the waves there grows a long shadow like a cloud: the coast of the magic kingdom.

II

THE WIND DROPS AS THEY COME TO THE
mouth of the river Laun, and the pinnace breaks out
its oars. The caravels must wait until two long galleys
come to draw them up river between the green fields.
Sharn stares at the countryside: it is the same as anywhere else; but no, it is not. A softness about the short
grass, an old and gnarly quality about the trees, elm
and oak and willow, curious effects of mist and sunlight.

He sees Nerriot, the lute-player, wrapped in a dark
sea cloak, staring out over the pleasant landscape with
an expression of intense and stony sadness.

"What do you see, Master Nerriot?" asks the king in
alarm.

"The towers of Wencaer, Sire."

"Your old home?"

"If beggars have a home, Sire," says Nerriot gently.

"By the Goddess, man," says Sharn, "you must not
be the prey of cruel memories. You have bettered your
estate!"

Long before the grey walls of Lindriss come in sight,
the river winds among villages and towns, closely following one upon the other, with tall warehouses and
silos at the water's edge. The houses, dark with age, are
strange and crooked; here and there the tall tower of a

118

keep rises up, grey or red or white, with banners flying
from its narrow windows. The river winds on and on;
three or four mighty watergates are passed; the city lies
all about them, offering bright vistas then snatching
them away as the mist closes in.

The wharves are less strange, only a larger version of
the harbor at Balufir, with a dozen frowning stone
roundhouses as dark as the Blackwater Keep. As the
Nixie and the *Golden Oak* are brought to their moor-
ings, Sharn Am Zor and his companions go down into
the saloon and peer through the portholes to appraise
the landing arrangements without being seen. Tazlo is
sent to reconnoitre, and the young man from the north
soon comes back with good news.

Effrim Barr, whatever his success with the nobility of
Eildon, has done his work well elsewhere. The livery
stable he engaged has provided decent horses for the
guards as well as three or four well-mannered and
docile steeds for the king to inspect.

"A herald?" asks Sharn. "A brace of knights?"

"Not yet, my king," say Tazlo, his spirits dampened,
"but all is in readiness . . . see there."

The young men peer through a different porthole and
behold a large carpet, red and white like a Battle board,
laid down below the gangway and beyond it some kind
of striped barrier like the lists of a tournament. The
king is uncertain whether or not to go on deck. Perhaps
his appearance will touch off a satisfactory welcome as it
has done so often in the past.

"Come then," he says impatiently, "let us put ourselves to rights and stand in the waist of the ship. Tell
the escort on board to stand close about the gangway."

The king and his champions are then "put to rights,"
their gorgeous attire checked by the valets. As they
emerge behind the backs of the escort to see better,
still without being seen, a herald has appeared on the
gaudy checkerboard, together with a trumpeter. After
the trumpet sounds, the herald roars out a welcome in
the common speech: they must all strain to catch the
words in his Eildon dialect.

"Shennazar," says the king. "Shennazar of Kemmelond."

"Two gifts," says Zilly. "Begs you to accept two gifts, Sire."

The king nods to his own herald, mounted on the bridge, and the man bellows in his turn. King Sharn Am Zor gives thanks for the herald's welcome and deigns to accept the gifts.

The scene is still eerily deserted. The guardsmen at the next mooring, some already mounted and looking very fine in their green and gold uniforms, stand stock still. Suddenly, to a burst of harp music and the jingling of bells, a figure clad in motley, red and white, bounds on to the mat and cartwheels about.

"A fool! A fool! A fool!" cries the fool in a loud, brazen voice. "A fool for Shennazar! Half of a fool and the other half of a fool!"

A strange figure in a long black mantle teeters onto the mat and stands towering over the fool, who is an undersized man about four and a half feet tall with thick dark red hair twisted up into three peaks like a fool's cap. Now he prods the "giant" at his side, and the black mantle billows out. Three very tiny creatures, dwarfs or midgets standing on each other's shoulders, fall about on the checkerboard then group beside their leader, making their music. Sharn Am Zor feels his lips drawn back in disgust; he remembers an old fear he had of dwarfs and little people. In any case he has never liked fools.

"Great King! Mighty Shennazar, come from afar," cries the fool. "Here is the second gift."

Another trumpet call sounds, and a young kedran in white livery leads onto the carpet a splendid white horse caparisoned in green and gold. It is, happily, not the kind of fiery steed that the king would have to reject out of hand. It is in fact a heavy, aged charger, well-mannered, docile. The kedran has it gently stepping from square to square of the mat, and now she feeds it a tidbit. The horse waits patiently with its head held up.

"Well, what d'you think, Sire?" asks Gerr of Zerrah.
"It looks a remarkably suitable beast. Their best horses
come from the island of Ariu."

"Yes," nods the king. "Yes, I like the horse. It has a
look of my good Redwing."

"Wait, my King," says Tazlo Am Ahrosh. "Let me go
down with an officer and examine the horse."

"Well, we have time," says the king. "Have a round
of schnapps sent up from the galley."

Tazlo and the second officer of the escort march down
the gangway and examine the white horse upon the red
and white carpet.

"Strange welcome," says the king. "When will we
know where we are lodged?"

Tazlo and the officer lead the white horse about and
it responds with perfect docility. At last they return,
and Tazlo says to the king, "Sire, I do not trust the
horse. Perhaps it is the strangeness of this place. It
would be better to have someone of your own weight
try out the beast."

"All seems quiet enough down there," says Zilly of
Denwick. "Let me go down and try this gift horse, my
King."

The king nods to his old friend. Denzil of Denwick,
clad from head to foot in gold satin of Lien, with a
white and green short cape, strides briskly down the
gangway with an officer. The fool and his group bow
low and play a musical accompaniment. As Zilly climbs
into the saddle and the kedran adjusts the stirrups,
Sharn Am Zor becomes aware of a murmur of sound,
beyond the music and the sounds of the common day
here upon the wharves.

Zilly sits firmly upright in the saddle, and the kedran,
unexpectedly, springs away several squares of the mat.
The big gentle horse flings up its head, bears its huge
yellow teeth, rolls a wild eye and begins to buck with
the agility of a mule. Zilly is thrown almost at once and
comes down heavily. There are shocked exclamations
from the guardsmen on land and on the ship; Tazlo and

the officer run to help Denwick who has scrambled to
his feet.

The fool dances about on the mat crying out in his
harsh, loud voice, "Fell down! Fell down! Shennazar
fell down and lost his crown!"

And behind the low barrier, there are suddenly knights
and ladies, mounted upon noble steeds or seated in
graceful open carriages. Banners wave and snap; the
sun comes through and blazes upon patterned stuff,
jewels, gilded armor, painted tissue and gauze threaded
with gold and silver. The denizens of the courts of
Eildon laugh and clap their hands.

Sharn knows instinctively, and with a quiver of revulsion for the magic of the thing, that the Eildon lords
and ladies were watching all the time, although the
newcomers could not see them. Now they have played a
cruel trick on him, struck at his right, threatened him
with injury, injured his trusted friend instead. But the
painted fools of Eildon have laughed too soon. Can they
really believe that it is the king who has fallen from the
gift horse? The fool still dances about, but his horrid
little companions have run to Denzil of Denwick and
are crouching at his feet in attitudes of submission.
Three knights have dismounted and are striding across
the checkered carpet in Denwick's direction.

The king says quietly to Captain-General Britt, just
in front of him, "Full flourish, Britt. And stand away."

The signals are given, the silver trumpets of the king,
three on the ship and three on shore, sing aloud their
full flourish. Sharn Am Zor stands forth at the head of
the gangway in Chameln dress of white, the long jeweled
tunic panelled with gold, a gold circlet just visible upon
his golden head. He does not acknowledge the presence of the Eildon nobility at all. He walks a few steps
down the sloping planks, in the silence following the
trumpet calls, and speaks to Denzil of Denwick.

Zilly, looking shaken but sound, replies, "No great
harm, my King."

The spectators, acknowledging perhaps that the jest
has not found its mark, cheer and applaud the appear-

ance of the king. The fool summons his followers and bows lower than ever at the foot of the gangway.

"King Sharn," he cries in his rasping voice, "in these days we celebrate the Feast of Fools. Your forfeit has been paid, and you have the fool's leave to enter the kingdoms of Eildon."

Sharn meets the eye of the fool and finds the man's gaze as hard and full of anger as his own.

"Is the white horse bewitched?" he asks quietly.

"No, my King," says the fool. "It is a clod-catcher, a yokel trap from the fairground. It bucks when a certain weight is on its back."

"What is your name, Fool?"

"I am called Farr the Fool, Majesty, and these are my three farthings."

The little creatures, apparently two men and a young girl, are muscular, well-proportioned midgets with long tresses of glossy black hair caught back with bone clasps.

"You may attend me, if you will," says Sharn with a first hint of a smile, "though I am sure there are many fools in Eildon."

The fool and his farthings tumble away from the mailed feet of the three knights who have reached the foot of the gangway. They make obeisance to the king, so far as their strip mail will allow, and the knight of the Hunters acts as spokesman.

"King Sharn Am Zor," he begins. And even in the accents of a knight of the realm, it is thinned a little into Shennazar. "We bid you welcome in the name of the orders of Eildon. I am Mortrice of Malm and this is the noble Sir Pellasur of Hay, knight of the Falconers, and the noble Sir Tarn of Whitrow, knight of the Fishers. Pray you mount up with this your noble company and follow. You are lodged at Sennick Fortress."

The king bows to the three knights, observing the ruddy countenance of Sir Mortrice, the dark glance of Sir Pellasur, the youthful brow of Sir Tarn. He nods to the Herald and to Captain-General Britt. The disembarkation proceeds smoothly. One of the stolid mounts from the livery stable, a brown gelding that does indeed have a look of Redwing, is brought forward for the king, and it bears him safely all the time that he is in Eildon. Now he rides forward, just as he had hoped to do, and receives the greetings of those who gathered to welcome him.

The ranking personage and the only member of the royal courts to welcome the king is a lady in an open carriage: Princess Gaveril Tramarn. By her smooth look, her wise and unfriendly dark eyes, he guesses that she is not wearing her years. Her long robe is entirely quartered with the arms of all her feoffs and possessions. Her spreading headdress of gauze is adjusted by a lady in waiting so that king and princess may speak face to face. Sir Pellasur speaks her name and titles to the king, who bows his head, unsmiling, and says: "My greetings to the noble house of Tramarn!"

The princess bobs her head with a broad smile.

"What did he say?" she demands out of the corner of her mouth. "Sir Gerr of Kerrick, is that you? Can you tell me what the King of Kemmelond said?"

Gerr rises to the occasion.

"Sire," he says loudly to the king, "the princess is suffering from deafness. She did not hear your greeting."

"Perhaps I gave none," says Sharn Am Zor, smiling terribly at Gaveril and riding on.

A ripple of laughter or surprise follows him. Led by the three knights and followed by his own champions, his escort, the Eildon folk who gathered for his curious welcome, and at last by the twenty officers of his guard, he sets out on his first long ride across Lindriss.

As the procession winds along fine streets, between high houses, or through many tracts of parkland the patches of mist still come and go. Vistas, glimpses of the city, are all that the king beholds. More than once, between the tall houses or on the brow of a hill, other groups of knights and their followers can be seen, as if there were several processions all crossing the city at once, hardly aware of each other.

At last, after riding for more than an hour, the three knights draw rein in the shadow of a mighty fortress.

Sennick stands upon a low hill above a warren of grey
houses and narrower streets, a village that has become
part of the great city. It has two massive round towers
of grey stone linked by a wall with a battlemented walk
upon the top. Each tower stands in a separate round
garden plot with a low rampart faced with stone and a
drawbridge crossing the moat. Yet there the likeness
ends. The tower on the left looks as if it has been
scrubbed clean or newmade; banners fly from its arrow-
slit windows. The garden below this tower is a perfect
round of soft, clipped, bright green Eildon grass with
two or three young trees standing in beds of mooncups
and daisies, yellow and white. The tower on the right is
of old, dark stone without banners. Its round garden is
grassy but unkempt with nothing but an old plum tree
struggling into blossom with a few spring flowers among
its mossed roots.

"King Sharn!" cries Sir Mortrice of the Hunters, as
the procession slowly comes to a halt. "You have come
first to the fortress and may choose the tower where
you will lodge!"

"Great Goddess, Sire," says Tazlo, on the king's left,
"there is no choice . . ."

As other voices are raised and the escort begins to
drift towards the bright tower, Sharn feels a gentle
touch on his right boot. He glances down and sees one
of the fool's small companions, the little maid, gazing
up at him with large, liquid brown eyes. She holds a
finger to her lips, and with her other hand points urgently towards the old, dark tower. Weary with the
long ride and the strange welcome, the king makes his
decision, feeling as if he were plunging into the icy
waters of the moat.

"Another trick," he murmurs to Gerr of Zerrah.

He raises his voice and says, "Good Sir Mortrice, I
trust Eildon hospitality. I will choose the tower yonder,
the one that wears its years!"

His words are understood by the Eildon nobles; there
is a burst of laughter and applause. The king's trumpeters sound his call, the drawbridge of the dark tower is

lowered. Farr the Fool and his three farthings play
their music and tumble about on the drawbridge, leading the king and his followers into the tower.

Sir Pellasur makes bold to say, "King Sharn . . .
Majesty . . . will you keep the fool then?"

"For the moment," says Sharn, "but the white horse
may go back to the fairground."

The king is dismounted quickly in a spacious inner
ward and brought through a warm well-appointed hall up
to a set of rooms with rich hangings, a pleasant fire,
gleaming oaken furniture of antique design. As he sinks
into a chair by the fire, Prickett is in the doorway
wringing his hands. Two guardsmen bring in Zilly of
Denwick, green as his cloak, and lie him on a settle.
The healer has been summoned.

"Zilly!" the king kneels beside his friend. "That damned
gift horse! What ails you, man? Something broken?"

Denzil of Denwick is now deathly pale, a terrible
color. He can only whisper, "Forgive me, old son . . .
we showed them . . ."

Then he faints dead away, his eyes rolling up in his
head. Captain Ruako, the healer, makes a quick examination, has the lord carried up to his bedchamber
overhead.

"My King," he says, "it is a brain-shaking. Nothing
worse. I believe there are no bones broken, a little
bruising."

"Can he be healed?"

"He must have rest, my king."

"We must all have rest." The king sighs. "Eildon is a
wearying country."

Tazlo Am Ahrosh and Gerr of Zerrah, when they
appear, are full of confidence again, praising the sta-
bles, speaking boastfully of the rightness of the king's
choice of a residence. Sharn Am Zor is encouraged by
their high spirits, but he has a flicker of doubt. Neither
of these two men—Gerr, the straight-featured Athron
knight, and Tazlo, the brash northerner—are strong in
judgment. He sees it for the first time.

When the king has dined, Nerriot the lute-player

offers a favorite Eildon air. Suddenly a sound of stranger music penetrates the dark tower; Tazlo, at a narrow window, cries out with excitement.

"Look there, my king!"

Below, in the afternoon sunshine, twenty bag-pipers, hairy men with bare knees, bright plaids and feathered bonnets, are caterwauling before the bright tower. Another party on tall horses and shaggy ponies is poised before the drawbridge with a welcoming escort of Eildon knights. A smaller escort than was sent for Sharn Am Zor.

"Yet they too have a prince," murmurs Nerriot. "See there, Dan Sharn: the tall man on the grey is Prince Borss Paldo."

Preceded by half a dozen pipers, a dark and ferociously hairy young man clad in a tribal kilt and bristling with dirk, claymore and eagle plumes, rides over his drawbridge on a black charger.

"Great Goddess!" says Sharn Am Zor. "That can only be Diarmut Mack Dahl, the King of the Isles!"

The arrangements in the bright tower, it turns out, are sparse and cold. The Chameln guards hear the men of the isles complaining through the wall that separates the two stableyards. The men of the isles are quarrelsome; all leave is cancelled among Sharn's followers.

At twilight a knight comes with his esquire to the drawbridge of the dark tower and sounds a call. Sharn Am Zor, rested now and dressed in fresh finery, goes down eagerly to greet his cousin, Prince Beren Pendark.

The young man who stands before him in the hall is no older than himself and of middle height, with light brown hair worn rather long in the Eildon fashion. He has an open, pleasant face, but his manner is very strained and stiff. He has come to bid the king to a grand ball at the Pendark Court, and, first of all, to collect the deed of the land pledge. Sharn smiles, asks after all the members of the house of Pendark, and offers, besides the land pledge parchments, a gift of jewels and woven stuff.

The king feels again a curious whisper of unease, as if

the noble old hall in which he stands were full of
phantoms, hidden watchers. Farr the Fool comes out of
the shadows to a burst of music and capers about before
the king and the prince.

"Shennazar!" he sings harshly. "Shennazar of Kemmelond and Beren of Pendark!"

He makes a doggerel verse for his song:

> *"Shennazar sits in Eildon Hall
> Beren and his watchdogs come to call!"*

His small companions join in the chorus:

> *"The king is a fool if he chance to roam,
> The fool may be king in his faraway home . . ."*

Sharn turns to his cousin and makes one last effort to
understand the prince and to make the prince understand his own situation.

"Cousin Beren," he says, "I have set some store by
ceremony in my own court, but now I wish it away.
How fair and pleasant it might have been to arrange a
marriage in our two families by a simple family gathering. I long to see your sister. I long to make her my
queen. I would this were enough."

Prince Beren flushes darkly and hangs his head.
"Cousin Sharn," he says in a low voice, "I am honor
bound to handle this as I do. Tonight you will meet my
sister."

The king is filled with hope and confidence again.
Prince Beren departs to bring the evening's invitation
to the King of the Isles in the neighboring tower. The
order of march is given: Sharn Am Zor will take only his
escort; the King of the Isles will be led first; then the
Pendark escort will form a buffer between the island
men and those of the Chameln. As he is wrapped in his
cloak, Sharn calls the fool to his side.

"Watchdogs?" he asks, "who would keep a watch on
Prince Beren Pendark when he visits his cousin?"

"Those who have him honor bound," says the fool crisply.

"The Council? His family?"

"Yes to the one and no to the other."

"A name . . . do you have any names for these watchers?"

"Paldo heads the Council. The patron of the Hunters. A huntsman works with beaters and decoys!"

"Fool," says the king, "how do I know that *you* are not some decoy?"

"How indeed?" The fool grins. "It is a wise lord who knows all his friends and liegemen!"

"I think I know what you are," says the king. "But I cannot think how you came to Eildon."

Torches are lit, and the procession moves off to the west, across the city. Lindriss is beautiful in these smoke-blue twilight hours with lights flowering here and there in the houses and upon the tops of the towers. Presently the Pendark Court is reached, a white mansion, just as Count Barr described it, and the scene is a familiar one, a torchlit courtyard with lords and ladies coming with their servants to a great festival. King Sharn hopes that all uncertainty will be at an end; he will meet the princess and her mother and be chosen as the most worthy suitor.

In the entry Sharn Am Zor comes face to face with Diarmut Mack Dahl, the King of the Isles. The chieftain is strongly built and somewhat above the middle height, although Sharn can give him several inches. He is well combed, his hair and beard, both lustrous, glossy black, are plaited and jeweled. His skin is tanned by the sun, and his eyes are a fine light blue. In his plaid velvet tunic and kilt he cuts a fine figure; he strokes his moustaches and shows his teeth in a smile. The king, thinking of Ferrad Harka, High Chieftain of the Durgashen, bows politely.

"Greetings to the King of the Isles!" he says.

"Greetings to the King of the Chameln!" replies Diarmut Mack Dahl in a thick and curious brogue.

He holds out a hand, and Sharn clasps it. Diarmut says

in a low voice, "By the moon, let's not quarrel. These lowlanders will give us strife enough!"

"Well said, noble Diarmut," replies Sharn.

So the two kings go in and their trumpet calls are sounded; they are led with their champions to opposite hearths and settled in the great hall of the Pendarks. The dancing floor is of polished tiles, white and blue, with patterns of fish and seashells. The Eildon nobles stare and laugh; the headdresses of the ladies billow about like ships in a gale.

There is a trumpet call and some sort of commotion at the end of the bright room. Music begins to play, then breaks off. An old man leaning upon a staff and supported by a young page moves unsteadily out into the hall. His white elf-locks and straggling beard, his long wrinkled face and bent back are all out of place. There seems to be, far and wide, no other person "wearing their years," not a grey head to be seen.

"One king!" trumpets the old man in a shaking voice. "Yes, yes, I see: the young highlander. Greetings to you, Mack Dahl, from the House of Pendark. One king and where's tother?"

He is brought round slowly to face Sharn Am Zor and comes forward on his staff peering at the King of the Chameln.

"By the Holy Tree and the Seven Stars!" roars the old man. "There is a king indeed! Is *that* the fine young fellow come from over the sea? I swear he has a look of Edgar! You there—Leffert, Lady Malm, Lady Evritt— does he not have a look of Edgar, my younger brother! Sharn, d'ye say? Sharn of Zor! Ah, it does my old eyes good to see such a fine young man and of my own house."

Sharn Am Zor looks into the faded brown eyes and comes to the musty embrace of his Great-Uncle Kilnan Pendark. By this time he is glad of a welcome; greets the old man heartily.

"How are they treating you?" asks the prince in a hoarse whisper. "Badly, I reckon. They're a clannish pack of bastards here in the city. I am out of the world.

I would sit down with you to a goblet of wine at the Gwanlevan palace, but I expect it cannot be. Good luck to you, and a great-uncle's blessing."

Prince Beren and a lady who must be his mother have appeared and are approaching down the hall. It seems likely that the old prince will be led away, sent back to bed. There are rustlings and titterings among the guests. The prince makes the most of his outing.

"I greet the company!" he says, bustling a few paces down the hall again. "And I am mighty glad to see all of you looking so well. I was never one for magic . . . eh, Merigaun . . . but I like to see a few heads of my color in any gathering. How would it be if everyone 'wore their years'?"

Sharn sees the Princess Merigaun raise a hand in alarm. Prince Kilnan straightens his bent back, lifts up his staff and utters a few words in Chyrian. There is a crackling of the air in the upper reaches of the hall as the spell takes hold, and then a general moan or gasp of despair. Before the eyes of the Chameln watchers, jaws slacken, skins are netted with wrinkles, bosoms and paunches bulge and sag, hair becomes grey or white with here and there a head of dyed hair surrounding a wrinkled face. The headdresses of the women totter upon their poor old heads, and the trunkhose or trews of the men hang upon their shrunken shanks. The mischievous old prince takes his leave. There is an instant murmuring from those stricken; each one unmasked makes his or her personal magic to repair the damage.

The king and his companions stare in horror. A moment past, Sharn might have welcomed some defense against the hostile crowd of nobles, but the presence of so much magic is unsettling. He turns his face away from the awful readjustments going on all about him and meets the calm grey eyes of the Princess Merigaun. She sinks down before him, and he raises her up at once.

"My dear cousin Sharn," she says in a bell voice. "Majesty, you see the best and worst of Eildon."

"Mother," say Prince Beren, "the king has had no easy passage in Eildon this day."

"Come," says Sharn, "we are all strong and undismayed, cousins. We observe your customs with keen interest."

Merigaun smiles, but Beren is still cast down. Sharn perceives that Effrim Barr described Merigaun very well; she is indeed a lady with ash-blond hair, slender, grey-eyed and handsome, but he has omitted, or did not see, her most striking characteristic. She is a magic being, resembling Nieva, the messenger of the Falconers, with silvery skin in certain lights and a silvery chime to her voice.

"We will start the dancing," she says now. "My dear cousin, I have chosen a Long Garland for you to dance with my daughter."

So the musicians begin to play a familiar melody for this slow, courtly dance of Lien, and Merigaun leads the king down the hall to a group of maidens and ladies in waiting. One stands forth: it is the Princess Moinagh. In a dream Sharn Am Zor bows low to her, takes her small cold hand and begins the dance.

He feels no shock of recognition; he imagined someone rather different. Yet there is no question about it: Moinagh Pendark is one of the most beautiful girls he has ever beheld. Neither the poets nor Effrim Barr did her justice. She is small and slender and her face is delicately modelled with high cheekbones and a mouth perfectly shaped. Her complexion is pale, flawless, glowing, so that she has her own aura. Sharn can see a blue pulse on her temple where the tendrils of her brown-black hair escape from a silver fillet. Her eyes, raised to his own, are very widely spaced and of a luminous grey-green with dark lashes and fine dark brows. Even before she smiles, shyly, and speaks to him, he thinks *She is still a child* . . . Her slenderness, her style of beauty is rather different from that admired in the court of Lien. She wears a maiden's gown, simply cut without a surcoat, but of rich silken cloth shot with many colors: sea-green, turquoise, blue and silver.

As Moinagh speaks to him, calls him "Cousin," questions him shyly but with perfect composure about his homeland, Sharn is enchanted. To have the care of this exquisite creature, to have her trust and love, to reassure, teach and protect her, these things are worth all his pain. Yet for the first time he is plagued by the unbearable thought that he may not win Moinagh's hand or be chosen as her husband.

Meanwhile that slow and stately dance, the Long Garland, goes on. Moinagh asks particularly about Sharn's journey and its starting point, the inland sea, the Danmar. He is aware that she dances very lightly and knows all the steps well, and he wishes that she were already his betrothed so that they might dance together all night long. He thinks suddenly of poor Denwick, lying sick in the dark tower, of Zilly and his dark beauty Veldis dancing away the seasons in Achamar, dancing on their wedding night in a shower of rose petals. He begins to understand their feelings and to search Moinagh's face for some mark of special favor, some sign of love.

They dance on, leading fifty couples in the simple figures of the dance. The scene is unrecorded, but the judgement of the chroniclers is clouded. In the Annals of Eildon, written at this time by a scribe of the house of Paldo, Sharn's visit is given three lines:

"In this moon came an outland half-king from Kemlon beyond Athron where savage tribes killed the liegemen of Princess Gleya, wife of noble Prince Borss Paldo, at Adderhill."

When the dance is done and he has led Moinagh back, as slowly as he dares, to her mother's side, Sharn returns to his two companions and receives their excited congratulations. Sir Tarn of the Fishers comes by to pay his respects and arranges partners for the next dance, a chain, for Gerr of Zerrah and Tazlo Am Ahrosh. He remains with the king, and they talk easily enough though Sham is a little distracted, searching among the dancers for the Princess Moinagh. In fact she does not dance this time but waits until the pipers begin to play a reel. Diarmut Mack Dahl leads her out, and though it gives Sharn an odd qualm to see her dance with another, he takes delight in her mastery of the steps. There follows a longer pause in the dancing, and the trumpets sound for a late arrival, Prince Borss Paldo. Sharn is disappointed to learn that the prince has not brought along his young wife, the Princess Gleya of Mel'Nir, whom he has been curious to behold. He spares a thought now for this young girl, the "unmarked child," shut up among strangers in a foreign court, awaiting the birth of her child, as his poor aunt Elvédegran once waited in the palace fortress of Ghanor, the so-called Great King.

When Prince Borss has greeted his hostess, she leads him straight away to greet Sharn Am Zor. The prince is tall and heavily built, no more than five and thirty. There is a weatherbeaten quality about his handsome, ruddy face that tells Sharn the prince is "wearing his years," his fine dark eyes do not peer out of a smooth mask. Sharn, who has a trick of seeing likenesses and sometimes judging people unfairly on them, sees a hint of his uncle, Kelen of Lien in this man. Kelen but without the good humor. Prince Borss stares at the young king, and his smile is closer to a sneer.

"Majesty," he says in rich tones, "you have gained much honor here today!"

Sharn will not smile at all but gives the prince a hard look and graciously inclines his head.

"We are proud to have our kinsman in the Pendark Court," says Merigaun quietly.

Now the music plays again, and Tazlo says, "I see the princess, my King, with young Tramarn."

The young Prince Gwalchai, slender and dark-haired, is nothing like his overbearing mother. There is a change of atmosphere in the Pendark hall. This, Sharn realizes sadly, is how it feels when the Eildon folk are pleased or contented. The lights burn a little lower, the music sounds more sweetly. The dance is a round dance called the Waves of The Sea, and Moinagh, dancing with the Prince of Tramarn, steps as lightly as before, yet he could swear she does not speak more intimately to the prince than she did to him. Sharn Am Zor heaves a deep sigh and wishes the dance were done.

The music strikes up next for a moon dance, and three young girls come smiling to the king's hearth and ask Sharn and his companions to join the dance. All around, the ladies of Eildon are bringing the knights and nobles out on to the floor. Sharn joins his partner with a good grace; she is a dark-blonde beauty who would have caught his eye at any other time. One figure of the moon dance is a chain, and sure enough Sharn comes in his turn to dance for a few moments with the Princess Moinagh. From her smile she is pleased to see him again. He can do nothing more than smile at her in return, press her hand, look into her eyes. Then she has passed on to the arms of Tazlo, of Gerr, of Sir Tarn—it is too cruel. He has the feeling that he will never see her again. Soon after the moon dance, the princess leaves the hall with her waiting women.

A movement of linkmen with their torches in the entry signals the time when guests may depart. The king goes forth and so does Diarmut Mack Dahl. When Merigaun takes his hand in farewell she looks gravely at Sharn Am Zor and says, "You must follow the way to the end."

Did she speak these words? Or did he hear her voice in his thought? The two kings ride home side by side behind the torchbearers across the unsleeping city.

Diamut Mack Dahl says to the King of the Chameln, "It is a bonny lass . . ."

"It is indeed," says Sharn Am Zor.

The King of the Isles falls silent again for a little while, then says, "At least we will be outdoors tomorrow, practicing for this Tourney of the Trees."

Sharn agrees heartily that this will be an improvement. The two kings begin to talk of hawking. Diarmut has trained a sea-eagle to fish for him. So they come to the Sennick Fortress and part very civilly. Sharn sits down to a nightcap with his two remaining champions, Tazlo and Gerr.

"You have gained much honor, my King," breathes Tazlo, "the Prince of Paldo said as much."

"Princess Merigaun seems to favor you," says Gerr. "Blood will tell!"

Alone once more, watching Prickett prowl the unfamiliar bedchamber with a sputtering Eildon candle, the king does not know whether to hope or to despair. His two champions have understood very little of the ways of Eildon. He thinks suddenly, as scenes of the day pass before him, that it should all be written down. When all is done, he thinks sleepily, I will tell it to Hazard, my dear old companion, and have him work it into a tale . . . the Tale of Shennazar.

CHAPTER VI

THE QUEST

MORE THAN TEN DAYS PASSED BEFORE THE Tourney of All Trees. The king rode out in high spirits to practise for the tourney in the wide meadows before the Hall of the Kings. The weather was so clear, untroubled by mist or rain, that the folk of Lindriss thronged the way to see King Shennazar and his guards go by. Surely, reasoned the king, he must meet the nobles of Eildon now on firmer ground and learn to deal with them. Surely the ladies would come to the lists to see their knights, and he would see his lovely childlike princess again, come to watch *him*.

Yet the days passed, and he saw none of the Eildon princes. Only the three knights—Sir Mortrice, Sir Pellasur and Sir Tarn—came and watched the king and his companions at their practice. No one waited upon his pleasure at the Sennick Fortress. The King of the Isles was more favored: he rode out to practise in the park of Earl Nollister, and more than once received heralds from the Paldo Court.

The king's efforts to woo the Princess Moinagh were all in vain. First he sent a jeweled fan, with a request to Princess Merigaun for an audience. When there came no reply, he sent Nerriot with his lute. Nerriot was not admitted, and the Pendark house kerns were dour and threatening as ever.

At last Sharn Am Zor rode out himself with Gerr and Tazlo one late afternoon and came secretly to the Pendark Court. He thought of an adventure: he would leap over the wall to that garden where the princess walked beside a pond. The white mansion was deserted. In the dusk a few guard lights sprang up, a ring of wildfire burned upon the walls. The solitary gatekeeper told them that the family had gone to Gwanlevan.

Sharn was cast down, then angry and petulant. After a miserable meal time, he tried to control his ill-humor and sat with Denwick in his sickroom. Zilly was no longer pale but flushed and feverish with a nagging headache; he was eager to hear of all that had passed. Presently Nerriot was sent for, and he helped compose a lying letter to Lady Veldis, leaving out all mention of her bridegroom's accident.

On his way to practice in the meadow, Sharn rode sometimes past the Paldo Keep, a mighty edifice of red and white stone with six tall towers and a gateway carved with stags and wild boar. On his way home in the evening, he had the escort ride another way, past the Tramarn Park. Gerr of Zerrah had once stayed in the old house of grey stone that could be glimpsed among the trees. The king ordered Gerr to visit the house where he had spent those bright moons as a new bridegroom, the guest of Prince Ross.

Gerr returned on the eve of the tourney angry and perplexed.

"I spoke with the Princess Gaveril," he said. "My King, she begged me to leave your service!"

"No more than that?" returned Sharn.

"I spoke up hotly," said the knight, "and said that for my honor and the love I bear the Daindru I could do no such thing. I protested over the treatment we have received here, my King, and so I took my leave."

"Ah, my King!" cried Tazlo Am Ahrosh, "they are afraid of us! They fear the King of the Chameln Lands and his champions!"

Gerr shook his head; this was not the cause of Princess Gaveril's appeal to him. Nerriot, at the window of the king's bower, called softly and played a chord of music. When they looked out, knights were passing; the nobility were returning to the city for the Tourney. Sharn Am Zor, fighting irritation and foreboding, wrote letters to Achamar: to Aidris, to Seyl. In the morning they would be brought to Captain Dystane in the harbor. The *Golden Oak* was sailing to Port Cayl, then on to Balufir. The king gazed around the chamber in the dark tower, saw its heavy trappings, gilded ornament, smelled the particular Eildon reek of neatsfoot oil, lavender and cherrywood logs and was overwhelmed with homesickness. He saw Yuri crouched by a settle and knew that the boy suffered from this sickness so badly that Prickett feared he would run mad.

Though Sharn retired early, he could not sleep. The dark tower was quiet; he felt no magical presence, no hidden watchers. He thought of the morrow and knew again an unreasoning fear, a foreboding of ill-fortune. Sharn Am Zor did what he had never done, had never intended to do. He crept from his massive curtained oaken bed and moved confidently through the dark chamber. He found his leather jewel case, unlocked it with his own key and took out his magical protection, the scrying stone that Aidris had given him, in its leather pouch. He carried it back to bed and sat propped on his pillows.

As he drew the stone out and cupped it in his hand, it felt warm to the touch. Still he did not look at the stone. He remembered Aidris, her look of care and urgency as she gave him the stone and said, quite simply, that it was her most treasured possession. Then she had gone on to speak nonsense, magical nonsense that he could not believe. He had the evidence of his own senses. He had seen his Grandmother, Guenna of Lien, seven years or so ago at the Hospice of the Moon Sisters in Hodd. He could still conjure up her pale twisted face, her hands fumbling with the coverlet, her mild gaze that flicked over him, unseeing. The old

woman—yet was she so old?—was half blind, unable to
speak. Her expression was peaceful; she tried to nod a
little when his mother touched her hand. Aravel spoke
the name of her eldest son several times. It was the last
time Queen Aravel was able to go abroad.

That was what stuck in his throat, thought Sharn,
crushing the stone in his hand. This was cruel nonsense
that Aidris had told him. Could Guenna of Lien still be
hale and sound, a mighty sorceress living in some secret place, with some poor invalid bearing her likeness
in the hospice? Could she do all this and not make
herself known to Aravel, her surviving daughter? Could
she not heal his mother's madness?

Still Aidris had sworn it was their grandmother "in
the world of the stone" as she called it. Could it be
some fairy spirit, some demon? He did not doubt that
he needed protection for himself and his champions.
The king took a sharp breath, opened his hand and
stared into the stone. It was a large oval stone, a green
beryl set in a silver rim. Around this rim was a little
band of sparkling mist, like the glittering trails of light
that certain fishes left at night upon the surface of the
sea. Before his eyes the mist began to fill the stone and
then to clear away again from the center. He saw another place, a forest glade, a huge oak tree. Sharn Am
Zor grew cold with wonder. Under the oak tree stood
two horses cropping the grass: a Chameln grey, a young
mare, and a plump white pony. Moon, balky, foolish
Moon, long since turned out to pasture in Achamar,
and lovely Telavel, killed in battle, the horse of Aidris
the Queen. And there under the tree stood a young girl
with crimped black hair looking down at a boy, a golden-
haired boy in a red tunic stained with earth. Aidris and
Sharn.

The image faded and was replaced by another. A
tabletop, an altar covered with a green cloth, just as
Aidris had described it. A crown lay on the altar and a
bunch of oak leaves and an angular twig of mistletoe
with glassy white berries. Sharn concentrated on the
world of the stone. The crown and oak leaves for him-

self, and the mistletoe, the sacred plant of Eildon, for
protection, for magic, perhaps the two together. The
stone became dark. Disappointed he slipped the stone's
silver chain over his head and lay down to sleep.

Next day at breakfast Britt, the Captain-General,
brought the king a letter. It was bound with a strip of
leather to the shaft of an arrow; the watch had found it
embedded in the trunk of the plum tree. In the night
an archer had fired it across the moat.

"Shall I open it, my King?" asked Britt. "There may
be some magic . . ."

"Let me," said Sharn Am Zor.

He untied the folded parchment, broke the plain
seals of blue wax, and his hand did not wither nor his
eyes dry up in his head. The letter was written in an
Eildon hand, not so fine as the Eildon script he knew
best, that of Rosmer, and addressed to "The High and
Mighty Prince, Sharn Am Zor, King of the Chameln,
who shares the double throne."

> You will bring no bride out of Eildon. Know this
> and, while you can, hold yourself and your cham-
> pions far from the Tourney of All Trees and the
> vigil that will follow. Do this for those who love
> you and respect your ancient line. There is still
> time for you to forswear this tournament because
> of the injury to the Lord Denwick or for some
> other ground. For if you once take part in these
> ceremonies, you will be bound, by Eildon custom,
> to follow the ritual or suffer a disgrace that is
> worse than death for a true knight. Heed this
> entreaty, noble Sharn, and know that the one who
> risks great pain and penalty to send this warning is
> your true friend.

Sharn made some sound of anger and disgust and
flung the letter down on the makeshift table, an oaken
press covered with a cloth.

"My king?" asked Britt, alarmed.

The two men were alone. The king woke early in

Eildon, dressed at once and ate by an eastern window of the tower.

"Read it," he said.

The Captain-General, a burly, hawk-faced officer from Hodd in the Mark of Lien, bent awkwardly over the table and read the letter almost without touching it.

"The watch saw nothing, Sire," he said. "Who would have sent such a thing?"

"Well, I have a friend in Eildon," said Sharn with a bitter smile.

One line of the letter had excited in him a cold fear: *You will bring no bride out of Eildon.*

"Sire," said Britt, "I cannot think that you, that your royal person, will be harmed at this tourney. Count Ahrosh, too, is an excellent horseman, and Count Gerr was never better in his tiltyard practice. I doubt they will come to harm. But the vigil afterwards when you are far from your escort. . . ."

"Come, Britt," said the king, "a vigil? It is in the temple, the White Tower where our own Skelow tree grows and all the magic trees of Hylor."

"What does this unnamed friend fear, my king?"

"Who knows? Some breach of their damnable ritual? I will not heed the warning," said Sharn Am Zor.

He folded the letter and stowed it away in the pocket of his tunic.

"Tell no one of this!" he ordered. "Send Nerriot to me."

"He took a night's leave from the tower, my King," said Britt, "to visit in the city. Dan Sharn, this letter is in an Eildon hand. Do you suppose the musician . . .?"

"No," said Sharn Am Zor. "Not he. Not Aram Nerriot."

Yet he knew, suddenly, that the smiling, gentle, pleasant musician was not his true friend, did not give two straws for the ancient line of the Daindru. Probably, he cared only for his music. Or was he loyal to that ungrateful girl, Merilla, and to Carel, the pair who had brought him out of Lien? The thought of his sister and brother, far away in the Chameln lands, aroused feelings of envy and unrest. *You will bring no bride out of*

Eildon. Could he fail? Could he fail so quietly and pointlessly, whiling away the spring days in this beautiful, puzzling city where he had done nothing but ride out to practice archery? Yet he had seen Moinagh; she was no dream, she was beautiful . . .

"Britt, my friend," said Sharn Am Zor, "we will all do our best! We will put on a brave show and gain what honor we can! I will speak to the men before we ride out. All is not lost!"

Upon this cry of hope, Tazlo Am Ahrosh hurried in, dressed in his riding costume from the northern tribes, booted to the thigh, with a blue cloak and a red bonnet.

"My King," he cried, "we will do great things! We will show these Eildon men and these men of the Isles!

Hard on his heels came Gerr of Kerrick, Count Zerrah, ready for another great adventure. Sharn Am Zor felt his spirits rise at last. When he was put to rights in his own gold tunic and brown breeches—he wondered that he had ever hated Chameln dress, handsome and practical—there was one more duty. He went up to Denwick's chamber and found poor Zilly half dressed in his satins, seated upon the bed. Ruako, the army doctor, stood over him. Zilly was close to tears.

"Dan Sharn," said the healer, "the Lord must not ride to the Tourney, even as a spectator. He has a fever . . ."

"By the Goddess," said Zilly in a shaking voice, "I will do it. I have lain here for twelve days—it feels like twenty. Sharn, my King, is there a litter? May I not watch in the stands with the women?"

"Zilly," said Sharn Am Zor, "it won't do. It is a damnable thing this brain-shaking, but the captain knows what is best. Stay here till I come. Let the captain bring you down to my bower. We will bring home crowns of oak leaves."

II

THE CITY OF LlNDRISS WAS SHROUDED AGAIN
in that drifting magical mist that the Chameln party
recognized from their arrival, but in the familiar green
fields before the Hall of the Kings the sun was shining
brightly. As they rode up, a great concourse of citizens
cheered Shennazar and then, to a skirl of bagpipe music, cheered King Diarmut Mack Dahl, who had ridden
another way. Far from being a stiff knightly contest, the
Tourney of All Trees was a popular festival. Heralds
and marshals stood about in the livery of the knightly
orders, and a way was quickly made for the two kings.
As they rode on slowly past the lists, the tilt-ground,
the race course, all decorated with green boughs and
garlands, Sharn heard the marshals sorting the folk into
"order of estate." He and Diarmut were presently dismounted, and so they walked forward alone, two kings,
towards the pillared porch of the Hall of the Kings, and
behind them were the Princes, Borss Paldo, Beren
Pendark, Gwalchai Tramarn and the Princess Gaveril
Tramarn, in riding dress, and the Margrave of March,
an aged lord from the west, together with his lady, and
the two dukes of the southern cantreyn, Greddach and
Wencaer. Then came the seven Eorls of Eildon, and
lords, carrying branched staves, and the knights and

144

their ladies, all blazoned with their own crests and
those of the three orders. Then came all the people of
Lindriss and the countryside, still sorted by the marshals into order of estate, until they gave up and let a
host of prentices, servants, tinkers, beggars mill about,
climbing on each others' shoulders to see what went on
before the hall.

The trumpets sounded a long fanfare, and there followed a silence broken at last by the sound of harp
music. Along the grey pillared porch of the hall came a
line of men in white robes, walking from the west and a
line of women in white and blue, walking from the east.
The druda and the priestesses, the dagdaren, all wore
their years; some were old, very old, the men white-
bearded, but others were still young, no older than
Sharn himself. Sharn Am Zor, afraid of his own impatience, prayed that the ceremony would not last long.
The strange music soothed him; he could hold out, he
knew it, and Aidris would have been proud of him.

The ceremony closed with a mighty chorus in which
all the men and women of Eildon gathered there in the
meadows sang together with great power and sweet-
ness. The druda and the priestesses were gone; the
games began.

Down on the banks of the brook the prentices of
Lindriss watched the oxen roasting or chased the greasy
pig. Archery, horse races, sword play and tilting went
on all at once. A kern or kedran might outshoot or
outride a knight or nobleman; only the jousting was for
knights alone. It was true that no prizes were given
except for garlands of oak and willow, but more than
honor could be gained. Bets were laid in coin or in kind
upon every contest and rich gifts of meat, game, fruit or
wine were lavished upon those who had brought the
gamblers a winning. When Tazlo won his first horse
race, he was cheered by a clutch of prentices and their
sweethearts and presented with a fat goose.

As he debated whether or not to accept the humble
gift—he was, after all, a king's champion—the escort
sergeant who acted as his groom hissed, "Take it, for

the Goddess, Count Ahrosh, we have trouble enough
with fresh food in this place!"

It was clear that the tourney held certain dangers for
anyone of high degree who deigned to take part. A
prince or lord who stood forth with all comers had
honor to lose while a contestant of humble estate had
not. The notion of a king, even the outland king of
Kemmelond, trounced at the shooting butts by some
sharp-eyed kedran or hardy forester, was enough to
shock the Eildon nobility. When Sharn Am Zor strolled
over with his escort, he found the fool at his side in
yellow and green motley with his midgets trotting at his
heels.

"Oh Shennazar . . ." sang the fool very softly and
sweetly,

"Unstring your bow, the wind blows cold,

Some country lad will hit the gold . . ."

"What do you mean?" asked the king.

"Does Shennazar really shoot so well?"

"Yes," said Sharn Am Zor flatly.

He strode up to the place where Britt and the escort
were holding his bows and called over his shoulder to
the fool.

"Place yourself a wager, my lord fool, for the honor of
our faraway home!"

The fool scowled and led his followers to a little
mound where they could watch the king. Sharn Am Zor
addressed himself to the targets, which were mounted
upon hollow "trees" made of straw and daub that could
be moved about by men inside their trunks.

So, hour after hour on that cloudless day in the
meadow before the Hall of the Kings, he shot with
tireless precision and grace. Foresters, kedran, country
champions came and went; the targets went to their
farthest distance; the short bow was used for "false
hares" moved on wires and "woodcocks" ejected from
the tops of the trees; still the king of the Chameln
hardly wasted an arrow. He was at first a gold mine for
those laying bets: a cartload of thank offerings grew

beside the fool and the king's guard until the odds
shortened.

Sharn Am Zor drank water and ate sparingly. Word
was brought from the lists and the race track: Gerr of
Zerrah held his own splendidly against a variety of
opponents and Tazlo fared well in the short distances.
Prince Gwalchai excelled in swordplay with the light
blade, while the King of the Isles and one of his champions defeated all comers with the broadsword.

So the king went on, untroubled, smiling at last, free
from care for a moment, as if he were practicing at the
shooting butts in the garden of the Zor palace or flying
his hawks on the side of the long valley. Few of the
better folk came to watch him, but the commoners of
Eildon saw and remembered his performance on that
bright day and said simply: "He shoots like a King." In
after years there was a common adage "to shoot like
Shennazar" meaning "to hit the mark."

About the fourth hour of afternoon the garlands were
given, to the king and to the two bowmen who had
lasted longest against him, an old forester and a young
esquire from the Tramarn household. There came a
trumpet call, and a marshal approached; the crowd
began to whisper and rustle with excitement. Sir
Mortrice of Malm came up, dismounted and came with
the marshal to the king.

"Majesty," said the knight, "you have won much
honor!"

"I have had a good day," said Sharn Am Zor, "and so
have these fine fellows."

"There is a custom to be followed," said Sir Mortrice.
"The Grand Champion will be decided by the use of
Ravedd's bow."

The marshal unwrapped a long silken package, and in
it lay a black bow, shorter than a longbow and strongly
curved above and below the grip, which was inlaid with
gold and ivory. The old archer, the forester, stepped
back shaking his head, and the esquire did the same.

"Sire," said Britt to the king in a low voice. "I think
there is some magic in the black bow."

"So do I," said Sharn Am Zor. "Tell me plainly Sir Mortrice, is there magic in this bow? Where does it come from?"

"Prince Ravedd Pendark brought it back long ago from an expedition to the Burnt Lands," said Sir Mortrice, "and there *is* magic in it. The bow will not allow everyone to handle it. Yet it is the custom to shoot with this bow every year in the spring and to wish for good fortune for the land of Eildon."

"These two archers have refused to shoot with Ravedd's bow," said Captain-General Britt. "Should our king . . ."

Pardon me, Captain," said the marshal, "these men are not of high estate. It is a matter of honor."

"I have been made an offer that I must not refuse," said the king smiling. "Peace, Britt, I have no fear of the black bow. The blood of Pendark runs in my veins, too."

He picked up the black bow, fitted the bow string and tightened it easily.

"I will use a Chameln arrow," he said. "What distance, Marshal?"

The marshal had one of the target trees set on a mark in the middle distance. Sharn tested the bow a little and felt in it a strong resistance, a strength greater than its size, which yielded to him.

At last he took the arrow from his own quiver and said, "I wish all in Eildon good harvest and good hunting!"

Then he stepped up, took aim and with a singing note of the bowstring, the arrow flew straight to the mark. The crowd cheered, but for Sharn Am Zor time had stopped, and the noises round about were hushed except for one loud cry and the clash of metal. The moment passed; the marshal took back Ravedd's bow. Sharn forced himself to smile upon all those who cheered and wished him well. He left the archery ground wreathed in green garlands, Grand Champion of the Bow, and strode off across the meadow towards the tent of his escort with its Chameln banner, near the lists. He saw Tazlo, on foot, wearing garlands himself, run-

ning towards him with two guardsmen and knew their
message before they uttered a word.

"My King," gasped Tazlo, "Gerr of Zerrah is down.
The knight Pellasur struck him down. They have brought
him to the tent."

Sharn quickened his pace, climbed a low hill to the
tent, seeing anxious faces. His guards and some of the
Eildon servants who worked in the lists scattered as he
approached, making a pathway. Then he was inside the
hot tent that reeked of crushed grass. Gerr lay on a
trestle, his head supported by a folded saddlecloth. His
face, tanned by the sun, now had an ugly greyish pallor;
his eyes were closed. Captain Ruako was wrenching off
portions of the knight's strip-mail, hacking with a knife
at his undertunic. A thick splinter of wood and metal
from Sir Pellasur's lance had penetrated the left side of
Gerr's chest, high up near the armpit. Now the healer
took a firm hold, motioned to his assistants who held
the fainting knight firmly to the table. He drew out the
splinter, and blood followed it; Gerr gave a loud cry of
pain and opened his eyes.

"My King . . ." he whispered.

"Praise to the Goddess that you still live, good Zerrah!"
said Sharn.

"Ill . . . fortune . . ." said Gerr. "By Carach, Captain, that salve of yours smarts . . ."

"Do not speak, lord," said the healer. "Give him a
sip of water, no more."

Sharn Am Zor came round the trestle, took the bea-
ker from the ensign and held it to Gerr's lips. He
thought of a high-vaulted old hall and a table covered
with featherbeds. Aidris lay face down on them, pale as
the linen, and Jalmar Raiz went to draw out the arrow.
An old woman, one of the elders of Musna village,
hustled him away down the hall, would not let him
watch. He heard Aidris, the bravest person he knew
besides his father, give a cry of pain.

Britt murmured in the king's ear.

"Sir Pellasur's esquire is without. The knight will
know how Count Zerrah is doing."

"Tell him he does well enough," said the king.

He moved away and stood with Tazlo in a corner of the stuffy tent. They tried to smile, and Tazlo told him haltingly, then with more heart, of the races he had won. Captain Ruako turned aside now and came to the king.

"It is not life-threatening, sire," he said. "Count Gerr will need some nursing."

"Did you see the joust?" asked the king.

"It was an evil chance," said Ruako. "Pellasur and Gerr were well matched. It was the last round but one. The knight's lance caught and splintered—luckily it was not on the Count's helm."

Sharn Am Zor felt a furious irritation; the whole world was bent on crossing him in great things as in small. Life was no more than a series of discomforts, even though he was a king. He made no reply to the healer, but frowned and went out into the afternoon sunshine. There was a strange silence; he was afraid that some other champion had been cut down.

The fool spoke up from among the tent ropes: "King Sharn, it is the Summoning!"

A small mounted procession came up to the tent, and a white-clad herald blew a brief trumpet call. An old man in a white robe and mounted upon a splendid white horse was the leader. He had something of a martial air about him, but he was not dressed as a knight. The king recognized him partly from his companions: a woman and a younger man riding darker horses.

"Sharn Am Zor," said Dravyd, the messenger of the Falconers. "We have come to summon you to your vigil in the White Tower."

"Now? At once?" said the king. "Good Master Dravyd, let me change my clothes at least and see to my people. My champion, Gerr of Kerrick, Count Zerrah, has been wounded."

"May the Goddess spare this scion of a noble house," said Dravyd. "You must come at once, King Sharn. You are honor bound to mount up and follow."

"Master Summoner!" exclaimed Captain-General Britt
with some heat, "This is our king you are summoning.
He cannot ride off unescorted. We, his guardsmen, are
honor bound to protect him!"

"The king may take an esquire," said Dravyd.

"My king . . ." murmured Tazlo Am Ahrosh.

Sharn saw a flicker of anxiety cross Britt's face; even
the young man from the north was not enough protection for his liking. Yet there was nothing else for it.

"Mount up then, Tazlo," said Sharn Am Zor in
exasperation.

He stripped off the garlands from his wrists and from
his neck and held them out to the fool.

"Farr the Fool," he murmured seriously, "stay with
my folk in Sennick Fortress and help them. I swear I
will give you all that your heart desires."

Then the fool bowed his head and his smaller companions seized the garlands. One of them kissed the
king's hand and said, *"Go well, King Sharn!"*

Tazlo Am Ahrosh turned his head sharply; the little
man had used the Old Speech.

The king mounted up on his trusty Eildon steed,
which was called Blaze, and Tazlo was on his second
mount, a bay called Trueheart. They followed the messengers across the field and saw the King of the Isles
summoned with as little ceremony from his tent by the
Swordsmen's Yard. Then they came further to the tent
of the Falconers, and there Prince Gwalchai was waiting, already mounted, with his esquire who was a kedran
officer. So they came past the stand before the lists, and
the Eildon nobility waved their hands and cheered the
two kings and the prince as they went by to their vigil.
The procession moved to the porch of the Hall of the
Kings again, and where the priests had stood, there
were now the heads of the knightly orders with their
banners. Prince Borss Paldo was their speaker:

"Go now, brave knights and warriors," he said, "go to
your vigil and your quest. You are honor bound to
return here to this place no sooner than the meeting

day, two moons from now, and give account of your-
selves. You may ask the Council a boon at that time."

The king's head whirled with questions. Two moons?
A vigil and a quest? A boon from the Council? What if
they all asked the same boon, the hand of the Princess
Moinagh? Would the business of contests, magic, the
formal and friendless life they had been living in Lindress,
begin all over again?

Dravyd and Nieva and Gil rode on in silence, taking
a path that led round the Hall of the Kings and through
smooth parkland. It was late afternoon; they were riding to the north. The setting sun hid behind a low hill,
and in twilight they came at last to the White Tower. It
was a very old and solid keep built of huge blocks of
crudely dressed stone, whitewashed like a farmer's cottage, with the original grey of the stone showing through
in places. It rose up on a flat green field without any
trace of fortifications; to the right and left were the
colleges of the druda and the dagdaren—long low buildings with hedged gardens.

On the green lawn before the arched entrance of the
tower grew trees of various heights, planted in no special pattern. It was hard to count these trees; as Sharn
Am Zor looked from one to the other, he was amazed
by each separate tree, by its beauty or its power or its
strangeness. That must be the Carach. Almost involun-
tarily he sent out a prayer to the Carach, saying "Care
for your countryman, poor Gerr of Kerrick Hall, injured in the lists!" There was an oak, twined with
mistletoe, and there a sea-oak, bearded with moss, and
there a conifer unknown to him, very narrow and dark,
and there a bulbous tree with roots hanging in the air.
As they dismounted, still in silence, young druda in
their white robes came and led the horses away. The
messengers led the way down a broad pebbled path to
the entrance of the tower, and at last Sharn saw the
black tree, the Skelow, grown a cloth yard high in the
year since it had come into Eildon. It stood to the left
of the path, and he wished he might run and kneel

down beside it. All he could do was call to it in his mind: "Skelow, I am here, come from the Palace of the Zor at Achamar, from your parent tree, my old dark companion."

III

HE WOKE WITH AN EFFORT AS HE HAD DONE
so many times before and saw that the candles beside
the altar stone had hardly burnt down. It was the fourth
night, and they were still on the cold stone, still keeping vigil, stripped of their rank, showered with the
sacred spring water and wrapped in curious garments.
Sharn fingered the stuff of his cloak: it was like nothing
at all, like mist, its color a brown-purple-grey, mole
color perhaps. It kept him warm, so warm that like all
the others he fell asleep in the huge cold hall during
the nightlong vigils. He saw that Gwalchai's kedran was
wide awake, while her master dozed, kneeling. The
woman, Edrith, was the oldest; then Kenzie, the esquire of Diarmut. Both the island men were sitting
cross-legged, upright, staring straight ahead, entranced.
Tazlo had fallen from a kneeling position a body length
away; if he slept too long, one of the druda would come
and waken him. Sharn drew up his long legs and hugged
his knees; his body ached.

The vast hall was open to the sky. He had watched
the stars overhead during these long nights: was that
the Hunter winking a red eye at him? There were
wooden galleries circling the interior of the white tower,
their pillars made of tree trunks, dwarfed by the ma-

sonry. The altar of the Goddess was a single block of white stone flanked by thick candles and decorated with stone urns of spring flowers. Sharn knew that visions were often vouchsafed to true worshippers during a vigil, but he had seen none. A trio of priestesses came in every night and swept and garnished the altar and the place before it.

The leaden hours crept by, and he passed them sleeping and waking, gazing at the altar until it swam before his tired eyes. Was it becoming lighter? Was the dawn coming at last? He thought he heard the birds singing and even a fluttering of wings. Yes, woodland birds had come in through the opening overhead; he saw them flying about the altar. A young druda in a long golden cloak stood at the altar. A bird flew down and rested upon his outstretched hand. Tazlo gave some startled exclamation, and Sharn glanced at him, blinking as he turned from the light. The young man from the north looked at the king wildly, then settled himself into a more comfortable position. When Sharn looked back, the young priest and the birds had gone. It was indeed getting light.

The vigil ended. They were led off in silence, each to a lonely cell. Sharn, feeling drained of strength but oddly peaceful, lay down again on his straw-filled mattress and fell asleep. When he woke, there was his daily ration: a jug of water, half a loaf of bread and beef-dripping to spread on it, two hard-boiled hens' eggs, two apples. He began to gobble up the food gratefully.

There was no door to the cell but a thick felt curtain. Now it was drawn back, and a man came in: it was the High Druda, the leader of the college, who had led the opening ceremony for the Tourney of All Trees. He was middle-aged and not as tall as he had appeared at first. Sharn heaved himself up from the low pallet and bowed to the High Priest.

"Sit down, Sharn Am Zor," said the druda gently. "I am called Gwion Goldenhand. We must prepare for your quest."

"Master Gwion," said Sharn, not quite sure how to address the priest, "I will do all that I am bound to do, but I am growing tired of Eildon and its magic."

"Do not think you know Eildon, my son, because you have spent some time in Lindriss at the princely courts and at the Tourney of Trees," said Gwion Goldenhand.

"I am a king," said Sharn. "I came here to court my royal cousin. Yet I have been ill-used and tricked and my loyal followers have been struck down . . ."

"Put aside all worldly thoughts," said the High Druda with firm authority. "What you shall do now in the Sacred Wood and in the countryside of Eildon is no courtly game; it is a quest!"

"What am I to understand by that?" asked the king. "Is it a search for some object, some magic place such as lost Ystamar, the vale of the oak trees?"

"It is a search for truth," said Gwion Goldenhand. "Everyone who goes into the Sacred Wood, in good heart, purified by a vigil, will learn as much of the truth as he or she is able to bear."

"But what truth?" asked Sharn impatiently. "The truth about life? The answer to some question?"

"The truth we need most," said the High Druda. "The truth about ourselves."

Sharn Am Zor fell silent. In spite of the warmth of the magic cloak, his only garment, he shivered.

"You are a king," said the priest again, "and you are a brandhul. Do you know what that means?"

"I am proof against certain kinds of magic," said Sharn. "I have known this for some time, long before the messengers told me. What else is a brandhul?"

"It is a strange quality," said Gwion. "I have seen brandhul who were very ugly, twisted and deformed. Others, like yourself, are well-made, handsome. Magic, especially the empty kind of trickery you have experienced in the city, bounces off the brandhul. A spell misaimed returns upon the sender. A spell aimed at a brandhul . . ."

Sharn understood before the words were spoken. He uttered a loud cry.

"Yes, it is true," said the High Druda. "A spell aimed at a brandhul strikes someone else."

The king stared open-mouthed at Gwion Goldenhand. He saw Zilly upon the white horse, heard Gerr of Zerrah struck down in the lists. He thought of many common "accidents" in war and in peace that had visited those near him while he went unharmed. Even the arrow fired in the Hain long ago had wounded Aidris while he escaped. He thought of the ride in the early snowstorm with Tazlo; a guard officer had died and others had suffered for *his* foolishness.

"Can I be rid of this?" he demanded. "Master Gwion, can I be healed of being a brandhul?"

"Think carefully," said the priest. "Some would say that this quality is no bad thing in a king."

Sharn shook his head but fell silent.

"You will go to the tiring room again," said Gwion. "Then ride out with Tazlo Am Ahrosh, your esquire, into the Sacred Wood. Take the road that beckons. Open your heart to the power of the Goddess."

"Is the wood very wide?" asked Sharn.

"About three times the size of the Hain, near Achamar," said the priest. "If your way leads out of the wood, you must follow it, but the power of the vigil and the quest will be on you, and you will come to no harm."

"Is the quest peaceful?" asked Sharn. "I have heard of knights who fought with dragons and so on . . ."

"Perhaps it was so in old time." Garion smiled. "But today the dragons have all flown to the warm lands. They do not trouble us. The quest is peaceful, and no blood can be spilt in the Sacred Wood."

It all seemed easy enough, Sharn thought, and in the same moment he distrusted the Sacred Wood. He clung to the feelings of peace, of emptiness that he retained from the vigil. In the tiring room, still under ban of silence, he grinned at Tazlo, and they dressed in their clothes from the Tourney, newly pressed and refurbished, but were allowed to keep their cloaks of the magic cloth. So they came out into the noonday sun beside the White Tower and followed two druda to a stableyard where their horses were waiting and were led by their two grooms over a flowery meadow between the colleges of the priests and priestesses.

They beheld the Sacred Wood on the other side of a little river, and Sharn's first thought was that it did not compare with the Hain. The trees were lower, with the gnarly Eildon look he had marked as his ship sailed up the river Laun. The elder of the two druda bowed and blessed them and pointed to a small bridge. They rode over the bridge, first the king, then Tazlo, and Sharn saw a decent path beside a bush of yellow broom, so he took it and they rode into the wood.

The ban of silence was ended; they both burst out laughing. It was delicious to speak aloud, to ride through the low green aisles talking and laughing over every cruel detail of the vigil.

"I saw no visions," said Sharn. "I wonder how the others fared?"

"On the last night I saw a strange thing," said Tazlo, "and I could have sworn, my King, that you saw it too."

"What, that tall blond priest and the birds?"

"A priest?" said Tazlo. "In the gold cloak?"

The young man from the north had reined in his bay horse. They stood on the edge of a clearing. Sharn felt for the first time that the wood spread out all around them, impenetrable. He looked about keenly and saw nothing that he could interpret as a magical sign leading him on.

"The man at the altar in the golden cloak, sire," said Tazlo uneasily, lowering his voice, "it was yourself. You lifted a hand, and the bird settled on it."

Sharn shook his head, wondering.

"Perhaps it was a chance likeness," he said. "I did not see the man as myself."

They rode on into the clearing and found the ashes of a fire in a ring of stones and hoofprints in the thick soft grass.

"Choose a path," said Sharn. "We must go further into the wood."

Tazlo turned his steed to the right under the branches of an oak entwined with mistletoe, and the path he had chosen opened up before them and became very beautiful, springing with wild flowers. The wood, as they went in deeper, was full of life. Squirrels chattered at them overhead; birds started up at their approach or ran off into the thickets; a badger swayed across the path. They had ridden so long that it must be near sunset, but the light in the wood was deceiving. Sharn felt as he had while crossing the city of Lindriss, that ways and paths closed up around him just before he caught sight of them, obscured by leaves as they had been by patches of mist.

Suddenly Tazlo drew rein with a rapt expression.

"Listen, my king!" he breathed. "The singing . . . !"

Sharn heard nothing but the sounds of the wood: the chirring and ticking of insects, the sleepy call of a bird. Tazlo swung his horse awkwardly to the right again and rode off down a narrow dark path. Sharn did not follow. Tazlo had been called to seek his own destiny, they would surely meet up again.

The king rode on; a horse whinnied close at hand, and he peered through a screen of alders across the path. There he saw a clearing, wider than the first, with a brook running through the glade. A black horse was tethered to a tree, and a man sat on his saddleblanket gazing into the waters of the brook. It was Diarmut Mack Dahl, King of the Isles. Sharn parted the alder saplings and rode through, giving a friendly greeting.

"Good company at last!" cried Mack Dahl. "This stream is alive with fine trout that we're not permitted to fish. I hope our saddlebags are filled with meat or game. Nuts and berries are not to my taste!"

Sharn dismounted, and they drank a sup from Diarmut's leather bottle, filled with island spirit, and examined their saddlebags. Grumbling a little, the two kings fed themselves on bacon, cold beef, bread and ripe pears.

"Well then, how d'ye go with this request?" asked

Diarmut, leaning against a tree and picking his teeth luxuriously with the point of his dagger.

"A blank," said Sharn. "I see no signs."

"I will go out of the wood," said Diarmut, slyly. "It is a long two moons until we come to account with the Eildon princes. I will meet my folk north of the wood a little and go to the city of Yerrick."

He gave a sigh.

"I am out of the running," he said. "Princess Moinagh is not for me. I have been offered a compromise."

Sharn could not hide his surprise.

"I will wed Nollister's lass," said Diarmut. "She is bonny and good-natured, though not so beautiful as the pearl of Pendark. It is as my auld carlin wife foresaw matters. I consulted this wise woman before I came down, and judged it worthwhile even at the sacrifice of my island."

"The golden island of Kaindelly," said Sharn. "What will become of this land pledge?"

"The Council will have it tended," said Diarmut, "and the mines worked by someone of their own faction. In this case Eorl Nollister, whose territory is in the north, in Imbermal. It is usually this way: a neighboring lord works the pledge on behalf of the Council."

Sharn stopped with a scrap of cold bacon halfway to his lips. He felt sick; a wave of nausea swept over him. He breathed in the cool air of the Sacred Wood and cursed under his breath.

"Man, what ails ye?" asked Diarmut Mack Dahl. "Are you away with the fairies?"

"They promised a revelation in this wood," said Sharn Am Zor, "and, by the Goddess, you have given me one, good Diarmut. I begin to think that my whole courtship, my love for the Princess Moinagh, was awakened only for this. There are those who would have my land pledge, the silver mine in the Adz of the Chameln lands."

"Pardon me, noble Sharn," said Diarmut, "but I have only the haziest notion of your kingdom: that it is bigger than Eildon more than threefold. Who d'ye think will have the care of your pledge?"

"The rulers of the Mark of Lien," said Sharn. "The Markgraf Kelen and his vizier."

He saw it all; he even saw, with the eye of love or with the help of the Sacred Wood, that Hazard was an innocent tool in the matter. Buckrill had been the link, and even he had been driven to rescue Hazard. Behind the whole enterprise was Rosmer. He, Sharn Am Zor, had been the willing victim, eager for a royal bride, a pearl, a princess of dreams. He felt a hopeless anger, which he could not give vent to. In his mind he saw Sharn Am Zor in his apartments at Achamar falling into a royal rage, striking the servants, smashing jewels, dishes, armor to the floor, ripping at the silken hangings, roaring aloud in his frenzy. He clenched his fists and bowed his head. He knew now that he must digest his anger and his failure; he would not bring home the Princess Moinagh.

"Alas," said Diarmut softly, "alas, my good friend, you have done better than any of us, I think. But for the princess: I think they will give her to Tramarn."

Sharn gave one sigh, which seemed to come from his very soul.

"Yes," he said. "I think they will."

In silence Diarmut Mack Dahl handed him the leather bottle of Usqubeg; Sharn took two good swallows, felt the spirit burn down to the pit of his stomach. The King of the Isles matched him drink for drink, and they spoke more companionably than ever. They drank to brotherhood; they exchanged rings. Sharn gave the King of the Isles his ring with the fox's mask, and Diarmut gave him in exchange a ring with a large topaz. When the twilit glade swam before their eyes, the two kings lay full length on the greensward, wrapped in their magic cloaks, and fell asleep.

When Sharn woke in the dawn, he was alone; the King of the Isles had ridden away. Sharn, as he opened his eyes, saw the fair green leaves overhead, heard the sweet song of the birds and remembered his failure, his misery, the way he had been set on to a hopeless enterprise. This would be his lot now: waking every morning to this bitterness. He remembered waking in Lien, as a young lad, and feeling the same pain: the king, my father, is dead, and we are in exile. Yet the Sacred Wood still soothed him a little. He rose up and washed in the brook and groomed Blaze, his horse. The thing was to find Tazlo if he could.

He mounted up and caught sight of a narrow path that led out of the clearing past a wild plum tree, which bore a few pink blossoms. He took the path, giving himself up to the power of the wood, as he had been told. The way led uphill and became so steep that he got down and led his horse up the grassy banks. In the distance he heard other horses and thought he glimpsed riders below him. Then he saw open ground up ahead and came out into bright sunshine.

He stood on high ground, a grassy clifftop that fell away at his feet in chalky tiers and down into a wide plain. Eildon spread out at his feet, a very green countryside, with clumps of gnarled trees in new leaf and stone walls and villages. To the north, beyond the reaches of the wood, he saw blue hills; before him, to the west, there was wooded hilly country and another blue haze that might be the seacoast. He admired the cantrys of Eildon, and at the same time he pined and longed for the Chameln lands. Eildon was hilly and rough, a little like the central highlands of the Chameln lands, and it was hardly bigger than the Mark of Lien. Why, the seacoast, yonder, was surely not more than a day's ride. He had a sudden urge, if he could find a path, to ride down the cliff and set out for the sea. Where was Tazlo? The king called aloud for his esquire, and the cliffs sent back loud echoes. He rode along the cliff and saw a path. The sunlight dazzled on a piece of metal; Sharn peered, shading his eyes, and glimpsed a bay horse far below, at a turn in the path.

He took the way down the hillside as swiftly as he dared, calling Tazlo's name anxiously. At last he reached the turn of the path, a wider shelf than it had looked from above, and found the horse, Trueheart, riderless and restless. There was Tazlo sitting on the ground trying to wrap a cloth round his head. Sharn leaped down and ran to him.

"What is it man? How are you hurt?"

Tazlo let the cloth fall. His face was swollen and reddened on the right side, his lips so distorted that he could hardly speak.

"Stung?" said the king, falling to his knees. "Here, let me . . ."

Something moved on the ground, and he saw that Tazlo sat panting, his eyes dark and wild. Sharn took his water bottle that he had filled at the brook and wet the cloth that Tazlo was holding to his face. The young man had been stung in three or four places, and the hornet had left a deep purpling wound each time. The wet cloth did little to ease the pain. A voice came to them, borne by the wind, and when Sharn looked far up to the cliff top he saw that two riders had come out of the wood. It was as hard to see upward as it had been to see down, but at last he made out a dark blue shield.

"Tramarn, I think," he said, preparing to stand up and wave.

Tazlo suddenly gripped the king's arm with both hands and shook his head violently.

". . . not call . . ." he whispered.

They remained stock still; only their horses could just be seen. The riders above soon rode back into the wood. Sharn took the young man's shyness for a kind of vanity. Who would be seen in such a state? Yet Tramarn or his kedran might have had a slave with them.

He looked helplessly at Tazlo, who was still in great pain, and was inspired. Both of them still wore their magic cloaks, hitched back on their thongs because the day was warm. He took a fold of the misty, magical stuff and laid it to his esquire's swollen cheek.

In a few moments Tazlo was able to say "Better, Sire!"

"Mount up then," ordered Sharn. "We will ride down to the plain. In a day's ride we can be beside the sea."

There was no particular sense in what they did; Tazlo swathed his head in his cloak, and they rode down to the plain and took a road to the west. They passed through two villages and at a third they found a kind of tavern where they dined on mutton pies, stewed leeks and bread and cheese: good Eildon fare. They were treated as knights and gave no hint of name or estate.

As they sat drinking their ale, Tazlo burst out awkwardly; "I am glad to be free of the wood! It was an uncanny place."

"I did not find it so," said Sharn. "It was peaceful. I saw and heard nothing unearthly."

His disappointment in this was only a part of the greater disappointment that he was concealing from Tazlo. He did not know how to tell the young man from the north that their journey must end in failure.

"The air was full of voices," said Tazlo, wild-eyed. "The power of the Goddess breathed from every leaf. I rode for miles and seemed not to have gone a step. I came to a stone shelter in the wood and heard some men of the Isles, waiting for their master. They said King Diarmut would wed another!"

"Nollister's daughter," said Sharn. "Yes, I heard it from Mack Dahl himself."

"They said Tramarn would have the princess, as if it were well-known," said Tazlo. "Then I turned and rode off, for they had not seen me. I came clear across the wood again and stood behind a great oak and saw where Tramarn lay sleeping in a grove. Sire, for your honor, I felt a sudden rage at the prince. I picked up a large stone and hurled it at him as he lay sleeping. The power of the wood turned it aside. Tramarn woke, and his kedran rode after me, out of a brake. I rode away as swiftly as I could, and brushed against the hornet's nest. One hornet pursued me, stung me dreadfully, drove me out of the wood. I came flying down the cliff path to the place where you found me.

"You must be mad!" said the king, furiously angry.

"You sully my honor instead of upholding it. You dese-
crate the Sacred Wood!"

Sharn Am Zor sprang up and left the tavern, full of
his royal rage. When Tazlo had paid their score, they
rode on, both silent. As the sun went down behind the
hills, directly in their path, they met a shepherd driving his flock to the fold.

"Ask him where the road leads!" ordered Sharn.

The man, who was sturdy and old, with a fringe of
white beard, took some time to understand Tazlo's question, but his answer was plain. The road led to Gwanlevan, the Pendark fortress. They remained standing in
the dying light as the shepherd and his dogs passed
over the way, following the flock.

"My King!" cried Tazlo, full of his old hope and
spirit. "My king, it is your destiny! It is a sign that all is
not lost. Oh my King, forgive me for that rash act in the
wood . . ."

"Yes, yes," said the king. "I forgive you. Come let us
make haste."

He still could not admit to Tazlo that all was lost
indeed. Yet he did feel that it was his destiny to go to
Gwanlevan. Perhaps he would meet the family on better terms, drink wine with old Kilnan. He envied Tazlo
his experiences in the Sacred Wood: the air full of
voices, the power of the Goddess breathing from every
leaf. He was a brandhul, he reasoned, and immune to
magic, as he had often boasted at home in Achamar.
The vigil and the talk with the High Druda, Gwion
Goldenhand, had brought him to the edge of some
experience, to some magical threshold that he could not
cross.

So they rode on through the long twilight and came
between low hills crowned with ash trees, their leaves
green-gold for the spring. They saw a gleam of water
before them and rode on through a tract of dark, reedy
country, empty of any farms or villages. As the moon
rose, they came to the edge of a lake.

Gwanlevan Fortress was an island in the midst of the
lake, a dark and forbidding pile. No banners could be

seen, and only a few feeble lights burned high in the towers. Sharn saw a line of low dunes at the western end of the lake, and when he pushed through the reeds and tasted the lake water it was brackish. The seashore lay beyond the dunes, and sea water flowed into the lake. They could see no jetty on this part of the lake shore, but there was a causeway that might lead to one.

"We must go to the north, by that causeway, my King," said Tazlo.

"No," said Sharn.

They both spoke in whispers. The lake, the island keep, the spreading tract of barren land by the sea, all silvered in the light of the moon, had cast a spell upon them.

"How will we come in?" asked Tazlo. "We must find a boat."

Sharn looked about, and in the moonlight, bright as day, he saw a stunted tree by the lake shore. When he came to it, he found that the ground nearby was firm and dry underfoot. A low branch of the tree had been used as a hitching rail, there was even a hollowed place full of fresh water for a drinking trough.

"Bring the horses," he called softly.

When Tazlo came up, the king said to him, "I must go alone into Gwanlevan. Stay here and make camp for the night. There is grass and fresh water for the horses. I will send a boat for you if we are to lodge at the fortress."

Tazlo began a vain protest. He could not let the king go alone. How would he come into the place? The two young men argued furiously in whispers, then Sharn Am Zor strode back through the reeds to the margin of the lake. He stripped off all his clothes, wrapped them into a long bundle with his magic cloak and slung it across his body. He waded into the water, which was cold but not icy cold as the waters of the Chameln lands could be. He set off swimming with firm strokes. Halfway across, he rolled on his back, floating, and saw Tazlo standing anxiously in the moonlight. He waved briefly and swam on, enjoying the water, which was warm now and buoyant.

He came to the fortress and paddled round a sheer black cliff, topped by ancient masonry, until he came to an old weedy stair. He scrambled up—it was slippery and dangerous—and stood at last upon the island, in a rocky niche of the outer wall of the keep. Listening for sounds of life, he dressed himself again and donned the magic cloak, which had kept his clothes dry. He climbed easily to the top of the wall and peered over.

He looked down into an ancient garden with fruit trees, full of blossom, trained against the walls. The keep rose up, old, frowning and unlit, yet with some noise of servants in the distance. At the end of the garden was a plain stone building with a round arched doorway and a wooden roof. It reminded him of a granary in Achamar, but a light burned inside and he decided it might be a chapel to the Goddess. He slipped down easily into the garden; no dogs barked; no men at arms came running. Following a white path edged with seashells, he came to the open door of the chapel and it swung wider without a sound to let him enter.

He came without warning into vastness. Gusts of sweet sound, half-heard, and waves of light cast him down and brought him to his knees on the stone floor. The very stones trembled, floating in the void, and voices spoke, but he had not the power to raise his head. He strove to do so, almost breathless, and beheld, far off, a figure clothed all in light who was three figures: three women, and all were one. It was the Princess Merigaun, transformed, full of power and radiance. Her voice came to him as many voices, and the question they asked was put in many different ways. "What is he?" "Is this man dark or light?" "Who is come to us?" and at last, in a whisper at his ear: "Who are you?"

He strove to answer, but no sound came. He shut his eyes against the light and made a mighty effort.

"I am Sharn Am Zor!"

And again, raising himself up a little; "I am Sharn Am Zor, who shares the double throne."

And a third time, as the voices began to mock and chide; "I am the king of the Chameln lands!"

A single voice rang like a bell:

"*Are you a king?*"

Then he crossed the threshold of his quest and saw into his life, as a man and as a king, afterwards he could not explain, even to those he loved, how this was done or what he saw except to say that it was like a dream. A cruel dream full of faces, a tapestry woven of bright and dark threads, a masque of kings, of one king, Sharn Am Zor. Old fear and hatred began to overwhelm his proud spirit; all his defenses were stripped away leaving only a frightened boy. Another voice spoke.

"*Enough, Merigaun! Let him alone!*"

"Who speaks in this holy place?" rang the voice of Merigaun.

Sharn raised his head, and the world was with him again. What he saw was still as strange as his dream, the revelation of his own life. He lay upon the floor of the chapel; Merigaun stood by the altar, and to his right the stone wall shone like a dark mirror. A woman in a glittering robe and crowned with light was to be seen in this mirror, and he knew her before she spoke her name.

"I am Guenna of Lien!"

"Sister," said Merigaun, "Is it you? Have you such power?"

"It has been granted to me. I have learned my art in secret, the art that you have through your birth. I am a mortal woman, the Eildon blood of the Vauguens is thinned with years in Lien. I risk much to come here, to show myself as whole and sound and versed in magic. Yet I must speak for this child, for Sharn Am Zor, my daughter's son."

"Will you say that he is a true king?"

"Not yet," replied Guenna, "but he has suffered much at the hands of our old enemy. Having seen into his life, Sharn will learn to be a man and a king."

Her calm faith sustained him. He felt that it was more, much more than King Sharn, the arrogant, wrong-headed, impatient, shadow king, deserved.

"Grandmother," he said, feeling hot tears upon his cheeks, hearing his own hoarse, altered voice, "Grandmother, I swear that I . . ."

Her image wavered.

"Sharn Kelen," whispered Guenna, "my dearest child . . ."

"Oh stay!"

He came to his feet, held out his hands, but the image faded, and Sharn could not stand. He groped his way to a stone bench in the shadowy chapel, and Merigaun was beside him, holding a stone cup of cool water to his lips.

"The Markgrafin spoke of an enemy," she said.

He looked up at her fearfully, but her glory had faded. She was the Princess Merigaun Pendark, no longer the avatar of the Goddess of the Priestess of the Moon.

"A deadly enemy," said Sharn, "and he has lived in Gwanlevan. It is Rosmer, the vizier of my uncle Kelen, the Markgraf of Lien."

"I will say his true name," said Merigaun. "He is Ross Demergue, born within the fortress, child of a young kedran in the service of the house of Pendark and of Prince Ross Tramarn, now become the Priest-King."

"I know his name," said Sharn. "He has done great harm to my grandmother."

"And to you?"

"Yes," he said. "He set me on to come to Eildon and sue for the hand of your daughter. He did it so that he might increase the territory of his master. Lien will have the working of my land pledge. But do not think that he is to blame for my coming. I was warned of all the pitfalls of Eildon, even the Messengers of the Fal-coners tried to dissuade me. There is a wise man in Achamar, called Jalmar Raiz, and he told me plainly all that I had to fear and that I would never be granted the hand of the Princess Moinagh. I would not hear them. I know that the House of Pendark could do nothing to warn me."

"The Prince of Tramarn *is* the favored suitor," said Merigaun. "You came in vain."

"No," whispered Sharn. "It was an ill-starred journey. I have brought injury on two of my closest companions, and I have wasted the substance of my kingdom. Still I have had this revelation, this vision that will surely work to the good of the Chameln lands. And believe me, Lady Merigaun, it was fine to see your daughter, for she is a rare jewel. I will always remember her."

"You do not know all," said Merigaun gently. "Tramarn is a noble youth, but Moinagh is no ordinary bride."

She laid a hand on Sharn's shoulder and turned about until he looked again at the wall where Guenna's image had appeared. As she spoke, the wall became a mirror again, and he beheld the wild seashore just beyond the lake of Gwanlevan. Dawn was breaking.

"You will have seen that I have no voice in the Councils of Eildon," said Merigaun. "I am set apart from the rulers and their courts. It is a fault to have no magic here, and it is a fault to have too much. I am of the Shee. My father was a Lyreth lord, living in the depths of the ocean, far from mortal men, just as the Eilif lords have withdrawn to the High Plateau, in the land of Mel'Nir. My mother was a daughter of a knight of the Fishers, who lived not far from here. I share her heritage. The land is my home, and it is the home of my son Beren. Yet some live between earth and water . . ."

They watched the little waves running up the white sands. From among the rocks came a bevy of young girls; their hair and the skin of their bodies was tinged with green. As they danced upon the sands, leaving the prints of webbed toes, Sharn caught his breath, for the eerie strangeness and the beauty of the dancers. The loveliest of all was Moinagh.

A dolphin leaped in the bay, and dark shapes slithered

down from the distant rocks. Not only seals but the selkin, the sealwives, with soft arms and women's breasts. Moinagh cried out in greeting. She led the way into the sea, plunged into the waves with her Lyreth companions, and he saw, by Merigaun's magic, how they swam deep down where even the bravest mortal swimmer could not follow.

"There may be other suitors," said Merigaun, as the vision faded. "The Kings of the Sea, the Lyreth. Moinagh is still a child; one day she will choose."

For an instant Sharn was filled with longing. To live in the ocean, to swim untiring in the silver flood, to share the nature of the sea creatures . . .

"The sea," he said. "The kingdom of the sea . . ."

"What will *you* do, Sharn Am Zor?"

He returned to land. He was new born; he hardly knew himself. He must bring all that had passed into some sort of order in his head.

"I will go home," he said. "I will go home now, at once. I pray that my two friends Denzil and Gerr are recovered from the injuries they received and that the men of my guard are holding together in the city of Lindriss."

"Your way will not be smooth," said Merigaun softly. "You are breaking the ritual of the quest."

"Perhaps you can tell me," said Sharn. "Why is this rule set down? Why should those on a quest hold themselves far from the city for two long moons?"

Merigaun smiled.

"There are certain grounds for this rule," she said, "although the Council holds to the ritual blindly without remembering the grounds. Those on a quest serve the Goddess and are no longer governed by the ties of court and family. Also, it was an old health measure. Those on a quest were feared as plague carriers who did not become ill themelves but brought sickness to others."

"I must leave Eildon at once," said Sharn. "I believe it is the right thing to do. I will follow the way to the end."

"Come then, Sharn Am Zor," said Merigaun.

She took his hand, and they walked out of the chapel into the light of the rising sun. There was a narrow gate in the wall of the fortress, and servants held it open. At the foot of the old stair there floated a round boat made of hides, a coracle. He said farewell, commending himself one last time to Moinagh, to Beren, to his Great-Uncle Kilnan. Merigaun held up her hand in blessing, and he saw that her eyes were full of tears. It was as if the Goddess herself wept for him, for that sorry prince, Sharn Am Zor. He stepped into the boat, and before he could look about for an oar, it bore him swiftly across the waters of Gwanlevan to just that spot where he had entered them.

CHAPTER VII

THE RETURN

TAZLO LAY SOUND ASLEEP UNDER THE TREE by the lake shore.

"Wake up!" said Sharn. "Come Tazlo, old son . . ."

The young man from the north squinted up at him, trying to wake quickly.

"Take your time," said the king. "There is food in my magic boat yonder. I will fetch it."

"My King, you look pale!"

"Tazlo," said the king, "I cannot tell you all that has passed. I am a changed man. This is the morning of the world for me!"

"The princess?"

"I am no longer a suitor for the hand of the Princess Moinagh."

"My king, what have they done to you?"

"I have seen the truth. The quest is over. Tazlo, let us eat a bite and quickly mount up. Good news, the best news: Tazlo, we are going home!"

Sharn smiled, gathering his energy. Tazlo stared at his liege, his face a mask of dismay.

"My king, you are honor bound! We cannot return for two moons!"

Sharn strode off to bring food from the coracle, with his esquire trailing after him, protesting, almost weep-

ing. The disgrace! The loss of honor! The broken prom-
ises! The king remained resolutely cheerful and would
not listen. At last, as they sat under the tree eating fruit
from Gwanlevan, the king said seriously, "Tazlo, you
have served as my esquire on this quest, but now I
release you from this service. Will this please you? I
have done ill by all the brave men who came with me
to Eildon; I would make amends. If it offends your
honor to break off at this point in your personal quest,
in and out of the Sacred Wood, then stay out the
remaining two moons. I have gold; you carry my purse.
Take what you need and come home when you choose."

Tazlo was deeply astonished. He stopped with his
apple halfway to his lips, staring at the rosy fruit as if it
might contain poison. At last he shook his head.

"No, my king," he said. "I will follow you."

They mounted up on Blaze and Trueheart and rode
out of the reedy country about Gwanlevan and found
the high road to come to Lindriss from the west. In a
day and a night of steady riding, they came within sight
of the city. It swam upon the horizon like a mirage in
the Burnt Lands. The king was eager and pleasant all
the way, and Tazlo could think that this was the Sharn
he knew of old, in the hunting field, perhaps. Yet he
saw now and then traces of humility and sadness in his
royal liege.

Between them they tried to calculate how many days
they had been absent from the city. It was not so easy.
Four days and four nights for the vigil in the White
Tower, but then how long had been spent in the Sacred
Wood. Sharn said it was only a day and a night, but
Tazlo claimed that it was much longer. He recalled at
least four days and four nights wandering the uncanny
reaches of the wood, while perhaps the king lay in a
charmed sleep by the brook where he met the King of
the Isles. Then a further day's ride to Gwanlevan and a
night spent in the fortress by Sharn. Two days to reach
the city. This all added up to ten or eleven days,
bringing them to the end of the Birchmoon. After another night at an inn, they rode into Lindriss through

the west gate, early in the morning, with a tide of market carts.

They were near the Pendark Court. The air was clear and bright, with no traces of magic mist, and they found their way to Sennick with no trouble. At one point Sharn was recognized and cheered as champion of the bow, the Archer King, Shennazar of Kemmelond. So they came at last to the dark tower. In answer to their shouts and cries, a few guardsmen looked out fearfully and some appeared upon the top of the tower. The drawbridge was lowered, and they rode into the courtyard to find a few men on duty with a drawn look.

"What is it?" cried the king, leaping down. "Tell me the truth, Ensign Fréjan! In the name of the Goddess, have I come too late? How fares it with my two champions?"

"My king" said Frejan "they are very sick. It goes ill with us all."

Britt pushed his way through.

"My king, we were not prepared . . ."

The captain-general was haggard, a man beseiged.

"Come," said the king, "no ceremony, Britt. I will send to the docks. We are going home. The whole miserable business is at an end."

Captain-General Britt fell to his knees and kissed the king's hand.

"Goddess be praised!" he said.

The men round about echoed his words; the trumpets sounded as Sharn hurried through the cold, dark hall.

"What has happened?" asked the king. "What brought you to this pass?"

Britt poured out a doleful story. A fight with men of Paldo on the way back from the tourney left several injured, and in the scuffle both Britt and the Quartermaster were robbed of their money belts. Gold was scarce after that, and they expected a stay of two moons in Lindriss, eking out their winnings from the tournament. Britt persuaded the master of the livery stable to take back most of the horses in order to cut down on fodder. The king's two champions continued very sick, and now a fever had struck at the guard. They lay in their quarters, six or seven men stricken with this low fever.

"Two days past," said Britt, "I rode out with Count Zerrah, so weak that he could barely sit his horse, and we came to the Tramarn Court. The count asked for help for us all, and it was denied. He was offered lodging for himself alone and would not accept it, though I begged him to do so."

The king looked grim and pale. Captain Ruako came to the door of the king's bower, and he had the same look of care turning to relief when he saw the king. In the sunlit room Denzil of Denwick lay in a makeshift bed, wasted and feverish. His mind was wandering; he hardly knew the king. Prickett went about doing the nursing, and at the sight of the king he began to weep, silently, tears trickling down his ill-shaven cheeks.

"The boy, Sire," he whispered. "If he could come out of this place . . ."

Yuri lay sick in the dressing room. Gerr of Zerrah lay in the king's own bed, white from the pain of his swollen arm.

"Sire," he gasped, "I saw you in a dream yesternight and my prayers have been answered. I thought it was all over for myself and poor Denwick."

The king turned aside to Tazlo and said softly, "You see, Ahrosh? Is honor or ritual worth the very lives of these brave men?"

It was clapped up at once that Tazlo should ride to the docks with an ensign and prepare the *Nixie* and the pinnace to receive passengers.

"Where's Nerriot?" asked the king. "Has he been of any service?"

"He comes and goes on his own errands, my King," said Britt. "We have had the best help from this gentleman and his little ones."

"Come," said the king, "let us sit in the hall, my lord fool, and drink beer if there is no wine in the house."

So they came to the dark hall again, where at last a

fire had been lit. The garrison went about packing up, awakened to life by the king's coming and the news that their misery was at an end.

"Shennazar," said the fool, "there will be trouble. The princes will see it as a triumph for themselves and a disgrace for you and for the Chameln lands. You have broken off the quest before the appointed time."

"I should not have come to Eildon," said the king. "I know that now. I have had a revelation. I know what I must do as a man and as a king. I must take home these men, my champions and my soldiers."

Farr the Fool made no reply, but his small companions whispered to him anxiously.

"Well, what do you say, my lord fool?" asked Sharn Am Zor. "Is your masquerade over?"

"Sharn Am Zor," said the fool in an altered voice. "What do you know of us? What do you know of our cruel exile?"

"I know that you are all of the Tulgai," said Sharn, "and you, Farr, must be of the royal house! Your exile is at an end. You will all come with me. You will return to your forest home."

Farr bowed his head in silent assent, but the three Tulgai raised their heads and uttered a chorus of piercing bird-calls. Then for pure joy, they all capered about, tumbling in the dark hall and shouting in the old speech.

"My name is Ragnafarr," said the fool, "and these are my true servants: Theranak, Omberik and Lillfor. I was, I am the uncle of Tagnaran, the Balg of the Tulgai. When we are safely out of this land of Eildon, Dan Sharn, I will tell you our story."

In less than two hours the baggage wagons were packed, some being used as litters to transport the sick. The officers of the escort mounted the seven remaining horses; the guardsmen were ready to march to the docks. Tazlo returned with good news and bad. The pinnace for the baggage had sailed with the *Golden Oak*, the king's flagship, on a trading errand for Captain Dynstane. Captain Straith of the *Nixie* was ready to sail, but the smaller ship could not carry the whole party.

"I have spoken with the captain of another caravel bound for Balufir," said Tazlo, "and he will willingly give passage to the King of the Chameln, if the king will sail with him."

"I would sail with a sea-goblin to get my friends out of this place." Sharn Am Zor grinned.

The trumpets sounded briefly, and the king led his once-proud guard, still bravely clad in their gold and green, out of the dark tower of the Sennick Fortress. They set out on their last journey across Lindriss.

The weather had turned round. The day was overcast; lightning played around the tops of the towers and thunder followed it. Before they had gone half a mile, the storm broke, directly overhead; they pressed on through the deluge. The ways were hard to follow, and Ragnafarr gave directions from his seat before Captain-General Britt. A man loomed up before them, drenched, waving his arms. It was Aram Nerriot, the lute-player.

"Sire!" he howled against the storm, "The quest . . . honor bound . . ."

"The quest be hanged!" shouted the king. "If you will stay in Eildon, Nerriot, you may do so. Get your lutes from the wagon and go where you will!"

Nerriot did not take the king's offer. He drew his sodden cloak about him and fell in at the end of the small column of soldiers. So they went on, through the dark, wet, winding streets, past the high houses and the rain-lashed towers of the city.

Between one lightning flash and the next, the rain stopped, the clouds rolled back. In a green space the sun shone down upon the men of the Chameln lands. There before them, blocking the way, were three knights of Eildon in all their panoply, and further off men and women in the colors of the princely houses, the courts of Eildon.

"Hold!" cried Sir Mortrice of the Hunters. "King Sharn, Count Ahrosh, how can you show your faces in this noble city before the time is right?"

"Your oath is broken!" cried Sir Pellasur of the Fal-

coners. "Your honor is forfeit! You and all your household have become objects of scorn!"

"King Sharn," cried Sir Tarn of the Fishers, moderat-
ing his tone a little, for he served the house of Pendark,
"Have you not understood our customs? You lay yourself
open to these words of shame and infamy!"

"So be it!" said Sharn Am Zor firmly. "I will leave
Eildon. Let us pass and you will be rid of us."

The knights held their places, and Sir Pellasur said
with a curling lip; "It is some way to the docks,
Shennazar. Would you run the gauntlet of our displeasure?"

Then the king rode forward a little by himself into a
patch of sunlight. His garments were travel-stained, his
horse Blaze was wet and weary, but he still outshone all
those assembled: He was indeed the summer's king.
He spoke with a new fervor and authority.

"I came in peace in Eildon, and I will go in peace. I
am unarmed and so are my men. Pellasur, would you
strike again at Gerr of Zerrah, still troubled by that
shameful wound you gave him at the Tourney of All
Trees? Will you three, as knights and honorable men,
strike at us still with magic and trickery? Step aside or
let me parley with someone approaching my own rank.
Where are the princes?"

"Oath-breaker!" howled Sir Mortrice. "Foul incomer!"

He plucked from his saddle a star-shaped dart, which
he hurled at the king. Sharn Am Zor raised an ungloved
hand, and no one was sure what happened next. Some
said that the dart turned in the air and flew back to
strike the horse of Sir Mortrice. Others swore that the
dart fell short and a ring on the king's hand with a large
topaz caught the sun and dazzled the horse. In any case
it reared up neighing and deposited Mortrice in a mud
puddle. There was a gasp and an audible curse. Prince
Borss Paldo spurred out from the waiting clutch of
nobles and confronted the king, his face very dark.

"Brandhul!" he said, hoarse with anger. "Oath-breaker!
Miscreant! You have lost all!"

"I have lost no more than a piece of land containing a

silver mine," said Sharn. "My fair cousin, Princess
Moinagh Pendark, was always beyond my reach."

"Fool!" said Borss, "we might have offered you a
compromise . . ."

"What then?"

"The cure for your condition, man. Freedom from
this curse of being a brandhul."

"I will take my chance and trust in the Goddess!"

"You have committed a grave breach of knightly
honor!"

"I am not a knight," said Sharn Am Zor. "I am a king.
I have seen my duty at last, and it is to bring my poor
wounded champions and my followers out of this treach-
erous city!"

"Beware!" said Paldo, "beware you kemmling dog,
you have not felt the power of Lindriss!"

"You are very jealous of your honor, Prince, and free
with insults. Yet you have conspired with my enemies!"

Prince Borss flushed and took on a blustering tone.
Sharn knew that his surmise was right.

"What kind of foolish talk is this?" said Borss. "I have
not conspired . . . And where are you taking that fool
who was lately in the service of the courts of Eildon,
with his three dwarfs?"

"To his home in the border forest," said Sharn. "He
is my liegeman of the royal house of the Tulgai. Ragnafarr
and his people go with me."

"So you say!"

The prince raised his hand, but whatever it was that
he had in mind, a magic working or an armed attack, it
was halted by a wild cry.

"Hold! Hold!"

A young man on a roan horse came galloping through
the green park and drew rein between the two princes.
It was Beren Pendark.

"Prince Borss!" he cried. "Noble Sharn, I beg you to
part in peace. Let the King of the Chameln go to his
home, my lord Paldo."

"You take this man's part," growled Paldo, "You take

his part, young Pendark, and do yourself much harm in our eyes."

"I have been honor bound," said Prince Beren, "and I have kept within the limits of our code. But by my troth, I have seen no honor in what was done to my cousin!"

There was a freshness in his anger, a sudden breaking of the old bonds. King Sharn Am Zor knew at last who it was who wrote the warning letter. He knew that the ways of Eildon had been questioned at last, and he feared for his young cousin. Borss Paldo seemed to sense the recklessness of the young man, and he too drew back.

"Let be," he said. "Shennazar is an outlander. We are well rid of him. Take your way to the docks, King Sharn."

The king bowed his head and led off again. Prince Beren fell in beside him.

"I will ride with you!"

"No," said Sharn. "Noble cousin, do not tempt the wrath of the Eildon courts. I will say farewell and ask a boon of you before I depart."

"Anything, Sharn."

"Visit me in Achamar, good Beren!"

"By the Holy Tree, I will cousin!"

So they clasped hands and parted, and the Chameln party came to the docks without further incident. The sun continued to shine, and once more the King of the Chameln was recognized and cheered by groups of citizens.

The king did not see the glances he drew from his own men, from Britt and the other officers and from Tazlo. The way in which he had withstood the threats and insults of the Eildon knights and Prince Borss struck them as subtly different from his usual behaviour. The king *was* a changed man, there was more reason in him, less anger, less arrogance. Captain-General Britt thought this would pass: it was some effect of the vigil and the quest. The king would soon be his old self again with all that implied in impatience and exercise of the royal will.

The king's patience was severely tested at once. While the *Nixie*, under Captain Straith, was made ready to put to sea and carefully laden, the king approached the other caravel bound for Balufir. An officer of the escort, Lieutenant Kogor, a veteran soldier from the campaigns against Mel'Nir, went aboard to inquire for the captain and returned white-faced. He spoke aside to Britt and to Tazlo Am Ahrosh.

The king, together with Ragnafarr and the Tulgai, was attending to Denzil of Denwick, helping to unload the poor man's litter from a baggage wagon. He wrapped his friend in the magic cloak that he had received from the White Tower and looked about for Tazlo to take his cloak for Gerr of Zerrah, who sat on a clothing bale, still in pain. He noticed the anxious whispering.

"What is it?" he said. "Will this captain have more gold?"

Britt stood forth with a desperate look.

"Sire," he said, "this captain is known to us. I fear it is a fellow you would avoid at all costs!"

Tazlo burst out; "My king, forgive me! I did not know. I never set eyes on the impudent devil before. I served with the northern tribes! I was never within a hundred miles of the city of Dechar!"

The word tolled like a bell. On the gangplank of the caravel there appeared a tall, loose-limbed young man with golden hair and flowing moustaches. He was richly dressed in the swashbuckling garb of a merchant adventurer. The king recognized him at once, and so did Gerr of Zerrah, who uttered a cry. Sharn stood erect, gazing at the sea captain as if he saw a ghost.

"Captain . . . Raiz?" he said in a small, cold voice.

"Captain Mazura, at your majesty's service! I see that you need a swift passage over the western sea."

The pretender, the False Sharn, spoke well and without a shade of irony, but the hearts of those watching failed a little. What hope for a swift passage with this huge, golden caravel, at least as fine as the *Golden*

Oak, when its captain, more than any man alive, had struck at the king's right, his very kingship? Sharn Am Zor, still very pale, bowed his head.

"Yes," he said humbly, "I need a passage for these poor wounded men that you see and for myself."

He looked up again while Gerr, Tazlo, Britt and the others were mastering their astonishment, and astonished them even more. Sharn Am Zor smiled himself, for the irony of the thing, and met the eye of Captain Mazura.

"I am sure you will handle us most royally!" he said.

So the king saw his two wounded champions on board as well as the other sick men of the escort, then boarded himself together with Ragnafarr, Prince of the Tulgai, and his companions. The *Caria Rose* was spacious, and on consultation with Captain-General Britt, the masters of the two caravels disposed the whole party as best they could. The two ships and the pinnace set sail upon the Laun to catch the evening tide. Hardly three moons had passed since Sharn Am Zor and his followers left Achamar with high hopes and banners streaming. Now they slipped away from the magic kingdom of the west without ceremony. As the *Caria Rose* sailed out of the river mouth into the western sea, Tazlo Am Ahrosh, standing upon the high bridge with the king, gave a startled exclamation. His cloak had lost its magic, and the king's cloak, wrapped about Zilly of Denwick, in his cabin, lost its magic at the same moment. All that the king and his esquire had as a reminder of their quest were two purplish brown mantles of wool frieze.

The ocean began to demand its toll again; all but a few of the travellers were content to lie very still in their bunks, sipping strange cordials. The ship's healer was a woman, very beautiful, black-skinned and utterly forbidding. None of the ailing men dared to seize her hand except Yuri, the poor young valet from the cold north. She worked her magic upon him, gave him her cordials and a little silver charm. He believed she was his witch-mother from that hour; he had dreams all his life long of her lovely dark face and strange festivals in the lands below the world.

It was a charmed voyage, outside time, far from the uses of the world. Sharn Am Zor sat down to table with Mazura; Ragnafarr, unaffected by the seas' motion, bore them company. While the silent, dark-skinned servants plied them with dainties, the honor of the first and strangest tale went to the Prince of the Tulgai.

THE TALE OF RAGNAFARR

"It was eight years past," he said in his deep, harsh voice, "not long after Princess Aidris, the Heir of the Firn, had visited us on her way into exile. As is our custom, in the spring, I set out with a party of ten to hunt the high and low trails. There is a certain river in the forest that runs for miles underground through huge caverns, and we use it to come to distant hunting grounds.

"This year, as we sailed peacefully down the river, which flows southeast to join the Ringist, there was a great noise of water and a spring torrent filled the caverns. One of our boats was lost at once. My own boat was damaged. I was carried on with four others, clinging to our frail craft. We came to the accursed grounds. I mean those places where the trees have been cut down.

"We came ashore on a strip of underground beach beside a rocky chimney; our plight was desperate. My old arrow-bearer, Forberan, the father of Lillfor, had been dashed against the rocks and his head was broken. We had nothing but the clothes upon our backs.

"I can hardly bring home to you, King Sharn, or to our captain here, what it is to be of the race of the Tulgai. In the history of our tangled relations with the Longshanks, there are many runes that tell of cruelty and betrayal. To be a creature of a lesser size is to be delivered over to the will of others. Now our only hope for our wounded comrade and for ourselves lay in making ourselves known to some of the larger race.

"I climbed up and looked out upon a scene of terrible desolation. We were deep into the territory known as the Adz, some miles, as we found later, from the town of Orobin, in a desert place from which all the treasures had been taken. No one lived close to our lookout, but in the distance a faint light burned in some kind of cottage. The edges of the forest could be seen miles away over open ground pocked with old diggings.

"We were too weak and our companion Forberan too sorely wounded to reach the trees alive. We decided to approach the cottage. I went out myself, with Orombek, first of all. I had a good smattering of the common speech and was of course the tallest.

"We crept swiftly over the rough ground to the humped house and peered through a slit in the wooden walls. In a strange room full of shards and scraps there sat one old woman. She crooned over her fire and stirred a pot and there were cats with her and a singing bird in a cage. We were pleased to see that she was a very small old woman, no taller than myself, with a limp and a humped back. I took courage and knocked upon her door, and when she came fearfully peering out, I bowed low and begged for her help. At last I let Orombek come forward.

"The old woman was delighted. She bade us all come in by the fire and settled us in her second largest chamber, filled with straw and meal sacks. We made a place for the old man Forberan, and Lillfor his daughter watched by him.

"Our friend in need was called Mother Riddisal or Ilse the Herb Woman. She lived from the scraps of gold and the few remaining precious stones that she scratched from the old mine workings. Down in the town, she told us sadly, lived her three grandsons, grown children of her eldest son, who had died of pit-cough like his father before him.

"I promised that she would be well rewarded for her kindness. I wore an armband of gold and I said this was

hers, but it must not be shown in the town. She had
better melt it down once we had gone.

"Next day we kept hidden; no one came near the
cottage. About midday Forberan, our injured companion, died. We mourned his loss. Mother Riddisal took
some of her own findings and went down to Orobin to
buy food. We kept a close watch until she returned and
afterwards, not because we distrusted her but because
she might have let slip some word. When darkness fell,
we stole out and buried Forberan. Then we ate the
good food that Mother Riddisal had prepared and lay
down to sleep.

"There is a word in our speech "sashogan" meaning
"to be carried off in a bag"; it is what the Tulgai fear
most and what we of the royal house fear most for our
people. In the early hours of the next day while it was
still dark the old woman's three grandsons stormed into
her house and seized us all. She cheered them on; it
was her plan. We were brought down the hill to a
covered cart. Three laden sacks were flung aboard, and
then, before I was flung in with bound hands, I was
stunned by a blow on the head. That same morning we
were taken over the Ringist, and when I came to myself
we were deep into the land of Lien. Our forest home
lay far behind.

"The Riddisal brothers brought us to a fairground in
the town of Milnor and sold us there for twenty royals
of gold. The transaction was secret; it took place in the
tent of our new owner, a man called Born or Burrin. I
was the least valuable property, being merely a dwarf-
ish creature, not a "forest fairy," but I spoke up to this
Born. I told him I must stay or my companions would
pine and die. Also I was the only one who had the
common speech.

"Born was a middleman who hired or sold freaks and
misbirths for the fairgrounds. We met with the human
skeleton, a poor fellow with a wasting sickness, and the
dancing greddles and Gorbelly, the Fattest Man, and
Mistress Bart, the bearded woman. She took the measure of my companions and sewed them fanciful clothes

out of scraps of fur and leather. For me she found in some trunk a suit of motley. She told me to learn tumbling, to be a fool, so that I might have some worth and be sold along with my friends. We were all moved in painted wagons clear across Lien to a larger fairground."

"At Denwicktown where the two rivers meet," put in Raff Mazura, "or so I would guess. I went tumbling for a season or two."

"In the name of the Goddess!" burst out Sharn Am Zor. "Are stolen Tulgai on display in Lien? Are they bought and sold in this way?"

Ragnafarr and Mazura exchanged glances, and the Captain replied; "It is not lawful to put anyone on show against his will, Dan Sharn, and certainly unlawful to buy and sell human beings. But these laws are hard to enforce. I have never seen 'forest fairies' set forth, but I remember a Kelshin pair who traveled with a troupe of miniature ponies."

"This Born knew the law very well," said Ragnafarr. "He kept us well hidden until he found the ideal purchaser for his 'little treasures.' There came by night a sea captain and with him a courtier, a certain Lord Evert, who served an old, eccentric nobleman of Eildon, the Duke of Greddach, who kept a bestiary in his wide park. After a rough passage over the western sea, we were off-loaded in our cage, trundled through the misty countryside and set free in the old duke's park at Boskage. We all took to the trees again with goodwill. We lived a strange half-life, pleasing our new master by showing ourselves for visitors. We became 'forest fairies' indeed, popping out to frighten ladies and knights on horseback.

"Yet I saw that our life was not as it should be. We could no longer live like true Tulgai. When the old duke died and his domain went unwatched for a time, I decided that we must overcome our fears. I stole a pony cart; my friends rode under the hood, and we simply left Boskage one autumn afternoon and took to the roads of Eildon. In the first town with a fairground,

I found a band of tumblers and spoke to the master. Farr the Fool tumbled and sang for the first time with his Three Farthings. We were well received, and we earned our keep. We have done so ever since. We were safe enough. A little hairy man come out of the trees is something to be caught and sold, but a dwarf or a midget, living on a fairground, is a person of some estate, however humble.

"So we came at last to Lindriss. I knew more of the world by this time and understood that it would take an enormous amount of luck and of gold to get us home again. In time we became accustomed, as you have seen, to work in noble company."

"And you trusted no one with your story?" asked Sharn Am Zor.

Ragnafarr sighed.

"I tried the truth first of all upon a circus master," he said, "a powerful showman who rules over the Five Ways, the great year-round fair beyond the walls of Lindriss. He could hardly believe me. What did he know of distant lands, of a race living in the border forest? He pointed out a poor black man, old now and toothless, working as a roustabout, who had been billed once as the King of the Savages, from the Lands Below the World.

"More than a year ago we stood before Prince Ross Tramarn, whose magic allowed him to recognize many strangers. He spoke us fair and counselled patience. He matched one of my fool's couplets with another:

" *'Keep watch for the king whose way is long,*
For only a king will hear your song . . .'

"Now I understand the meaning of his rhyme. We worked before the courts of Eildon, and we were put into your service by Prince Borss Paldo as a piece of foolery, my King. You have answered our prayers. So ends the Tale of Ragnafarr."

Prince Ragnafarr and his listeners drank a round in silence, then Raff Mazura asked a question.

"Prince, you and your Tulgai have lived in the world. Will you be content to live in the forest?"

"I cannot tell," said Ragnafarr. "First of all we must return from the dead and see our loved ones again."

So the charmed voyage continued, and Sharn Am Zor went about on the caravel and sat at night on the deck, watching the sea and the stars. He came together several times with Raff Mazura, and they understood each other very well. As they sat one night watching the coast of the continent draw near, Mazura said, "The civil war in Mel'Nir is hot as ever. I spoke lately with a sea captain who had been in Krail, the city of the Westmark, ruled by Valko Firehammer."

"My sister Merilla was there once," said the king, "and Nerriot was in her service then, I think."

The musician who was not far off bowed his head and played melodies of Mel'Nir and the Chyrian lands.

"There is a certain warrior in Krail, in Valko's service," said Raff Mazura. "His name is Yorath, Yorath the Wolf, leader of a Free Company. Have you heard of this man, my King?"

"I have heard some strange tale from Dan Aidris," said Sharn. "Was it from you she had it then?"

"I warrant Nerriot has heard the story, too," said Mazura softly. "What d'ye say, Master Nerriot, to this Yorath of Mel'Nir?"

Aram Nerriot looked wise and nodded his head again.

"I saw this man once, Dan Sharn," he said, "and your noble sister, the lady Merilla, saw him on the same evening in the citadel in Krail. He is a mighty warrior, the tallest and strongest of all the warriors of Mel'Nir that I have seen. Also he has a rough charm and a native wit. I have heard him trade words with the Vizier of the Markgraf himself."

"So Rosmer was there, too!" said the king.

"Master Rosmer observed the warrior Yorath," continued Nerriot, "and afterwards I heard him speaking to the war lord of Krail, Valko Val'Nur. Master Rosmer swore that Yorath was of the line of the Duarings, the bastard son of Prince Gol."

"That was all he saw?" The king laughed. "If that were all, this big fellow would not interest us. The tale I heard placed him much closer to Lien and to the Daindru. He is the child of fair Elvédegran, the youngest swan of Lien, my mother's sister. Therefore he is Prince Gol's true-born son. Is this not so, Captain Mazura?"

"I believe it," said the Captain solemnly. "I will call Yorath my friend, my boyhood friend of one summer. Perhaps we should not bandy his parentage about."

Sharn Am Zor seemed eager to talk, but he fell silent and presently he sent away the officers, the musician and all who were on deck so that he was alone with Raff Mazura. They talked of Yorath and of Hagnild Raiz, Mazura's uncle, the Healer at the court of Ghanor of Mel'Nir, who had spirited away a marked child of the Duarings.

Then the king sat silent again, staring at the waves, and came out of his thoughts to say, "What have you to say of Rosmer?"

Mazura wrinkled his brow and stared into the gathering darkness.

"Once I thought him an intriguer, puffed up and overrated," he said, "but now I know his power. He is cruel, a monster of cruelty. I hope some champion will arise to rid the world of this evil creature."

Sharn Am Zor gave a sigh.

"Once I thought I might be that champion," he said. "I hoped to take revenge for the suffering of my poor mother. But I am unlucky, my feats of arms or of magic will never be equal to the task."

"He is well guarded," said Raff Mazura, "and has his spies throughout the courts of Hylor."

"In Achamar?" asked the king, and answered his own question. "Why not there, too. I must look about."

The king and the captain drank a round of schnapps, and Raff Mazura said: "King Sharn, you have offered payment for this passage over the western sea. I will take no gold from you if you will grant me a boon."

"What then?"

"We will anchor at Larkdel in five days, and your wounded champions and the sick men of the escort can be cared for at Wirth Hall and at the Hermitage of the brothers. I think you planned to escort Prince Ragnafarr and his people across Lien to the border forest."

"I had thought of this," said the king.

"I humbly beg you to go a little further in your travels. Cross over one of the mountain passes into Athron and visit Robillan Hazard at the Owl and Kettle Inn on the outskirts of Varda."

"Why yes," said Sharn, "yes, it is a fine idea. I might have come to it myself."

Then, glimpsing a strange expression on the captain's face, he asked anxiously, "Is he sick? Short of money? Does it go ill with my old friend after this cursed imprisonment?"

"I have been sworn to secrecy," said Mazura. "I can only send you to him, Majesty. He may not thank me even for this."

The king's fleet came to Larkdel again, and all those in need of healing were kindly received. Zilly of Denwick, already improved in health, came to the arms of his lady, Veldis; and Gerr of Zerrah also went to the manor house. Sharn Am Zor stood for the first time before a crowd of folk, gentle and simple, who had seen him sail off proudly, who had expected him to succeed. The ruin of his enterprise was plain for all to see, but no one had changed towards him. The Wirth family were full of sympathy. Sir Berndt cast off his Falconer's tunic and swore aloud, saying he would have no truck with Eildon if they handled the King of the Chameln, that fine young man, so ill.

The travelers still had far to go. The two caravels, the *Caria Rose* and the *Nixie,* sailed on towards Balufir with all those Chameln men fit to travel, save only four men of the escort and the king himself. Sharn Am Zor insisted upon traveling light; he would take no valet. Prickett stayed in the Hermitage to care for poor Yuri and bring him home with the other men sick of "Eildon fever" when they were well. Tazlo Am Ahrosh, under protest, agreed to go on to the Danmar and ride as courier straight to Aidris the Queen, in Achamar, to bring her the king's letters. The king sent more letters to Seyl of Hodd. He pondered a little and sent a very brief letter, together with the topaz ring that he had received in the Sacred Wood from the King of the Isles. The letter went to Lorn Gilyan, the Heir of Chernak.

Captain-General Britt, standing on the bridge of the *Caria Rose* with Tazlo as the king stood on the dock waving them farewell, shook his head in wonder.

"He is a changed man," said Britt.

Tazlo Am Ahrosh scowled and bit his lip, but he could not deny that his master had changed. The ship's trumpet sounded, and the king exchanged a last salute with Captain Mazura as the caravel set sail up the wide river.

II

SHARN AM ZOR CHOSE A STEADY BAY FROM
the Larkdel stable and set out riding across the Mark
of Lien. By his side rode Prince Ragnafarr of the Tulgai,
dressed as a prince, in Chameln breeches and tunic,
and mounted upon a black pony. His companions
Orombek, Theranak and Lillfor rode before the men of
the escort. The countryside was at its most beautiful;
this was the rich summer country of which Hazard
wrote and other poets of Lien. The early roses were
coming out.

More than once in the woods of Lien the travelers
found a pool and swam and sunned themselves. As
Sharn Am Zor swam in the river depths he thought of
Moinagh, child of the sea; as he lay in the grass, he
remembered the river fields at Alldene, his companions
Jevon Seyl and Iliane. O lost, elusive Moinagh, O lost
foolish Iliane. He had been continent for too long. Yet
he still had hopes of love and fulfillment. He looked into
his grandmother's scrying stone, hoping to find the
answer to a certain question he meant to ask, but the
stone was dark all through the journey.

The party crossed the Ringist on a stone bridge from
the town of Athory and entered the Adz, riding through
that part of the mining lands that surrounded the

Silverbirch mine. Sharn saw all about him his subjects whose land would be governed in the future by the Mark of Lien. There was no word in the land pledge of men and women, only of land.

In Corth, the largest town of the region, the folk recognized their king, wondering, then cheering; the word flew through the streets. Sharn was received at once by the reeve, an old and leathery individual called Baskin, and sat down with him alone. The King admitted his failure, his loss of the land; an agreement must be made with Lien. The folk could stay or go; those who chose to leave the district—though there was no saying that Lienish rule would be harsh—would be resettled at the king's expense.

Baskin the Reeve heard him out and comforted the young king. It was a trick, an Eildon trick and a Lienish one, he burst out, to come to the Silverbirch. He would say no word till all was arranged, but he knew the folk; many would stay, but some might take the chance to resettle. Mining was a hard task, and the younger men fretted under its yoke. So the king, taking comfort from the Reeve of Corth, allowed himself and Prince Ragnafarr to be given a feast on that summer evening in the town square.

The journey continued, and they came this time to Orobin, on the fringes of the worked-out lands of the Adz. Now it was time for Ragnafarr to stand forth and parley with a new reeve. The seizure of his person some eight years past was not known in the town. Mother Riddisal was dead, but what of her grandsons? A movement at the back of the puzzled crowd was quickly halted, and the eldest of the Riddisal boys was dragged forth. The third grandson tried to steal away, but he was caught, too; only one had left the town years before.

Prince Ragnafarr dealt out swift justice with the help of the Reeve. The waste ground above the town where the old woman's cottage still stood must be cleared and ploughed by the Riddisals and made ready for planting. In the following spring, tree seedlings would be planted;

the Tulgai would bring them to the edges of the forest. Slips or cuttings from the townsfolk of Orobin would be welcome in the New Woods, to be planted in the name of the Goddess, who had spared Ragnafarr and his companions.

It might be thought that there was nothing left for Prince Ragnafarr but to go into the forest with his friends, taking to the high trails. But the Prince of the Tulgai excused himself to Sharn Am Zor; he too was honor bound in this place and would hold to a certain ritual. So the party rode on, sticking to the highroad that led northwards across the great border forest to the town of Vigrund. Nights upon the road they camped in well-used clearings beside the highway; a host of unseen watchers went with them all the way, by day and by night. At last they turned up a well-made road leading to the Wulfental Pass and came about midmorning to the hospice of the Brown Brothers.

It was exactly as Aidris the Queen had described it to her cousin Sharn. There was the perfect round tarn and the bathhouse in a wide green meadow and the sturdy wooden bridge over a ravine. The Brothers came out bowing low, delighted to see the king and his companions, overwhelmed by this great honor. Sharn was a little cool, recalling the harsh welcome given to Kedran Venn and the lovely Sabeth Delbin, traveling into exile.

Ragnafarr and his companions Theranak, Orombek and Lillfor went slowly across the green meadow towards the wooden bridge, the Litch Bridge of the Tulgai that crossed the Lylan, the River of Souls.

Sharn Am Zor went by the prince's side, and presently Ragnafarr said, "It is time, my King!"

The king and the prince embraced and bade each other farewell and promised that they would meet again before too many years had passed. As Sharn retreated a few steps, giving his hand to the little ones, the guardsmen and the brothers and the travelers from the Hermitage, all come to watch the strange ceremony, began to point and cry out. On the far side of the ravine stood a slight figure wearing a golden crown, with two or three others of his height. The edges of the forest teemed with the forest people; the trees were laden to their topmost boughs. The men and women of the Tulgai lifted up their voices in bird calls and ancient chants. Ragnafarr, their prince, walked over the bridge. He returned from the dead with his three companions and was received by Tagnaran, the Balg of the Tulgai, and taken back into the forest.

Sharn Am Zor stayed long enough to use the excellent bathhouse and to eat a meal at the hospice, then he pressed on over the Wulfental Pass into the land of Athron. There was a chill lurking in the narrow valley, even with the summer sun high overhead; they were all glad to come to the watch post that marked the border. A kedran captain came out and saluted.

"Will you let us pass into Athron, Captain?" asked the king, smiling. "I may say that I am a friend of Gerr of Kerrick if that will let me through."

"By the Carach, sire," said the captain, looking from one to the other, "I am sure you are his friend and a royal friend at that. I served Frieda, the Lady of Wenns, and I rode with the Morrigar, the Giant Killers."

So the king, thinking of his cousin as she rode into exile, came to the top of the pass and looked down, as Aidris had done, upon the magic land of Athron. It was a bright and ordered countryside, beautiful, green, newly washed with a light rain. Yet Sharn had a pang of uneasiness; the scrying stone had come to life and stung him a little, so that he drew it out as he rode along. There was nothing to be seen but a sprig of rue in the world of the stone. As the party rode on towards Varda, they passed their first Carach tree and admired it, but the king would not get down and ask the tree's blessing. He quickened his pace on the good high road, and they came swiftly to the outskirts of the capital and to the Owl and Kettle Inn.

The host, a little bouncing man, came running into the yard.

"Good morrow lords!" he cried. "Have you come out

of the Chameln lands? Welcome to Athron! You honor
our house. I am your host, name of Polken."

"Good Master Polken," said Sharn Am Zor, "I thank
you for the welcome. I think your inn is already honored. I have come to seek my friend Robillan Hazard."

There was a low cry from the shadowy doorway of the
inn. She came striding out into the yard, a slim, dark
woman, almost a beauty, in an Athron gown of dark
blue. She moved so well that one hardly saw the injury
to her left side. Sharn Am Zor, dismounted now, stood
over her without smiling. The innkeeper, too, had a
strange look on his clown's face, all the smiles wiped
away.

"Little Queen," said Sharn Am Zor, "are you the one
who writes for my friend?"

"I am called Taranelda," she said. "I am in my right
wits, King Sharn, no queen at all. What do you want
with my poor Hazard?"

"He is my friend," said the king. "I owe him a visit."

"You were in Eildon," said Taranelda, "with a fleet of
ships and a troop of attendants . . ."

"Little Queen," said Sharn, "I am still not betrothed.
My enterprise has not prospered, but the magic kingdom has granted me some understanding. I returned
with my followers on the caravel *Caria Rose* and the
captain, Raff Mazura, bade me visit Hazard."

"Ah, he swore an oath!" cried Taranelda.

"He did not break it," said the king. "In the name of
the Goddess, is Hazard very sick?"

"Come!" said Taranelda. "Follow me, Dan Sharn."

She led him through a side door, past the staircase
and the taproom and the noisy kitchens. They came to a
sunny corridor, and at the end of it was a door that
stood ajar. Taranelda, still with her stricken look, put a
finger to her lips and pointed to the door. She gave the
king a push.

Sharn Am Zor went on tiptoe down the corridor,
fearful of what he might find and swung the door open
wider so that he could step in. The room was full of
sunlight and the scent of garden flowers. Hazard was

seated at a table before the open casement; he looked so like himself, even to his old buff-colored waistcoat, that Sharn could barely keep from crying out his name.

The poet's hair was greyer than it had been. On the table before him was a wooden box with many small compartments and a metal tray about the size of a large printed page. Hazard selected wooden letters from the box, packed them into a narrow metal frame—was it called a rod? a stick?—and transfered one or two lines to the tray. He ran his fingers over the letters in the stick and in the tray, mouthing the words he had made. He stopped suddenly and lifted his head, half turning towards the door. The king saw his friend's face, unchanged, a little thinner perhaps, brown from the sun. His large hazel eyes were wide open.

"Nell, is that you?" asked Hazard.

The king shut his own eyes against the sunlight and against a keen shock of pain. *Hazard was blind.*

"I know someone stands at the door!" said Hazard. "Who is it?"

"Hazard . . ." whispered Sharn Am Zor.

"Dear lad," said Hazard in a trembling voice that he soon mastered. "Is it you? Who has peached on me? Was it Buckrill?"

Sharn Am Zor crossed the room and laid a hand on the poet's shoulder. The pain he felt as he gazed into his friend's smiling face was surely more than he could bear. He dug his fingernails into the palm of his right hand and bit his lips so that these slight physical hurts would stop him from sinking down, from crying aloud. He thought of the madwoman in the white tower at Swangard, beating her faded golden head softly and repeatedly against her bed frame. He uttered a sob.

"Steady," said Hazard. "It will pass. I do truly believe that it will pass!"

"I come too late by five years or so," said Sharn, "but now I must request your service, Rob. You will come with Taranelda to Achamar. I'll brook no refusal."

"To live in your court?" asked Hazard warily.

"To live however you will and wherever you will in that good city."

"What have they done to you in Eildon?" asked Hazard. "Lad, how is it with the princess?"

"She was beautiful as your songs," said the king, "but I was not meant to win her hand. We fared badly in the magic kingdom of the west."

"I set you on to this wooing," said Hazard.

"Not so," said Sharn Am Zor. "It was my own doing. I was too headstrong. Yet some good has come of this ill-starred adventure and more may follow."

And to Hazard, in his darkness, these words were a proof that Eildon had worked magic upon the king.

The King of the Zor came home at the end of the Applemoon, and the Queen of the Firn rode out to meet him with a small escort. The Daindru were re-united just beyond Zerrah, where the road struck out over the plain to Vigrund. Aidris had seen her cousin go forth proudly on the Danmar, accompanied by his champions and his escort in a string of painted boats. Now he came home with four officers and a blind man driven by his wife in a little pony cart.

She saw at once that the rumors were true: Sharn Am Zor, clad in worn Chameln dress, was a changed man. The miracle that she had prayed for had been granted; the young, feckless king had been made to care. Aidris was stricken with pity and regret. Was he still the Summer King? Had he suffered so much? She urged her white mare, Shieran, forward to meet him, and they embraced.

"Ah, Goddess!" cried Sharn. "How fine it is to come home!"

"How fine to have you back again!"

"You must meet Hazard! You must speak with his wife, the little queen from Dechar."

"Gladly," said Aidris. "But first, do you see who rides with me?"

There, a little apart from the kedran of the escort,

was a tall dark-haired girl mounted upon a spirited black horse. Sharn stared and could not speak.

"She wears your ring," said Aidris.

Sharn Am Zor slipped from the saddle of his Lienish bay and strode across the yellow-flowered meadow. Lorn Gilyan had dismounted, too, and they stood at arm's length. Then the king knelt and took her hands and pressed them to his lips. Lorn Gilyan spoke, and as Sharn stood up and took her in his arms, she uttered a soft cry. No one but the king heard her words.

"I have loved on, my dear lord, though hope was gone . . ."

Sharn was an eager bridegroom. He was wed to the Heir of Chernak upon his birthday in the first days of the Thornmoon, and a shaman from the north performed the ceremony.

PART III

THE KING'S DESTINY

CHAPTER VIII

SECRETS

SNOW HAS FALLEN IN THE NIGHT. IT CURLS upon the gables of those two wonders of the world, the royal palaces of Achamar. The palace gardens are white and still; the square before the hall of the Dainmut is thickly carpeted and untrodden except by some cheeky fox or marten that has come to the city looking for food. It is the first day of the Ashmoon in the year 1177; it is the hour before dawn.

No one is supposed to be awake, but furtive candles gleam here and there; lights can be seen flitting past the windows of the palaces. In the South Hall the kedran garrison have lit their fire, and the smoke rises up into the frosty air. A horse neighs and stamps by the open south gate and is hushed by its young rider. A knot of dark figures have gathered in the shadow of the gatehouse: a small procession is being formed. The gilded sleigh is laden, its burdens secured.

A tall man says, "Whose idea was this?"

Before his head is covered, he is given warm wine to drink. A woman begins to laugh, it spreads to the entire party.

The boy on his grey horse, hitched to the sleigh, says in an urgent whisper, "Oh do hush! You will spoil it all!"

Gravity is restored. The boy receives a sign from a single kedran riding ahead and follows her. They move off slowly through the silent streets: the boy drawing a golden sleigh and two strange figures, one shaggy and tall like a tree walking, the other clad in a green-hooded robe trimmed with fur. Lucky children, looking out at the right time, see them go by: the Winter Man, the Green Woman and the Moonchild, bringing in the tree on a golden sleigh laden with good things.

On the ringroad in a soldier's house, a young boy and his sisters see the sleigh go by and call to their mother.

"But Ma," says the boy, "it was surely going to the Zor palace."

"Is that so?" Mistress Britt, wife of the Captain-General smiles. "Well, your father can tell us if it came there safely."

"Do they have all the gifts?" wails the youngest girl.

"Go into the warm front room," says her mother, "and see if a tree was left for us."

Sure enough, when they rush down the stairs, there is a tree by their own fireside and a sack of good things to nibble all Ashmoon long, until the Feast Days.

Meanwhile the Moonchild has drawn the golden sleigh right up to the palace. Guardsmen open the doors; the sturdy Chameln grey goes up the ramp, and the sleigh is drawn right into the hall of the Zor, into a warm, whispering darkness.

A voice cries, "Lights! Lights!"

Candles and torches flare up; the fire is stirred into life. On the grand staircase, hanging over the bannisters, standing before the wide fireplace are children, everywhere children, dressed or in their nightgowns. Mothers and nursemaids hold up the little ones; even babes in arms have been brought from their cradles. High up on a landing, a pair of young malcontent bachelors wonder aloud where all the little beasts have come from. Tazlo Am Ahrosh gives Prince Carel his candle to hold and draws forth a flask of schnapps.

"For shame!" hisses the countess Caddah, going down

the stairs, dragged by two well-grown four year olds.
Merilla's twin Chiel-brats, notes the prince.

Before the fireplace the Countess Palazan Am Panget
has commandeered one of the large golden chairs. She
too has a motherly role to play, and it has given her a
new lease on life. Her two young wards stand by her
chair, they are persons of such interest that the old
dame is received everywhere on their account. The
king himself and his consort have visited her ancient
townhouse on the ringroad.

The young man with a shock of white-blond hair is
Ilmar of Inchevin, one of the royal cousins. He is looking for an opportunity to slip away and join his boon
companions, Tazlo and Carel. His sister, a year older,
wears a star-maid folk costume from the east of the
Chameln lands, a stiff white robe of felt, glittering with
sequins and precious stones. She outshines these brilliants: Derda, the Starry Maid of Inchevin, is white and
gold, a lady of the Zor with a grave, old-fashioned
beauty. She knows her duties as a lady in waiting and is
quick to hand Countess Palazan her muff, her lozenges,
her pine cone rattle. A rumor says that she rules the old
woman, not the other way about. After so long with few
persons to love, the Countess dotes on her two young
charges and certainly they wear her jewels.

The tree, a noble blue tannen, is lifted from the
sleigh. The Winter Man strides about to the sound of
pine cone rattles; he is dressed in a spreading robe
heavy with evergreen twigs: tannen, fir and pine. His
headdress is trimmed with golden branches that curl
like antlers. The Green Woman is just as fine, her robe
of velvet trimmed with ermine, her mask of silver leaves.
The Moonchild is a dark-haired boy of eight in Chameln
dress of white and grey and a fur hat with a moon
emblem: Prince Sasko, Heir of the Firn.

Now the Winter Man, with a whooping sound like
the wind, comes to the staircase. There stands Danu
Lorn, the queen consort. She carries in her arms Gerd,
her son of three moons; at her side stands a dark-haired
girl, two and a half years old. She is bright-eyed, tall for

her age; her beauty is something to wonder at, for the
waiting women to whisper about. She is Princess Tanit,
Heir of the Zor; this is the first raising of the tree she
will remember. The Winter Man bends down and lifts
her up in his arms. He smells of the forest; his branches
are rough. She sees his eyes glittering deep under the
gold and green mask, like the eyes of a wild beast. It is
too much; Tanit's lip begins to tremble, though she
tries hard to be brave.

"Oh sweetheart!" says the Winter Man, reaching for
his headdress.

Uncle Denwick, hovering nearby with his own boy,
little Hal, lends a hand, and the headdress comes off.

"There now," says Queen Lorn.

Tanit is overcome with surprise. The Winter Man is
her father, with a few pine needles in his golden hair. It
is like magic, as if he shared a secret with her, as if this
whole exciting morning with the tree, the candles, the
waiting in the dark, was arranged for her alone because
she is his darling. Tanit and Sharn smile at each other.
Their eyes are exactly the same deep brilliant blue—
the eyes of Queen Aravel, the last swan of Lien.

Now those rough country boys Till and Tomas Am
Chiel have captured the Green Woman, and when her
hood falls back, a mass of brown hair shows that it is
Merilla, their mother.

"Come then!" she cries. "You must help me give out
these favors!"

Sasko stands by his horse's head. Morrah, a patient
fellow, lets the younger children take turns sitting on
his back. The prince, surrounded by his cousins and
other trusted friends that he sees every day, is still
pleased when his own sister Micha comes storming up
with Nila, their nurse. Privately he decides that the
tree is better raised in his own palace, but Cousin
Sharn must have a turn at playing the Winter Man.

Sasko's father is riding back from the tribal lands in
the north; his mother waits in the Palace of the Firn
with his newborn sister Maren. He saves up amusing
incidents to cheer her. The snow fight that Huon Kerrick

begins on the terrace; the way in which Carel and
Count Ahrosh and Ilmar Inchevin slide down the bannisters. The children are overexcited; there are tears
and scoldings. The young prince sees how that proud
full-blown lady, Iliane Seyl, now the mother of Seyl's
little son and daughter, speaks aside to her former waiting woman, Veldis of Denwick, and makes her cry.
Sasko hates to see grown-ups weep or quarrel.

The incident cannot be hushed up; Veldis is led away
half-fainting by her younger sister, Mayrose of Wirth,
come to Achamar for the Winter Feast. Danu Lorn
catches the eye of the king, and he gives the signal to
end the early morning revels. Babies and older children
are whisked away, not without protest, to their warm
nurseries. The day is now a day of rest with nothing
planned until evening.

Sasko is permitted to drive his sister and Nila, the
nurse, home across the city in the gilded sleigh. The
Countess Am Panget, wreathed in her furs, is assisted
to her waiting carriage. The hall of the Zor is almost
empty now; the tree stands in place with tubs of sweetmeats and candied apples at its base. Servants carry
away scattered twigs and cones, the Winter Man's headdress, the Green Woman's silver mask.

Now a gilded chair before the pleasant fire has been
occupied by an old soldier. When a guardsman passes
by, he beckons.

"Lord Zabrandor!"

Captain Fréjan salutes the old warrior.

"At ease, Captain," says Zabrandor. "See if you can
find me some breakfast and an urn of herb tea or that
newfangled Lienish drink."

"At once, General!"

"Keep watch, Fréjan," says the old man. "See that no
one comes too close."

He gives the captain a wink.

"I have a tryst with two beautiful ladies!"

The captain is as good as his word. When Merilla Am
Zor comes down the stairs to sit with Lord Zabrandor,

she finds steaming kaffee waiting. She embraces the old lord and sinks into another of the chairs.

"It is exhausting being a mother," she says.

"Sometimes," says Zabrandor mildly, waving a hand at the tree, "I wonder how all this came about."

"The ceremony?" asks Merilla. "The raising of the tree?"

"No," he says, "that is a very ancient usage, a hope of spring in the midst of winter. No, I mean the transformation of this court and its king. I visit Achamar once a year, sometimes once in two years. I have hardly heard the tale of your brother's Eildon journey before I find him married to our own sweet maid, Lorn Gilyan, a loving husband and father of two children. Those banished have been recalled; even the Inchevin have returned to court. The king sits still at meetings. You know me, my dear princess, I am a devoted liegeman of the Zor and subject of the Daindru, so I may ask: Is the king so much changed?"

"Yes," says Merilla in a low voice. "Yes, he is changed. In Eildon his spirit was touched . . . subdued. Since then he has been a better and a happier man. Some would say that he has simply grown up."

"I ask for a particular reason," says Zabrandor. "I have a notion that the king's wisdom and patience may be tested."

The old lord who has been watching the several doorways to the hall breaks off and rises from his chair. A young woman in a long grey cloak trimmed with fox fur comes in from the terrace. Her armed servant prowls before the door.

"My lady," says Zabrandor, "pray come to the fire."

Derda Am Inchevin bows gravely to Lord Zabrandor, clasps hands with her cousin, and brushes Merilla's warm cheek with her cold lips. She is very deliberate in manner, almost unnaturally self-possessed.

"This is a strange hour for our meeting," says Lord Zabrandor. "I hope you had no difficulty . . ."

"The old aunt is sleeping," says Derda with the hint of a smile.

Merilla finds the Starry Maid a puzzling figure, more difficult to befriend and to love than she would have thought, knowing the warm-hearted family of the Chiel and her dear Aunt Parn. Yet Derda is very beautiful—another beauty at court, no denying it—Merilla admits with an inward sigh.

"If you will talk to me of marriage," says Derda, "I will hear but make no bonds. I may accept only small tokens of a suitor's affection."

Zabrandor shakes his head, taken aback, but Merilla laughs.

"I expect you are plagued with foolish suitors, cousin," she says.

"My kerns will whip them if they offend me!" says Derda.

"My lady Derda, Dan Merilla . . ." begins Zabrandor.

"Why do you use such a title?" interrupts Derda. "Why do you say Dan Merilla when she is no longer the king's heir?"

"For my part Lord Zabrandor need use no title at all," says Merilla. "Speak on, my lord."

"I make a patrol of the east and the northeast every year," says Zabrandor. "What I heard beyond the river Chind, in the foothills and about the town of Threll, was disquieting."

"My father hunts in those lands," says Derda, unsmiling. "He will not have the game disturbed and the fishing spoilt. By incomers."

"Yet there are incomers," says Zabrandor. "The brigands of the Skivari and their leader Rugal. What do you know of him, Lady Derda?"

"He dares nothing in our lands," says Derda. "We are the Inchevin. Elsewhere he destroys the villages, takes what he needs, women and so on. He impales the village elders if he believes they have gold. He is said to be very rich."

"There have been rumors as far south as Chiel Hall," says Merilla. "But this terrible brigand has not approached our land."

Derda laughs aloud.

"The Chiel have no land!" she says.

"Has your father, Lord Inchevin, gone to the aid of the free towns and the villages attacked by Rugal?" asks Zabrandor. "It would be better, my lady, if he did. For I tell you plainly that I have heard he makes common cause with this savage chieftain, that he has received him in Inchevin Keep!"

Derda lowers her eyes then looks up through her lashes, first at Zabrandor then at Merilla. It is a flirtatious trick that does not become her; she smiles, but her eyes do not smile.

"We have made no bond with the Skivari," she says softly. "Rugal came once to the keep. He sued for my hand. He had heard of the Starry Maid of Inchevin."

"Derda," says Merilla earnestly, "you have close ties of kinship with the house of the Zor, you have friends, you have come to court. This brute Rugal is not fit to approach you or any young maid of high estate!"

"My mother is dead now for five years," answers Derda harshly. "She lived in exile, and my father had no benefit from her once the dowry was spent. I am the Heir of the Inchevin! The runes have told that I will bring golden treasure to our house."

So saying, she rises up from her place by the fire, nods to Merilla and Lord Zabrandor and sweeps off out of the hall. Zabrandor gives a deep sigh.

"Poor child!"

"It is not easy to make amends to the Inchevin," says Merilla. "They are a wild folk."

"I remember Inchevin," says Zabrandor. "I remember Zarah Am Zor, the king's heir for years, until Sharn Am Zor was born. She was something of a beauty, as I recall, very quiet, not so cheerful and lively as your Aunt Parn, her younger sister. Ilmar of Inchevin was young, proud, dashing, always a little outlandish. What kind of man is he now? I fear for his whole clan!"

"What of this brigand, Rugal?"

"I must speak to the Daindru. We will send troops to the northeast. I hope Inchevin is warned by his daughter and casts off all links to the Skivari."

Merilla gives a rueful smile.

"Derda has been spoken of as a bride for Carel," she says, "but she is too fierce, and he will not take any wife just yet."

"Perhaps Inchevin and his daughter should be given what they crave," says Zabrandor. "Gold. Gold from the treasury of the Daindru as the price of their loyalty."

The old lord raises his head as if he sniffed the air. It is broad daylight now, but the wintry sunshine hardly penetrates the hall. Zabrandor bends forward and stirs up the logs in the long fireplace with an iron poker.

"I think we are observed," he murmurs. "The captain stands yonder in the entry, but there is a fellow on the landing of the stair behind the tapestry. I would not have all this known . . ."

"Perhaps it is one of the children," says Merilla, just as low. "There is a door behind that hanging: one of the secret passages. We used them for hide-and-seek."

Soon afterwards she takes her leave of Lord Zabrandor and goes sedately up the grand staircase. Suddenly, at the landing she whirls about, pulls back the thick tapestry and wrenches open the small door hidden in the old reed panelling. Nothing. Merilla peers into the cold, echoing passageway. Far away she hears the sound of running footsteps. Something catches the light at her feet. Merilla stoops down quickly, then closes the door and lets the hanging fall. She shakes her head to Lord Zabrandor below and goes on up the stairs. She glances at the shining object, which the watcher let fall: It is a small oval of ivory or bone, highly polished, shaped like a giant thumbnail. If this token does not lie, Merilla now knows who watched and listened and it fills her with a dull sadness.

The king has lost none of his restless energy; on winter afternoons when the whole court is stricken with drowsiness, he goes upstairs eagerly to the room where he once gave his little suppers. There he finds a "new man," one with energy and obsession to match his own.

Trig Grünweg is a master-builder come out of Lien, a dry and unimposing little man, a genius.

On a large trestle table there is a model, slowly growing, complete and perfect in every detail. Sharn Am Zor, absorbed, shakes sand upon a pathway then turns to cutting out a parchment balustrade. Master Trig, who simply tolerated the king at first, has discovered that he is skilled with his hands. More important his taste is good, if unformed.

Trig Grünweg and his royal apprentice are designing Chernak New Palace, a gift to the king from his shrewd and loving queen. It is a project dear to his heart, an occupation. In the first days of their marriage, she rode out alone with him south of Chernak Hall to a piece of land, well-watered, flat, with richer soil than is usual upon the plain and hence a grove of fine trees. They walked about, arms entwined, and planted two acorns, which Lorn found there. The seeds were sown. There will be a new palace of stone, together with gardens, walks, fish ponds, storehouses, all the appurtenances of a palace. The king is just as interested in perfect drainage as in rooms of state.

Grünweg, designer of the royal rose gardens of Lien and of the Wilderness rose park, has lacked employment of late. His patron, the Lord of Grays, is at loggerheads with the Markgraf and his vizier. The talk continues, year in year out, that fair Zaramund of Grays, the Markgrafin, will be put aside because she is childless. Grünweg has come gladly into the Chameln lands and found the commission of his lifetime, his true memorial.

It is in this room that Queen Lorn acquaints the king with the very thing that the Lord of Grays has feared for so long. She comes in, one afternoon not long after the raising of the tree, and sits quietly by the fire, waiting for Sharn to finish his consultation over the orangery. He sees at last that she is cast down; he hurries over to take her hand.

"What is it?"

He has never in his life been so close to anyone. He

is impatient with words and wishes he could know her thoughts.

"I have spoken to poor Veldis," she says, "and to Mayrose, her sister."

"Come," says Sharn, "do not share their tears. It is some little thing . . ."

"No," says Lorn. "I fear it is not. Do you recall the third sister, the youngest, Fideth of Wirth?"

"Yes." He nods. "I remarked all three sisters at Zilly's wedding and later at Larkdel. Veldis is the beauty of the family; Mayrose is a bit of a hoyden, I think—she reminds me of Rilla. Then there is sweet Fideth, fair-haired and well-behaved."

"She has come to harm," says Lorn. "She is in Balufir at the house of an old gentlewoman, her Aunt Vane, and she has come to harm, as the saying goes."

"In the name of the Goddess! That poor child Fideth?"

He can only think that the poor girl has been the victim of an attack.

"She has been seduced by a nobleman," says Lorn. "Poor old Sir Berndt feels this dishonor very keenly and so do her sisters. Iliane Seyl made some slighting remark."

"Is Fideth with child?"

"Not yet."

"Could she not marry?" asks the king.

It seems to him an ordinary misfortune.

"The man is married," says Lorn. "He is of very high estate, in fact the highest in the land of Lien . . ."

"But that is the Markgraf! Uncle Kelen!"

Lorn bows her head. Sharn is ashamed and disgusted.

"He is nearly fifty years old!" he exclaims. "And the girl . . .?"

"Not yet seventeen," says Lorn. "The Markgraf has promised marriage. He will put aside the Markgrafin Zaramund at last."

The king casts a glance at Grünweg, busy with his plans by the window, and thinks of the rose gardens in Balufir.

"Poor Zaramund," he says. "She was always a friend
to me and to Merilla and Carel when we were in exile."

"There is more," says Lorn. "Mayrose has the story.
The old knight, finding that this Aunt Vane had so
betrayed his trust, sent Brother Basil, their house priest,
to poor Fideth. This brother met with the head of his
priestly order, the Brother Harbinger from Swangard.
These two approve the match! Fideth is for them the
spoiled vessel, the besmirched woman who will bring
Kelen to the light by her sin."

"That is hateful!" says the king. "This lord of light
puts forth some dark doctrine. There will be trouble in
Lien . . . the Lord of Grays . . ."

Abruptly he raises his head and calls to Grünweg.
The Master-builder leaves his work unwilling and comes
shuffling between the tables with his fine quill still
poised. He bows to the queen and seems to recollect
himself.

"Master Grünweg," says Sharn Am Zor, "what kind
of man is your former patron, the Lord of Grays?"

"Surely, Sire, you knew him . . ."

"I saw him at court in Balufir," says the king, "a
grandiose figure, more richly dressed than Kelen himself. How will he behave when his worst fears come to
pass, when his daughter, the Markgrafin Zaramund, is
declared unfit for marriage and set aside?"

Grünweg wrinkles his brow and smooths a hand over
his bald pate.

"He will foreclose!" he says promptly. "The lord is
very choleric and stubborn. He will try to collect all the
outstanding monies and mortgages owing to him from
the Markgraf and his friends . . . nay, from the state
coffers, the realm of Lien itself!"

He looks at the king and his queen politely, having
given his opinion, and returns to his drawing table by
the window.

"Now I must beg *you* not to be cast down," says Lorn
softly. "These are not your troubles, my dear lord."

"By the Goddess," he says, teasing. "I hear of too
many young women, chits of girls, troubling the rulers

of Hylor! If it is not Derda Am Inchevin and her clan, suspected of consorting with brigands, then it is poor Fideth of Wirth, causing scandal and unrest in the court at Balufir!"

"Scandal in that court is nothing new," says Lorn, smiling.

"Something should be done!" says the king. "I will speak with Aidris. We may send some envoy into Lien."

Thoughts and memories of Lien trouble Sharn Am Zor all through the Ashmoon and the feast days. Watchers in the palace often see the king stride across the grounds through the snow to a small gateway in the wall. In the street he dismisses his two guards who wander off gratefully into a pleasant quarter of Achamar called the Old Market.

The king knocks upon the door of an old roundwood house and stoops down to enter Hazard's new home. The poet has a gift of settling, taking possession of a place and making it his own. Taranelda, who had resigned herself to the role of a blind poet's wife, leading a hand-to-mouth existence, now finds herself the mistress of a lively establishment. There are two scribes and a maidservant, not to mention the three cats, the dog and the garden goat.

When Taranelda goes marketing down the broad street among the quaint wooden houses, she finds herself in an elaborate setting for a masque. The Old Market is full of old friends. There is Jem Toogood, the poet, scribbling away at his place by the tavern window. There in the new printing shop is Hogrim, Buckrill's own master painter, lured away from Lien. There is Emyas Bill, the painter of portraits, and surely that old woman told fortunes in Balufir, not far from the Tumblers' Yard. Aram Nerriot, the musician, frequents the quarter, and a nest of minstrels from Athron have moved into an old stable.

Taranelda buys her bacon and a goose for the Feast Days from the stall of a man who calls himself Hunter. Has she seen him before? Clean-shaven, sandy hair streaked with grey, a look of the forest about him. He speaks little, but she could swear that he has a Lienish accent. Hazard should take a look at the man. Taranelda stands still, holding her market basket, and is engulfed by a wave of despair.

Hazard has been examined by the healers Jalmar Raiz and Gradja Am Gilyan. Several things may contribute to his blindness: years of reading and writing by candlelight; a period of darkness and privation in the Wells; a brainsickness of the kind that takes away the use of a healthy limb; a magic spell of unusual power. Any or all of these things may be at work. Hazard looked his last upon the world one summer morning in Balufir, in a boat rowing out to the *Caria Rose*. A master magician, his enemy, stood upon the dock.

Now in an upper room of Hazard's warm house, Sharn Am Zor sits down with his old friend. He reads back a chapter of that long, fine mock-heroic work "The Tale of Shennazar," a devastating picture of the courts of Eildon. He drinks mulled wine and peels roasted chestnuts for Hazard. The blind poet and the king gossip and laugh and conspire harmlessly together.

They seldom speak of Rosmer. Hazard has been expressly forbidden the use of spells, charms, potions, for their working cannot be calculated. Sharn Am Zor, seeing the vizier's grand design take shape, how this piece of territory, then that, is added to the Mark of Lien, has some hope that their enemy may be sated and release his hold upon his victims.

Word comes in the new year that Ghanor, the Great King of Mel'Nir, is dead. The old tyrant, wounded on the battlefield, has lingered for many moons in his Palace Fortress. Now Gol, the new king of Mel'Nir, has made a truce with Knaar of Val'Nur, the young lord of the Westmark. By the time the snows have melted, the whole continent of Hylor is at peace.

The brigand Rugal has drawn back into the northeastern mountains. Bajan Am Nuresh, returned from the northern tribes, has no disputes to report. Even the quarrelsome Aroshen of the mountain feoff of Vedan, Tazlo's folk, are peaceful. The Daindru have ridden out together to the Turmut, two years past, and will ride out again in three years.

In the spring, in the Willowmoon, Aidris Am Firn makes a progress through the central highlands to the city of Nevgrod. The royal children and the children of the court, those who saw the rising of the tree, go with her and continue on to spend the summer at Zerrah. Nursemaids, cooks, pages crowd into the wagons and carriages, along with mountains of linen.

It is easy on such a bothersome journey for Jalmar Raiz, the queen's healer, to slip away southwards. It will be given out, if necessary, that he has gone into Athron, to fetch herbs and simples. Even Sharn Am Zor does not know exactly where the healer is going, and he does not wish to know. He fears that this great secret, the hidden presence of Guenna of Lien, in some magic retreat, might be plucked from his brain while he sleeps.

The king is wary of spies, and observes the folk at the courts of the Daindru very carefully. The one person he has come to suspect seems harmless enough and easily diverted. This is part of Hazard's teaching.

First the king asks; "What should be done with a spy?"

And Hazard replies, laughing; "Oh a spy should be encouraged!"

"What do you mean?"

"The spy should be given plenty of freedom, watched most cautiously, fed harmless information . . ."

"And then?"

"The spy may be turned around, made into your own spy, or else arrested and imprisoned."

These wintry conversations with the blind poet are ended with the approach of spring. It is time for Sharn Am Zor to ride out with his queen to Chernak Hall, to go hawking again in the long valley; soon it will be warm enough for swimming. Above all, it is time to visit the site of Chernak New Palace. An army of men and women have made camp upon the plain: stone masons, bricklayers, laborers and their families. Building is going on everywhere; Denwick builds on his estate beyond the Hain; Seyl has his own hall at North Hodd on the road to Dechar.

Jevon Seyl, heir of an ancient line, numbers among his ancestors Holy Matten, the prophet of Inokoi, the Lame God, as well as many noble men and women of Lien who ran more true to type. His ancestral land, the rich province of Hodd in the northeast corner of Lien, has come gradually into the power of the state. Seyl's widowed mother, Lady Bergit, has no more than the old manor house and its park. Like Denzil of Denwick, a younger son with few prospects, Seyl has done better to throw in his lot entirely with King Sharn, his close friend and cousin, and found his own dynasty in the Chameln lands. For Seyl, at first sight a courtier, shows more and more the makings of a man of judgment, a chancellor for his king.

It is fitting that he should travel into Lien as an envoy from Achamar to the court at Balufir. His mission is to greet the Markgraf Kelen in the name of the Daindru and express concern about the succession. He sets out on this small and peaceful progress with his wife Iliane, quantities of fine clothes, gifts of jewels for the Markgrafin and an escort of guardsmen and kedran. So it is that the Daindru have an excellent witness to a cruel episode in the history of the Mark of Lien.

II

SEYL ARRIVES IN EARLY SPRING AND FINDS
all as fresh and fine as ever in Balufir, with no unusual
tension at the court. Between Kelen and fair Zaramund
there is not so much a coolness as the kind of resigna-
tion that grows between those long married. The
Markgraf makes discreet visits to his new love, Fideth
of Wirth, but she is never seen at court. On the other
hand, the Lord Merl of Grays and his three sons are
going about at court in great spirits. Some would say
that they are proud and overbearing, at least the lord
himself and his heir, Dermat. It is clear that they have
a hold over Kelen and his vizier, Rosmer. Zaramund
will not be put aside. Iliane Seyl, who has a gift for
intrigue, comes upon a very strange rumor. Rosmer has
a new candidate for the succession, a young man shut
up in a tower, a giant of a fellow not quite in his right
wits. In the middle of the Willowmoon, the court sets
out on its annual progress through the countryside and
comes to Nesbath to take the waters.

The old town on the Dannermere, at the confluence of
the two rivers, has a dreamlike beauty. Its wide streets,
lined with linden trees, are filled with summer villas of
pale stone. A wide promontory spreads out into the
inland sea; shoals of pleasure craft complete the vistas of
Nesbath as they move past on the endless blue.

The Birchmoon passes, unusually warm; all the roses come into bloom before the Villa Pearl, the royal residence. There are displays of fireworks. There is a regatta, somewhat marred by lack of wind. The prize is carried off by Dermat, the Heir of Grays, in his magnificent new sailing boat, the ketch *Huntress*.

Untroubled, Jevon Seyl observes the summer pleasures of the Lienish court. Privately, he and Iliane admit, at last, that these fine folk have become boring. Achamar, at the end of the world, now suits the Seyls better; there is more to do. Iliane misses her two little children, Jevon and Ishbel, now with their nursemaids at Zerrah; even the flattering attentions of the young men have begun to cloy.

Seyl has an interesting encounter with the Lord of Grays on the terrace of the Villa Pearl, typically at dawn after a nightlong revel. They drink kaffee and watch the sun rise over the inland sea. Lord Merl, in an elaborate wig, the latest mode, and a bewildering effulgence of brocade and jewels, has taken off his high-heeled shoes to cool his aching feet upon the tiles. Jevon Seyl, dreadfully sober, realizes that the old lord is asking for the support of the Daindru. A compact, an alliance. Some firm agreement over the succession, with the implication that Zaramund, daughter of Grays, will never be put aside. Seyl agrees that this treatment of the Markgrafin would indeed offend King Sharn and Queen Aidris. As for the succession, he will not be drawn.

Some days later Seyl and his lady accept one of the rare invitations from Rosmer. The vizier has requisitioned an old villa near the northern tip of the promontory; he keeps somewhat apart from the rest of the court. The day is called Swan Greeting, traditionally the beginning of summer. There will be a procession to the harbor, and the Markgraf's grand barge will sail to the floating pavilion, an artificial island anchored in the Dannermere.

Rosmer has invited a most select company to see the festival; the Seyls meet Zelline of Grays, Duchess of Chantry, Hal, Duke of Denwick and his red-haired consort from Balbank, and merry old Lord Trench, a local dignitary who happens to be Iliane's uncle. From the upper balcony of this villa there is a perfect view of the dusty, white tree-lined street, the small harbor for pleasure boats and the wide sweep of the inland sea. The company moves continually between the dark chamber, its old-fashioned oaken table set with dainties, for Rosmer has an excellent cook, and the bright balcony.

Rosmer pays particular attention to Jevon Seyl, who believes he is being sounded out over his recent talk with the Lord of Grays. The two men walk in the lovely untended garden, and Rosmer confides that the villa is the property of the Raiz family. He admits, slyly, that Jalmar Raiz might not take kindly to his tenancy.

"Jalmar Raiz has certain gifts, I will allow," he remarks, smiling, "but his brother, Hagnild Raiz: there is a master of his craft."

He adds cryptically; "I had proof, living proof, of Hagnild's magic, and the fellow slipped through my fingers. For a Duaring, he was unusually clever. Gone . . . gone . . . swum over the Bal, I don't doubt, back home to Mel'Nir."

He pauses by the sundial and checks a large pocket watch. Overhead the sky is cloudless; it is exactly midday. Rosmer has changed his black scholar's robe for one of olive-green; he wears a soft falling ruff without starch. He begins to complain of the Lord of Grays, a tyrant, holding the realm of Lien to ransom for a few paltry debts. Jevon Seyl puts in a word at last: the Daindru are concerned by rumors about the succession.

"Have no fear," says Rosmer gently, with his sidelong look. "The Markgrafin Zaramund will never be put aside."

They are hailed from the balcony by golden-haired Zelline and Iliane with dark ringlets tumbling over her smooth shoulders. The procession is approaching, the ladies cry, the refreshments have been served.

Seyl has racked his brains ever since as to the exact sequence of events. What can he recall? The chamber, dark after the sunlight, the marvellous wine. Rosmer

certainly is absent for minutes at a time but always
returns unruffled. On the balcony the Duchess of
Denwick gives her hearty laugh. The procession is made
up of decorated carriages drawn by young men dressed
as birds, animals and trees. It is pretty enough but
badly organized, full of amusing mistakes.

There is a lengthy pause in the proceedings while the
royal barge is made ready. Beside it at the wharf is
moored the *Huntress,* also hung with garlands. The
Markgraf Kelen can be seen striding about on the deck
of his barge, all in white with a red hat. Zaramund, his
consort, is wearing blue; the ladies agree that it suits
her. The sky is no longer cloudless. Seyl remembers a
breeze that blows in his face, a south wind? A west
wind?

The royal barge begins to move, poled by sturdy
boatmen, and then sticks fast. Denwick's footman is
sent running to the harbor to find out the cause of the
delay. Even before the man comes running back, Iliane
points to the *Huntress,* which has always been ready to
sail. Now Zaramund may be seen going aboard her
brother's new boat, together with a lady-in-waiting.

The footman reports that the royal barge is unseawor-
thy; it has sprung a leak and is filling with water. The
Markgraf is angry with his sailing master, and he has
refused to sail with the *Huntress,* in the company of his
wife's relatives. Zaramund has saved the day, saved the
ceremony by going alone. There is a good deal of mischievous amusement on the balcony when this tale is
told.

Meantime the *Huntress* speeds out into the inland
sea, spreading her painted sails, drawing in her wake
long flower garlands in honor of Swan Greeting. The
floating pavilion shimmers in the haze of early afternoon about two miles from shore. The wind is blowing
strongly now, a warm wind that comes in gusts. When
the *Huntress* rounds the pavilion, rockets are fired,
white and green.

Seyl, seeing that the traditional cruise will be com-
pleted very quickly in the sailing boat, goes indoors to

replenish his glass. The room is stifling; old Lord Trench sits in a corner singing to himself. Rosmer comes from the direction of the stairs, a tapestry lifts as he passes. They stand together at the end of the table, Rosmer with his cuffs turned back, his hands clasped, nothing up his sleeves. Out on the balcony Iliane begins to scream loudly.

Jevon Seyl races out again, overturning a chair as he goes. Iliane goes on screaming until Mechtild of Denwick slaps her face briskly; Denwick is leaning perilously over the balcony shouting for his servants. Zelline stands very still, then when Seyl comes to her side raises her hand and points.

The Dannermere has been whipped up into grey foam-crested wavelets. Where the *Huntress* sailed, close hauled upon a jibe, there is a depression in the water, a patch of turbulence. There is a streak of red that Seyl recognizes with horror as the long masthead pennant. As he watches, this too is drawn under into the waters of the inland sea.

There is hideous confusion on the wharf below; a tangle of small craft attempt to go to the rescue. Seyl sees two boatmen from the royal barge plunge into the water and begin swimming. The floating pavilion appears to have slipped its mooring in the squall and is canted crazily in the water with the few servants who let off the rockets clinging to its deck. Seyl turns his head and sees Rosmer still with his hands clasped standing on the balcony. His face is expressionless.

"Put down this wind!" cries Seyl. "Have you no powers?"

"It is too late!" says the vizier.

Zelline gives a soft moaning cry and falls in a faint. Iliane, very pale, her teeth chattering, seems about to do the same. Seyl seizes his wife by the wrist and begins to drag her away. He says to Rosmer; "The Lord of Grays?"

"He was aboard," says Rosmer, "alas."

"A clean sweep then!" says Seyl recklessly.

"What can you be thinking?" protests the vizier with

a modest smile. "You are my witnesses. Could you believe that I had any hand . . ."

"Yes!" says Seyl through clenched teeth. "Yes, by the Goddess!"

He catches sight of Denwick and his wife, clinging together, their eyes fixed upon Rosmer. Poor Lord Trench, sobered, is trying to revive Zelline. Seyl drags Iliane with him and rushes from the house, panting down the stairs out into a storm of summer rain. The two kedran left to wait with the carriage have gone; now the older woman comes running up from the harbor.

"Lord! Lord! The ship, the sailboat . . ."

"Bring us away," orders Seyl.

He settles Iliane into the carriage in frantic haste and leaps in beside her.

"Bring us to the Villa Pearl and by the north road, not the avenue!"

The second kedran comes up just in time to chase after the carriage and leap up behind as they gather speed. Even the back road to the royal villa is not empty; men and women are rushing to the harbor. Seyl, hanging from the window, brushed by overhanging boughs, sees a ghost, a young man struggling uphill from tree to tree. He shouts to the kedran to slow down and flings open the carriage door.

"Here man, get in!"

The young man scrambles in; he is wearing a tree suit, a domino covered with green silk leaves. Iliane, seeing him, chokes back a scream, then begins to wrap him in the carriage rug.

"Garvis, oh Garvis, Poor boy," she weeps, "you were not aboard!"

The young man, shocked and pale, tries to draw breath.

"Murdered!" he says at last. "All murdered! Dermat, Tam, the Old Man . . . Zaramund, my dear sister Zaramund! Goddess, what shall I . . ."

"Hold firm," says Jevon Seyl. "Remember who you are!"

"Yes," says Garvis at length. "I am the Lord of Grays."

After his headlong flight from Rosmer's presence, Seyl regains his self-possession and observes the aftermath of the tragedy. He sends off two kedran at once to bring word to the Daindru. They leave Nesbath while it is still in confusion, and with them, in kedran dress, goes Garvis of Grays. Once they are on the Nesbath road to the Chameln border, he slips away, mounted on a gift horse, a trusty Chameln grey, and returns to Lien.

Seyl watches from his apartments in the villa and sees Kelen brought home, his face a mask of anguish, his white robes wet and foul as if he had cast himself into the sea. Seyl speaks later with Sharn Am Zor over the Markgraf's complicity in the murders. Kelen knew and did not know. Perhaps he knew what must happen but not the time or the place; all was left to Rosmer, and he worked so skillfully that even witnesses close at hand could not say that the vizier had worked one jot of magic. The witnesses were carefully chosen: persons of high rank.

In the twilight of the long tragic day Iliane calls her husband to another window.

"I have been watching the roses," she says. "They are all accursed! The Goddess has put a curse upon the land of Lien."

Jevon Seyl protests that it is her fancy, the roses were crushed by the summer rain. Yet even he believes, looking at the rose gardens. Soon there is not a rose in all the land of Lien to deck the funeral pyre of fair Zaramund. The doomed ketch *Huntress* lies fathoms deep, but the bodies of the drowned are washed down the river Bal to a beach by Lesfurth called Dead Man's Strand and there are burnt, lord and sailor alike, even the body of the Markgrafin.

So there begins a dark, unsettling era in the history of the Mark of Lien. The long revels of the court are at an end. Kelen takes Fideth of Wirth as his wife in the Maplemoon, and from that time forth she makes their life together a penance. The priesthood of the Lame God go about for good or ill; pastime and merriment are at an end. The taverns and disorderly house are shut down in Balufir; the prisons are overflowing; the Tumblers' Yard has gone dark. The Markgraf Kelen walks barefoot to Larkdel in the Ashmoon and there gives thanks at the sanctuary for that which he has craved so long: Fideth, his wife, has borne him a son: Matten of Lien.

In the spring of the following year, 1179, when the carpenters and masons were preparing for the raising of the roof trees of the great hall of Chernak New Palace, a solitary visitor came into the Chameln lands. The east wing of the palace more or less complete; Sharn Am Zor and Lorn, his queen, were already camping there, with many of their court; it was like a perpetual picnic.

Now they rode out to meet Queen Aidris and the visitor, Yorath Duaring, child of Gol of Mel'Nir and that fair, lost swan of Lien, Elvédegran. There he was at last, the child whom Hagnild Raiz stole away to his brown house in Nightwood to save him from the wrath of Ghanor, the Great King. How could anyone short of a master magician hide this Yorath? He was a giant, even among the giant warriors of Mel'Nir, a natural wonder, his hair and beard of a rich auburn, coarse and thick, his face handsome and open with a touch of melancholy, almost a wistful look. His light blue eyes seemed fixed upon some distant horizon. He talked well and pleasantly and laughed, and Sharn Am Zor puzzled over a resemblance. Who was he like, this cousin Yorath? King Gol, his father, certainly, but who else?

Yorath went off into the distant north with his companion Zengor, the white wolf, to seek a retreat in the mountains and live like a hermit. Long after their day together had passed, the king remembered. In Yorath he had caught a look of his own father, King Esher Am Zor, that unhappy man, his co-ruler murdered, his queen mad, his realm threatened by the Great King. Esher had not been a good father, and Sharn could see the reasons for this. He blew hot and cold, was preoc-

cupied, had no natural touch with children, yet he was
an honest man, and he had loved his son and heir.

Autumn had come. In the night, in the Zor palace,
after the visit to the nursery and the king's couching,
Sharn and his queen sat in their bedchamber, in the
midst of their large golden bed. Sharn sprawled upon
the pillows, and Lorn fed him green grapes. He told
her of a hunting trip, his father's last gift, the last time
they had spent together. It was more than a year after
the time in the Hain when the children were attacked
and Aidris wounded by the arrow. Aidris had been far
away in Thuven Manor; Aravel's sickness had grown
upon her dreadfully. It had been a bad time, and so in
the spring Esher Am Zor had taken Sharn and a few
followers and set out along the road to Dechar. His
father did not insist, for once, upon too much riding;
they took a pony trap, and Sharn was allowed to drive
it. They struck out eastwards across the plain and traveled for several days, making camp at night, and came
to a lonely hunting lodge upon the river Chind.

"I must go there next year in the spring," said Sharn,
"eastward to that river. Zabrandor will see that the
brigands are put down."

"And the Inchevin?" asked Lorn with a frown.

"I will try to speak with the old lord."

"I wonder if your hunting lodge still stands?" she
asked. "Is it near the Inchevin lands?"

"Nowhere near. It is on this side of the river, a place
that has no name. I will have it built up again, and one
year when all is quiet, I will take a hunting party . . ."

"Take Carel," said Lorn.

"Yes," said the king. "Yes, Carel. I do it for a memorial, you know. For my father."

He took her hand and was silent.

CHAPTER IX

OUTLAWS

THE THREE RIDERS CAME ON STEADILY ACROSS the plain of silvery grass; there was no wind, the tresses of hair on the spirit trees hung limp and still, not a thread stirring. Prince Sasko looked to his left at his mother, Aidris, and saw himself in her smile, in her smiling green eyes. He looked right and saw Sharn, his cousin, the very model of a king of the Zor, and riding better than ever on Redwing.

"They are coming . . ." murmured Sharn.

Sasko gripped Morrah's rein more tightly and told him to hold firm. The outriders from the northern tribes came on very fast, uttering their strange cries and hanging perilously from their saddles. Aidris lifted a hand, caught a streamer of dried flowers and gave it to her son. A rider in a blue cape came wheeling in close, and Sharn laughed and raised a hand to Tazlo. Sasko watched, as they came among the lodges and the swirling crowds, until he saw his father, in his tribal dress as High Chieftain of the Nureshen. Bajan lifted his son to the platform, and he stood between the Daindru, hearing the cheers, hearing the cheer for Dan Sasko, Heir of the Firn.

The Turmut, the second since the restoration of the Daindru, was remembered as another great success;

even the quarrelsome Aroshen were gentle as lambs. It was an hour of triumph for Tazlo Am Ahrosh, son of old Kall, the High Chieftain. He proved that his years in the capital, far from his tribal home, had not been ill spent. He was the trusted servant and friend of the King of the Zor, and Sharn showed many marks of favor towards the Aroshen of Vedan.

Between the king and the young man from the north there had grown a coldness, a distance that neither of them cared to acknowledge. It was not simply that Sharn had married and had a family to claim his duty. As Merilla wisely said, the king had grown up and Tazlo's hectic vigor was no longer so much to his liking. Yet at the Turmut they were close as ever, and even Aidris was persuaded that the friendship had helped the Daindru to a new peace among the tribes.

When the folk-moot was done, the Daindru went separate ways, for there was work to do in which Aidris would have no part. Her last warlike expedition, she said, had been the Great Ambush at the Adderneck Pass. She returned with her son and the kedran of her escort to Achamar. Sharn went on with Bajan Am Nuresh and a troop of chosen riders from the northern tribes. They rode to the east, passing through the lower hunting grounds of Vedan and through the rich grazing land about Lake Oncardan, still the subject of a dispute between the Durgashen and the Aroshen. So they rode on, turning south, and followed the course of the river Chind, a thin foaming stream that fell through the gorges with a noise of thunder. After five days they camped by a ford, not far from the remote town of Threll, on the edge of the territory of the Inchevin, and there Zabrandor came to meet them with his own southerners and a troop of guardsmen from Achamar.

They had not come with any particular secrecy and were planning no ambush, but what followed worked like one. Scouts came back at nightfall from across the river; a large band of the Skivari were approaching Threll from the east, through the foothills. The scouts swore there were five hundred of the devils, some mounted on their hill ponies, some running. Rugal himself was their leader.

There followed a slow ride through the ford, then through the dark trees of a larch forest growing down to the banks of the Chind. At the gates of Threll, a knot of men with torches whispered, "Where is the king?" and when they saw him, tall and golden-haired, they smiled and gained heart. Sharn was led to a wooden watch tower in the stockade with his bodyguard; he took a short bow and his favorite black-feathered arrows.

The attack came, as expected, promptly at dawn. Rugal and his Skivari were creatures of habit, savage-looking men in pointed hats whose only tactic was to roar and hack and press on. They were soon defeated. A horseman at the tower's base sounded a horn for the retreat: Rugal's trumpeter. Sharn saw the terror from the east at last, seated upon a fat, shining little horse, brown and white. Rugal was a youngish man, very short and broad, with his black hair shaved in patches and a string of human skulls decorating his saddle. The king let loose another arrow, and again it found its mark.

"Winged him, by the Goddess!" cried Tazlo, who had come to bring word of the victory.

Rugal bore the arrow in his shoulder as if it had been a bee sting. Sharn shot again, but the chieftain was out of range. When the king and his guards came down from their eyrie, the town was littered with dead Skivari; a troop of riders from the northern tribes was pursuing the fugitives.

Sharn went about examining the dead brigands with Zabrandor and the Athaman of the town.

"Are they all Skivari?" he asked.

Many showed the features of this tribe or race: they were short, smooth-skinned, yellow-brown, with coarse straight black hair. Others were more ordinary, they could have been men of the Chameln lands. They came to a man of the Zor, tall, pale-skinned, yellow-haired, without a pointed hat. He had the look of one of the palace guards, a trumpeter. The man's right hand was tightly clasped around a small leather pouch.

"I will see that," said the king, pointing.

He glanced up at the sky and the oak tree in the town square while the town elder brought his boot down on the dead hand. The pouch contained an eagle's claw, mounted in silver, together with a lock of white-blonde hair. On the mount were runes for good fortune and the device of a double star, the arms of the Inchevin.

"An amulet, my King," said the Athaman. "He might have stolen it."

They followed a guard officer to the hall where there was food and drink for the defenders of Threll.

Zabrandor said wearily, "Is this proof, Dan Sharn?"

"Almost," said Sharn. "When Bajan and the northern tribesmen return, I will ride for Inchevin Keep."

"Let me send a herald . . ."

"No, I will go myself," said the king. "This lord is my uncle, my father's sister's husband. The Chameln lands are wide, and it is easy for a man to feel forgotten, here at the end of the world."

"Inchevin was too proud," said Zabrandor. "When he bore all the debt in that ill-fated trading venture, he might still have remained in Achamar. He could not bear to live in the palace as a pensioner of his wife."

"And my mother?"

"She made it clear that both of her sisters-in-law were out of favor," said Zabrandor. "A king or queen will have an inner circle of friends and courtiers."

Sharn Am Zor sighed, remembering a king who had upbraided his sister cruelly and banished her. He bent his head and went into the smoky hall of Threll. There he found the women of the town in their best clothes, smiling, after a sleepless night, offering him breakfast. So he sat down at the high table and accepted their hospitality graciously. He kissed and blessed any number of little children, brought to see the king, and Lieutenant Dann, who carried his purse, ran out of gold and silver coins.

Then, before the pursuit of the raiders was ended, before the king rose from table, there was a trumpet

call at the gates of Threll. The Lord of Inchevin had
come. The king kept his place and had Zabrandor clear
the hall.

Presently the lord came in; Sharn saw him approach
through the smoky haze in the big airless room, a dark
halting figure. Ilmar of Inchevin was about five and fifty
years old, somewhat above middle height and strongly
built. At a short distance, with his dark hair and stiff
carriage, he looked well-preserved, young for his years,
although he limped and walked with the aid of a staff.
Then he came closer, and Sharn saw that his lank,
ill-kempt black hair was heavily streaked with white, his
wedge-shaped face was wrinkled, the skin of a yellowish
pallor; his teeth were long and decayed. He stood,
panting a little, below the high table on its platform,
and cried out, "Dan Sharn! So I have brought you
here!"

"Uncle Inchevin," said the king, raising his voice as if
speaking to a deaf person, "Uncle Inchevin, sit down
with me!"

Ilmar of Inchevin heaved himself up on to the platform and took the proffered seat. When the Athaman's
wife came forward, bowing, to draw tea from the silver
urn, he struck at her absently with his staff.

"The runes do not lie!" he panted. "What great news
have you brought? How fares the Starry Maid, my
daughter and heir, in Achamar. How fares young Ilmar,
my son? How will the Daindru make amends?"

"Your children do very well," said Sharn. "I hope
your health is good?"

"I am sound as a gold piece," said the lord. "They
say, king, that you were in Eildon."

He lowered his voice and leaned across the board.
The king, who had gone hunting and campaigning in
the Chameln lands where the soaps and perfumes of
Lien were unknown, had never been close to a man
who stank so vilely as his Uncle Inchevin.

"Do they practise the true and noble art there?" he
whispered. "Do they have great adepts in Eildon, wizards and star callers?"

"You mean the art of magic?"

"The art that is the end of all magic," murmured Inchevin. "The turning of base metal into gold!"

Sharn Am Zor could not help but meet the eyes of Lord Inchevin, black and glittering, with red rims that told of sleepless nights. He knew that the man was mad.

"I have heard that some magicians in Eildon and in Lien have tried to do this," he said, "but none have the secret."

"Yet hear me," said the lord, grasping the king by the sleeve, "there are wizards and great sages beyond the mountains, far to the east. They have tamed the spirits, have climbed to the topmost bough of the jeweled tree of life and plucked the golden bird from its nest. This Rugal has a wizard in his tent city. If I could but take this yellow devil and force him to raise spirits for me . . ."

"Is that why you dally with these brigands?" demanded Sharn. "Is that why you have Rugal in your keep?"

Inchevin drew back and slapped the table with the flat of his hand.

"Don't talk to me of loyalty," he said. "We are here at the world's end. Yet our day will come!"

"I am your king!" said Sharn Am Zor, not loud but firm. "We have taught the raiders a sharp lesson with only this small force. Hold yourself far from them, Ilmar of Inchevin, I command it!"

The lord writhed and scowled on his chair, but not as if he rejected the king's sovereignty. Rather he was a man feeling the pricks of conscience.

Sharn pressed on. "You will need gold," he said, "if you are to defend the frontier against Rugal and the Skivari . . ."

Inchevin's face lit up like the face of a child seeing the raising of the tree. Sharn spoke aside to Lieutenant Dann who hurried out of the hall.

"Mind you," said Sharn, "it is a hard task, perhaps too much for even the greatest lord in these parts."

"No!" said Inchevin. "No, by the stars, I can raise men and weapons. With gold I will do great things, my King!"

The Lieutenant came back with Tazlo helping him to lug the small coffer that had been brought all the way from Achamar. Inchevin waited, the tip of his tongue showing between his teeth, as it was placed upon the table. Sharn Am Zor broke the seal of the Daindru and flung back the lid, then pushed the coffer across to the lord. Inchevin drew out reverently a goblet of pure gold and began to count gold pieces, stacking them neatly before him.

"There are forty new gulden," said the king, "and forty gold royals of Lien."

Inchevin went on stacking and counting as if entranced, then seemed to recollect himself and swept all the treasure back into the coffer.

"My King," he breathed, "we begin to understand one another. I will drive out the Skivari, never fear. Rugal will not show his face again. Ha! I will build a great wall across the mountain passes . . ."

He laughed aloud. The king presented Tazlo Am Ahrosh, who sat down with them, and Inchevin called for spirit to seal the bargain. Gold had indeed worked on him like a charm. The king turned the conversation to hunting, and Inchevin told tales of the grey bear who lived beside the river Chind, further south, and the fish-otters and wolf-cats that were still trapped in this part of the world. Yet he could not long hold back from his obsession.

"The runes have told me that my daughter, the Starry Maid, will marry one who is blessed with gold," he announced. "How stands your noble brother Prince Carel, my King? Could a match be made pleasing to the Goddess and the race of men, as the saying goes?"

Sharn was proof against embarrassing questions.

"In these matters I let Aidris Am Firn mediate," he said firmly. "Carel has no great estates, although he is a prince of the blood. I will commend your daughter, the

Lady Derda, to the care of the Queen of the Firn, who shares the double throne."

The taming of Inchevin was complete. A day-long feast followed in the town of Threll, for the miserly lord would not entertain the king at his keep. Bajan Am Nuresh returned, having chased Rugal and his brigands almost to the mountains. As they rode away back to the river, Zabrandor confessed himself well pleased with the king's diplomacy; but both the king and his general agreed that Inchevin was a madman, hardly to be trusted.

Bajan bade farewell to the king and returned to the north, leading home the raiders from the northern tribes. The losses had been slight, but there were men and women from the north and the south who did not come safe home. The king continued on with Zabrandor and his southerners and the men of his escort down the river Chind. Sharn Am Zor, weary with campaigning and disgusted by the encounter with Ilmar of Inchevin, was soothed now by the countryside.

It was a sweet, wild country between the plain and the mountains; the river was now a broad stream. Once, at dawn, Captain Kogor of the escort came to the king's tent, whispering. Sharn rose up, just as he was, and wrapped himself in his cloak. There, directly across from the camp, were two grey bears fishing in the river: an old bear, taller than a man, and another, half-grown. Tazlo appeared at the king's side as he peered round a tent and urged the king to try a shot with his longbow. Sharn Am Zor refused, smiling. The bear was a noble animal, under the special protection of the Goddess.

So the king came to that hunting lodge upon the river Chind that he had visited long ago with his father, King Esher Am Zor. There it stood, a sturdy six-roomed loghouse, fallen into disrepair but still used by hunters and trappers.

Sharn wondered whether he should send a party from Achamar to repair the lodge, but Zabrandor said, "Only a few days more, my king, and we come within sight of Chiel Hall. Your aunt, the Lady Parn Am Zor and Am Chiel, will gladly send out a party to repair the lodge."

The king came, as he had planned, to Chiel Hall and experienced with some relief a return to civilization. His Aunt Parn kept a good house, fall of comfort and good humor, even though she was not rich. Having spent gold upon the vile Lord Inchevin, the king felt doubly beholden to the Chiel. His Aunt Parn, a plump and bustling woman, soothed her nephew.

"I have never wanted land," she said. "Since my dear lord's death this is as much as I can manage. I have been granted great riches. My dear Merilla brought, you may recall, a decent dowry, and now she has given us those two rascals, Till and Tomas, twin sons. If you would make me any gift, dear Sharn, let it be simply your continued love and favor, and maybe some new hangings from the city looms. Our old ones are getting shabby."

So the king's hunting lodge on the Chind was rebuilt, and it was called Greybear. Every second year or so the king rode down to North Hodd and from there struck out across the plain with a few chosen companions and spent a moon in spring or late summer in the east of the Chameln lands. He put the lodge in the hands of old Engist, his former master-at-arms, now in good health again, and other veteran soldiers and huntsmen. They spent a good deal of time in that marvellous countryside and did not mind that the young sparks at the court called the place "grey-beard" instead of Greybear.

The news from Lien was unsettling as ever, but it did not touch the Chameln Lands directly. The Grand Design went forward. Now Lien laid claim to a great part of Balbank, the finest land in Mel'Nir, this through the Duchess of Denwick, widow of Hem Brond, a nobleman of Mel'Nir, who had brought large estates to her marriage. Other Balbank estates lay untenanted following the civil war, and in the year 339 of the Farfaring, as dates were measured in Mel'Nir, King Gol agreed to the Balbank purchase. He sold off a tract of land to the

Mark of Lien, and Rosmer came to a holding he had coveted far many years.

Within Lien itself, tales were told of the Green Riders who came swooping down by night upon the justices and tax collectors as they went about on the highways. The great house Grayholm, by the Ringist, tenanted now by bailiffs out of Balufir, was an empty shell, stripped of its treasure so that none of it fell into the hands of the state. Garvis of Grays, leader of the Green Riders, had become an outlaw, living in the woods and in the border forest, over the river. He went about with a price on his head, and none would betray him. Disaffected young nobles and commons, a growing band, ran off to join him. Songs and ballads told of the Green Riders and their dashing young leader. Some said that he had a lady-love, a young woman of high degree, fled to the woods to join him. In Larkdel, the thriving town of the Holy Sanctuary, the old knight, Sir Berndt of Wirth, had become reconciled to his youngest daughter Fideth, the Markgrafin. He mourned now the loss and the dishonor of his second daughter: Mayrose of Wirth; that wild girl was nowhere to be found.

II

ON AN EVENING IN LATE SUMMER IN THE YEAR 1183, Aidris Am Firn rode across the city to the palace of the Zor. She came unheralded with only a kedran officer, and found Sharn Am Zor seated in his garden with Lorn, his wife, and his sister, Merilla. The yearly ritual had altered. Chernak New Palace would never be quite complete; there would always be some work going on to amuse the king and his master builder; but in fact it had been habitable for several years. The court of the Zor went there in the summer, and their children used the children's wing. Now there was a delightful breathing space at the Zor palace when the adults had come back but the children were still at Chernak. Servants were ladling out cool drinks; Nerriot played a country dance.

Aidris sat down, smiling, drawing out the greetings a little as if she did not wish to break the spell. She bade Nerriot play some melodies of Lien, including the Rose Lament, with Hazard's famous lyric, so apt in these days, though it had been written for the Markgrafin Guenna more than twenty years past.

When the song was done, the queen said, "I have news for this family."

Sharn Am Zor and his sister began to speak both at

once; she deferred to the king. He dismissed the servants, gave Nerriot a purse of red brocade and asked the musician to attend him the next evening after supper. As Nerriot made his last bow, his music case fell and scattered its contents upon the grass. Merilla helped to pick up the odds and ends.

"Nerry," she said, "I keep finding your lute picks in strange places."

When the family was alone, Aidris said, "I think that one who has remained hidden will leave us altogether."

There was a sigh, a word or two of sadness; Lorn laid a hand upon her husband's arm.

"She will see us in the stone," said Aidris to Sharn. "She will see the Daindru."

"Come, cousin," said Sharn Am Zor, "shall we walk to the lakeside, to that young oak?"

The Daindru walked over the lawns side by side and sat down on a stone bench facing the garden lake. Aidris drew out the scrying stone, the blue-green beryl that she had from her mother, Hedris of Lien. It had gone with her into exile in Athron and it had gone with Sharn Am Zor into Eildon. In the world of the stone, they saw their grandmother, Guenna, very pale, her hair silvered, her hands thin and fine resting upon the altar or table, as if she were sitting in a chair.

"My dear children!"

Her voice was at last the voice of an old woman.

"It is time," she said firmly. "I cannot stay."

"Grandmother," said Sharn Am Zor, "will you not have a healer? Will you not come to us in Achamar?"

"No, my dear Sharn." She smiled. "The day is done. My wraiths must be called home before the dark. You two and Yorath have been a light to me in this exile."

"Will you remain in Erinhall?" asked Aidris.

"I will be set in a boat and brought to the hospice of the Moon Sisters in Hodd, across the river, and there laid to my rest," said Guenna. "I charge you both . . ."

"What, grandmother?" asked the king.

"I have failed in the struggle. Perhaps my life and art

have been wasted. Yet do you hold fast to the hope of
freedom for Lien, freedom from our common enemy."

"We will hold fast," said Aidris in a breaking voice.

"No, no my brave queen," said Guenna, "do not
weep. Let my good Hazard write some song or catch for
me. I will give the poor folk back their roses."

Then the light from the world of the stone grew and
shone up all around them, where they were sitting by
the lake shore; and there, far an instant, stood Guenna,
robed and crowned in silver light, holding out her
hands to them. Her voice came from far away: "Farewell . . . farewell, my dear children . . ." and the light
faded. Aidris gave a cry of grief, and in her palm the
scrying stone began to break; it crumbled into dust, and
she held only the silver rim.

"Hush," said Sharn, putting an arm about his cousin.
"We must not weep for her. She has gone to the halls of
the Goddess."

The Daindru walked back across the lawns and sat
quietly with Merilla and Lorn. They remained so long
together that servants and couriers came out to peer at
them across the twilit gardens of the palace, wondering
what it was that held them thus, so quiet and downcast.

So passed Guenna of Lien, a mighty sorceress, mother
of the Markgraf Kelen and of the three lovely swans of
Lien: Hedris, Aravel and Elvédegran. Her magic was
not entirely lost. When autumn rains lashed the border
forest and Garvis of Grays, camped with his followers in
a ring of rude huts, began to regret that he had no
better roof over his head, an old man was brought into
camp by the scouts. He hailed Garvis by name and promised him a great gift if he would mount up and follow.

Many thought it must be a trap. Mayrose, the leader's outlaw bride, came from her hut and questioned
the old man, and he gave her a leather bag containing a
large ruby, framed in gold. It was a scrying stone: it
showed a part of the palace at Balufir, always the same
room, and the people who came and went in that place.
This was only a part of the gift, the old man said; Garvis
must follow him.

In the end Garvis and Mayrose and some trusty knaves followed the old man on foot through the forest, taking their own secret trails and keeping a sharp look out. They came at last to a huge oak tree not far from the river; beyond the oak was a tangled thicket and a ruin. So the old man bade Garvis of Grays strike three times with his sword upon the trunk of the oak tree.

The young lord of Grays did as he was told, and at the third stroke of his sword, there was a sound in the air like a chord of music. The outlaws beheld a fair green park where the sun shone, and between two wooded hills there was a small keep with towers and turrets. The old man led them on and bade them welcome to Erinhall, a magical retreat, to be theirs until the Lord of Grays came into his own again.

With Hazard, who had long known the truth, Sharn mourned not only for Guenna but for the Mark of Lien. There seemed to be no help for that poor country. The roses might return, but the Lien that had produced so many poets, players, artists and musicians seemed to have gone forever.

More and more folk, gentle and simple, sought refuge in other lands. The players, two full companies, went to Varda, in Athron, and to the Chameln lands; there was a fine playhouse in Chernak New Palace and another in the Old Market in Achamar. At last, in this autumn, which came in very wet and cold, there was a knocking upon Hazard's door late on a rainy night. When the servant opened up, there was a figure on the threshold that Taranelda could hardly recognize: a tall, sagging fellow, a fat man grown thin. He had a heavy satchel of books and papers and type; under his cloak he carried a bedraggled black cat. It was easy to believe that Buckrill had walked every step of the way from Balufir to Achamar. So he was taken in kindly and brought to a place by the fire.

The old wives of the Chameln land who read signs of the Goddess in the stars and in the patterns of clouds and in the trees and grasses, predicted a winter of leave-taking. They meant that there would be changes, sudden partings, there would be deaths. No one paid much attention to such messages of gloom, least of all the young bloods at the courts of Achamar.

Beyond the Old Market in a tangle of poor streets by the city wall, there was a tavern called The Sun. It had long been the haunt of young malcontents, nobles and the sons of rich men, together with their huntsmen and grooms. They drank hot punch, swore brotherhood and went out into the streets of the city in search of adventure. There were stories of citizens robbed, tormented, sometimes badly hurt if they tried to defend themselves. This was the work of the Salamanders: a glimpse of a broad hat and a red scarf in the streets after nightfall sent honest folk far out of their way.

Who lurked behind the red scarf? There was no leader, but young Ilmar of Inchevin was what the Salamanders called a "plucky boy," one ready for any devilry. Carel Am Zor called the tune, although he did not know it. His presence and his contempt for authority worked upon the young men. It was common talk that the courts of Achamar had become very dull; at the same time it was agreed that King Sharn Am Zor had changed for the better. Yet was he so much changed? Or had Sharn Am Zor changed towards all the world but not towards his brother?

Tazlo Am Ahrosh was one of the Salamanders; he came and went and knew that he could take the leadership of these likely lads at any time. His ambition and his love were still directed towards the King; given time, he would be Sharn's henchman again. Meanwhile, he roamed the streets in his red scarf and broadbrimmed hat, saved Carel from the watch, paid court a little to Derda of Inchevin, the Starry Maid. The Salamanders often gathered, late at night, in the kitchen of old Countess Panget's home from the ringroad and sampled her apple brandy. Derda, cold and aloof but beautiful, had eyes only for the prince, for Carel Am Zor, her cousin. Carel was frightened of her, yet fascinated, as a rabbit is fascinated by a snake. She made him a gift of an eagle's claw set in silver with a lock of her hair and some runes for good fortune. It was a charm, she said, that she gave to her true servants.

One night in the last days of the Maplemoon, Tazlo Am Ahrosh had a strange adventure in the streets of Achamar. The Salamanders, three or four, spoiling for trouble, chased the servants of a rich merchant bringing his carriage to the livery stable, and were chased in their turn by the watch. They scattered, and Tazlo found himself alone in the Old Market. A man went past his hiding place wrapped in a cloak, and Tazlo jumped out with a hoot and seized him. In an instant the young man from the north found himself on his back in the gutter with the point of a knife at his throat.

The man heaved Tazlo to his feet by his red scarf and said in a hoarse whisper, "Take care, Count Ahrosh! I learned street fighting when you were eating berries in your stinking birch lodge!"

Tazlo, afraid and furiously angry, could only show his teeth. He knew the man; surely it was a fellow called Hunter who ran a stall in the market.

"Have no fear," said the man, tightening his grip. "I'll not hand you over to the watch. Achamar has seen the last of me. Would you do a service to the Daindru instead of waylaying honest citizens?"

"What service?" gasped Tazlo.

"There is a cursed spy out of Lien in the king's household this many a year," said Hunter.

"How would you know?" demanded Tazlo, regaining his courage.

"The spy serves Rosmer, the old scorpion, and once I served this same master," came the reply, still very low. "I fell foul of him and was cruelly punished. Only the mercy of Queen Aidris Am Firn saved me, and I honor the double throne for that. But I still remember much from the old days in Balufir, and I know that this man was one of Rosmer's most secret knaves."

"Would he talk with Rosmer by magic then?"

"Likely they use wizards' tablets," said Hunter. "Little wooden frames filled with a greasy stone, red shale or grey. They are charmed in pairs. Writing on one tablet appears on the other at a far distance."

Tazlo made some sound of disbelief.

"I do not lie," said Hunter.

"Where are you going?" asked Tazlo, full of mistrust. "Why not bring this intelligence to the king yourself?"

"I am going home," said Hunter. "To my first home, which is Lien, and to my second home, which is the forest. There is a leader there after my own heart, and I will do him good service. I will seek out the Great Outlaw, Garvis of Grays."

"Good luck to you," said Tazlo. "Tell me the name of this spy."

Hunter drew the young man from the north back into the shadows and began to whisper.

It came to a death in the first month of the new year, in the Tannenmoon, when the snow lies heavy. The king was spending an evening hour in the nursery of the palace in Achamar, a bright room hardly changed since his own childhood. A noisy game of two crows was going on at the round table with Hal Denwick and the king taking tricks from Zilly and Tanit, with Gerd holding the purse and keeping score.

Sharn, looking about at the children, marvelled at their difference, their cleverness. Surely he and old Zilly had been singularly blessed. He saw how grave and lovely Tanit looked, how well she reckoned up her score and helped her brother manage his hoard of gilded acorn money. He marked the good looks of Hal, like his mother Veldis, but with all of Zilly's good humor. The king heard a cry outside. Perhaps it was just the wind on the balcony. Instinctively he wished away all harm from these children, as if he clutched at an amulet.

The cry came again, close at hand this time and play was broken off. The nursery door flew open, and there was Princess Merilla, pale and dishevelled. She held a twin by the hand, Till, the one with more freckles, and the boy was shocked and gasping.

"Sharn!" she cried. "Have you done it then? How could you choose this way?"

"What is it?" demanded the king.

"*Nerriot!*" she hurled the name at him. "It is Nerriot, stabbed to death!"

"In the name of the Goddess, Rilla," said Sharn Amn Zor, "the children . . ."

"*This* child saw all!" she said. "He and Esher were crossing the court. Will you say you had no hand . . ."

"I swear it!" said the king. "Who has done this?"

Till Am Chiel broke away from his mother and ran to open the balcony doors. They followed him, everyone crowded onto the deep snowy balcony; far below they saw the north court. There stood Esher Am Chiel and officers of the guard. Nerriot could be clearly seen, lying in the snow in the midst of scattered music sheets, his lute by his side. A guardsman picked it up, and it gave off one last sad note, echoing up to the watchers overhead. The children were very still. Tanit took her father's hand on one side, and on the other she put an arm around her brother.

Hal Denwick said, "Nerry is dead?"

"Yes," said Zilly. "It seems so, old son. Come away."

The Countess Caddah had appeared; she shepherded the children back into the nursery. Only Till and Merilla and the king remained on the balcony. Sharn knelt down and spoke to his nephew.

"You saw it then?"

The boy nodded.

"I held his head," he said, "while Pa called the guard. The other man ran off through the arches."

"You are a brave fellow," said Sharn. "Was there some fight or quarrel? Was only one man with Nerriot?"

"Only one."

"Can you say what he looked like?"

"I knew him," said Till, "and so did my father. It was Tazlo Am Ahrosh. We saw him very plain as he passed us by."

"Go in now," said the king. "Sit by the fire. Lady Caddah will give you a posset.

"There is more," said Merilla in a low voice. "You must tell the king."

"Nerriot said some words," said the boy, moving his feet on the snowy floor. "He said, very loud, *'The Treble is false!'* Then he said, *'Inchevin . . . the golden bird . . .'* Then he murmured low to himself. The guard came. Nerriot spoke no more."

"Thank you, Till," said the king. "You have done bravely."

Merilla kissed her son and let him go into the warm room, where he was claimed by the Countess Caddah. The king and his sister remained standing in the cold.

"Will you believe me?" asked Sharn.

"Yes," she said. "But why would Tazlo . . .?"

"To win my favor," said the king. "He must have learned what I have known, what you have known too: that Aram Nerriot was Rosmer's creature."

"He was a poor boy, a beggar," said Merilla, "with nothing but his gift for music. He was an easy victim."

"I know it!" said the king. "I have had thoughts about him since the return from Eildon. I tried to keep him far from our councils, and I saw that you did, too. I might have charged him with being a spy one day, but I would never have had him killed."

"Will you send out after Tazlo Am Ahrosh?"

"Tazlo will show himself, never fear," said the king. "Let us go in. I must search Nerriot's chamber."

For more than ten years the musician had lodged at the palace in a small room under the eaves of the west wing. A guard officer found the door unlocked; Sharn Am Zor went in alone. He saw the few possessions of Nerriot strewn about, his bed made untidily, his makeshift desk piled with music, written in Nerriot's personal, crabbed notation, written upon paper, parchment, cloth. Two lutes rested on a shelf. A mirror hung upon the wall, and Sharn peered into it anxiously, but saw no more than his own face, shadowed and dark, more like the face of Nerriot.

The king, who had consulted with Hazard, knew what he was seeking. At the small window, with a view over the city towards the palace of the Firn, there stood a vase with a sprig of evergreen, resting upon a flat reddish stand that looked like a tile. Sharn lifted the vase aside, sat down on the edge of the bed and placed his lighted candle upon the broad windowsill. He looked about for a stylus and found it in the vase. So he waited, staring at the greasy reddish stone of the wizards' tablet, and after a long time, about the second hour of morning, his waiting was rewarded. Words appeared on the tablet, and in a familiar hand. *"What news?"* wrote Rosmer, far away in Lien. The words faded, and the king took up the stylus. *"You will die, old canker, and the world will be healed!"* His words faded too, and he wrung from his enemy a reply of surpassing cleverness. *"Courage, little king; darkness comes to us all."* A quotation from *The Masque of Warriors* by Robillan Hazard.

The line faded, and the wizards' tablet heaved and twisted; it became crumbly and dry, unfit for messages. The king ordered all the music to be brought to his sister's apartment. He went away feeling sick and puzzled by Nerriot, his gift, his treachery, his narrow room, his violent death. What had Rosmer and his creature to do with Inchevin and with the Golden Bird, a reference to the old miser's magical obsession with the so-called noble art, the attempt to turn base metal into gold?

Tazlo Am Ahrosh soon learned that he had lost all. Sharn walked with his former henchman in the palace gardens and told him, with some embarrassment, that he was banished. Both men held themselves in check; there were no recriminations, the mood was one of leave-taking. The king gave room for hope that the banishment would not last forever. At the last they stood together by the railing before the Skelow, the black tree.

"I hope the sapling grows well in Eildon," said Tazlo.

"The Skelow grows slowly," said the king.

He stood in a patch of winter sunlight; his cloak was of white fur, ermine and fox. He was at that moment no longer the young king but an ageless being, an embodiment of the Zor, white and gold.

Tazlo cried out, "I struck for your honor, sire! I killed a spy!"

It was as if he hoped to wring a few angry words from Sharn Am Zor. The king gazed at the young man from the north with a mild and pitying look that stung much more than his old harshness. Tazlo turned and ran off across the snow. In two moons the old land dispute flared up and was at last decided. The king insisted upon a division of the lands, a notably fair decision approved by all but the Aroshen.

Aidris the Queen was puzzled and displeased at first by the tale of Nerriot, musician and spy. As Sharn tried to tell the story at her fireside, she recalled a scene years past when she had sent the two pretenders, Raff Raiz and Taranelda, off into the snowy night to freedom and had spoken of the mercy of the Goddess. Surely this was what had been shown to Nerriot, the master musician? He had been tolerated for his great gifts and kept from doing too much harm. Yet at the heart of the affair there seemed to be a hint of the fear that she hated: the fear of Rosmer, the night-flyer, the eater of souls.

Sharn had spoken of his children and of his nephew Till Am Chiel, who had done so bravely when Nerriot was struck down. Aidris could sigh for a time when her children were still so young; now she had a son full grown, almost a man, fourteen years old and taller than his father. The palace of the Firn was the home of striplings and growing girls, from the wild beauty Imelda Kerrick, of marriageable age, to the green-eyed Princess Micha, shy and woman-shaped at thirteen. Huon Kerrick, barely a year older than Prince Sasko, started climbing out of the palace at night and sporting a red scarf and a broad-brimmed hat. Countess Sabeth wept; Gerr, his father, stormed; and Aidris let her power be felt. The kedran of the garrison fell upon the Sun tavern, rounded by the Salamanders with scant regard for their high estate, and let them taste a day and a night of the dungeons of the South Hall, unused since the Protectorate.

Before the winter ended, there was another strange death in this season of leave-taking. The watch heard shouting upon the ringroad: Jalmar Raiz and his son Pinga, the greddle, were walking by and saw the lanterns. A frail old man, dressed as a steward or house servant of the better sort, was hammering upon a house door. The healer recognized the old man.

"Surely it is the old ballad-maker," he said to his son, "the old fellow who serves the Countess Am Panget."

"His name is Lett!" piped Pinga. "And that is the house of the old countess."

Jalmar Raiz pushed through the small crowd and addressed the wild-eyed old man, who was shouting in the old speech.

"Master Lett, what is it? Where is your mistress?"

The old man drew breath and told the tale. He had been awaiting the countess in her southern manor, but she had not come. All her servants had come on to the manor house and all the baggage.

"My lady was promised an escort from her eastern cousins . . ." panted Lett.

"The house is deserted," said Raiz. "Perhaps the countess has taken another way."

"Good Master Raiz, I fear she is within!"

The watch had the doors open now, and old Lett ran in, followed by Jalmar Raiz. They called softly, and no one answered. In the torchlight the rooms were disordered. At last the two men came to an upper room, to the bedchamber of the old countess. There she sat in her chair, her eyes wide open; she had been dead for many days. The chamber was icy cold; snow had drifted in through a broken pane. The jewel boxes lay scattered empty about the room; the rings had been stripped from the old woman's fingers, and the brilliants torn from her earlobes. Of her two beloved wards—Derda, the Starry Maid, and young Ilmar of Inchevin—there was no sign.

CHAPTER X

THE HUNTING OF THE DARK

THE SUMMER OF THE YEAR 1184 WAS LONG and hot; by the time of the Elm Moon, the alarms of the winter were burned away, almost forgotten. From his apartments at Chernak New Palace, Sharn Am Zor beheld the wide, decorous expanse of the formal gardens, descending beyond the stone balustrades first to the long walk, then to the south lawn. Further south upon the plain, a whole town had grown up, first to build, then to serve and maintain the new palace.

Sharn was a creature of habit, but at the same time he loved surprises. The day must not run just so; or if it did, the king welcomed a diversion. One morning in the Elm Moon he was enjoying a leisurely breakfast with his queen and their good friends the Denwicks in the garden room of Queen Lorn's apartments. The royal children and Hal Denwick came by, ready to set out beyond the palace grounds to collect herbs and simples: the "holiday task" of Princess Tanit.

The children were permitted to join their parents at table and drink kaffee, which was not good for them, heavily laced with milk. Presently there came a distant trumpet call, which no one could read; a guessing game followed, but only little Gerd guessed right.

"By the moon!" said Zilly. "It *is* Seyl! What brings him from the Danmar?"

"I hope it is nothing bad," said Danu Lorn.

Jevon Seyl, who came in without ceremony, had a fierce look as he handed a packet of letters to the king.

"We live in stirring times, my king."

So the king quickly scanned the letters, which came from Countess Barr, taking the waters at Nesbath and doing a little newsgathering for the Daindru. In a swift action by the newly formed army, the Mark of Lien had added the coastal state of Cayl to its territory. The time being adjudged to be right, new patents of nobility had been wrung from the courts of Eildon: Lien was proclaimed a kingdom. Kelen Vauguens was king, his son a prince; he would be crowned in autumn, together with Fideth, his beloved young queen. The grand design was complete.

There was excitement in this and a certain finality, as if such news must come. Hal Denwick, a handsome boy, nearly ten years old, asked a question, "*Why* must the Markgraf Kelen and Aunt Fideth be king and queen?"

The grownups smiled and looked from one to another. Tanit who found the question vaguely shocking listened wide-eyed.

"Some would say it is good to hold high rank, old son," said Zilly. "Question of prestige, if you know what I mean."

"Yes," said Sharn Am Zor. "Uncle Kelen wants his estate to measure up to the crowned heads round about."

"More than that, Sire," said Seyl. "He will make clear that the *Kingdom* of Lien is larger and more important than the old Mark of Lien, Ydillians Pledge, between the two rivers."

"Ah, it is my sister's doing!" cried Lady Veldis softly. "I am sure she will have a crown for her son!"

"Yes," agreed Queen Lorn. "King Matten of Lien—it sounds well. I hope the poor boy is equal to his task and has good advisers."

"It is unsettling," said Sharn Am Zor. "Can kingship

be plucked from the air? Is it a matter of an Eildon parchment?"

"Hope a copy was made in Eildon!" said Zilly with unexpected wit.

Everyone laughed aloud at the notion of Kelen's patents of nobility changing upon the page as Eildon edicts were wont to do.

Tanit put in primly, "Kings and queens . . . the Daindru . . . have their right from the Goddess!"

"Yes!" said Seyl. "The princess has shown us another truth. I warrant that King Kelen deems *his* right to come from Inokoi, the Lord of Light. A new kingdom, a new religion."

"Too much remains the same," grumbled Sharn. "The architect of the new kingdom, the gatherer of all this territory, is still Rosmer."

"Hush," said Lorn. "You will spoil your breakfast."

Presently Tanit persuaded her father to walk to the end of the palace grounds with the party of herb-gatherers, and the Denwicks went along. Only Queen Lorn remained with Jevon Seyl, pouring him another bowl of kaffee.

"Alas," he said. "No one has a word to say for Cayl, that poor neglected place. What did it have but a few ports and market towns, a few bumpkin lords . . ."

"I think of the people there," said Danu Lorn, "and hope they have not suffered."

"There was a certain interest in Cayl," said Seyl, "though I am not sure I would point it out to the king."

"Tell me, good Jevon. . . ."

"It had no ruler," he replied. "No overlord. It was governed by a council of free towns where lords and commons sat together. Could men live without kings and queens, I wonder? Could they form some kind of commonwealth and make shift to govern themselves?"

The neighbors of Lien were more wary than ever. Only Athron had an intact natural barrier to divide it from the new kingdom: the mountains that rose between Athron and Cayl. Lien had spread out beyond

the Bal into Mel'Nir and had a small foothold over the
Ringist in the Adz. The new king's ambition, it was
rumored, embraced not only land but water. King Kelen
would claim half of the inland sea as his own and
dispute the fishing and the pearling rights.

Within their wide boundaries, however, the Chameln
lands were still at peace, though there was a feeling
abroad that the peace was fragile; it might be broken.
Perhaps the summer days, perfect, hot, without even
the relief of a thunderstorm created this anxiety. The
king spent time with Tanit, working upon her holiday
task. The expeditions in search of feverherb, sourwort,
nightshade, lissmenil, led beyond the lakes and gardens
of the palace.

Towards the end of the Oakmoon, after her birthday
feast, a high point of every summer, Tanit came home
one afternoon from riding with her brother. They had
left their horses and were kicking stones on the long
walk. Above them, half hidden by the spray from the
fountains, they glimpsed their father and mother, side
by side, leaning upon the balustrade. Tanit was about
to run and call, but Gerd tugged at her arm.

"Something has happened!" he said.

They came to the next staircase and went up slowly,
peering through the balusters. At the top they were
gathered up by Lady Denwick; she drew them aside
murmuring of a messenger out of Lien. A knot of courtiers in their fine summer clothes stood by the blazing
beds of redsage and wind-flowers. Far away the king
leant upon the balustrade, and Queen Lorn stood very
close with a protective hand upon his shoulder.

"Is somebody dead?" whispered Tanit. "Is King Kelen
dead, or anyone of his family?"

She remembered just in time that Lady Veldis was
sister to the new queen.

"No," said Veldis of Denwick, distracted. "No one
from the court. The messenger was a house servant of
the Duchess of Chantry."

Her voice shook.

"The messenger was sent directly to Dan Sharn, here in the gardens . . . for a surprise."

The king was suffering from the greatest surprise of his life; for Sharn Am Zor it was as if the sun whirled in the heavens. Queen Lorn had run to him, hearing the name Chantry, the name of his mother's chief attendant. She saw the blood drain from his face as he recognized Zelline's fair round script. She drew him aside to a stone bench while he broke the seals of the package and read what was written. He uttered a cry; then he could not speak.

Lorn took the letters from his lap and read them. Zelline, Duchess of Chantry, had written with wild informality in violet ink, her words eating up a whole pink page from a lady's writing case.

> *Sharn, my dear friend!*
> *You may hear in some roundabout way, as news travels between Balufir and Achamar these days, that your lady mother, Queen Aravel, has been removed from Swangard to the royal manor of Alldene.*
> *It is generally believed that her condition has worsened, and indeed the poor lady is in weak health. But the truth concerning the queen is wondrous and strange and can no longer be kept from her family. A change began to show itself some five years past and continues to this hour. Please read this letter that I send to you and share the joy and thanksgiving of all who attend the queen.*
>
> > *Your true friend and servant,*
> > *Zelline Chantry*

The second letter, with a plain red seal, was written on a large sheet of parchment, ruled with faint lines like a child's copybook. The handwriting was very even and round, with no blots or crossings out, as if the letter had been copied several times to make it perfect:

*To the High and Mighty King, Sharn Am Zor,
who shared the double throne.*

   My Dearest Son,
   *I write this at Alldene, in my old chamber, which
I shared long ago with my dear sister Elvédegran.
The room has hardly changed, only the world outside has changed amazingly, and the woman I see
reflected in the windowpanes has changed out of
all recognition. My true servants will not let me
have a looking glass, but I will prevail on them.*
   *I have wakened from a long, evil dream, and I
truly believe that I will not fall into this dream
again. A cloud has been lifted from my mind and
spirit so that my nurses speak of a miracle. There
are new gods worshipped here in Lien. I hope I
will not offend good Brother Less, the house priest
of the Duchess of Chantry, if I say that I firmly
believe this is a miracle of the Goddess.*
   *At the royal prison of Swangard there was a
young man, Yorath Duaring, who is for me a great
part of the miracle. He is believed by all to be
Elvédegran's own son, now grown to manhood. He
made his escape from captivity and had a thought
for the poor wretch who shared the tower with
him, for his mother's sister. He possessed a healing
medicine of great and magical power, and he sent
it to me by this same Brother Less. It has restored
my reason.*
   *What can I say to you, my dearest son, after so
long?*
   *What can I say to Merilla, my sweet girl, and
Carel, my baby. The children I knew and loved so
well even in my darkest hours have long gone, but
so it is with all children. I joy to hear that you are
all well. I am proud to know that you are king,
long since, having held to your right as your poor
father would have wished. Commend me to all
those I once loved and send me news of all my
family.*

*Commend me as well to Queen Aidris Am Firn,
child of my dear sister, Hedris. I fear that I used
her ill, years past, when I first fell into my sickness.*

*I am not strong, dearest Sharn, and I do not
know how long I will be spared to ravel up the
threads of my life.*

*Do not grieve for me if we never meet again in
this world.*

*Praise the Goddess who has given me these days
of peace and accept a mother's blessing.*

The signature was bold and steady: *Aravel*.

Sharn Am Zor walked stiffly to the balustrade
and leaned upon it. When Lorn followed him, holding
the letters, she found that he was weeping. Tears
coursed down his pale cheeks, but he uttered no
sound.

So they stood there together for a long time, and at
last the king said, "I must tell Merilla and Carel."

"Will you write to them?" asked Lorn.

The king's sister was spending the summer with her
family at Chiel Hall, her home in the east; his brother
was at North Hodd, choosing a new horse from Seyl's
stud.

"No," said Sharn. "Carel comes to Greybear Lodge
with me. I will tell him on the way, and after the
hunting we will visit Merilla."

He smiled at his wife and kissed her cheek, then
beckoned the nearest servant, a page who came running up.

"Danu Lorn will walk with me to the clipped yew
trees. We will take refreshment there, and the children
may come to us after supper."

The setting sun made the windows of the east wing
light up in rows. Lorn and Sharn walked slowly towards
the dark shapes of the yew trees, which stood like
sentinels about an oval lawn with marble benches.

"I was an ill-governed boy," said Sharn Am Zor,
remembering. "None of my mother's women or the

guard officers could restrain me. I saw too much. I saw that my mother was distracted. A scene of violence—I cannot remember all of it—her hands were bound and the fingers bandaged, for she bit them until the blood came. I saw my father's pain, heard my mother's voice, so untuned and shrill. I have told you something of this before; it was winter, a bad time in winter. The snow lay thick, and there were snow houses in the palace grounds. I was seized with a great sorrow and despair. I did not wish to live."

"Sharn, you were a child!"

"No, wait," said the king. "I went out into the night, stole out into the cold and climbed the fence. I crossed a ditch full of snow and lay down beneath the Skelow tree. Yet it did not harm me. Perhaps it knew me for a brandhul, its own kin. I woke up in the morning disappointed, feeling a warmth under the ground, coming from the tree's roots. An old gardener, he is long dead, leaped over the fence and dragged me away. His hands came out in a rash, but I was unharmed by the Skelow and the freezing night."

"Who knows of this?" asked Lorn.

"Merilla might know," said the king. "Some of the servants. My father knew, of course, and to cheer me he took me on that first expedition to Greybear Lodge. Now I have lived to this hour, to learn that my mother has been miraculously healed. The ways of the Goddess are strange to mortal men."

On the first day of the Hazelmoon, the harvest month, Sharn Am Zor rode off to North Hodd with an escort of guardsmen. It was the hottest summer for a hundred years; the grass of the plain was burned brown; a few wells had dried up, and the shepherds brought their flocks to better-watered pastures—to oases such as Chernak New Town and North Hodd. The king started off very early in the morning while it was still dark. The children were allowed to get up in their nightgowns to bid him farewell.

As they stood in the stable yard with their mother watching the dark shapes of the horses and their riders

go jingling off down the broad avenue of half-grown
linden trees, the young prince, Gerd Am Zor, burst
into tears. Queen Lorn looked at her son in surprise.
He was seven years old, tall and well-built for his age,
with a thatch of blond hair, bleached almost white by
the summer sun. Gerd was overshadowed by his sister,
beautiful and lively. Now he wept in the stableyard and
would not be comforted. Neither Lorn nor Tanit nor
the servants could get any sense out of him, unless it
was that Papa and Redwing should not go away.

The king remained at North Hodd only two days. He
paid his respects to Seyl and Iliane and rode out again
with his brother. Carel had chosen a brown stallion
named Ayvid, four years old, spirited but well-schooled.
Captain Kogor and Lieutenant Dann, two veteran soldiers, made up the hunting party, together with Yuri,
the king's younger body-servant.

The king was in a strange mood, not sullen, but given
to long silences as they rode out upon the plain. Carel
was in high spirits, like his new mount, and took it ill
when the captain suggested that he was using his horse
too hard in the summer's heat. Sharn Am Zor, waiting
in the shade of a wilting birch grove, hardly knew the
young man who came riding out of the heat haze. Carel
was like no one at all, only like himself: brown-haired,
brown-faced, still inclined to plumpness, his eyes
blue-green.

Sharn Am Zor tried to come closer in their conversation to things of childhood, to Alldene and Queen Aravel.
The letters in his pouch, which should have been a
cause for rejoicing, now weighed upon his spirit. He
saw how far divided he was from Carel and believed
that the division was mainly his fault. The prince was
tense and alert, his jokes all seemed forced. He shied
away from Sharn's faltering attempts to speak of the
past in Lien and had no patience with tales of Achamar.

Because the summer was so hot, they rode by night
and made a detour to a sheepfold with a good well and
shelter for the horses during the heat of the day. As
they moved on from this place, Sharn became con-

vinced that they were following the very same trail that
he had taken years ago with his father, driving the pony
cart. The countryside began to change; they saw before
them the forest and grassland that spread out from the
river Chind, and in the hard, blue distance, the eastern
mountains. At last, early one morning, they came riding up to Greybear Lodge among its sheltering trees.
A thread of smoke rose from the chimney, horses whinnied, a dog barked. Out came Engist, grey-bearded
indeed, and a thickset Firnish fellow with a dog at his
heels: Jarn Réo, the elder hawkmaster.

It was sixteen days since the king left Chernak New
Palace, ten since the party set out from North Hodd.
The travelers rested and swam and explored the river
banks. The king went out several times with Réo and
the hawks that were kept at the lodge. On another day
the whole party forded the river a mile downstream
from Greybear and hunted for small game until nightfall, bringing home more than they could use.

The king would spend his birthday at the lodge; he
set no store by it, but the men thought of feasting their
lord and drinking his health. A cask had leaked in the
storeroom so that the wine was running low. It was
arranged that Lieutenant Dann and old Réo would ride
to Chiel Hall for more wine and dainties for the king's
feast and bring Princess Merilla and her family a gift of
gamebirds.

The hunters had seen no one in the wilderness: no
other hunters, no shepherds or travelers upon the plain.
Chiel Hall seemed worlds away. Sharn Am Zor sat
outside the lodge in the twilight watching the stars
come out. A trout leaped in the silver waters of the
Chind; Carel walked about snatching at fireflies; Yuri
sat with his back against a tree. When the king had
gone indoors, Yuri followed him shortly, saying that a
fire could be seen over the river to the north. Everyone
went out and stared at the small flickering light in the
darkness over the river. Engist, who knew the countryside well by this time, said that it must be a campfire
on the side of Bald Hill. The king and his brother took a

nightcap of apple brandy, and the whole party turned in. Carel had come up with a plan to take a longer ride in the morning. His horse, he said, was fretting for lack of proper exercise and old Redwing was positively fat from the lush grass near the lodge.

Yuri did not hunt and was not called upon to take part in the early morning ride. The king dressed himself and so did Prince Carel. When Yuri awoke, there was only a smell of breakfast in the air; he was alone. He turned over and went to sleep again.

It was a cool morning; the summer was coming to an end at last. Carel led the way upon Ayvid and then came Captain Kogor upon his black gelding; after them came the king on Redwing and Engist upon Sorrel, a massive light-colored Lowlander. They rode far out on the plain, five miles or more from the lodge on the riverbank. The prince was in fine fettle, putting Ayvid through his paces, breaking off to chase a hare that rose up in his path. At length he turned back in a wide curve and led the party to a shallow valley at the foot of a down, a place they called the Valley of the Stones.

One huge flat stone or piece of masonry lay in the midst of the valley and smaller stones, very worn, grew up out of the grass; it was like a giant's hall with a table. The king had wondered, when he first saw the place, whether the table formation was in fact a grave, the resting place of some ancient chieftain. Now he dismounted and sat down at the head of this table on a convenient hump of rock. Engist brought out food and drink from his saddlebag. It was getting on towards midmorning and the day was warm but not bright; a film of cloud hid the sun.

Carel, who was more restless than ever, made some sound. The king looked towards the north. A clear line of demarcation could be seen between the brown grass of the plain and the green of the river lands, tree-shaded. A party of riders had come out of the tree half a mile away; the leaders, four horsemen in dark cloaks, came on at a steady pace over the plain. The king felt a thrill of alarm even though these were Chameln riders, his own subjects. Kogor and Engist seemed to feel the same; they both stood up and moved towards the king.

Carel said in an ill-governed voice, "Do you see who it is, brother?"

The king did not see; no one saw who it was. Then, as the leaders were very close, one, mounted on a Chameln grey, came forward. Kogor spoke sharply to Engist; the king did not stir.

Carel cried out, "It is Tazlo! It is Count Ahrosh!"

Sharn Am Zor cursed under his breath, cursed his brother. His first thought was that Carel had arranged this "chance meeting" upon the plain so that Tazlo could plead for an end to his banishment. In after years it became a matter of hot dispute: Had the prince done only this innocent service for his friend? The young man from the north rode forward to the very edge of the giant's board; he stared boldly at the king. Tazlo Am Ahrosh had a desperate look; he had not come to plead for anything. At his back his three companions remained hooded and wrapped in their black cloaks in the heat of the day. Further back there was a movement as armed riders dispersed north and south to surround the Valley of the Stones.

Tazlo cried out, "Greetings to Prince Carel Am Zor! What is done here was the blessing of the Goddess!"

"I doubt that," said the king quietly. "Who rides with you, Count Ahrosh? Why are you so far from home?"

"Be still!" said Tazlo. "Your time is spent! I have found you out!"

Engist and Kogor both spoke at once. The old master-at-arms strode forth angrily.

"Count Ahrosh, have you lost your wits?" he demanded. "Address King Sharn as you should. Answer his question!"

"Old man," said Tazlo, "you are deceived! King Sharn Am Zor, my true liege, is not here. This false king that you serve is a changeling come out of Eildon!"

There was a silence, then the king gave a short laugh, nervous and scornful.

"This is madness!" said Engist.

"Not so!" said Tazlo. "Who would deny that the king is changed, sadly changed, since he returned from the magic kingdom of the west. I have seen the truth. This is an imposter!"

"Tazlo Am Ahrosh," said the king, "you were long my friend and rode with me. Will you turn traitor?"

"I rode with the king!" said Tazlo.

"So did we all, Count Ahrosh," Captain Kogor said cautiously. "We ride with him still. Who would believe this foolishness?"

He exchanged a warning glance with the king. His question was answered. The three dark riders threw back their hoods and spurred forward: a shock-headed young man, Ilmar of Inchevin; his sister, Derda, in white Chameln dress; and their father, Lord Inchevin. He was a fearsome sight, very pale with wild hair, his inflamed eyes glittering under matted brows. When the king saw the mad old lord, like Tazlo more than a hundred miles from his own territory, he knew what must be played out, here upon the plain. He was delivered into the hands of his enemies.

Derda, the Starry Maid, spoke up first in her clear mincing voice. "Prince Carel Am Zor, will you not say that the king has changed?"

Carel had followed the whole encounter in a state of bewilderment, breathless, looking first at Tazlo, then at the king. He had, although he did not know it, the power to lessen the danger to his brother, to gain some breathing space. He hesitated, staring at the king. He gave the same nervous laugh as his brother, fascinated by the sublime unreason of the thing.

He said loudly, "Changed? Yes, I suppose . . ."

Tazlo plunged in again.

"The true king is dead! This Eildon spirit came to me out of an old water fortress called Gwanlevan and it goes about in his image. I doubted him at that moment. He had no sense of honor. We came out of Eildon in disgrace. We came in the caravel of the Pretender, the False Sharn from Dechar who struck at the king's right. Was this my old liege and master?"

"No king!" croaked Inchevin. "No king but a mischievous spirit out of Eildon!"

"Uncle!" said the king sharply. "Was it a spirit who recalled the Inchevin to court and gave them gold?"

"Yes," said the mad lord, nodding his head. "Yes, yes, you did all this. You must appease us."

"Father," said Derda. "We must honor the true prince, Carel Am Zor."

"So we must!" breathed Inchevin. "My royal lord, mount up and ride with my daughter. Come to us!"

"Hey boy!" cried Ilmar suddenly. "Hey Salamander! Come to horse!"

Derda lifted a hand and removed a clasp so that her golden hair flowed over her shoulders. Her arms were bare, and her tunic of fine linen showed the swelling curve of her breasts.

"Come, my dear lord," she said. "Ride out with me."

Carel flushed, looked at the ground and made no move. As a temptress the Starry Maid was awkward and cold.

Tazlo Am Ahrosh said, "Carel, you must come. For your honor!"

The king tried to catch his brother's eye and draw him closer.

"Go along with them!" he ordered, as low as he could. "They will not harm you. Save yourself!"

"Hey, hey secrets!" hooted young Ilmar. "Speak up, false king. Will you poison our true prince with your lying talk?"

Kogor and Engist were drawn again and roared out in protest. The king stood up at last.

"Carel!" he said loudly. "Ride out with the Inchevin. They will not harm you. Do you see what is played out here?"

Carel stared at his brother and shook his head.

"No . . . No, I . . ."

"It is treason!" said Sharn Am Zor. "It is a clumsy attempt to seize the throne of the Zor. They will put me and my children aside with this weak-brained notion of an Eildon imposter. You will inherit, wedded to the lady Derda."

"But I am not . . ." faltered Carel.

The king came to his brother's side.

"No!" he said, low and fierce. "You are not the heir. They have taken me, they will try to take Merilla and her children. Ride with them. Save yourself. Warn the Chiel."

Prince Carel sprang away from his brother and mounted Ayvid. For an instant it seemed that he might ride off alone, southwards or to the river. His horse was as fast as any there and he rode well. He might have drawn off some of the lurking horsemen in pursuit. Instead he walked Ayvid round the valley to the north. Derda came to his side, smiling, and so did young Ilmar; the three young people rode off together. Carel's words came back to those left behind.

"What will they do to my brother?"

The king laughed sadly. Then the three riders were out of earshot. Inchevin raised his hand. Captain Kogor drew his sword and almost came to horse before he was struck down. Engist, who had almost lost his king once before, flew into a sort of godrage. He hurled a lump of rock at Tazlo and caught him in the shoulder. He flew at a man on foot and attacked him with a hunting knife.

"Mount up, my king!" he shouted.

Sharn grappled with the swordsman who had killed Kogor. Engist gave a choking cry and fell back across the table stone with an arrow in his breast. Two men on foot had seized the king, but he flung them off and came to Engist. He knelt down, cradling the old man in his arms. Engist breathed the name of his king once and died, blood pouring from his mouth. Sharn Am Zor rose up slowly wiping his hands on his tunic. He stared at the men at arms, and some could not meet his eyes.

"Hear me!" he said. "You are all lost men! Tazlo! Inchevin! Your lives are forfeit from this hour!"

Then he was seized and his arms pinioned.

"Show yourself!" said Tazlo Am Ahrosh. "Take your true shape!"

"You must be sure that I have no other shape!" said the king.

"Tell us your true name, spirit!" said Lord Inchevin.

"You know it well!" said the king. "I am Sharn Am Zor, and I hold to my right!"

Yuri woke from a long dream of the lands below the world. Black men and women linked arms, chanting and stamping on the packed earth. It was night in his dream; suddenly a wailing cry arose, and he knew that it meant danger. He was wide awake in his pallet bed in the storeroom of the hunting lodge. It was late, almost noon by the pattern of the sunlight on the wall. Two men were outside the lodge, strangers, walking their horses. The sense of danger was overpowering. Yuri seized his breeches and boots; he crept on all fours to the south window of the storeroom. The wooden shutters were unfastened; he went out over the sill and lay in the long grass.

The men strode into the lodge and went from room to room. He watched them from behind a shutter: strange men at arms, grim-faced men. One man said, ". . . *if it is the king* . . ." The other had a blood-stained green scarf wrapped around his right forearm; it was Engist's neckerchief from his hunting dress. The men took nothing from the lodge; he heard them go into the thatched lean-to, which served as a stable and as a mews for the king's hawks. There was only one horse in the stable: his own Chameln grey. Presently there were shouts and cursing, then the men laughed. The great hillfalcon soared up over the lodge and across the river: the men were setting free the king's hawks. Yuri did not wait to see any more; he stole from tree to tree until he was out of sight of the lodge. There he dressed himself and ran headlong down the track to Chiel Hall. He ran by day and by night, hardly resting, and on the second day he met Lieutenant Dann and old Réo returning to the lodge. When they heard his story, Dann returned with Yuri to Chiel Hall to raise the alarm; old

Réo rode on with his dog to scout about and find out what he could.

The conspirators and their prisoner rode to the north. For Sharn this was the worst of all, a dull agony of mind and body. At first his hands were bound behind him so that he fell to the ground from Redwing's back several times; then his hands were bound in front so that he could steady himself. He was swathed in a stifling black cloak and hood; he could not see the way; Redwing made sounds of pain; the horse was on a leading rope. Sometimes his senses were acute; he listened as they rode and at night in their camps. Besides Tazlo Am Ahrosh and Lord Inchevin, there were eight men-at-arms, four who were followers of Inchevin and four from the Aroshen.

At night he lay in a narrow tent; he was fed on rye bread and given water to drink. A man of the Aroshen brought him wine and scraps of mutton. Sharn's throat was dry; he could hardly speak. He asked after Redwing; the horse should be well cared for. The men had orders not to speak to the prisoner.

Once he woke from a long peaceful dream of the Zor palace and felt a hand tugging at the rings on his fingers. He cried out. Tazlo Am Ahrosh knelt before him, half inside the narrow tent.

"Where is the seal ring?" he demanded. "The ring with the double oak!"

"In the valley of the stones," said the king. "I slipped it off and hid it in the grass by the table stone."

"Work some magic!" said Tazlo. "Or Inchevin will have you shot like a hind!"

"You are a murderer," said the king. "You murdered poor Bladel, the southerner, long ago in that snowfall. I have remembered how he set me upon Redwing and you came by."

He shut his eyes and tried to dream again.

On another night he got wind of his Uncle Inchevin close beside him in the darkness.

"Spirit," said the mad lord. "Spirit, you will be saved.

Only climb to the top of the tree and pluck down the golden bird."

"I am no spirit, Uncle."

"I have the knowledge," said Inchevin. "I have consulted a great wizard of the south."

The king, weakened from his captivity, began to tremble.

"Tell me . . ." he whispered.

"I must confront a spirit in its true shape," said Inchevin, "and order it to bring me the formula."

"I am your king," said Sharn Am Zor. "I am your liege lord and your kinsman."

"Ahrosh has seen the truth," said Inchevin. "Relent, spirit, or you must run the long field . . ."

"Uncle, I am a mortal man!"

The king shut his eyes and called in his mind again to Aidris, his co-ruler and to his sister, Merilla, and Carel, his brother. Did they not all have the Eildon blood that would heighten their magical powers? He dreamed of his dear wife Lorn so clearly that he believed she must see him in her own dreams and feel his touch. He saw his children sleeping, saw how they moved in their sleep. He dreamed that Hazard came to him, smiling, no longer blind, and said: "This is your birthday, lad!" He awoke in the chill morning upon the plain and could not tell how many days had passed.

At last the path beneath his horse's hooves began to wind uphill. His enveloping cloak was flung back by his captors. For a long time he was dazzled by the sunlight, then he understood where he was. He had been brought far to the north; the party was riding up a trail on the eastern shore of Lake Oncardan. They came to a green plateau high above the lake, ringed with fir trees. Among the pointed firs, at the end of the long field, was a troop of riders in pointed hats.

The leader came prancing forth on a fat, shining little horse, brown and white. Lord Inchevin and Tazlo Am Ahrosh hung in their saddles a moment before they spurred round the king, their prisoner, and rode out to parley with Rugal of the Skivari. Sharn Am Zor, unkempt, filthy and in pain, straightened up a little.

"For shame!" he said. "For shame, you lords of the Chameln lands!"

He became aware of the cliff edge at his back and below the waters of the lake. A sudden, swift movement—poor Redwing would obey, would ride upon the air for his master. He would cheat these madmen and traitors. At this moment he saw the tents at the end of the field and colored markers on either side, among the trees. He saw the shape of the course that would be run and he clung to his life a little longer, thinking what might be done.

Now the king was urged forward by his guards of the Inchevin and the Aroshen. He was brought face to face with Rugal. The Terror from the East had a fierce golden countenance; his slanted eyes and strong mouth, ornamented with the drooping threads of his moustache, reminded the king of no living man but of a demon mask in the museum at Balufir. Rugal, in his turn, beheld a pale, straight-featured man, taller than the tallest Skivari, with bright hair and wild eyes of a deep and brilliant blue. So each man looked upon a foreign devil.

To the king's surprise Rugal had the common speech; his voice was clear and light.

"A king?" he asked, looking at his Chameln allies. "A king or a demon?"

He indicated that he would speak to the prisoner alone; Tazlo Am Ahrosh and Lord Inchevin reluctantly gave way.

Rugal said to the king, "King or demon, you are caught in a trap!"

"How goes your arrow wound that I gave you by the town of Threll?" asked Sharn.

Rugal smiled. "That proves you are a demon," he said, "for I cannot be harmed by mortal men!"

The king saw that he was joking. Rugal knew him for a mortal and did not share the madness of Lord Inchevin.

Rugal said then, "The Skivari will have all these lands

round about. He will come and come again until we get
them. Grant me Vedan and the Inchevin lands, and I
will save your life."

"Rugal," said the king simply, "I would rather die!"

The war lord bowed his head and rode off down the
field. The king was brought after him to a tall green
tent of the Skivari, standing apart from the rest of the
camp. He was allowed to wash himself and was offered
hot food, but he ate very sparingly and lay down to
sleep.

No one was supposed to enter or leave the camp on
the long field, but during the hours of darkness one
man of the Aroshen slipped away. He came down to the
farther shore of the lake where the horde of the Aroshen
were encamped and the followers of Lord Inchevin
and, in wilder country towards the gorge of the Chind,
the Skivari. He knew that they waited for the raising of
the banners. He saw a splendid white birch lodge built
by the Aroshen and hung with banners of the Inchevin
and the Zor, in white and gold and sky-blue. This was
to house the "True Rulers," the Starry Maid and the
True Prince, but he could not tell if they were within.
The man of the Aroshen passed quickly through the
camp of his countrymen, stole a horse and made off into
the lands of the Durgashen. The king was held on the
plateau for a day and a night and another day. At
midnight on the second night, the sound of a drum was
heard in the camp by the long field. A shaman had
come down from the hills.

Esher Am Chiel rode out with ten kedran as soon as
Yuri's tale was told. He found the lodge empty and
rode out upon the plain; a solitary vulture circled above
the Valley of the Stones. When he saw the signs of a
struggle and blood upon the table stone, Esher sent
two kedran riding to North Hodd. He rode out to a
certain point on the plain and lit three signal fires, then
returned to the Valley of the Stones and continued to
search. Under the table stone a kedran found the seal

ring, with the double oak, together with a leather pouch of letters, hidden in the grass.

In a grove of trees, just north of the valley, the bodies of Engist and Kogor were found in two marked graves. While Esher and his followers stood by these graves, old Réo, the hawkmaster, came out of the trees. He had placed the markers, he said, and prayed for his old companion Engist and for the king's captain. He pointed out that one party of horsemen had ridden to the north and that a smaller party, perhaps only three riders, had forded the river. He had followed this trail, and it had led him to a large camp of armed men behind Bald Hill. They had a banner for the Inchevin. He had not been able to get close enough to see if the king or the prince were held there. He believed that he had seen Derda, the Starry Maid, at this camp. So Esher returned to Chiel Hall; riders were sent out, and the plain was red with signal fires.

Princess Merilla could hardly take comfort from the letters telling of her mother's recovery; half-mad with anxiety for her two brothers, she gathered together a rescue party. These were all the able-bodied men and kedran from Chiel Hall and the first lords and their followers who answered the call from the surrounding countryside. More than a hundred strong, they crossed the Chind and rode to the northeast, heading for the camp of the Inchevin at Bald Hill. Merilla urged them forward, unsleeping. She rode ahead like a battlemaid. Her standard-bearer carried an old silken banner for the Zor household, sky-blue, and it could be seen weaving in and out of the trees on the riverside, pressing on with frantic haste.

On the second day of this wild ride, just at dawn, Merilla looked over the Chind and beheld the first vision or sending of the king, her brother. She saw him clad in hunting dress, mounted upon Redwing, just at a bend in the river. She uttered a cry and the vision faded before her eyes. Merilla thought of the early snowfall by Achamar; she had seen the king, and he had still lived.

The camp behind Bald Hill was deserted except for one man-at-arms, terrified and in pain. He had broken a leg in a fall from his horse; his companions-in-arms had splinted his leg with branches and left him behind. They had ridden off when they saw the signal fires. The followers of the princess threatened the man, demanding to know the fate of the king and Prince Carel. Merilla went into his tent and sat with the man alone. He gasped out all that he knew, holding his life for lost at the hands of the Chiel if he did not die of wound fever.

He had ridden out with a raiding party from Inchevin Keep, far to the east. The lord had ridden with them and the Starry Maid, the Heir of Inchevin, and the young lord. They had met with Count Ahrosh and a small troop of the Aroshen and made camp behind Bald Hill. There was some talk of riding south to make a raid on Chiel Hall. It was all in the service of the true prince, said the man, the true prince, who would wed the Starry Maid and claim the throne of the Zor. The king was an imposter who must be set aside. Lord Inchevin had spoken of a spirit who would bring him gold, heaps of gold; riches and honor would be given to all his followers. His lord was mad, the man said, but he and his fellows had argued among themselves that it was a heaven-sent madness. The power of the Goddess was in Lord Inchevin, and the Starry Maid was as fearless as she was beautiful.

Just at the point in his story where he might have learned something of the fate of the king and his brother, the man had suffered his accident. In pain, in his tent, he had not learned much. All the leaders had ridden out, of that he was certain, and he believed there was a signal fire lit on the far side of Bald Hill. The Starry Maid and her brother returned, and there was one who rode with them, that was all he knew. No one had been held prisoner. The Starry Maid was displeased, had her body servants whipped and rode off with her brother and a small escort a day or so later. He could not swear that Derda had been headed for the muster point of the rebels, the ford of the Chind near Threll; he had some notion she was riding for Inchevin Keep. At any rate the troops behind Bald Hill were almost leaderless; they took fright when they saw the signal fires and headed for the muster point themselves.

Merilla, when she heard all this, sent the wretched man in a litter to Chiel Hall to be healed. She had the countryside and the camp site searched many times. She searched in her dreams for a sign, even for a grave, and woke in terror of a search that might never end, all her life long. Surely Carel had been at this camp. Had he turned traitor? Had he been lured away by Tazlo and the two cruel young Inchevin? She joined Esher and the army of the south, gathering strength every day as they hurried north over the plain.

The weather had already broken in Achamar; signal fires were washed out. The news had come to Chernak New Palace; Queen Lorn had begun her long vigil; the guard had ridden out to North Hodd. Aidris Am Firn woke at night from another fearful dream, with thunder rolling overhead. She caught up her scrying stone, the rare carbuncle, and the star in its depths became the face of Sharn Am Zor, very pale. The queen cried out; Bajan woke at her side; her cry was echoed through the Palace of the Firn. The north court was alive with kedran of the guard. Messengers had come from Chernak New Palace: the Chiel had called the south and east to arms. The signal fires were always three-fold; this meant *"Danger to the realm and to the Daindru."*

"It is Rugal!" said Bajan. "The Skivari have come down. We must ride to the southeast."

"No," said Aidris. "Trust me. We must ride to the north, I know it."

Aidris led out all the kedran of the guard and the garrison in great haste, and on the northern road they met riders from the Nureshen. The Aroshen were up in arms and had joined with the Skivari and Lord Inchevin. The rebel horde were massing round Lake Oncardan. The queen urged her kedran forward and sent a rousing call to all the loyal tribes in the north.

"We may come too late!" she said.

"The tribes will hold these rebels till we come, my queen!" said Jana Am Wetzerik.

"These rebels have the king!" said Aidris Am Firn.

So the queen and her kedran rode on into the lands of the Nureshen and then into the northeast. There came messengers from Ferrad Harka, High Chieftain of the Durgashen; a deserter from the Aroshen had come into his camp with a strange tale. Lord Inchevin and Tazlo Am Ahrosh held the king prisoner upon the long field above Lake Oncardan, and Rugal of the Skivari was with these traitorous lords.

The shaman entered the green tent where the king sat all alone. A bronze lantern hung overhead casting a feeble light. Sharn was wrapped in a silken robe from the Skivari, and he sat upon silken cushions; his hands and feet were bound with long chains. The shaman sat down close to the prisoner.

"My king," he said, "I cannot save you."

Sharn Am Zor saw that the shaman was a thin, tall, elderly man with black hair flowing in waves over his shoulders. He wore a mourning band around his head, and his hair was unplaited in token of mourning.

"You have often served the Daindru," said the king. "You wedded me to my dear wife."

The shaman bowed his head.

"I wedded Queen Aidris to Count Bajan," he said, "on the edge of the forest, by Vigrund. I have blessed the Dainmut and the Turmut."

He had left his drum outside the tent. Now he sounded a wooden rattle and prayed in the old speech. When he had done, the king asked for word of his brother. The shaman had no news of the prince. He told of the planned uprising, as much as he knew. The king was composed and serious; he sent word to Aidris, his co-ruler and gave the shaman an account of all that had passed at the Valley of the Stones.

He sent tender messages to his wife Lorn, to his daughter and son and to his sister. He bade Tanit Am

Zor hold to her right and heed the word of Queen
Aidris, the true Regent, until she came of age. He told
the shaman the story of his mother Aravel, how she had
been healed.

"I have spoken with Yorath Duaring," said the shaman. "I showed him a map in the camp of the Nureshen,
before he went into the distant north."

"Where is he now?" asked the king.

"He has found his refuge," replied the shaman. "He
dwells in lost Ystamar, the Vale of the Oak Trees."

Sharn Am Zor gave a sigh, and his eyes filled with
tears. The shaman urged him to sleep a little, but the
king drank some water and continued to speak. He sent
word to his friends and torch-bearers: Seyl, Denwick,
Barr and Zabrandor. He spoke of his friend Robillan
Hazard. He went on to speak of many servants and
retainers of the Zor household, naming them all by
name, sending his blessing to them and their children.

It was about the third hour of morning; there were
sounds in the night. Thunder rolled about the mountains and made the horses restless. Armed men stood
watch outside the tent.

"I will not go alone," said the king. "What do you
know of a magic working that is called the Hunting of
the Dark or the Ox-felling?"

The shaman held up a hand.

"My king," he said, "you will be avenged a thousand-
fold. Inchevin and Count Ahrosh . . ."

"I know it," said the king. "They are doomed, and so
are their poor benighted followers. I am a king and a
brandhul!"

"But this dire working, the Hunting of the Dark!"

"I will bring it down upon another enemy," said the
king. "He has worked his evil too long. He has even
had dealings with that madman, my Uncle Inchevin."

The shaman was silent.

"Help me!" said the king. "It is a work of vengeance,
but I will do it!"

The shaman sighed and felt among the charms and
amulets that hung at his girdle. He opened a flat wooden

box and drew out a single black leaf. The king and the shaman spoke in whispers, and then the king lay down to sleep. The shaman continued to pray softly.

The morning was very still and clear. It was the seventh day of the Thornmoon, the month of sacrifice. In the night a man of the Inchevin, the lord's guard captain, who had awaited him at the long field, fell down raving and had to be bound up and left in his tent. There were six men of the Aroshen and five followers of Inchevin; there were twelve men of the Skivari. They all rode down the field when the sun was well up and took their places among the trees; they were all armed with the short bow. Before their tents stood Tazlo Am Ahrosh, Lord Inchevin and Rugal. The mad lord rode back and forth, then dismounted and went among the trees, saying he must hear the words of the spirit as he ran the course. Since the captain failed, Tazlo Am Ahrosh blew a note upon a hunting horn for the ceremony to begin.

The prisoner was brought from the green tent by two of Rugal's slaves, big, hairless men trained as executioners. His chains had been removed, and when they reached the starting place, one held his arms while the other stood near with a spear, iron-tipped and very sharp, to goad the prisoner if he would not run. Sharn Am Zor stood before the long green ride, edged with dark trees; the sky was blue, but a head of cloud, a thunderhead, was moving down from the mountains. At a word from his master, the slave released the king's arms and stripped off his silken robe. He stood naked except for a loincloth, straight and tall and golden-haired, the image of a man and of a king.

Sharn Am Zor held up his clenched fists; he cried out in the old speech; he began to run. His voice rang out unnaturally loud and was echoed by a peal of thunder and by the notes of the bow strings.

Half a world away in the city of Balufir, King Kelen was rehearsing for his coronation. The day was cool and foggy with a fetid mist rising from the harbor. A crowd of men and women coming to the markets had collected near the Temple of Light, an old city mansion now dedicated to the service of the Lame God. It stood in the center of the city at the end of a broad avenue leading from the palace; carriages were bringing nobles and court officials to prepare for the great day. The crowd gave a desultory cheer for the Duke of Denwick; some fell down reverently at the entry of Jurgal, the Brother Harbinger, with his escorting priests.

At the foot of the steps to the temple, behind the backs of the market women, stood two men dressed in frieze cloaks and hoods, like porters. The older man looked down into his hand where he held a small, shining stone.

"Patience, lord," he whispered. "This precious gift from Erinhall will show us if his guard is down!"

"And if it is never down?" asked his young companion. "If he has magical protection forever?"

"Hush!" said the other. "He is coming . . ."

The crowd had fallen silent as the dark blue carriage rolled up. The king's vizier had some way to walk before he reached the steps. Rosmer had no guards, he walked always by himself, clearing his own way, in a protective circle of emptiness and silence. As he set his foot upon the lowest step, there came a rumble of distant thunder. The soft autumn air of Lien was cleft by a wave of sharp sound, the echo of a voice. Rosmer looked up, alarmed, and a voice near at hand cried out:

"Strike now, by the Goddess!"

Garvis of Grays leaped out of the crowd, flung himself upon his enemy and plunged a dagger into his breast. He struck and struck again and waved his blood-stained blade at the frightened crowd.

"Justice!" he cried. "I avenge the house of Grays!"

He sprang from the steps again into the crowd and made off into the alleys of Balufir unharmed, led by Hurne the Harrier.

Rosmer lay on the steps in his death agony. When Kelen of Lien came from the temple with lords and courtiers crowding after him, it was too late. Only one brother, said to be the house priest of a noble lady, had enough courage or enough charity to comfort the hated vizier. He heard his last words and told them to Kelen, the man Rosmer had made king. The dying man had uttered a name: *Sharn! Sharn Am Zor!* then, very low, he had murmured *Darkness comes to us all*. With Rosmer gone, there was no one to remind King Kelen that these words were from Robillan Hazard.

Still the thunder rolled overhead, a magic storm, the voice of a mighty working, sounding through all the lands of Hylor. The thunder spoke in Mel'Nir, in Nightwood, where old Hagnild raised his head from his book, and on the High Plateau, last bastion of the Eilif lords. In Eildon the sound reached to the very throne of Ross, the Priest-King; the trees before the White Tower bent down their boughs and Princess Merigaun, upon her battlements, cried out to the wild sea waves.

The thunder spoke in Athron, where the Carach trees began to murmur; it rang through the green aisles of the great border forest, driving the Tulgai down from the trees. Far in the north, far from the ways of men, all the oaks of Ystamar began to move their branches and cast down their leaves; Zengor the white wolf howled. Yorath Duaring and his son turned to Gundril Chawn, the Owlwife. She whispered, "It is for the king. It is for Sharn Am Zor!"

In Chernak New Palace, Queen Lorn, sleepless and pale, came to an eastern window. The thunder spoke, and the children, Tanit and Gerd, came to their mother's side. A cloud had come down from the north, suddenly. All three saw the bright day fade before their eyes; they saw the sun go out.

Upon the plain, in the van of the army, with Zabrandor and Seyl and her husband Esher Am Chiel, Merilla saw the lightning strike the ground ahead. She called a halt; already the host stood still, tongues of fire glistening upon the points of their spears, their pennants all outstretched although there was no wind. The thunder sounded again, and it seemed to many of the soldiers that a horseman stood before them, under the lowering vault of heaven.

Further north the thunder spoke very loud; Queen Aidris Am Firn reined in her white mare; she rode in the midst of the northern tribes with Bajan and Ferrad Harka. They were not yet within sight of the rebel horde by Lake Oncardan. The sky overhead was black with cloud; a clear yellow storm light played upon the dark northern trees; a woman began to raise the keen. Aidris was cold, cold to the marrow of her bones; her old wound ached, the arrow wound in her left shoulder. She knew the approach of an unending sorrow.

In Achamar the thunder spoke to a dejected and frightened city. The air was rent over the palace of the Zor, and lightning played about all its cornices and gables and seemed to hang there so that the whole towering structure was outlined in fire. There was a soft pounding on the door of Hazard's house in the Old Market, and Taranelda opened it herself, for the servant girl had gone to seek for news. Buckrill came in, white-faced.

"The king . . ." he said, very low, looking about to see that Hazard was not present. "Nell, they say the king is dead!"

"Has word come?" asked Taranelda, looking towards the stairs. "It is a rumor! It must be!"

Buckrill shook his head.

"I was with Jalmar Raiz when this storm broke. He swore it was the sign of the king's passing and some great magical working besides. He has sent me to Rob, to question him."

At that moment Hazard called from above in an altered voice.

"Nell? Nell? Could you come up?"

There was so much urgency in his call that they went tumbling up the stairs and burst into Hazard's study. The poet stood at the window with the curtains flung back and the shutters open. The Zor palace reared up against the grey sky burning with its unearthly light.

"What is it?" cried Taranelda. "Rob . . . sweetheart!"

"What has Raiz to say to all this, friend Buckrill?" asked Hazard without turning his head. "You have come from his house . . ."

"He says the king is dead," said Buckrill, slow and hoarse.

Hazard turned to face them; he smiled, and his eyes were full of tears, which he dashed aside, the better to see them with. For it was plain that he could see again.

"Sharn is dead," he whispered. "And, by the Goddess, so is Rosmer!"

There were no more wonders to be seen. The storm that centered on the long field worked even more terribly upon the rebels than it did upon the armies of the Daindru. Lord Inchevin never took the field; Tazlo Am Ahrosh rode down like a madman from the heights and called for the raising of the banners. Even before this was done, the army of the south was seen approaching and the northern tribes came within sight of the lake. Derda Am Inchevin stood forth from her birch lodge, but of the true prince there was no sign. Rugal of the Skivari had come down from the heights just as headlong, but his morale was better and he had a good position by the gorge of the Chind.

The wretched Aroshen bore the brunt of the attack; they fought with traditonal ferocity and paid dearly for the disputed land by the lake. They died for their high chieftain and their high chieftain's son, just as the followers of the Inchevin died for their mad lord and the Starry Maid. Within a day and a night, the Aroshen had been beaten back into their mountains, leaving hundreds slain; the Inchevin had fled back to the line of the Skivari. The way to the long field lay open; Captain-General Britt and the veterans of the escort went to seek their king.

The place was peaceful, unmarked by fire or storm; dead men lay unburied in the grass. The horses had been led away, and the tents, all except one green tent, had been torn up and hastily carried off. The ceremony of the long field was known: it was an old, cruel rite of the Dark Huntress, used against those possessed by demons. Ten men lay dead upon the field. Lord Inchevin lay shot to death, as if he had run onto the field into the path of the arrows. Not far from the fallen lord were two men of the Aroshen and four followers of Inchevin who had dismounted and gone to drag him to safety. The lightning had struck first one then the other; they were twisted together in their shirts of mail like the links of a chain. One man of the Skivari had been felled by a single arrow that had traveled clear across the field. Another warrior, one of Rugal's officers by his breastplate, had been struck down by lightning, together with his horse.

Sharn Am Zor lay where he had fallen, face down in the grass; he had run more than half the course and taken many arrows. In his right hand, lightly clenched, Britt found a leaf of the Skelow tree. It crumbled into dust before he could read the letters written upon it.

As the men stood with bared heads, they heard the sound of a drum. The shaman came from among the trees.

"The ground is hallowed," he said. "The king must lie here forever."

The king sleeps in the northeast above Lake Oncardan. Two young oaks have been planted by his grave, and further off a Skelow tree. Pilgrims climb up to the long field alone, whatever their estate. It is the custom among the northern tribes to speak with the dead and tell them all that has passed. There is much to tell the king. The Skivari have been beaten back. The northeast will be better governed. The lands are at peace. The harvest is good.

Young Inchevin died fighting with the Skivari. Tazlo Am Ahrosh fled to the south; he was killed by a grey bear on the banks of the Chind. Derda, the Starry Maid, rode off with Rugal to his tent city beyond the mountains. She became one of his lesser wives and died in childbirth.

Carel Am Zor has never been found. Even his horse

Ayvid has not been found, though Redwing and the horses of Engist and Kogor were rounded up on the aftermath of battle. Merilla, searching still, regards this as a hopeful sign.

On winter nights the long field is very still and white; the moon hangs over the plateau; wolves howl in the distance. There are no ghosts on the long field. The restless spirit of the young king has been seen everywhere in the world: in Achamar, at Chernak New Palace, in Balufir. On summer nights in distant Eildon, the Archer Shennazar shoots with a golden bow before the Hall of the Kings. Here, in this quiet place where he lies, all these phantoms can be seen for what they are: a last tribute to the summer's king.

Hazard makes the long journey in summer, all alone. He climbs up wearily, full of protest, to the bright meadow, and stands at the grave, bereft of words. When at last he turns to go, he sees that a kedran is waiting at the top of the cliff path. As he comes closer, he sees that it is the queen herself, Aidris Am Firn. Far below a large escort with banners has drawn up next to Hazard's quiet grey mare. The poet bows his head.

"Majesty . . ."

The queen lays a hand on the poet's arm.

"Wait for me, Master Hazard. We will go down the hill together."

Rob a Pharaoh and you've made an enemy
not just for life . . . but for *all time.*

FRED SABERHAGEN
PYRAMIDS

Tom Scheffler knew that his great uncle, Montgomery Chapel, had worked as an Egyptologist during the 1930s, and after that had become a millionaire by selling artifacts no one else could have obtained. Scheffler also knew that the old man, fifty years later, was still afraid of some man—some *entity*—known only as Pilgrim. But what did that mean to Scheffler, an impoverished student with the chance to spend a year "house-sitting" a multi-million-dollar condo?

What Scheffler didn't know—and would learn the hard way—was that Pilgrim was coming back, aboard a ship that traveled both space and time, headed for a confrontation in a weirdly changed past where the monstrous gods of ancient Egypt walked the Earth. And where Pharaoh Khufu, builder of the greatest monument the world had ever known, lay in wait for grave robbers from out of time . . .

JANUARY 1987 • 65609-0 • 320 pp. • $3.50

ROBERT A. HEINLEIN

"Heinlein knows more about blending provocative scientific thinking with strong human stories than any dozen other contemporary science fiction writers."
—*Chicago Sun-Times*

"Robert A. Heinlein wears imagination as though it were his private suit of clothes. What makes his work so rich is that he combines his lively, creative sense with an approach that is at once literate, informed, and exciting."
—*New York Times*

Seven of Robert A. Heinlein's best-loved titles are now available in superbly packaged new Baen editions, with embossed series-look covers by artist John Melo. Collect them all by sending in the order form below: